The EarthStar Solution

Arlene L Williams

ISBN: 978-1-938151-39-2
Library of Congress Control Number: 2023916350
Arlene Williams Books
Edmonds, Washington
www.arlenewilliamsbooks.com
PO Box 3142
Edmonds, WA 98020

The story, all names, characters, and incidents portrayed in this production are fictitious. No identification with actual persons (living or deceased), places, buildings, and products is intended or should be inferred.

Publisher's Cataloging-in-Publication Data
Names: Williams, Arlene L.
Title: The earthstar solution / Arlene L. Williams.
Description: Edmonds, WA : Arlene Williams Books, 2023. | Summary: In this contemporary climate fiction mystery, Kaye must solve her brother's death, change her father's mind, and alter the outcome of the climate crisis across time—but it all springs from one moment of connection.
Identifiers: LCCN 2023916350 | ISBN 9781938151392 (pbk.) | ISBN 9781938151385 (ebook)
Subjects: LCSH: Climatic changes – Fiction. | Families – Fiction. | Political activists – Fiction. | Oregon – Fiction. | BISAC: FICTION / Nature & the Environment. | FICTION / Mystery & Detective / Amateur Sleuth. | FICTION / Science Fiction / General.
Classification: LCC PS3623.I45 2023 | DDC 813 W—dc23
LC record available at https://lccn.loc.gov/2023916350

Hope does not deny all the difficulty and all the danger that exists, but it is not stopped by them. There is a lot of darkness, but our actions create the light.

— **Jane Goodall**

This is a not-for-profit book.

All proceeds from this edition will be used to support the mission of The Climate Story Garden, a free newsletter to promote climate fiction with hope and heart. To learn more, go to climatestorygarden.com.

Chapter 1

There's that light again. I've seen it for the last three nights, flashing across my laptop screen, a burst of sparkle exploding through the glass. The first night, I thought a drone light might be creating a strange reflection. Last night, I guessed fireworks. Tonight, I'm thinking it's a light show for the party. *Ba-bum-ba-bum. Thrum. Thrum.* The beat of the music outside pulses against my window, but nothing on the terrace looks like a band's light display. Instead, everything's dimly lit—just strands of silver globes laced among the trees and electric torches lighting the pathways.

I confront my laptop. Something must be wrong with it. My hand reaches toward it, and then jerks away as if touching a key will zap me with strange electric current. The thought of losing my machine to a system crash leaves me desolate. These past two months it's just been me, sitting alone, loading photos, tweaking their pixels, embedding them into my digital art. Yes, my art, my photos—no, I can't lose my work. It's time to start a backup.

A whoop from a musician announces the end of a set. There's a final roll of the drums and a pathetic smattering of applause. That's embarrassing, no one's listening, but even so, it's good to have the music stop. Still, all that chatter from the crowd, punctuated by some tipsy shrieks, propels me into an ugly mood, one that's cranky and raw.

Glaring out the window at the party mob—strangers who know Margot and Dad—I delete them as a source of potential links. I haven't had a real conversation since we moved here in June, but I could never imagine speaking to any of them, especially that woman drunk-dancing through the garden bed. *Stomp, stomp, stomp.* She's crushing coneflower petals into the earth as if it's her favorite game.

Ugh. She's what's wrong. Her! Them! Making my night so utterly wrecked! They overflow the nooks and crannies and surge up my stairs, defying gravity, forcing me to lock my door against them. They're why I'm not down on the terraces, gossiping about the next big deal or the latest fad diet or what someone's shoulder bag cost. Instead, I'm up here, staying put.

That woman's driving me crazy, still stomping her way through the greenery. Grabbing my camera, I storm down the hall to perch on the balcony overlooking our garden. It seethes with the party crush, people swarming the pathways, just ants in their nest. Behind them stand the tall Doug firs, watchers like me. I breathe in their evergreen scent, fresh in the warm summer's air, and for a moment, I tower like the trees, capturing a bit of their magic until it vanishes.

The woman plows through some rose beds. Focusing my lens, I wait until she flattens a coral zinnia. *Click. Click.* Photographic evidence. For what? Who knows? But it's a victory, a small one, in a night of dismal feelings, wishing I were forty miles away.

We just moved to Mossy Hills from Portland in June, and the party is a housewarming for this brand-new, monster mansion. My dad paid millions to have it built, but why? It's designed boxy-modern but trimmed in rustic touches that clash like pickles and cake. It's nothing like our Portland place, a restored Craftsman bungalow, expanded but still cozy with a wide front porch and wood-wrapped windows. That was a real home. I lived there my whole life, seventeen years. Mom never would have let Dad sell it, and so I'm boycotting this ugly house, this dreadful party.

My camera sweeps the terrace until it spies Margot, my stepmother. The lens frames her milky face, pale like her bleach-blonde hair. There's something sad-banshee about her eyes as she scans the crowd, desperate to find someone—hopefully not me. I stand still as the trees. No luck. She heads in my direction.

Swaying below me like she's already over her limit, she calls, "Kaye, come down. I want you to meet someone. She'll be a senior at Moss High this year like you."

"No." My glare pierces the shadows around her. "And it's Mossy *Hills* High."

Hands on her hips, her mouth pinches. "You can't keep doing this. You need to get established. Meet people. Make a good impression."

My eyes become two daggers. My camera grip is extra firm. Her life is one big phony impression that doesn't mean a damn thing, so I'm already breathing fire when she says, "You've got to learn to make connections."

A plastic cup full of stale soda balances on the balcony railing. With the flick of my finger, it splashes down beside her, a near miss. Spinning away, I knock over a tall, empty planter. It's brass, so it clangs like a cymbal. Kicking it aside, I tip a painting sideways as it hangs in the hallway—just to piss Margot off. Slamming through my bedroom door, I lock it tight and march across the room, ready to shut my windows against the heat of the night.

A laugh stops me. It's not deep, but still earthy, a generous laugh that spreads like warm molasses. It could be my brother's laugh, but it's not. It echoes through me as I search for Marty's impish face among the party crowd, just in case the impossible has happened. Just in case he's here.

Turning to my laptop, I tap a key to wake it up. No electric shock. No puzzling light. It's safe. Whatever the problem was, it's gone, and the backup has finished, so I scroll through all my laptop files, looking for photos of my brother. There's one from the night of his big blowout seven years ago before heading off to college, the night he gave me his old camera. *Take photos*, he said, *post them so I know what's happening*. This picture of him is surprisingly good for my rookie ten-year-old attempt. He's dancing, hands to the sky as if sparks shoot from his fingertips, his eyes ablaze, bright as the stars.

Searching my phone for a voicemail saved from Marty—sometimes I play it just to hear his voice again—I tap the screen to listen, but the phone *dings*.

A text comes in. It's from a Craigslist ad. *Do you still want the car?*

I text back: *If it runs, yes.*

$2500. Firm.

That's fine. When?

Tomorrow at 10 AM.

Where?

Mossy Hills DMV. Bring cash. Look for the car. I'll park toward the back. I'm Herman.

How about 10:30 so I can get to the bank?

Sure.

Send the pix again.

A photo comes through. It's a small white hatchback. There are some scrape marks below the right front headlight. *It's perfect. See u then.*

My next move is to check my bank balance. "Hey, Mom," I whisper, "there's just enough." Technically, it's Dad's money, but I always think of it as Mom's money because she's the one that demanded it—an allowance every month going straight to my bank account. "She's got to learn about money," Mom insisted. She even made me do chores for it. Wisely, she wrote it into her will. Dad can't disappear it in a stormy fit.

With a smirk, I lock my phone. Dad will be furious. He just bought me a little coupe, brand new. It's metallic red. Bleh. And he didn't even let me choose the color! I can't see myself driving around town, calling attention to my 1 percent status with a brilliant red car for everyone to stare at. That's no way to fit in. And didn't Margot just say I should learn to connect?

Tomorrow—my own car. I'm all twitchy with the thought and head straight for my walk-in closet. It's mostly bare, it's so big. A half-empty suit-case holds some dress-down clothes for meeting the car guy. There's a torn T-shirt, but it's a brand label. Still, its blue is faded into blotchy patterns like a bad tie-dye. Who will guess? On the floor is a pair of capris, nicely stained. Scissors snip off the pocket flap with its monogrammed designer logo. Grinning at myself in the mirror, I announce, "The princess breaks out of the castle."

I study my long, thin frame, my somber stare, the clench of my jaw. Is that really my goal—to escape Dad's realm of riches? I definitely gaze at his hedge fund universe like an outsider, at least that's what I think. Am I right? All I know is my days are spent exploring the land of pixels, creating my art, working on photographs, searching for meaning but not finding it in the lavish world Dad's given me. I have more than I could ever need but not what I want: goodnight wishes, arms to hugs me, the smile of a best friend.

My fingers drum the windowsill, inspecting the party mob, finding a hundred reasons not to like any of them, so I launch myself across my bed, searching for images among the random patterns of the ceiling texture. These beige splats of drywall mud, knocked down to flat plateaus, are harder to concentrate on than my sprayed popcorn ceiling back in the old house, but I manage to spy a skyscraper, a bus, a man running down a street. I miss the city.

Getting edgy, little prickles of energy running across my skin, I jump up, pacing, not sure how to stand another minute here. We just moved into this upscale neighborhood above the town of Mossy Hills, but each lot is at least ten acres so you can't even see the neighbors. This is the loneliest place I've ever been—beautiful, quiet—but it's been two months of pure boring living here. That includes the town below. Nothing happens there that I can tell, though it's still the dead months of summer.

A man's surly voice ruptures my restless feeling. He's talking on his cell in the shadows below my window loud enough for me to hear because the band's on break. "I don't care what the policy is, fire him." He listens for a moment. "It's not retaliation if you substantiate it." Another pause. "So, make up something. He's too smart. He'll catch on."

After a moment he says, "Yes, he'll catch on, but not about the carbon tax. Everyone knows Big Oil is backing us against it."

The carbon tax? Dad's against the carbon tax too, something that will hurt his investments in oil and gas. Is this guy talking about that? I lean into the window screen to catch every word he's saying.

"It's the project. He's snooping around about it. I know he is."

His tone sharpens. "Yes, it's a sure thing … I've got insider knowledge it will happen."

"I can't explain it, but it's true. It's like a crystal ball or something." He sounds exasperated. "I don't know when it will happen, but I'm certain of it."

"No, I haven't found it yet!" he shouts.

A woman calls through the shadows. "Tom, there you are. I thought you'd left me here."

The man lowers his voice. "I've got to go," he says. "Just fix it, or I'll do more than fix it … and you'll be next."

I shrink back from the window—the threat in those words as pungent as rotten fish. Does Dad know him? He knows a lot of nasty guys like him. Mom kept them away. She set the boundary firmly: "Not in my house. No dinner parties for clients." Even Rory, Dad's business partner, was only a name to me when Mom was here. These ruthless, wealthy men never invaded my life until Margot appeared. She thrives on having them around. When they show up at the door, I announce my urgent need to study for a test.

After fiddling with my aperture and ISO settings, making sure the flash is off, and dialing in the photo burst, I lean forward. My camera's steady on the sill, ready to capture Tom's face despite the darkness. Tom takes the woman's arm and steers her toward the side of the house where his face is illuminated by a security light at the corner. *Click-click-click-click-click.*

Tom looks up. His beard is graying. His thick eyebrows scowl above a stare that's as harsh as a dusty desert, reminding me of the threat he just made. Maybe that's the way the world works at the upper levels of business. Someone has a plan, but someone's in the way, so rules get broken all for the pursuit of money. Ugh.

I gulp down a breath. "There was an owl in the trees. Trying to catch a photo."

With a smile, the woman breaks the spell Tom's cast. "Looks like a great camera, but it's strange to see a teenager with one. Why not your phone?"

I focus on her, not him. "This one's special. My brother gave it to me."

She nods and tugs Tom away, waving. "Good luck with the owl."

As they round the corner, Tom looks back, his eyes shadowed by the darkness. I raise my camera to deflect the venom in them. He blinks and turns away, but a chill settles in, washing me in the drab of browns and grays. Desperate for the reason he alarms me, I make one big guess—his piercing look shouts it—Tom knows exactly who I am.

With a shudder echoing in my bones, I rush to my desk to touch Mom's rose-scented candle, its wick still white, its beeswax intact. Mom gave it to me ten years ago—her last gift, one as precious to me as Marty's camera. I never lit it because how could candlelight replace her? Just a glance from her would push away the gloom. It wasn't the brilliant blue of her eyes that would save me. It was their warmth, glistening in the highlights. I need some tenderness now to melt the frostiness of that man.

But even Mom's candle can't do the trick tonight, so I pace, scanning the crowd, searching for a path back to stillness. And then it's there, yes, in the stone fountain rising on the high terrace. That tall granite pillar, softly curved like the waves in Mom's hair, wraps her warmth around me. She's hugging me, whispering: *I'm always here.* That hug, even imagined, reminds me who I really am: a dreamer, an artist, someone who searches for what's important, just like Mom taught me.

My camera scans the crowd again—a huntress to frame my world. That's why I love it, and not my phone. We become one—the camera, my eye—and the smooth rotation of the lens feels exquisite as my hand focuses it. *Schwish. Schwish.* My phone is just for quick pics, always ready but so distant. Besides, all these camera dials challenge me, generating some *zing*, and it has a larger sensor for capturing low-light images, fast action, and cool effects.

Spotting Dad on the terrace, I follow him in the viewfinder, his hair speckled like salt and pepper, his eyes steel gray and hard as the metal. I take after him—black hair, long, narrow face, except my eyes are pale blue, a bit limp. Neither of us have that fair Irish skin. Mom had that. Marty had that too, plus a zillion freckles. The one thing true-Irish about Dad is his name, Paul Malloy. Malloy means noble chief and it fits. He definitely knows how to take command. He moves toward the fountain and stands alone, staring at the water sliding over it in gleaming sheets like he's remembering her—Mom, our angel of light.

It had always been a silent understanding that this fountain was Mom's memorial. Ten years ago, she chose it for the garden back in Portland. Dad brought it with us when we moved here, and as far as I can tell, he's never told Margot about the connection to Mom because, if he had, for sure, it would be a target for stepmom jealousy. It's the one secret that still connects me and Dad, even though it's never spoken between us.

And now I feel guilty about the car thing, wanting to rush down to him, put my arms around him, tell him it's okay, that I miss her too. It's not just the party that stops me. It's him. It's me. So instead, I head for the balcony again, camera clutched tight. Raising it, centering on Dad, I snap a photo, once, twice. *Click. Click.*

Dad's moving back into the crowd, turning away as my finger taps the shutter release one more time, but another face behind him captures my attention—high cheeks, strong brow, a face that says life's been lived. My lens captures the lines beneath the eyes but also a crinkle at their corners when he grins. A spark blazes in them like a star shooting across the sky. It's not Marty, but it's good. *Click.* I check the screen. Great exposure. Sharp focus. *Click. Click. Click.* I take at least ten more—his cheerful grin's so captivating—but then I stiffen.

Behind me on the upstairs landing, a woman giggles. A man releases an obnoxious burp. "Shh!" the woman hushes.

My arms wave at them wildly. "Hey, this is off-limits! Shoo. Shoo."

They just wobble in front of me, too drunk to comprehend, so on comes my camera flash. *Click.* I blind them with it and chase them down the stairs with the light bursting across their backs. *Click. Click. Click.* Back in my room, I print out a sign: *NO ENTRY*, which gets taped to a chair placed at the top of the stairs.

Retreating, I lock my door and collapse at my desk. Marty's photo is still open on the laptop, and my mind boomerangs into focus at the sight of him. Yes, that's what's troubling me, what has turned me into such a grouchy, gloomy, jumpy mess tonight. Counting on my fingers—March, April, May, June, July, August—I do the addition. That makes six months, and it's August 5th. This is all about Marty.

Soon the only photos lined up across my laptop screen are ones of Marty hamming it for the camera. I've chosen his goofiest: hanging from a tree limb monkey-style, his grin jam-packed with glee; a big-eyed, high-dive belly flop, his mouth baboon-wide; plus countless prank scenes, like tiptoeing up on people with arched hands and wicked winks. And in every picture, his eyes gleam with giggles and hugs. Marty's *joy-light*. That's what Mom used to call it.

Mom and her words. Ordinary things turned special just by the names she gave them. The sun was the *EarthStar*. Clouds were *angel-mist*. Trees became *The Wise Watchers*. And my favorites as a girl—*yummy-dippers* and *grub-stabbers* were the names for spoons and forks. Mom was an artist like me, but she used words to paint her pictures. I keep a tight hold on them, her special words, to keep her close.

Just when I feel back in balance, from Mom-words and Marty-antics, I click to close a photo—one with Marty in the middle of a wild skateboard tumble, but the cursor freezes. A burst of light skips across the screen, once, then twice, the second flit of brilliance less intense. The third time, the light creates a halo around Marty, quivering, pulsing, until it sputters out and fades away. I blink, searching the room, but nothing shimmers midair, so I study the photo. It hasn't changed. Marty's still all crazy arms and legs as his rebel skateboard veers off-frame, yet I get the eerie sense those tiny pixels have actually been in motion, even if only for a second, and they're just now settling back into place. The hairs rise on my neck. Something is there, something that makes me tremble like thunder rumbling through the sky.

And then it's gone. But the thunder stays, boiling, churning, building a storm. I dread the lightning heading my way.

Chapter 2

It takes minutes, but it feels like hours, till I can budge, the storm of
emotion ebbing. Through the fir trees, I imagine Marty drifting there, a
ghost of mist. Tonight makes six months without him, the worst night to
celebrate anything. Obviously, Dad and Margot have forgotten, but how
can we have a party, especially a housewarming party, with no Marty? I
can't—I won't—mostly because I miss him, but also because it's just so
wrong without him. He would have loved this night. The laughter. The
chatter. The desperate flirts. The drunken clowns. The wine, the beer, the
weed, but not the coke that I assume is going around. I hesitate on that
point. Am I right, Marty? Did I even know you?

It's hard to admit that he almost became a stranger after he left for
college. He was mostly absent from social media, claiming he despised the
hatred it generated, though he still had some halfway-neglected accounts.
I scoured them for information about dates, girlfriends, parties, events,
but came up short. Photos showed him studying in the library and playing
ultimate Frisbee. There were videos of him singing his crazy songs while
playing his guitar. I did notice how his look had changed—trendy hair,
stylish clothes. Those hinted Marty had escaped from the nest, but it wasn't
till later that I realized he had broken free of Dad, of me. After grad school,
when Dad set him up in his own lab south in Salem, he barely came by for
a visit. He was always doing research that I didn't understand, and every
time I saw him, he seemed shrouded in stress and secrets as dense as the
river mist.

My laptop seems normal again. Still, I run a diagnostic. As the program spins through my machine, I reach for my camera to avoid the pain of what that scan may bring. Scrolling through my latest pictures—the cheerful partyman, gloomy Dad, creepy Tom, the flower-stomping drunk, I linger over one from yesterday of a yellow moth clinging to some mossy tree bark and then a cute white cottage being torn down in town. It's a shame. Mossy Hills is growing too fast, and its old-fashioned charm is endangered.

The diagnostic comes up clean, but I start a virus scan to make sure nothing weird is lurking, like a ransomware attack. That scan comes up zero threat, so I strike random keys. It's all routine, just a crazy mix of characters. Next, I open Marty's picture. All clear. No strange light or anything. I try to reconcile my brother's cheerful face with the police report. It doesn't make sense. He couldn't do it. Not on purpose. Just look at him.

To shake free of my suspicions, I load my camera's SD card and open that magnificent partyman face. There he is, dark hair, sun-leathered skin, his eyes splashing starlight from the screen. Staring into those joyful eyes, I wonder: *Have I smiled today? Yesterday? Have I smiled at all since Marty died?* I know I have, but it's hard to remember.

And then it's time to get to work, deepening his merry crinkles layer by digital layer, enhancing the light in his eyes, pixel by pixel. Sitting back to study my efforts, I turn off layers, one by one, announcing, "I'll call you Ned. And you're a natural. You don't need anything."

Deciding the secret's in the crinkles, I click a photo of my father by the fountain and zoom into his face. A corner of his mouth has a gloomy droop. Wishing I could pull it higher, make him smile, I touch the screen. His eyes, so grim—did they ever used to crinkle? Yes, when I was young, he took me to a park to play on the swings. He pushed me high and then sat on the plastic seat hanging empty beside me, swinging just as high himself. We laughed so hard as we passed each other going backwards and forwards in opposite directions. There were crinkles in his eyes that day. I decide to give them to him again.

Cloning some crinkles from the partyman, I place them onto a new layer, moving them to the corners of Dad's eyes, scaling them down, mixing them with the colors of his skin. My hand is patient as I build the illusion layer by layer. It feels so good to be working on Dad, fixing him. Was Dad always so alien, lost in the world of hedge funds? Not when Mom was here. She always knew how to bring him back to us.

I run through the blend modes to see which setting works. Each mode mixes the layers in different ways, enhancing or modifying pixels like I've got a magic wand to enchant them. The one called *soft light* does the trick—Dad, you need some softness. I adjust the hue/saturation sliders and set transparency to sixty percent, so Dad has a touch of human in him again. Perfect.

It's great to see Dad brighter, at least in the eyes. "Stay that way," I whisper, a wish that won't come true. Dad grows darker, more rigid, as the months slip into years. He's a rich man, making millions from the hedge fund that he runs. Every dollar in the bank costs him his soul, at least that's what Marty said the last time he was home. He was on the phone, fuming that, without Mom, Dad's just all about the money now. Money. Money. Money. Marty blamed Margot for changing him.

Needing a break from thoughts of Dad, I switch back to the photo of Ned, wondering who he is, inventing his story. He's an artist. He paints pictures of the universe—stars, planets, galaxies, but like Van Gogh, he gives space some personality. Van Gogh set the sky in motion, swirls among the stars, but Ned focuses on depth, reaching into the sky to touch a star. I'm not sure how he would paint that, maybe concentric circles of blue, ever darker, ever smaller, like a tunnel into the sky. As he paints, he wonders who is out there in the universe beyond that tunnel he's creating.

Yes, someone's out there, their voice the pulse of light beams. That's what Mom would say. One time she even did, staring into the vastness of the sky, her face glowing. "There are worlds out there, Kaye. A universe of people I want to know. Can you imagine it?" I close my eyes, doing just that, imagining that connection she reached for. It comes to me so warm and rich, like sips of hot chocolate sliding down my throat. Ned knows that feeling. I see it in his eyes. They're like doorways to a different world. I want to walk through them to find that world too.

I do it. I step into those eyes. I open the door and gaze around, ready for a new world, but I can't see it. My mind goes blank. It's beyond me. It's like all the times I've reached out to Marty, imagining I can talk to him, but in the end, I can't.

Twang. A guitar in the band brings me out of Neverland. The music resumes. It seems louder, but maybe I'm just tired and grumpy. Could a snap of my fingers make the noise disappear? That's not possible, even though I try to imagine it, so I focus on a stack of cardboard boxes still waiting to be unpacked. Somewhere in those boxes is a photo of my mother, deep red hair like Marty's, large blue eyes, a splash of freckle. I hunt through a box looking for it, hoping Margot hasn't disappeared the picture in her ongoing quest to take Mom's place.

The photo isn't in the box, but I bring out two classic DVDs that Marty and I used to watch. We loved to stay up late on nights like New Year's Eve and Thanksgiving, binge-watching them. Marty's favorite of the two was *Robin Hood*, an Errol Flynn megahit from 1938. I always felt more in sync with the other one, Flynn's earlier film, *The Prince and the Pauper*, about a prince and a beggar who trade places because they look exactly alike. I want to trade places too, with someone who's my double, to see what it feels like living a different life.

Weighing the DVDs in my hands as if I were the goddess of justice, blindfolded while deciding a tricky case, I ask: outlaw or prince? Which movie? *Robin Hood* wins, in honor of Marty. Besides, it's in Technicolor instead of black and white. Tonight, everything's so blah that a bit of color might perk me up. Slipping the DVD into my laptop, I shut the windows and turn up the sound. Robin Hood steals from the rich to give to the poor. Maybe there'll be some pointers for shaking down the hedge-fund crowd.

As the movie begins, the munchies overtake me. Marty and I always had a plate of eats to feast on when we watched this. We would sneak down to the kitchen to raid the fridge, and the fridge must be full of treats tonight. A scene with Prince John doesn't help. He's carving up a plate of meat while snickering about King Richard being captured, leaving England in his evil grip. That's it. I need a plate of wings.

Pausing the movie on Prince John's loathsome face, I open my door and listen. There's a buzz of conversation in the great room, which is really a living room with a vaulted ceiling and a bulky stone fireplace that absolutely overwhelms. I'll have to pass the eddy in the crowd that's churning through the French doors toward the hallway, but I'll keep my head down, avoiding anyone who wants to talk. I'm not a party creature like my brother.

Yes, Marty was my opposite, outgoing to the max. He'd be the life of this party, and he would approve of the way Margot has orchestrated it, her one talent. He might even forgive her, at least for the evening, for barging into our life. We both held it against her, even though it happened five years after Mom died. She invaded that special place in Dad's heart that Mom had always held. Of course, I'm not sure Dad still has a heart to steal. Around me, he's pure icicle.

Tiptoeing to the upstairs landing, I watch for signs of movement down below. This is my lookout post where I guard the whole top wing. Behind me are three empty rooms, plus my own across the hallway. Right now, those extra rooms are filled with boxes. Someday, they'll be guest rooms, but for now, this is my domain.

Dad's study is near the bottom of the stairs. A loud curse escapes from it. "Damn carbon tax. We need more media buys." It sounds like Dad's on a phone call, yelling at someone about that tax he hates. It would put a fee on fossil fuels, which is where he makes a lot of his money. The rest of his rant is muffled because the door is solid-core, hand-hewn oak, teeming with carvings of knights in battle, holding swords and staffs and crossbows. It's a hideous door, part of the faux-rustic vibe that clashes with the sleek contemporary lines in this mammoth house of ugliness. Did Dad always have such bad taste, or is it Margot's influence?

No, it's Dad. He had this ghastly house built. I call it Bleak House—no connection to Charles Dickens; it just sounds right. For one thing it's about five times as big as we need it to be with eight bedrooms and fifteen thousand square feet. This place is triple the size of our 1920s bungalow in Portland. Our old home had been renovated and expanded, but it was still filled with the warm glow of oak floors and handcrafted cupboards built into the most surprising places. Here there's no warmth. My bathroom has a tub you could almost do laps in. One whole wing is still empty except for an exercise gym. Margot hasn't decided what to do with the rest of it yet except for vague plans for a home theater. That's the tip-off that it's way too much house for anyone. Even Margot doesn't know how to spend enough money buying stuff to fill it. What a waste.

Around the corner, I bump into Rory Mason, my dad's business partner, leaning over the upturned face of a pretty blonde. It looks like the opening move of a kiss, but they're talking, or really Rory's talking. She's just nodding, caught up in his words. I've never liked Rory, his pudgy nose, his pasty face. He's such an overt fiend, too handsy, too ready with suggestive jokes and compliments. He even flirts with Margot when Dad's not around.

I call out. "Hey, Rory. Where's Trish? I was hoping she'd be here tonight, and we could share music videos or something."

Rory steps back from the blonde, his brown hair dangling over his eyes. "Oh, she's in Paris for the week."

"With the family? How's baby Jeremy?"

The blonde's puzzled.

"And tell your wife hello from me when she calls." I add that for clarity so Rory will have to be honest about what he's looking for. Rory's a born salesman. He sees life as one big, schmoozy tall tale, but Dad depends on him because he's great at reeling in the clients. Dad hasn't got the knack these days.

The woman looks at me and then Rory. "Excuse me," she says, and leaves.

Pleased with my sabotage of Rory's sleazy plan, I cross the stone-and-glass foyer and slip into the kitchen. It's a beauty with stunning white quartz counters, dark mahogany cabinets, and a deep cast-iron sink. There's a built-in sub-zero fridge, separate wine cooler, a professional-grade gas range with a warming drawer, plus a convection wall oven and an induction cooktop. This over-the-moon kitchen is a gourmet chef's delight, ready to cook for an army, except no one in this house cooks much. Margot's not domestic. When she needs food for a party—one like tonight or just a dinner party—she has it catered. Dad wouldn't think of cooking, and I have zero kitchen talent. I could teach myself, I guess, but this is not a Cinderella story. I'm not becoming Margot's galley slave.

Beyond the trays of appetizers spread across the central island, a girl my age gazes out the window. She's small and thin, almost sprite-like, hair dyed black and violet. When she turns, I'm surprised at her thick eye makeup, the shadow smoky and dark. It makes those eyes a bit haunted, especially floating wide like saucers on her pale face. Her eyes pull me in. They say: *bet you don't know who I am.*

"Oh, hi," she says. "You must be Kaye. I'm Shelley Rodington. Margot thought we might hang out tonight."

"Well, I've been busy with a project." She gives me a spooky feel.

"It's okay. I'm out of here. I've called someone for a lift." Jingling some car keys in her hand, she says, "My parents are completely wasted. I'm taking their car keys, so they don't kill themselves tonight."

"I don't blame you" is all I have time to murmur before her phone dings and she speeds toward the door.

Margot charges around the corner. "Did Shelley leave? I invited her for you."

"She had something to do. She called a friend."

"Well, at least you two met." Margot grins, her botoxed eyes resisting any crinkling at the corners. She tosses her long, blonde hair back like a model on a photo shoot, which she once was. There's still some lingering beauty left, but it's a bleached-out one, brittle on the ends. "Shelley's Tom's niece. Her parents, Becky and Angus, live nearby."

"Who's Tom?" I ask.

Margot gives me a blue-eyed blink, puzzled that I don't know. "He's Paul's friend."

Now it's me that's puzzled. "Dad's friend? Never met him."

"I'm sure you did. He was at the …" She stops herself, and then blurts out awkwardly. "Oh, these toasted raviolis are getting cold. Would you mind heating them up in the microwave for me?" She gives me a head-to-toe review. Her scowl makes clear that my scrounged capris and T-shirt don't meet with her approval.

"I've got a movie waiting." I spin around, grabbing a plate of Thai chicken wings.

Back in my room, the bass of the music thrums through my wall, distracting me from the movie. I can't block it out, even though all my windows are shut. The glass buzzes on the low notes, which is worse than the full blast of music, so I open my side window just wide enough to ease the pressure against it. Below me, two voices rise through the swirl of summer heat. I strain to listen.

"Paul, Paul. Listen to me. Don't miss out on this."

Paul's my father. Who's talking to him? Is it Tom, the guy from earlier? I swerve back to turn off the movie so I can eavesdrop.

"I'm not interested," Dad says.

The voices get stronger. They're right below my window. The other voice is Rory. What's he trying to talk Dad into now?

"You should see these bunkers," Rory says. "You'll want one too. Talk about luxury. Five thousand square feet. Some even have a sauna. It's a whole community too, with a technical team, a maintenance team, and an extraction team that will whisk you and your family from anywhere within four hundred miles when catastrophe strikes."

My forehead's scrunching up. Huh? What kind of catastrophe is he talking about?

"How many units? Five hundred?" Dad sounds skeptical. "That means five hundred rich guys that are just as cutthroat as me. When someone realizes he'll have more supplies by killing off the rest of us, it will be bunker war. No thanks."

I recoil at that scenario—bunker war—but I haven't got a clue what Dad's saying.

Rory's adamant. "Well, I'm buying one. I'm not going to wait to be caught up in some climate collapse."

Chapter 3

Climate collapse? I'm a marble statue, not even blinking, waiting for Dad to respond to Rory. Dad knows all about the climate hoax. He's got all the evidence: the weather's always changing; the science is still in doubt; we're due for another ice age soon. Plus, the rate of warming has even slowed, so there's nothing to worry about. But that's not what Dad tells Rory right now.

"Be my guest. That's in the future." Dad sounds fully detached. "Nothing matters right now except the Galveston deal."

"But what about our kids?" Rory argues. "I've got a new baby."

Huh? My eyebrows pinch. That doesn't compute. Rory's worried about his baby so he's buying a bunker? I mean, Rory has been working with Dad to oppose the carbon tax, a state initiative that's on the ballot next November. It's called the Initiative for the Climate, but Rory calls it the Initiative for Eco-Lunatics. How can Rory do that, yet buy a bunker in case of climate collapse? He's working to create the future he fears. It's like a stupid fairy-tale dream gone crazy.

"Don't worry," Dad says. "It's going to be fine. You'll see. We have Big Leap. The project will save them."

Grabbing hold of his conviction, I take a deep breath. Dad's right. Something will save us, maybe this Big Leap thing, whatever that is.

Their voices trail off. A door shuts. They must have gone into the side door, heading to his study. Did Dad halfway agree with Rory, maybe-sort-of? Just for a minute? At least Dad said not to worry. I clutch at those words. Still, he said: *That's in the future*, like he knew it was coming.

The darkness beyond the window is alive with shifting shadows from the party—dancers, musicians, twosomes in urgent conversation—like ghosts in the woods. My jaw grips tight—that conversation doesn't add up, so I settle down at my laptop, aching for the comfort it always brings. Instead, it beckons like an enchantress, urging me to search the web for truth—will the climate really crash? I resist the grip of that question for one simple reason: Dad has never believed it will happen. Or maybe that's just an excuse. I never focused on sorting out the details because Dad's opinion was the easy default setting. Besides, who wants to think about how wretched I'll be decades from now? I prefer to focus on the misery I'm already feeling.

Still, I've got to check this out. Slamming fingertips against the keyboard, I hit the *B*, the *U*, the *N*, the *K*, the *E*, and the *R*. I add *luxury* and search. The first link is from an old news article. A showroom bunker fills the pixels on my screen. Its vivid color photos resemble a glossy real-estate brochure, but I can't quite take in the flagstone lap pool or the wall of glass beside it, looking out on a simulated backyard with artificial light. How far beneath the ground is this? It's absurd. Do they really think bunkers will save them from disaster? And the fact that these things really exist scares the hell out of me.

I've never embraced pure climate doom, but I can clearly see, if it came to catastrophe, those luxury bunkers wouldn't cut it for umpteen zillion reasons, not the least of which is what Dad said. I know these guys. Rich guys can be ruthless. They're not the type to sing *Kumbaya* and hold hands when food runs out and it comes down to you or them.

A drip of sweat rolls down my forehead. My fingers tap out a random line of SOS on the keys. I get up and pace the room, and then stare out the window at these people below, these men and women with the means to buy bunkers. Do they believe that disaster is coming? If so, why are they dancing and drinking and not doing anything to stop something that terrifies them?

Of course, the one thing about Dad is he's always been right about the world beyond the window. I remember the day he took me on my first roller coaster. At five, I was thrilled to go on such a grown-up ride, but also petrified. He settled his arm around me and told me to trust him, so I did. Nestling against his T-shirt, breathing in its fresh-pressed smell, relishing the fierce wind rushing past my ears, I didn't scream even when I wanted to. Instead with him there, I felt safe. Sometimes you need to trust someone, right? Dad might be remote. He might be lacking in kindness and caring, but he's always kept my world together. And if he says the climate won't totally tank, I still believe him, kind of.

I open the graphics file I made of Dad, looking for reassurance. Instead, his face frowns at me from the screen, despite the crinkles. It's those words he said to Rory: *The project will save them.* Save us from what? But Dad wouldn't lie to me—not about the climate, not about something that could tear apart my future. My heart clings to that, yet the more I stare at his picture, the less I believe him. Questions, doubts, bits of memory churn in my brain. I can't sort it out, so I block it. That's Dad's usual strategy, deny, deny, deny, especially when it's talking about Marty. I don't want to deny what I heard, but unless I ask Dad if he's been lying, there's no way to prove or disprove anything.

My mind drifts into memories of the last time I saw my brother. He was arguing with Dad. They were down in the old study back in Portland. As he opened the door to leave, Marty shouted, "What about the future? My future? Kaye's future?" I always supposed Marty was talking about trust-fund management or he was mad about Dad selling our home to move to Mossy Hills. I never suspected another reason for that argument until this minute.

What if Marty knew? He was a scientist. Unlike me who spent zero energy thinking about the climate, what if Marty had? I glare at Dad's photo. What if my brother realized everything Dad said about our future was a lie, and Dad just didn't care?

With a sharp click of the mouse, I attempt to close Dad's picture and shut down my suspicions, but the cursor is frozen again. There's another flash. It's that explosion of light like before. It's gone in a second, but something in the background of his photo catches my attention. It's a distortion in the pixels, a swath of grayscale that's out of place among the rich, rosy color of Mom's fountain behind it. What is it?

Squinting, leaning close, my mouth puckers into sour-lemon mode. These grayscale pixels are all wrong, appearing out of nowhere. They're a defect, an aberration, an out-of-place disturbance in my atmosphere, so I select every unruly pixel with a lasso tool and try to delete them. They don't disappear. I can't even erase them. Spot healing and cloning are useless too. I grit my teeth and hiss. Even masking doesn't work. Nothing happens except those shades of gray get stronger and darker as if they're double-layered. The pixels sharpen too. In a moment, it's clear what I'm looking at. It's an eye.

My stomach goes weird, all butterfly flutters. I've lost touch with the chair I'm sitting in. Yeah, I'm floating, even though I'm really not—my feet still rest firmly on the floor, but the sensation is zero gravity. Slamming the laptop shut, I launch myself across my bed, holding tight to the covers. Above me, the drywall texture looks storm-tossed and jumbled. It's all chaos, and I'm a-jitter, or maybe it's more the world is set to jitter, a full 100 percent, like a digital brush with permission to go totally random so you have no control over its shape, its size, its angle. Scrambling to my desk, I reach for my stylus as if it can take back control of reality, but it gives no relief, so I reach for my phone instead and open my voice mails to find Marty's. I need to hear him. I hit play.

First there's a music intro—Marty playing a few chords on his guitar—and then he says, "Hey, sis. Sorry I missed you. Look for a letter. I'll mail it soon. Love you. Brighten the moment. Don't forget, ever."

Brighten the moment—Marty loved that phrase, one of Mom's. After she died, he made it his own, serving it up with a smile, a wink, a hug, sometimes a little dancy-skip. Whenever he said those words, my smile blossomed, like it does now. I play the message again. And one more time, pushing the corners of my mouth higher. Despite the noise outside, despite the chaos in my brain, his words calm me.

And then I think about the letter. I never got his letter. Why would he send a letter, not a text, or at least an email? Of course, it's obvious why he might have sent a letter right before he died, but I refuse to consider that, so I fight to keep the smile Marty's given me. "Brighten the moment," I tell myself, but my words have lost his rhythm, and my smile goes flat.

Trying to keep hold of Marty any way I can, I turn on *Robin Hood*, pretending he's here. My smile returns at times, restored by the memory of him beside me long ago. During one scene, Robin of Locksley skirmishes with guards in Nottingham castle. It was right at this very moment when Marty would jump up with an imaginary sword, battling the sheriff's men. That was Marty, standing up to anyone he thought was in the wrong, though he'd try charming them first before crossing swords with them.

The next scene flashes across the screen—all the Freemen in Sherwood Forest swearing an oath to protect the poor. Marty and I would take that vow too, as we watched this, but now it brings a shudder, prickling the back of my neck. It's my old suspicion, one I've had since he died, that Marty had a battle brewing round him till his very last breath. All these months, it's been so unsettling not knowing what really happened to him.

Why did Marty die? A thought tries to whisper its answer to the question. A word's there, waiting, a word to keep far, far away, so I slump against my pillow and sing one of Marty's silliest songs. "Crow, crow, hey, naughty crow … Don't you eat my burrito."

Still, the first letter of that word lurks like a phantom in my brain. And then it slips through—the *mmm* drawn out like a hum—followed by a *U* and an *R*. But I can't let it finish, so I turn up the movie to drown out other unwelcome letters even though the movie doesn't grip me anymore. Despite the blaring soundtrack, I sense the next letter ... *D*. Yes, *D*. I know the one that follows too. I just refuse to think it.

Focus on the movie, Kaye, on the Merry Men gathering in the forest.

Yet, as those men in green crowd around Robin Hood, another thought breaks through the noise, one that's just as disturbing. If I were in this film, I wouldn't be in that band of men. Just living in this house, being in this family, I'd be the enemy, the ones they're fighting against.

Chapter 4

Bright morning sunshine splashes across the hillside beyond my window. Dad knocks on my door. "Kaye, I'm just going out for a minute."

The door opens. My eyes shut. My body's still. Will he detect what's revving up my breathing? I should confront him, but my nerve is gone today. All these years, I've trusted him about carbon and warming, but after hearing his *that's in the future* line and his talk about a project to save me, I'm at least 60 percent sure he's lying about climate change. He's lied about the future before, telling me Mom would get better because he had the best doctors in the world to fix her up. I wanted to believe him, and so I did, but when he let her die, it crushed me. He was supposed to stop it. He couldn't.

And now, climate collapse is added to the sins of my father. I think back to the climate strike at school. Everyone in my Photography Club debated it, but I never took a stand, keeping my mouth shut, working on my projects instead. Dad was my excuse, and what could I do about a global problem anyway? Yes, climate change was easy to deny because it never touched my life—well, besides those heat domes last summer and all that smoke from mountain fires. Can I go back to pretending there's no crisis? I study the ceiling splatter for an answer to that question, but nothing reveals itself in its ridges and gullies.

Flinging off my doubts with a flick of my hand, I force myself to stand. This morning is all about the car, so I pull on my worn T-shirt and stained capris, brushing my hair just enough to get out the worst kinks.

Downstairs, there's only dates stuffed with goat cheese to nibble. They're left over from the party. In fact, they're the only thing in the fridge. I guess this wasn't the goat cheese crowd. The cleaning crew should be here soon to take care of the disaster that surrounds me. Plastic plates decorate every surface. Spilled wine pools across the floor. Avocado dip is smeared over the cushion of a black leather love seat. Outside, broken wine glasses make the patio a no-man's-land of shards. People, especially the richest ones, can be pigs when they've overindulged in wine and drugs.

Dad has forbidden me to use rideshare because of a local kidnapping attempt. I've told him it could happen in a taxi too, but he's a stubborn old goat always ready to lock horns with anyone. Besides, he's the one who pays the bill, so I call the taxi and wait outside, pacing, checking the time. It's almost ten o'clock.

When the taxi shows up, I do my best not to snap as I tell the driver to get to the DMV, stat. To keep away the small talk, I play videos on my phone until I remember the cash. Luckily, a branch shows up in my bank app directly across from the DMV.

As we wind down from the hills, the tall firs and cedars give way to strip malls and tract homes. Fast-food chains and warehouse stores dot the scenery. As a child, Mom would take us exploring to see what the real world was like, and I was always curious about other kids, the ones in a big box store or movie theater. My dream back then was to live like them in a normal house with a bathroom to share and a dog in the backyard and kids next door to play with. I've always had the feeling that I belonged somewhere like that.

I still feel it. In fact, my first month here, I fantasized about finding my real family, the extended one, my grandmas, grandpas, aunts, uncles, and lots of cousins. They'd live in small houses in one of the new suburban tracts on the edge of Mossy Hills. I'd visit them every Sunday for a family meal. We'd share stories of great grandpas and grandmas. They'd hug me and applaud my photos and tell me how talented I was.

But I haven't found them. Instead, my house, this town, seems lonelier than the city. When I look out my bedroom window to the hillside behind it, there are only fir trees and ferns, plus plenty of gray-green, dried-up summer moss—not people. And when I go to town, I only meet strangers.

We reach the village center where century-old storefronts of brick and stone shape downtown. After passing through those cozy blocks, new buildings pop up again, including the bank and the DMV. Rushing from the cab, I discover the ATM has a withdrawal limit, so I dash into the bank for the cash. "I need to make a withdrawal," I say like I'm in total charge, even though my voice is quavering. Banks are an alien landscape. Dad takes care of money things.

The teller reacts as if I had said, "This is a stickup." She eyes my shirt and jeans and asks for extra ID. At first, I shrink from that demand—it feels like an accusation—but as I hand over my license and fill out the slip she gives me, it suddenly feels good to be treated like a suspect. It gives the morning the aura of Robin Hood.

The guy is already in the parking lot beside the car, which is twice as dented as the photo. He looks a bit rough too. White. Unshaven. Tattooed. His T-shirt is even more torn than mine. I hope this is legit.

"Herman?"

He nods and hands me the key. The engine seems to hum, though I'm no expert. I squint at the knobs and buttons on the dash and punch one, pretending to know what it does. The four-way flashers turn on. "Does the air conditioning work?"

He shakes his head. "Sorry."

"How about the radio at least?"

"You only mentioned it needed to run. It runs good."

Getting out, I walk around the car, frowning like a tough customer, even though I already know I will buy the thing. I'm surprised I'm not nervous. That's a good sign. "One tire is a little bald."

"I'll knock off fifty bucks. That's it."

I wave the whole bundle of cash. "You can take it all. Just let me know what else is wrong so I can have it fixed."

"Not too much. Perhaps the brakes are due soon."

"Okay, brakes."

"Battery is five years old."

"Okay, battery." My stance is firm. My voice is solid. I'm doing this. "Will it pass emissions?"

"Already did." He hands me something that appears official. It's two weeks old.

I study it, though it could be written in Greek. "Will they take this?"

"Sure."

That's doubtful, but still, I love the car. It looks everyday, average, a car that normal people would drive, people who don't have tons of dollars.

He signs over the title and takes off across the lot in a sprint, leaving me staring at the paper in my hand, hoping it's not a forgery. With a shrug—what can I do?—I slide behind the wheel and just sit. This is my first car, well at least the first car that's all mine, bought by me, chosen by me. The steering wheel's a bit grimy. Stains decorate the seat. It smells of tobacco and weed. I can't wait to get it cleaned and fixed. Feeling a glow, like when you get a crush, I decide I'll call her Charlotte.

Locking her up, I snap a picture on my phone before heading into the DMV. It's a smaller office and the lines aren't long. Hanging from the ceiling above the front desk is a big sign that says *START HERE*. There's a woman in front of me with a little kid in her arms—a girl, very shy. She peers over her mother's shoulder timidly. Her hair is wispy brown, and her eyes are hazel. She's got very pink cheeks. I play hide and seek with her through my fingers and make her giggle. Her mother turns. "She likes you," she says. "She doesn't often take to strangers."

"Maybe she's just picking up on my mood. Got my first car today. I feel like total bliss."

"Congratulations." She reaches out with her free hand. "I'm Jane. And this is Elyse." Jane is tall and slender. Her complexion's almost olive, a sharp contrast to her daughter's rosy one, but she's got the same hazel eyes as Elyse. Those green-brown eyes say *welcome.*

"I'm Kaye." I shake her hand. "Hey, do you know a good mechanic? Charlotte needs a little work."

"Charlotte?"

"Yeah, I was going to go with Carlotta, because, well, she's a car, but Charlotte has more class." I show off my photo of her like she's a brand-new baby.

Jane smiles as she studies it. She must be amused—my gushing over a clunker of a car. She's kind about it though. "Take Charlotte to Joe Mandell's shop over on Kettle Street. He'll take care of you. Tell him Jane Zell sent you."

"I sure will." I'm beaming as she steps up to take her turn. I've bought a car, found my mechanic. I'm set.

But a minute later, the woman at the desk—a sallow, cranky-eyed one who has no energy to be pleasant—barks out a new hurdle to clear. A huge one. "To register, you'll need insurance," she says.

Insurance. Ugh. I should have researched online, but my head's been so distracted lately by all things gloomy. "Can I drive it home at least?" I ask.

"Yes, you have thirty days to register, but you must get insurance before you can drive it."

"Okay," I say weakly. "Thanks."

At least Herman was right. They'll take the emissions test—finally a reason to draw a good breath.

Still, I slink out of the office, feeling like an idiot. The pavement feels spongy beneath me, the sun pulses against my back, and the sky fills with sudden chaos. It's those crows swarming across it, a whole flock. Their squawks echo in my brain, croaking and cawing, mocking me for not knowing what I'd need to buy a car. I'd better get it home in a hurry since I don't have insurance.

Unlocking Charlotte's door, though, my mood picks up. I did it! I bought my own car! Driving her is even better. She runs great. She takes the corners in stride. As I glance into the rearview mirror, those chaos crows disappear, heading beyond the trees.

Driving down Main Street, my smile greets all the people strolling along the sidewalks. I've got a car, a normal car that's perfect for this suburban scene. No heads turn when I drive past. I'm so giddy that I almost miss a red light. Screeching to a stop, I thank goodness that the brakes hold up. Damn, I shouldn't be driving without insurance.

While waiting for the light, the old brick post office becomes a pencil sketch in my mind, imaginary lines emphasizing the curved details over each window and the boxy parapet. I love historic buildings like these, especially my old Northwest Craftsman in Portland. I start to think about my room back there in the city, Mom helping me decorate it, choosing the colors carefully—we settled on sky blue and lavender. As we painted, Mom stopped me from slopping it on. "Concentrate on each and every stroke," she said. "Stay in the moment. Moments have power."

A steady people-stream flows through the wrought iron post office door. That's when he descends the steps. He's a guy about my age, maybe a year or two older. He stands at the corner, waiting for the light to cross, talking on his phone with a clipboard in his hand. His eyes are happy just like Ned's last night, except his skin is darker, a rich ebony. I can't take my eyes off him. He's gorgeous.

Honk! I missed the changing light. Stepping hard on the gas, *grr-vroom*, my thoughts return to this new car and the sense of freedom it brings—escape from Bleak House. "Yes!" This is the day I declare my independence. Out the window, I *whoop* at a help wanted sign in a store window.

Maybe I'll even get my own job, just an ordinary one in a store or a fast-food restaurant. Dad would have a fit.

Luckily, Dad isn't home yet. I park Charlotte as far over on the edge of the drive as I can, hoping he'll be too busy to notice her. If I'm lucky, he might believe she's the maid's car. In the kitchen, the party cleaners have come and gone. Everything's spotless, but the fridge is still empty except for those stuffed dates. I settle on an apple from the fruit bowl and head upstairs, chomping away at the crisp, white flesh.

Needing some pixel time—digital drawing calms me down, helps me think—I remember my vision of Ned painting tunnels into the sky and open his photo to admire his face again. I decide to try that—hollowing out the sky, digging into the spray of stars, the pen tool as my pick and the brush tool as my shovel. What a poetic way to spend the day, eh?

NASA's image gallery is full of star scenes. There's a perfect one taken from the space station, a dark sky above the atmospheric rim glowing around the Earth. Downloading the high-res version—lots of yummy pixels—sinking into that core of patience inside me, layer by layer, I build the space tunnel, working with gradients, scaling each blue-black oval smaller and darker, creating perspective as I drill into the cosmos.

Timelessness takes over. It frees me. Working in this software always does, and without the grind of time, I float. It's only moments like these that I feel genuinely happy anymore. Stepping out beyond myself into this deep-space image, I walk among the pixels of the stars. I love this.

I zoom into the photo, staring down the tunnel like it's the bull's-eye on a target. That target grows larger and larger. Now I'm locking onto the darkest core of it, but I'm startled by what's there—the legendary light at the end of the tunnel, and it's not just a flash of pixel light either. Its glow expands like a supernova burst, leaving behind a grayscale blur that grows larger and larger as it nears the max percentage of zoom on the screen. It's the eye.

My jaw snaps tight. No, no. This eye looks sad, too sad for me. It drains me of color, tinting me somber, so I hide all my layers except the original NASA image. There's no eye, not anywhere, no matter where I zoom. My breath slows, almost normal again, but when I turn on my layers, right in the core of that tunnel, the eye is back. It's bigger even, visible at just 200 percent. This time I'm gripped by the pull of its mystery. Whose eye is this?

I clone it, flip it. Now two eyes stare at me—no movement, no blinking, but there's a depth to them that defies the flatness of the screen. They're pleading with me to not turn away. And I can't. I'm hooked, needing to figure out the puzzle. Zeroing in on the slant of each eyelid, the enlarged pupils, tucking themselves under the lids just a bit, I recognize that look from all my digital work on faces. It's the squint of pain.

Yes, it's pain, but more. These eyes are whispering, *I'm lonely*. I picture a series of images: shattered glass, bleak, burnt-out buildings, a bit of empty, dusty street. The street has one long gash down its center, splitting the grainy asphalt. It's a deep and jagged crack, and there's a desolate shadow filling up that dark rift. It rips through my heart, but I can't escape it.

More scenes rise up and splash before me: Dad's face when he got the call that Marty died; the words he said, so flat, so dead; and then it's me alone in the cemetery, staring at two tombstones, one beside the other. Loneliness—*that* I understand.

A man's voice breaks into my sorrow. "Hello, Kaye."

"Huh?" I jerk back from the screen. My eyes bulge. My mouth hangs wide.

"I've been waiting for you." His voice is soft, like water lapping against the shore. The sound's too vibrant to be coming through a laptop speaker.

"What?" My heart won't stop hammering. "Where are you?" I'm on my feet, opening my closet, opening my bedroom door, checking the windows, looking for the man behind the voice as if I'm checking for the monster under my bed. I'm shouting now. "Who are you?"

My laptop speaks again. "I am Sol." There's a hint of accent. *El sol* is the

Spanish word for sun—maybe he's Hispanic.

"What do you mean? S-O-L, like the sun? Or S-O-L-E? Are you alone?"

"It is S-O-L. Short for Solomon. But yes, I am alone." His tone is so tender, my heart aches.

I glance around the room. "Where are you?"

"I am far away, somewhere too far for you to reach."

My ears go on alert—compelled to listen. "Are you hurt? Do you need help?"

"Yes, I need your help."

My muscles tense. "Should I call someone? The police?"

"No. I will explain it later."

I look over my shoulder, expecting him to appear. Minutes go by. Nothing. The eyes still watch me from the screen, but even though I wait for it, he doesn't speak. I'm surprised that desire to wait is so strong, like there's no choice in this. *Later*. He said *later*. When? How long must I sit here till he tells me? I'm patient. I can stay here. I can watch the tunnel I built in the sky. I need to hear his voice again, but I don't understand why. I should be glad he's gone.

Pixel by pixel, the eyes fade. I scan the room. Nothing's changed, yet something has. I realize it's me. I feel fresh, alive, all my nerves tingling. I can't shake the sensation that I've been someplace far away and have just come back. Last night that eye scared me. Today it claimed me, touching an ache, one that longs to connect. I take a step forward, and when I do, I'm unhinged from gravity, caught up in some virtual eternity.

It takes several minutes for me to walk across the room to check outside my window for the man. It's the window that brings connection to the real world again. The fir trees outside remind me of solid ground, the buzz of bees, the fragrance of flowers. Slowly the room conquers the present—I'm here inside it. Plucking a dark, stray hair off my T-shirt, I drop it. Gravity works. My amazement has left me. Doubt seeps in to fill the void, along with grumpy questions: *Was I imagining it?*

Back at my laptop, I hunt through my photos for the grayscale eye. It's gone. Not just in the sky tunnel, but in Dad's photo too. Grasping for explanations, I wonder, was this a ghost? A space alien? Was it the apple I just ate, a curse from the wicked witch? Perhaps someone drugged me. Could it be Charlotte? Could Herman have spread something on the steering wheel that seeped into my skin? Can drugs do that?

Running out of ridiculous explanations, my eyebrows pinch, facing up to the only sensible, logical reason left. I deflate, no longer buoyed by the mysterious. "It's obvious." I mutter at my PC. "I've been hacked."

How I've been hacked, I don't have a clue. And more crucial, I don't know why. I must admit, they really knew how to get to me, and it seems a very personal hack to pull off randomly. Clearly, they had talent. I run the virus program again, but there's no evidence of malware. Feeling helpless for a second, I search my ceiling for answers and then pick up my car key. I need a new machine.

Back at my laptop to search for a computer shop, I peer at the keys on the keyboard as if the hacker's hiding beneath them. It seems he is because, when I type in *Mossy Hills + computers* into the search bar and hit enter, that eye appears in the middle of the results.

"Very funny," I say, ready to close the search page, but another explosion of light pulses across it like a surreal GIF. There's a snippet of text, all italic, below the eye. It simply says: *EF0 tornado today at 4:00 p.m. on Clement Valley Road near Treasure Pond.* The text is linked. I don't click it, but it doesn't matter. A web map pops up anyway, showing Clement Valley Road a few miles west of town, where the hills spill into the valley leading back to the city.

An arrow marks Treasure Pond. I've been there, hoping to find a family-friendly spot to soak in the sun—people fishing, kids playing in the shallows, teens basking on the shore, maybe someone friendly. Instead, it was empty, only two tables, no restroom, and a scummy pond.

"Stop this!" I stare at the map, searching for an eye, a glow. Nothing shimmers. The text fades. No voice calls my name. I shut down my laptop, doubly furious because this machine, my lifeblood, my passion, now seems sinister. Why did I feel so touched by that voice—kind words thrown my way like a doggie treat? I won't need his kind words anymore. I'll stop being lonely. And I'm going to figure out who he is.

My charge down the stairs is interrupted when Dad opens the study door. "Kaye, I'm leaving now for Galveston. I'll be back in about a week."

"Okay. Are you going to give me a to-do list?" I stare at him expectantly, but the long pause between us is filled with tension. The tension is normal. What isn't normal is his hesitation to speak.

He peers at me, eyes narrowed in prosecutor mode. "Did you throw a soda at Margot last night?"

"Oh, for bunny-grumble-sake. It was an accident." I'm using Mom's kid-friendly code-word for *time to calm down*, hoping to lighten the mood, but it triggers the opposite reaction.

Dad eyes narrow even more, and the corners of his mouth turn down. "She said you were angry."

"When am I not?" I glare, ready for the lecture.

Instead, he asks, "Whose car is that in the driveway?"

In revolution mode, I can't help but blurt out, "Mine. I bought it this morning."

Dad's face reddens. He's holding back, just barely. "And what about your coupe?"

"That's not my car! That's your car! You didn't even ask me what color I wanted."

Dad's stumped for a reply, a flash of recognition in his eye.

I head to the door, saying, "Have a great trip."

His hand grips my shoulder. "You can't drive that."

"Why not?" I turn back, ready to draw my arrow, send it straight into his heart. "Not rich enough for you? The only thing that bothers you is what other people will say."

Dad's eyes squeeze. He takes a deep breath and says with his firmest of Dad tones, "It's not insured."

"So, insure it." I raise an eyebrow, daring him.

"I don't have time for this."

"Well, too bad. I've got things to do. I'm going."

"No, you're not. Give me the keys." His hand is out—not begging. He's demanding.

I bite my lip and stare him down.

His voice lowers. That's always worse. "I'll ground you."

"You're leaving. Who will enforce it? Margot? She's probably still drunk from last night."

"If you don't give me the keys, Kaye, I'll put a hold on your credit card."

Ugh. Flinch time. The credit card belongs to him.

Dad sees me waver. He steps forward, his hand still out. "We'll talk about this when I get back. In the meantime, drive the coupe."

Clank. The key drops. I glance away as he picks it up. "I just have one key. I haven't had a chance to copy it." How I wish that weren't true.

With the key in hand, he asks, "Did you get a title?"

"In the glove compartment."

He nods and heads into the study, so I stomp back upstairs, searching my phone for a rideshare link. No taxis for me anymore, and I am not going drive that ugly red car.

Chapter 5

Mom always picked cars that were white, like Charlotte. Her preference was for more cream in the tint than my car, but Charlotte's so dingy from sun fade and grime, she's totally off-white. White isn't cool, but Mom liked it anyway, which was strange. With her bubbly spirit, you'd think she'd drive something orange or yellow, but people are more complicated than they seem. I mean, why did she choose Dad? She was beautiful. She was smart. Everyone adored her, but she picked gloomy, driven Dad. That's complex.

I'm complex too, in a different way. I wouldn't pick my flinty, storm-gray dad if I had a choice. I'd pick someone full of blazing color, golden yellows and orangey-reds, like Mom and Marty. And where Mom always smoothed things over and let Dad have his way, I can't. Glowering at the rideshare app, I close it. I'll jimmy Charlotte's lock, instead, and learn to hot-wire her, maybe buy my own insurance. I search online for insurance tips and quotes. Adding my car to a family policy seems to be the cheapest, which means asking Dad. Ugh. That's not going to happen.

Dad's in the hallway outside my door. "I'm leaving, Kaye."

My eyes close in case he peers in, but he leaves without opening it. Despite how angry I am, that hurts, which doesn't make sense. I for sure didn't want to talk to him. Still, my pillow rockets through the air in frustration toward the shut door.

Dad wasn't always this stony. One day after Mom died, my ice-cream cone tumbled and landed in the gutter. Dad stooped down to my level and wrapped his arms around me, wiping away my tears. He didn't hesitate. He didn't hold back. In fact, tears filled his own eyes for a second before he stood up and took my hand. We walked back to the store and got a new cone. He even bought me extra sprinkles—for Dad that was empathy.

Shelving car insurance plans, I tiptoe halfway down the stairs, listening to the roll of the suitcase and the click of the front door closing. I almost call out to him. Almost. Instead, I scurry down to the foyer, peering through the glass beside the door, watching his taxi leave. I hate that taxi taking my dad away.

But as the taxi heads down the long cement drive, another memory rumbles inside me. It was the day of the wedding, Dad's and Margot's, and I refused to unlock my bedroom door even though it was time to get into the car to go. Dad pounded on it forever, and then everything went silent. Footsteps headed down the hall. Soon they returned and something slid beneath the door—a bunch of scraps, paper scraps. I picked one up and recognized what it was—a piece from my sketch of the two of us walking through the garden beside Mom's fountain. He had ripped up my drawing to give me a message: he chose Margot over me. Defeated, I finally opened my door. He just glared at me, not at all pleased that he won.

Sunk by that memory, I walk to his study and kick at its ghastly Medieval door. It creaks open, leaving me shocked. I've only stepped through that door twice, both times when Dad was handing down some sermon about credit-card limits. Today, he must have been so furious, or so rushed, that he forgot to lock it. This is his forbidden room. Everything that he claims as his, and his alone, is captive here, probably including my key, so I can't resist. I tiptoe inside like a thief.

Dad's study is a hybrid between an office and a museum. Old first editions of classic literature fill the shelves, and expensive art lines the walls. At the desk, I try some drawers. They're all locked, but that won't stop me from checking out the usual places to hide a key. The photo of Margot is suspect, but nothing's behind the backing. The walnut paper weight beside it is way too bulky, but there's no seam to indicate a secret compartment. I kneel on the floor, running my fingers along the underside of the desk. Instant payoff! It's a small, rectangular box, and when I lay on the floor to examine it, the bottom slides away, revealing a key. I'm sure it will open the drawers.

But it doesn't. I try all the closet doors and cabinets. The key doesn't work on any of them. I'm not really surprised. Drawers and cabinets are too obvious. Dad likes to reach beyond the obvious. I check behind the pictures on the wall and the books lining the shelves. There's a large, long wall mirror tucked into a back corner, partially hidden by a bookcase, and a basket on a shelf beside it, holding a comb and an electric razor. This could be a place to preen for last-minute meetings, maybe virtual ones.

Or it could be a place to find a keyhole!

I gaze at my reflection in the mirror, its pale blue eyes searching mine, challenging me to answer the question—do I really want to know where this key leads? Dad's world of deals upon deals has always been a mystery I've never wanted to crack. And since Margot arrived, everything else about Dad's been one big secret. That's even truer now after Marty's death. Nothing's been right, but I haven't wanted to investigate what's making me so uneasy. Will I find out why Dad and Marty argued, or maybe something even worse? Is this about that Big Leap project Dad talked about? Or is this about the carbon tax he's fighting? I need to know what the key unlocks. And besides, I need to find my key for Charlotte. I need to drive my car.

The mirror's firmly attached to the wall, so I work through the books on the bookcase beside it. The last book by the wall is large and wedged in tight. I pry it out and peek beneath it. There it is, a dark indent in the wood, finger-wide, like a button. When I push on it, a tiny door slides open in the wall beside the shelf. The keyhole stares at me, whispering a dare: *Try me.*

When we were young, a favorite game of Marty's and mine was finding Dad's hiding places. I was always first to guess Dad's spots for secrets—it's the one thing I could do better than Marty. We weren't really interested in what we found, but the finding of it was a thrill. Today, though, that thrill is mixed with dread.

My hand trembles slightly as I slide the key in. Before I can turn it, the front door slams. Did Dad forget something? Yanking the key back out, I go into reverse, pressing the button. The tiny door closes over the keyhole again. As I struggle to get the big book in place, more books fall off the shelf. Stifling nervous giggles, I hurry them all back, dash to the study door, and peer out.

My knees sink a bit as my breath releases. It's just Margot. I shut the door and lock it, thinking through my options—either explore where that key leads or wait till Margot's busy and won't come looking for me. Yes, I need my car key, but if Margot catches me, she will certainly tell Dad, so no. Now is not the time to investigate.

Placing the key back in its box under the desk, I scrutinize the jumble of books. What's Dad's plan for them? It's not alphabetical. I close my eyes to picture the shelf as it was before. The books had been ordered by size, so I reorganize them to make sure they rise toward the oversized one at the end. Dad wouldn't want that book to look out of place.

Satisfied I've broken the book code, I poke my head into the hallway and slip out to peer at Margot's copper roadster in the parking roundabout in front of the house. She's still here, but there's no loud TV in the family room, no whir of the spin cycle, no faint chatter on the phone. Did she leave again, perhaps with someone else? It's so quiet she could be a ghost by now, dying without my knowing. It's Bleak House, the perfect place to haunt.

I check the master bedroom. Just stepping inside gives me shivers. Dad had this room fortified. It's the safe room in case of home invasions.

I'm not sure I could sleep in here, reminded of that. Wandering into the bathroom—everything is marble, the tub, the shower, the vanity—I peek through the glass door of the home sauna, the only thing not stone. Its rich cedar interior is empty except for a small packet on the bench. Inside is something white. Is Margot using drugs again? And Dad just left a half hour ago.

Margot had a drug problem two years back. A month in fancy rehab cleared it up, but I don't think Dad would forgive her if she had to go back there again. Hopefully, she won't. Despite my anger toward her, I wouldn't wish that on anyone. Maybe that white powder is air freshener or cleaner for the cedar wood. I spin around, not wanting to look too closely, and head for my room.

Down the hall, there's a *clunk* in the kitchen. It must be Margot. Instead of scurrying up to my room, I get an idea. "Hi, Margot." I practically skip across the kitchen tiles. "Great party."

Margot's taking a bottle from the wine cooler. As she tugs on the cork, she stops, looking at me. "You stayed locked up in that room of yours the whole night."

"Not all the time."

"Well, I'm glad you enjoyed it." She's not smiling as she pours Chardonnay into her glass.

"The best part was the band. Who were they?"

She squints at the ceiling. "Oh, I forget their name. Becky recommended them." She returns to filling her glass.

"So, where does Shelley live?"

Margot's softening up, her voice rising. "She lives just up the road on Crisscross Mountain." She points out the window.

Since Margot's smiling, I keep talking. "I thought she was interesting."

"Becky is really nice too. We should all go have lunch together. Mother-daughter time."

I try not to wince. She's not my mother, no way, but for a few minutes I pretend. "Sure. Shelley can tell me all about Mossy Hills High."

Mossy Hills is the new school I'll go to in September. Dad always fought against public school with Mom, but now that it's my only choice, he's cool with it. I'm curious what it will be like. Maybe I should try connecting with Shelley after all, even if her family's rich, which of course they must be if they're on Margot's radar.

Now that Margot's warmed up, I make the play. "I bought a car today. I need to add it to the insurance policy. Dad left before he could."

Margot goes blank. I'm counting on that. After she's been drinking all night, her memory gets patchy, so maybe she doesn't remember I have the coupe.

"What about the red car?"

Damn! She does. My nose wrinkles. "That car's hideous. Dad will have to take it back. In the meantime, I bought one for myself, but I need insurance. I can call and do everything. I'll just hand the phone to you to give the okay."

I speed to the stairs to find the phone number for the family policy. I know I've got it somewhere. "I'll be in the gym," Margot calls after me as she heads into the east wing of the house to sip her wine between turns on her spin cycle. My eye roll is automatic.

Pulling Charlotte's title from my desk drawer—yes, I lied to Dad about where it was—I dial the number. By the time I'm back downstairs, an agent is already on the phone, and I'm reading out the VIN number for Charlotte. I call loudly, "Here's my mom. She'll approve everything."

Margot lights up when I call her *Mom*. She just wants the label, though, not the domestic burden, such as buying groceries. I usually fend for myself until she remembers to shop for food online. I would do the shopping, but I'm stubborn.

That's not the only domestic failing for Margot. Family meals mean dinner out. Laundry, that's for the maid, though I prefer to handle mine myself. Loading the dishwasher—how hard can that be, Margot? Scrubbing toilets, vacuuming, dusting, sorting recycling, clearing up random debris off horizontal surfaces, that's all for the maid too. Margot's never attended a school performance of mine or a parent-teacher conference. What excuse will she make when it's time for me to graduate? Probably food poisoning, her favorite one. It was harder to deal with Margot when I was younger. I've gotten used to her. But a mom? She's not a mom. Not even barely.

I hand her my cell.

"Hi, it's Margot Malloy speaking." She announces this as if she's Woman of the Year and gets all chatty because the agent is a man. And then she says, "Yes, I'll be on the title."

My mood slumps, diving into mud-brown territory. Margot on the title? How do I manage that?

After she hands me back the phone, she spins out a story about how her trainer, Terry, who should be arriving any minute, worked with Olympic athletes a few years ago. To escape, I volunteer to let him in. She's delighted.

The foyer becomes a cage to prowl, pacing, pacing, waiting for him. All I need is the car key and somehow, Margot's name on the title. Dad would be pissed, but it would be too late.

Letting Terry in, I say the required greetings, and then walk him to the gym. He's tall, strong, and gorgeous, with sandy hair and green eyes that sweep over you like a kiss.

"Terry!" Margot gushes as he steps through the door.

My grin becomes charged, a current of wishful thinking that Margot will run off with him and leave me in peace. Dad has too much money, though, for Margot to ever let go of him. Still, if Margot would ever cheat with anyone, it would have to be this guy. But what would be *his* motivation? Margot's pretty, but not at all his age. Nah, I can't pawn Margot off on Terry.

Margot will be working with him for maybe an hour, so I head back to the study, slip through the heavy oak door, and lock it. Grabbing the key from under the desk, I remove the book and press the little button. With the keyhole exposed, I listen for any sign of Margot's cackle. She always laughs extra loud around her trainer because he's a guy who thinks he's funny. She never wants to disappoint men, so of course, she overdoes it. It's quintessential Margot: phony and obvious.

The key twists a quarter turn, and the whole mirror begins to move, swinging out toward me. It's narrow, so it misses me, but still, I jump back, wincing at a twinge in my ankle as I catch myself on the bookshelf.

Behind the mirror, there's only solid black, except it's not a wall, it's a steeply sloping corridor leading downward into darkness. I can't tell how far it goes. As I step across a threshold, floor LEDs blink on, leading the way. Inching along, following the trail of light, my heart pounds like I'll meet a mad scientist or serial killer, maybe both, any minute. Another door greets me. It's more like a submarine hatch or an airlock on a spaceship with a heavy-duty handle to pull. I stop, reluctant to touch it.

My breath is deep, so deep. This is crazy. I'm in a house, my house, with real secret corridors, real secret doors, and they're not old doors in an old house. This house is brand new, which means Dad had these secrets built into it. I set my jaw, putting my hand on the hatch handle, yanking it hard. It opens too easily, and I stumble back.

The room I step into is furnished with a couch, comfortable chairs, and a dining room set made of mahogany, probably harvested illegally like the cabinets Margot had built for our kitchen—yes, she winked when she hinted they were not sustainable, savoring the wickedness of it. On the left, several doors are shut. One is just a closet. I check a file cabinet inside, hoping my car key is waiting there, but it's empty.

This must be a guest house somewhere out back. Ten acres might be bigger than I imagine. Maybe this is on the other side of the hill that rises behind the back garden. I haven't explored there. Another door leads into a bedroom, very large, but without windows. Don't bedrooms have to have windows? An uneasy shiver grips me.

Beyond the living room is a small kitchen with all-electric appliances, upscale but compact. There are dishes in the cupboard and a pantry full of packages that appear to be dehydrated dinners. There are even boxes of powdered milk and jars of instant coffee. Dad would never drink instant coffee—that's the giveaway. A jolt hits me. My gasp slips out like air releasing from a pinched balloon. Sinking back against the countertop, I clutch the gleaming quartz for support. All I can think of is that photo on the website of the lap pool in the bunker. This is one of those, a climate bunker, the kind Rory was talking to Dad about. Dad didn't need one like Rory's because he already had his.

Absolutely wrecked, I nibble at a hang nail. It's as if I've been living on an ice floe that's suddenly cracked in two beneath my feet. Old headlines splash across my memory, dire warnings rising like banners of doom: firestorms, melting ice sheets, coral reefs bleaching beneath an ocean where stronger storms churn and swirl. I focus on the ceiling, trying to beat back the rising seas, the deadly heat, all the things that might happen. It's true. Climate change is true, and Dad believes it.

The room goes wobbly, or is it my legs? Ugh. This must be underground very deep, not a thought I'm very happy about. Mental compression lines form across the floor. The ceiling almost seems to bulge from the weight of all that earth above me like a digital filter has been applied to it. For extra effect, I tint the walls gray, and not just a cool gray without a hint of warmth, but a dull gray textured with depression—those dreary days of living through a catastrophe with nothing but these four walls forever.

I gaze around the kitchen and then stagger into the main room, my knees giving way beneath me. Imagine being stuck in here for months, even years, using up all the oxygen in this cramped, surreal place. Urgency propels me toward the door. I've got to get to the surface, up where there's fresh air and a sense of normal all around me. Stumbling through the hatch, I stop, and turn back. There, on a hook on the wall, is Charlotte's key. I clutch at it, triumphant!

But triumphant doesn't squash the queasy feeling. Groping my way up the tunnel corridor, I feel so weak. By the time I reach the study, I'm suffocating. Long breath in. Long breath out. Hey, Dad, I'm your kid. What kind of future are you giving me? I actually pass out for a quick second, but when I wake, the truth hasn't receded into some misty fog of forgetting.

Dad has built a bunker in Bleak House. He knows sometime in the future, maybe decades from now, maybe sooner, the climate crisis could collapse our lives, along with the natural world around us—a world that feeds us, gives us the air and water we need to live. Does he believe the only thing he needs to do is build a bunker to hide in when it all goes crazy? Meanwhile, he's working to make sure the nightmare comes true.

The corridor lights are out, but down that dark hallway, the bunker hatch is still open. Maybe it closes automatically. If not, Dad will know someone's been in there. I'll have to go back to check, but not till I can wrap my mind around this. Not till I have the courage to face it again.

Chapter 6

I replace the tall, thick book over the button in the bookcase but don't put the key back under the desk, slipping it into my pocket instead to remind me of what Dad's doing. My shock has faded. Now all that's left is anger. Why did I believe him all these years? He's opposing the initiative and spouting climate hoax lies. There must be tons of money he's contributing to all this.

Slipping out the side door near the study, I sit by the terrace fountain and let the sun chase the jitters out of my brain. This is my special place to spend time with Mom. She's in this fountain, at least in memories. "Why is Dad like this?" I whisper. "Was he like this before? Did I just not know it?" Peering into the reflection pool beneath the rosy granite pillar, I long to see her face beside mine, but there's only me.

The garden is quiet. It's actually quite peaceful, which is so welcome as I rebound from the shockwave of the bunker, but my world has shifted like a 9.0 quake. That jolt is like a bandit ready to rob me of the calm. When the gravel crunches behind me, I spin around. Nothing's there. Maybe it's just the gardener, Jose. I search the terraces, but no one's walking through the lush greenery. Shaking it off, my thoughts return to my father. I long for the old story—Dad being right about this climate thing—but the new story is whispering to me, one that begins: *Dad lied. About everything. He did.*

A rustle in a bush makes me jump. It's a small bird flitting from branch to branch, its busy hops and tail flicks distracting me from dwelling on ways to confront my father when he returns. All these years I've longed to reach out to him, but instead, I've resisted him, sulked about him, and avoided him. Now with these new issues looming—climate change, bunkers, all the lies—there's no easy path forward.

Beside the fountain sits a clump of yellow flowers. I'm drawn by the cheerful color and a sweet nectar scent. A bee lands on one, and my phone snaps its picture. It's a clumsy, fuzzy bumblebee. How can something that cute sting? It explores the flower as it searches for pollen, its deep black body pulsing against the yellow petals. A bright golden stripe radiates across its abdomen. Does Jose use pesticides here? The gardener in Portland did. I kept finding dead bees all around the yard. He was spraying the flowers, which of course killed the bees that were needed to pollinate them. Ugh.

I read about bee gardens at school last spring. Maybe I can plant one to help them survive. Bees need flowers. Flowers need bees. Scouting for a likely spot beyond the terraces, I head up the hill. One flower I've always wanted to grow comes in brilliant reds and purples. It's called bee balm— what a wonderful name. It's that word, balm. Right now, I could use some balm—Kaye balm. I wish there was a plant like that for me.

There's a crunch behind me on the gravel again. The flash of a rabbit bounces through the greenery. It breaks free of the garden and disappears between the scaly trunks of the firs, leaving my heart racing as fast as the bunny. Wondering what else is up there besides trees, I follow it, longing for escape from my gloomy, grayscale thinking. Why haven't I explored this place before? I've been brooding in my room all summer.

Beyond the top of the hill is a small ravine brimming with ferns and leafy shrubs. Moisture's in the air—the scent of damp earth and fresh, green moss. Water's trickling like a child's happy song. Between tall shrubs, I catch the glint of that water sliding over rocks beneath me. It's a creek! The scene makes me think of Marty and Mom. One day we went on a camping trip when Dad was out of town for a month. I wasn't sure I would like it, but Mom said I would. She told us stories of when she was a kid, camping with her family. She made it sound like fun.

And it *was* fun. We played in the creek beside our campsite, racing sticks to see whose floated fastest down the current. After supper, we toasted marshmallows, sipped hot chocolate, and sang songs around the fire. I asked Mom why we never go camping with her family. She got quiet. "They live a long way away," she said, as if it explained things.

Years later, I asked Marty what that really meant. The best he could understand was that there was a schism in her family. Mom had been cast out. I couldn't really believe it. Who wouldn't want Mom? But Marty said that's why she was so devoted to Dad. He rescued her from a bad scene, living on the edge. With Dad, she felt safe. After she died, none of her family showed for the funeral, and Dad refused to talk about it to Marty. I, of course, never asked.

Scanning the tangle of green that hides the creek, thinking how much Mom might like it, I feel in sync with her. She was cast out of the family. I'm cast out too. She was rejected, yet she found herself a new life. That's what I must do, find the place that I belong, figure out where I need to be, find something I can be part of. In the meantime, I need to stay sane in this wretched house, like by planting a bee garden.

Vacillating between exploring the creek and planning the bee garden, my heart sides with the bees. I claim a garden spot on the hill toward the far side of the house, away from parties and the gloom of Bleak House. It faces east. The morning sun will shine here. Searching my phone for bee gardens, wondering what to plant—there's so much information, so many flowers—I decide to focus on the basics first, like water.

At the edge of the garden is an outdoor faucet. I'll have to dig a trench to it and get the gardener to lend a hand to hook it up. As I walk along the hill, devising a plan, a squirrel scrambling up a cedar grabs my attention. It dashes across a fork in the trunk, dislodging a wire from the moss nestled there. Dangling from the wire is a black plastic tube.

The tube holds a long cylinder. Its wire leads into the branches above where I can't see. Standing on tippy-toe, I peer down through the fork of the tree to where the tube had been aiming. Whoa! My father's study. It's looks like someone's snooping.

On my phone, I search for *spy cameras* and *surveillance equipment*. Some sites pop up with all sorts of gadgets for listening in on conversations. Studying the photos, I find one that matches—a laser microphone. The product description says it can record conversations in a room just by capturing vibrations on the glass. It talks about a separate receiver, which might be higher in this tree, but needles block my view. I yank the device free of its wire and gaze at it balanced in my hand. How can this even work? It's so far away from the study. And what are they listening for? Investment secrets? Stock tips? All these mysteries are just burying me.

And then I find a clue. Down by my feet there's a business card trampled into the mud. Its print is scratched and faint. Only half the words show through the smear of the dirt. There's *Fossil* and *Tom* and a partial last name that begins with *Roding*, part of a phone number, and a Mossy Hills post office box with some numbers missing. Handwriting on the back says: *Call me tomorrow.* Shelley's last name is Rodington. Tom is her uncle. This card could be his, but why would he be spying on Dad?

Calling Dad to warn him, I only get voicemail. "Hey, Dad. I've found something strange in the garden. Call me." And then I remember the bunker, but what can I say: *I've found your secret bunker, so what else are you keeping from me?* I wouldn't dare put that in a voicemail, so I just hang up.

My fingertips press into the rough bark of the tree beside me until it hurts. It's hard not trusting Dad. Without him, there's nobody. Dad was an only child of only children. His parents died, and Mom's family is a mystery, so I've just got Dad, a man of secrets. Can you be angry with someone, hate him most days, and still need him? I press the bark harder and harder until I want to scream. It's like I'm on that roller-coaster ride with Dad again, but this time he's not keeping me safe.

Stuffing the business card into my pocket, I touch the key lurking there—the key to the bunker—and shudder. The key and card become linked in my brain, drowning me in darkness and danger. Beneath my house or the garden or this tree, perhaps even right below my feet, a hidden bunker waits. It's scary-crazy. Hackers. Surveillance. Bunkers.

Before I know it, I'm rocketing off, dashing down the hill, running to somewhere, anywhere, far away from this house that I hate. And then I remember the laptop I need to buy. Maybe I need a few spy gadgets of my own to figure this out—perhaps video in my room to make sure no one's sneaking in when I'm not there, or worse, sneaking up on me when I'm sleeping.

Rounding the corner of the house, I see Margot in the doorway, waving to me. "There you are. Come inside. I want to ask you something."

I'm not in the mood for fake mother-daughter conversation. Besides, she looks all wicked witch today, coaxing me closer to cast a spell or stuff me into her oven. I smile and wave back like I can't hear her. My grip on the car handle is strong, a thunderbolt of adrenaline surging through me—why does she do that to me? I yank the door open, toss the laser device into the glove box, and put Charlotte into drive.

Peeling out, screeching down Willow Mountain like a race-car driver, my imagination takes off into totally weird strands of thinking. There's Sol. He must be working with this Tom guy, spying on us. Shelley is Tom's spooky niece who may not belong with the living. Margot is the evil queen, masterminding everything. Dad? Maybe he's been taken over by aliens. This is all stupid, I know, but I can't help conjuring up the ridiculous because reality is just too bizarre. I grit my teeth and drive. A bicyclist on the road wobbles, clearly rattled by my speed. I should slow down, but I can't. It's as if Margot's really cast her spell.

My breath is shallow and quick. Will I make the next bend, or the one after? Squeezing the wheel tight, taking a deep breath, and then another and another, I start letting off the gas. The car slows—that's better—but I can't stop the trembles in my arms, my legs. Tears come now, like a flash flood. Everything's so upside-down, and I'm all alone, and I'm just a kid. I can't do this by myself. My tears drench Charlotte's seat, but curve after curve, a shaky resolve starts to build in me. I need someone to talk this over with.

I brainstorm ways to find that help I need. A therapist is out. They'd probably have to talk to Dad first. The police would think I'm crazy because there's no convincing evidence. No, I need a friend, someone who shares my interests. Maybe there's a club in town for photography. That'd be perfect for me.

Just as I'm settling into my plan, the brakes go soft. The car barrels forward too quickly to make the next bend. I get confused about where the parking brake is. On the red coupe, it's a button, but this is an older car. It's a lever. When I yank on it, the brake pedal comes back hard at the same time as the emergency, and my wheels lock. Charlotte spins sideways until she screeches to a stop on the shoulder. Dust rises beyond the window like dancing spirits—snaky, writhing ones.

Gasping, gazing down a slope below me, a vision rises of waves crashing on a rocky beach. The hill is steep and covered with bigleaf maples and oaks. There's no ocean at the bottom of it. We're not even close to water, but still, I'm imagining Marty, dropping through the air, the surf coming closer, fast, fast, very fast.

With a determined blink, I pull back from that free-fall feeling before Marty hits the water. I've reconstructed this accident in my head a hundred times, but it's not helpful to keep obsessing, so I focus on the aftermath: my doubts about the police, how it doesn't add up. I've recited the list over and over: Marty didn't have drugs or booze in his system, he wasn't depressed, and there wasn't a note, but they ruled it a suicide. They claimed nothing was wrong with the brakes, and so there wasn't a reason for his car to go over that cliff unless he drove it over himself.

Suicide. I never believed it, but what if the trigger was that last argument with Dad? Did it upset Marty so much he got in his car and just kept driving? He was in Washington. What was he doing there? And his letter that never came, the one he promised me in the voicemail, would it have explained why he did it?

Staring into the ravine, I feel Marty close to me, and somehow—I just know—suicide doesn't explain it. "They're wrong! It wasn't you, Marty. It was just an accident … no, not even that." My brain aches from thoughts racing through it. If it wasn't a suicide, wasn't an accident, what does that leave? All that's left is that word. I've known it for months but refused to set it free. It begins with *M*. It ends with *R*. The word is *murder*.

Chapter 7

Joe Mandell listens quietly. He's an older man, bushy white beard, heavy set, sea-blue eyes, Santa-jolly. His eyes crinkle nicely. I like him right away. His garage is a converted gas station, painted in gray and black. It would be dull-blah, but he's got a mural on the back wall of the shop behind the car lift. It's a mountain scene, one of the Cascade peaks rising above a misty sky—a solid Northwest image.

"Jane Zell sent me," I say.

"Oh, Jane's a good egg. She's got a sweet little daughter."

I nod, remembering Jane, my first good connection here. "So, what do you think about the brakes?"

Joe is studying me, figuring me out. "How long have you owned the car?"

"One day."

His eyebrows squeeze. "Ouch."

"I just bought it this morning. The guy said the brakes might be due. It's intermittent. The pedal goes soft, then the next thing you know it's okay."

"Could be the master cylinder. When they get old, they can do that."

My forehead's all pinched. A part called master cylinder sounds important. If it's gone bad, Charlotte could be in the shop for a week. "Can you tell by looking?"

"Not always. Sometimes it's an internal leak."

I have no idea how much repairs like this cost or if I'll have enough room on my card for the new laptop. "Is it expensive?"

Joe's head wags back and forth, his lips press tight, turning that question over. "Can't say. It could just be old fluid. We'll start with that and see how the linings look."

"Do whatever you need to fix it. I don't want Charlotte to go over a cliff next time." I pat the hood. "That's what I call her. Charlotte."

Joe's voice is firm. "Don't worry. I won't let your car out of my shop until those brakes are safe. Go get some coffee somewhere and relax."

In desperate need of coffee, I head down the sidewalk, my thoughts beginning to fog. I'm on overload, trying not to think of the *M*-word, but as soon as I try to ban it from my brain, it flashes neon bright inside my head—*MURDER, MURDER, MURDER*. I've always been able to pack that word up like an unwanted gift and store it away in the mind-attic where all crazy ideas go to die. And in the bright, sunny light of Mossy Hills, surrounded by cars and people and buildings, it does seem crazy. Nobody would hurt Marty. He had a gift for calming frenzied dogs and soothing grumpy strangers.

Besides, I crave coffee, and there's a cute cafe across the street, cozy with a bright green awning and rainbow flags flying beneath its top cornice. I design a flyer for it, the red brick walls rising from a giant plate of salad, a friendly woman waving from the doorway.

Waiting to cross at the light, I spy movement on the opposite corner—a bobbing head and a smile like gleaming diamonds. It's the face from this morning at the post office, the one that grabbed my guy-radar. He's holding a clipboard again and talking to an older woman. Her rosy cheeks turn toward him like a flower seeking the sun.

I'm crossing the street, a moth drawn to light. I've got to meet this guy, maybe make a friend. He may not be a photographer but look at him so shiny-bright. I'm getting goose bumps just walking in his direction. The woman's writing something on the clipboard, signing up for whatever he's selling. Just hearing his voice—those deep tones thrill me—I decide I probably will too.

As the woman walks away, he turns to me. "Hi. Hey … you registered to vote?"

My mouth drops open. Voting? That's what this is? "No, I'm not old enough."

"But will you turn eighteen by November? Election day?"

"September."

"So, great news. You can register for the general election." He puts out his hand to shake. "I'm Fremonte Clay, but they call me Free." His hand has a friendly grip. It's solid too, in a good way. It says *I-got-you*, as in dependable.

"I'm Kaye. So, what's going on with the voting?"

"Heard about the Initiative for the Climate?"

"Oh, yeah." I curb my response, wondering whose side he's on.

"What's your position?" Free is super intent.

"I'm not sure." There's a flyer in his hand, but the only word I can read upside down is *YES*. He must be for it. And I am too, I think. Yesterday I was against it, simply because of my father, but now that I know he's been lying, I should step up to this.

"So, let me break it down for you. Coffee?" Free points to the little cafe.

"That's where I was headed."

As we cross the street, Free jumps into his pitch. "Give me a pro and a con to the initiative. Pro first."

I squint into the sun. He's tall and thin. "We need to stop emissions or we're doomed?"

"That's solid. Now the Con."

I know what Dad would answer, but I'm embarrassed to say it. "It will hurt the economy?"

"That's what they're saying, but will it really hurt us? You've heard about the rebate, right?"

I shake my head, feeling embarrassed to be so clueless.

"Half of the tax will go back to the people. And the other half will go to mass transit, renewables, and efficiency. Installing rooftop panels will boost the local economy instead of the bottom line of far-off oil companies. See?"

My nod is too eager. "Sounds good to me."

Free's laugh spills out like a jazzy melody. I can see why they call him Free. "Oh, so you're already convinced? Maybe I should head back to my street corner so I can convince that old man standing there."

"No, no. Convince me more." I realize now I'm flirting with him.

"I'm down for that … maybe," he teases. I'm pleased he's flirting back.

Our coffee talk becomes one long climate-change lecture, but Free is so passionate it seems more like a storytelling masterpiece. It's personal too. "Oh, man. The impact is already hitting. It's hitting everywhere. My cousins have been flooded out in Houston from thousand-year storms every year. And my neighbor came down from Alaska. She says the permafrost is melting, the roads are bulging, the house walls are cracking, and forest trees tilt like they're all drunk. Can you imagine?"

As he talks, something builds like there's a bond between us. It's definitely magnetic, at least for me. He's got charisma, and it's working its magic, drawing me into the tale that he's telling.

Free keeps going. "There's a lot happening though. No need to get discouraged. A startup right here in Mossy Hills is working on a new type of battery for energy storage. You've got to know, batteries are top priority."

"Really?"

"Oh, yeah. If we get good storage of solar and wind, for when the sun doesn't shine or the wind doesn't blow, we'll have natural gas beat for price, even with their subsidies."

"They have subsidies?"

"Taxpayer-funded subsidies. You know, like write-offs, tax deductions. Gas and oil and coal. Billions a year." Free shakes his head.

"Now I see why we need a carbon tax."

"Exactly." Free talks about breakthrough ideas for renewable technology and capturing carbon from the atmosphere. "But the forests—no one has to invent those. Forests take out quite a bit of carbon. We've got to save them." He looks down at his hands, suddenly quiet.

I'm nodding but the light in him has dimmed. "With all the fires, I don't know how we can do that."

"Yeah, I know." Free's fingers drum the tabletop. He's staring into his mug. There's a flash of sadness in his eyes.

"Hey," I say, softly coaxing. "What's wrong?"

He looks at me, eyes filling with pain. "This summer I worked on a fire crew. It got bad. My last fire, there were tornadoes of flame as tall as a mountain." He's lost that casual tone. "Some on my crew were trapped in their fire shelters on a different flank of the line than mine. All those red-hot gases stole their oxygen. They suffocated."

My breath pulls in quick. "Suffocated?"

"I quit right afterwards. Instead, I'm doing this."

I'm gripped. Death. Grief. I know that terrain, but it doesn't seem right to explore it, so I ask a safe question. "You were fighting forest fires?"

"To raise dollars for college. It was good money too, but with the surge in heat from all things carbon, it's getting scary out there. I've got to do something about it, I'm just saying … for them."

"Your crew that died?" It's a fine line I'm walking with him. Where does he need to go with this?

"Yeah." The passion in his voice becomes reverent. "I've got to put some meaning to it, what happened."

I touch his hand. "Let me help."

His eyes redden with tears. He straightens, turning away, reaching into his pack for a voter registration form and pen. "Okay. So, let's get you registered to vote, and then we'll sign you up to volunteer."

"Sure." After what he told me, I can't refuse him. Besides, it's not just sympathy for Free. It's my anger at Dad for lying, and it's Marty too. With all he knew about science, he would be voting for this. Since he can't, I must. As ink flows across my form, it feels good to be thinking of Marty. Last night, I was so raw over losing him, but today after spinning out—settling the suicide question—I've finally made some peace with it, even though I still miss him.

After one last sip of coffee, I hand Free back the paper. He finishes his half-full mug in one big gulp and stands up, heading out the door. "Come on. I'll introduce you to everyone."

The office is a few blocks away, just off Main Street. It's in an old store-front with weathered shingles for siding and peeling orange paint on the trim around the windows and the door. Inside, a large open room has a few rudimentary walls set up in the back for offices. There's a banner across the side wall that says *Initiative4Climate.org*. Folding chairs fill the center of the room and long tables surround them filled with clipboards and papers. People mill around—young, old, all colors and ethnicities. Everyone is smiling, a crowd scene with a good vibe. It feels so alive in here that I can't help it—I want to stay.

"This is much bigger than I imagined. Is this the main office for the whole state?"

"No." Free chuckles. "Hey, you should check out Portland headquarters' page. They've got so many volunteers they're like in a huge warehouse." He leads me to a table where he turns in the voter forms he's collected. "Twenty-eight," he says. Cheerful crinkles radiate from his eyes again.

The girl behind the table has a long, thick braid and dark eyes that take your breath away; they're so calm. "Almost a slow day for you."

Free sweeps his hand toward me. "Yes, Mariela, but I captured a new soul for the cause."

"Well, sign her up."

Free leans against a column next to the table, wearing *casual* like it's in his genes. "Kaye, what are you doing tomorrow?"

I'm drawn to him, a bee to the honey. "Absolutely nothing." Am I too eager? I am, and my cheeks blush.

"I have a tabling event at the mall. Join me?"

I don't know what that is, but I'd table anywhere with him. "I'd love to."

"So, hey … tomorrow. Noon. Here," Free says, but before I can ask anything about it, someone calls to him from a back office. He walks away, his stride lanky. I love the way his short twist of braid brushes against his strong brown neck.

"Just sign up here." The girl points to a clipboard on the table. She grins at me. "He's a good guy."

Blushing even more, I fill out my name and contact info on a sign-up slip for the tabling and pick up some material to take home to read. One page has a list of opposition groups. A name connects: Citizens for Tax Free Energy. Ugh. That's the group Dad's part of. I go all queasy, a hundred million nerves from brain to stomach igniting. Will these people accept me, the daughter of a wealthy man who's opposing them? Scanning the room for Free, I spot someone else staring at me, eyes wide.

He's a white guy in his twenties with a fade cut on the sides and a longer brush-up on top. His shirt has a block-print floral pattern in red and black. He's not interested in me—that's not what's behind his stare—it's just his alarm bells ringing, those brown eyes fixed on me like they've got a question in them. I grip the back of a chair, the winds of knowing battering me—he recognizes me. When he glances away, I slip out the door.

Heading back to the coffee shop to wait for my car, my heart thumps wildly until Free texts me: *Where'd you go?*

My fear of being recognized by that guy vanishes. I work my thumbs fast:

I have to pick up my car. It's in the shop.

Noon tomorrow?

That's definite.

Free sends a little sun emoji, and I beam back at it, bouncing with each step. I'm so looking forward to a date at the mall with Free. It's not a date, I know, but it's the first good thing since I've been here except Charlotte.

In the coffee shop, nibbling a scone, waiting for Joe to text me, I browse on my phone for all the climate latest. There's good news. The cost of wind and solar power has been dropping dramatically. There's bad news. The permafrost is melting, letting methane gas escape, and methane is a potent greenhouse gas that traps the heat. Also, in the creepy news category is an article about pathogens that could be lurking in the frozen soil above the Arctic Circle. Before I can read it, Joe texts me: *Charlotte's almost ready.*

The sun on the sidewalk is dimming. Towering columns of cloud rise to the west, their bottoms flat and black beneath mounds of puffy white like triple scoops of vanilla ice cream piled high. They're deliciously mesmerizing, so I watch them, feeling buoyant, as if the updraft sweeping them higher and higher is lifting me as well. The stoplight changes and the spell breaks, but the floaty feeling doesn't leave me. It must be Free. He's going to be a good thing. I know it.

Back at the shop, Joe's just finishing up. "It was old fluid. I replaced the pads and the rotors too. The cylinder is fine."

I'm all smiley with relief. "How much?"

"$449."

I can't hide my gasp. "Is that all? Great."

He winks. "I gave you the Jane Zell discount."

He hands over the key, and I slip it onto the ring with my house key. As I shake his hand, a twinge of guilt spasms in my stomach. He probably thinks I'm hard up, dressed like this. "Thank you so much. You're the best mechanic I ever had." I giggle. "Of course, you're the only one I've ever had."

Joe chuckles. "I'll still take that. Any kind of compliment goes down good in this garage." Right before I drive away, he calls to me. "Just because you have new brakes, don't be reckless now, young lady."

"I'll be back, I promise, all in one piece."

Heading through town, not thinking about the brakes or spinning out, I'm all grins. Maybe my eyes are even crinkling at the corners a little bit. Something's changing. I'm changing. I've made two friends, and it came so easy. Joe's so nice—I was lucky to find him—and Free might be amazingly perfect for me. He's like Marty. He's like Mom. He's got that zest for life I need, the way he walks, that beaming smile of his. I imagine us walking into the mall tomorrow, hand in hand. Yeah, I'd like that.

Just before the turnoff to Willow Mountain Road, I take a side road going west, the opposite direction from Bleak House. I'm not ready to go home, not yet, so I'm cruising back to the city. I'll show Charlotte our old house. I'll park out front and tell her stories of life with Mom and Marty till the sun sets. It's not like I need to be back for dinner or anything. Margot wouldn't notice for a week.

At the edge of Mossy Hills, though, I'm already slipping back into gloomy thinking. I can't believe Dad's built a bunker. I can't believe someone's spying on the house. And my computer—how can a hacker create all those strange effects, the lights, the floating feeling? Plus, there's Marty. What happened to him?

Stopping at a pullout on the crest of a hill, I turn off the engine. Ahead of me, hills fall away into a tree-filled valley. Down below is a pond. On the horizon, thunderclouds are building. The towering columns of gray and white move steadily closer. I check the time on my phone. It's 3:45 p.m.

Even though I don't want to admit it, I know why I'm here. It's the prediction. This is Clement Valley Road. Below me is Treasure Pond, and out there, somewhere, is a swirling mass of wind, a budding tornado. Or maybe not.

I should go home. I should get somewhere safe. Instead, I sit and wait.

Chapter 8

It's almost four o'clock. The sky gets strangely dark. I gaze upward, feeling dizzy like I'm spinning, but it's the clouds that are spinning, slowly circling round. Something's close. Is it the darkness or the clouds or a sinister feeling? The wind picks up the dust around the car. Lightning flashes, once, twice, again and again. Mammoth spots of dirty rain hit the windshield. I search F0 tornadoes on my phone, that's what Sol said it would be. A weather link explains that F0 tornadoes are the weakest, with only minimal damage. Winds are between sixty-five to eighty-five miles an hour. That's not deadly, at least I hope not.

My hand finds the key waiting in the ignition. It wants to leave. It's smarter than me. I start the car, just in case, but open my phone to get a video of this. The screen says 3:59. Will it happen?

At first, it's just a tail of cloud dropping down about a mile away, but then it begins to form. A thin funnel dives like a magician's rope dancing and swaying. Some debris, maybe tree limbs, get churned up at the base. It's heading straight for me, and I'm locked in a trance like that gray eye is staring at me from the laptop again. It enters the fir trees at the edge of the park. There's rain, ferocious rain, all around me. I turn the wipers on high but can barely see the funnel anymore. Before it reaches the pond, it wiggles left, twisting away along the shore below. In another second, the funnel has writhed upward back into the clouds, vanishing. The downpour stops. I blink about ten times, my heartbeat fluttering honeybee fast.

Did I just see that? I check my video to confirm it's there. Trapped in the screen on a phone, it doesn't seem so scary—just a tuft of cloud spun into a snaky swirl—but since it's true that a small tornado came to Treasure Pond at almost exactly 4:00 p.m., what does that mean about Sol? Can you hack the weather?

Heading home, my hands grip the steering wheel. I'm feeling a bit whiplashed and wish I had someone to share this conundrum with, but who would believe me? No one, that's for sure. Passing through town, life seems normal. The mall is packed. Shoppers stream in and out of the doors. A group of teens head across the parking lot, and the lot is dry as a bone. It didn't catch a drop of rain.

Every car I pass has zero tracks of water sliding down its windshield, signaling they never got hit with a shower. Pulling over, searching my phone, not even the weather service has a post about the tornado. I check for my video, just to make sure it's there. What strange universe can have a tornado that no one sees but me?

Without an answer for that, I clench my jaw and focus on the cars, the traffic signals, the yellow line dividing the highway, anything to stop think-ing of that question. Still, driving home up Willow Mountain becomes a challenge. At the spot where Charlotte spun out, I get shaky again. I've had this shaky feeling before about this snaky road. I even yelled at Dad about it as we were driving here last spring. "Why did you have to pick a road like this to build a house on? Remember Marty?" Dad just turned away from me, driving on. He never wants to talk about my brother, but I crave it. I have so much to say and no one to say it to. Why can't Dad hear me?

Pulling into the driveway, it hits me—I've forgotten the computer store. I'll have to find one at the mall tomorrow after working with Free. Yes, Free. Just the thought of him raises my energy. I skip into the house, upbeat like the tune I'm humming. I don't even frown at the empty fridge or a note on the kitchen island, scribbled in Margot's writing. It says: *Kaye, if Paul phones, remind him to call Tom about the campaign. And I found a letter addressed to you. It's on your desk.*

A letter? Where did she find a letter? I burst into my room. A business-size envelope is propped against Mom's candle, addressed in Marty's scrawl. It's stamped but not postmarked, with a crease mark down the middle like it had been folded in two. My name and address at the old Portland house are legible—Marty was doing his best, for once, to write carefully—and the seal isn't broken. It's hard to believe Margot left it unread, but maybe even she understood what this letter would mean to me. With a pocketknife from my drawer, I carefully slit the edge of the envelope, sliding out a piece of letterhead from Malloy Genetics, his lab.

Hey, Sis,

I passed your name along to a good friend. He will contact you. So, pay attention. Listen to him. He's got a lot to say.

I'm working on something big. I may be out of sight for a bit. Don't worry. Here's a flower I want you to have. It's a camas. One of Mom's favorites.

Brighten the moment. Don't forget, ever. And always, look to the EarthStar!

Love,

Marty

PS: There's a guy named Carter Brown. Don't go anywhere near him.

Slumping onto my desk chair, I stare at the dried flower, pressed flat like a deep blue star. Its stem is bent from the crease in the envelope. I smooth it out—reverent toward this bit of Marty-treasure. The flower, the letter, and *EarthStar*, one of Mom's special words, are all signs from Marty. I was right. He didn't kill himself. He was on a mission, doing something big. I mutter that like a mantra, six months of tension being shed. "Something big. Something big."

I read the postscript again—*a guy named Carter Brown.* Marty knew someone dangerous, someone to avoid. The *M*-word wraps around that name—*murder, it was murder!* This letter is evidence, but I'm not sure who should see it. Dad?

Opening my laptop—I'll just ignore the hacker—I type into the search
bar: *Carter Brown*, which brings up a million hits. A dead end. On a
hunch, I pull out the mud-smeared business card in my pocket—the only
other clue, well, besides the shudder of dread Tom gave me the night of
the party—and go to advanced search, narrowing it by adding words from
the card. First, *Tom*. Still a million hits, so I add *Fossil* plus *Rodington*. The
top link is for FossilLite Industries. I click on it and find a news release
from six months ago with a quote by Tom Rodington about the carbon tax
initiative, saying, "We don't need a new tax in this economic climate. There
are better ways to address this, like cap and trade." What's the difference
between a tax and cap and trade?

A search of the FossilLite website reveals it's all about natural gas. Tom
Rodington is mentioned in a few more press releases, but there's no photo.
I widen my search to the whole internet, filtering for photos, and find
some images to scroll through. Most are of old men, but one looks about
forty. There's something about his eyes that makes me zero in, a coldness to
make you shiver. Yes, this is the face at the party, the one illuminated by the
security light. The beard isn't there, but the eyebrows scowl. I keep scrolling
and find another photo of him with a beard. He's standing in a group
of three beside a Confederate flag. The caption talks about an alt-right
convention in Georgia.

I pull up my photo of Tom from last night. It's pretty grainy. Still, it
seems like the same man from my online search, harsh eyes, drawn-down
brows. He definitely fits the spy-on-Dad type. And that last thing I overheard him saying, *just fix it or I'll do more than fix it*, hinted of bad news
for someone who worked for him. But Marty? What's the connection?
For sure, Tom is capable of darkness, but there's no link between him and
Marty. Still, I just don't like this man.

I keep staring at his grainy photo. Something else is bothering me. It's
those cold-hearted eyes. Dad looks like that some days, but it's not just

that. I've seen those eyes in person but can't remember where. It was long before the party.

And then, to the right, behind that sullen Tom-face, something shimmers, flashing on and off, resembling heat lighting. There's a burst of light, followed by a splotch of grayscale, not grainy like the rest of his photo. Instead, that splotch is high-resolution sharp. I zoom in, knowing what I will find. Yes, it's the eye.

Planting my feet firmly on the floor, resisting zero-gravity, I close my laptop, stat. Whatever that hacker's doing, I'm not buying it.

Margot calls through the door. "Kaye, come see what I bought for you today."

"I'm tired," I yell back.

She opens the door anyway. I need to train myself to lock it.

"It was on sale." She holds up a silky blouse that has a wild spray of colors and lacy trim, so definitely not me. Her mouth is open, her eyebrows raised, her head tilted slightly.

I know what she wants me to say. "That's great. It would look better on you than me. Why don't you keep it?" My voice is flat, but I try not to offend when I decline her gifts. It's easier that way.

She holds it up to herself in the mirror. "Really? You think so?"

"I do. I'm going to sleep now, okay?"

Margot's so pleased that she rushes toward the door. Before she leaves, I ask, "Where did you find that letter?"

"Oh!" She stops to think. "It was in that box of your brother's clothes across the hall. I was sorting through them to donate. You might look to see if you want to keep anything."

"Marty's clothes?" I sit up straight, eyes wide. "I'm keeping it all. Don't you dare touch it, I ..." Pausing for breath, I dial back the anger because at least she gave me the letter. "Sorry, I'm just tired. Leave it for me. I'll get it tomorrow."

Margot nods and closes the door. I lock it, open my laptop—no eye greets me—and read up on Tom Rodington, but it's hard. He seems to be one for the shadows and not the limelight. There are a few mentions of him connected to some alt-right news sites, but nothing specific. If he's conservative, that's no surprise. So is Dad. Something nags at me though. I close my eyes, trying to remember where I've seen him, until with a shudder, I sit up straight.

The funeral! Tom was there. His eyes looked so severe as he surveyed the scene, like a detective staking out the crowd. Dad never spoke to him. Margot certainly did. She always speaks to the men. Why does Dad put up with it?

I scroll to the folder with the photos from that horrible day six months ago. Margot had asked me not to bring my camera to the funeral, but I needed it to get through those torturous hours. My heart was a broken drum that longed to stop beating. My stomach could only manage empty. I didn't want to attend, but Dad expected it, so I did.

To avoid talking to anyone, I hid behind my camera, focusing on the crowd, the flowers, the shadows in the corner, hoping my lens would let me see into the place Marty had slipped into, willing my camera to find him. Even now, I'm still longing for a sign of him as I search my pictures, but there's only Tom in several shots. And then in one of them, I see that guy from the Initiative for the Climate office, the one who was watching me. He's talking to Tom.

Whoa! Revelation! This guy is connected to Tom, who is connected to the opposition, which leads me to a wild guess: he might be Carter Brown. If so, what was he doing at the office? My conclusion comes quick: infiltration. I need to warn Free.

But as I pick up my phone, I stop. How do I tell Free what I know? The only way to do that would be to tell him who I am. I set down the phone. Not tonight. And not tomorrow either. I want one day to pretend. One day to feel a bit better. One day to see if something more will ignite between us, and then hope Free will understand about my father. And if not, if he turns away because of who I am, at least I'll have a day out of the house wrapped in the breezy warmth of him.

A new worry pops into my head: *will the guy from the office snitch on me?* He could tell Free, and then Free won't want me working with him. Or maybe he won't say anything because it would throw suspicion on him too. Still, if I could find out what he is up to, I could be the hero and not the villain.

Staring at the photo of Tom and the infiltrator as if I can read their lips to grasp their devious plan, I see it again—the blaze of light. The same grayscale blotch pops up embedded in some shrubbery above the patio of the funeral parlor. A soft glow hovers around the eye. I zoom in, my heart taking leaps inside my chest, my stomach all weightless flutter. It's that surreal feeling that the eye brings.

This time, I'm making an unlikely connection, one between the funeral, Marty, and the eye. "Is it you?" I ask, watching the eye, waiting. "Does Sol mean soul? Is it you, Marty, your spirit? Are you a ghost? Can ghosts predict the future?"

Nothing.

"I miss you. Just blink if it's you." I lean close, my body tense, my eyes scrunched up with pleading.

Nothing.

"Blink once for yes. Blink twice for no."

But the eye doesn't blink. It just stares at me.

Chapter 9

Certain it's Marty, I sit, ferocious as a lion. There's a roar inside me: *Marty, come back to me.* And then the screen goes dark, my laptop slipping into sleep mode. After hitting the down arrow, the image comes back, but the eye is gone.

Almost. A bit of grayscale is left. I zoom to the maximum to see a handful of pixels right where the pupil of the eye had been. Staring at it makes me almost dizzy. It's that hypnotic sensation, riveting me, but nothing about it says *ghost* or *dead-spooky*; and though I want to believe it's Marty I'm connecting with, his spirit on some astral plane, I get the sense it's not. Those little blocks of pixel black are pulsing, a bit electric. *Strong. Fade. Strong. Fade.* Deep and luminous, that black has come alive.

But Marty isn't alive. I know that, even if I don't want to believe it, even if I wish it weren't true, because the voice from the laptop wasn't Marty's. My mood sinks, anchoring me in my room. That eye is just a clump of dark squares in a photograph. Zooming back out on the screen, I lose track of those pixels, so I drag the photo into a folder and label it *eyes.* I search other photos that I move there—the one of Dad, the NASA image, and the grainy one of Tom. The eye is missing now in all of them. I'm relieved.

Closing down my laptop, I catch the irony. If this had been Marty, contacting me from the grave, I would embrace that eye, longing to see it, longing to hear him. Since it's not, I'm downgrading the drama, blaming it on a hacker, forgetting it happened. Well, not forgetting, really. I still want to find out who is doing this and make them stop.

Glancing at Marty's blue camas on my desk, I connect my hacker and my brother's letter. It must be Carter Brown. There are no other candidates. Marty warned me against him, and now he appears at the initiative office and in the pixels on my screen. He must be the reason that my world is upside down. He's cyberstalking me to the extreme. Marty said not to go anywhere near this dangerous man, but it's hard to avoid someone that can lurk inside your photographs.

Obviously, I need more information, and there's a box of Marty's clothes waiting. Maybe there's another letter, another clue about Carter. I race across the hall, looking for a box marked Marty. A dozen giant ones hold Margot's clothes, but back in the corner is a smaller box. I rush to it, sinking my hands into Marty's jackets, jeans, shirts, even a pair of hiking boots. The smell of worn leather is strong.

Sweeping the box into my arms, marching across the hall, setting it beside my bed, I paw through it, hunting for more letters. There are only clothes, so I grab a navy-blue hoodie of Marty's and pull it on, settling back against my pillow. My hand slides into its wide front pocket, touching something hard. It's a thin, black, metal cylinder with a sharp point—a point that looks like the end of a pen but isn't. Unscrewing the cap, I find a real pen hidden beneath it and scribble across a pad of paper on my nightstand. It gives a great line.

Settling Marty's pen beside the notepad, snuggling down between the covers, hugging his hoodie close, I whisper, "That's better."

And it is better. When I wake in the morning, I feel like I've just stepped out of a hot tub all warm and relaxed. I hide Marty's letter in a desk drawer and set the blue camas beside Mom's candle. Heading outside, I wash Charlotte, scrubbing out the stains on the seat and the smoky smell, humming as I work. Sunshine glints off the hood. I can't stop smiling. *Brighten the moment.* Yes, Marty. This morning I can do that.

Back inside, I draw a glass of water from the faucet. Margot's voice drifts in from the living room. "How's Galveston? Any good restaurants?" After a pause, she says, "That's good. That's good. I'm glad it's going well."

My stomach starts growling. Some old granola bars at the top of the pantry cabinet are not completely stale, and I manage to swallow them.

"It's lonely here." Margot sounds pathetic. "When will you be back?"

She's talking to Dad. I listen, but I don't get a clue about when he's returning. I'm not looking forward to the fight we'll have about Charlotte.

After a shower, I hunt for an outfit that syncs with my day of working with Free. It should be upbeat but not too revealing, bright, yet conventional enough to not to turn people away. After all, I want to get their attention but not be in the spotlight. Free can be the spotlight, and I can be the backlight.

I pick out a solid bright-green top and some tapered capris in an oak and acorn print. The next thing I fret over is my hair. It's long and dark and shaggy. It hasn't been trimmed in a month. Thinking of Free's braid, I make a braid of my own, a simple one with a green silk scarf woven into it. The trees, the scarf, they send off a subtle green-vibe message. Trees are important, right?

Besides Free must love trees. He was fighting fire, trying to save them. What was it like watching trees burn? I remember his face, talking of his friends who died. Often, I get all wheezy just from hazy skies filled with distant wildfire smoke. They were right in the middle of it. It killed them. I try to shut down a vision of suffocating in a firestorm. Thankfully, Margot barges in.

"I'm planning that lunch with Becky and Shelley. Are you free today?" Margot's hyped, rather breathless. How can this mean so much to her?

"I'm doing something."

"So, tomorrow?"

I grit my teeth, trying not to break my promise to her, and then inspiration hits me. Now, I've got bargaining power. "Sure, but I need a favor. I need you to come with me."

"Where?"

"The DMV."

Margot recoils like it's a shopping expedition to the Mossy Hills dollar store, as in common and cheap. How in the world did she get her license? Does she even have one? I wouldn't put that past Margot. She acts like she's above those sorts of things.

"Remember? You told the insurance guy your name would be on the title? It will only take a minute. You just need to be there. Please, Mom."

I'm surprised how effective the mom thing is. Thirty minutes later, I'm in line at the DMV information desk again. This time I get an actual number to be called up by a registration clerk, so I claim a bench to sit on. Margot fidgets beside me.

As we wait for number seventy-nine to be summoned, I ask, "Where are we going for lunch tomorrow?" It's small talk to distract Margot from the older man in paint-stained work pants who has settled down beside her. She sees him anyway, moves her purse, and inches my direction. To cover my embarrassment, I nod at him, and smile. He smiles back and takes out his phone, ignoring us.

"I thought I'd let Becky take the lead on that."

"How did you meet her?" Do I sound curious enough? Probably not.

"It was at a library fundraiser."

That's rare—Margot getting near a book? "I didn't think libraries were on your list. I thought it was more art and opera."

Margot scoffs. "There's not a lot of art and opera here in Mossy Hills, but libraries seem to be big."

"I like libraries. They're quiet."

"That library party wasn't." Margot snickers. "It got wild."

A big-bellied woman walks by, tugging a blond cherub of a toddler who's whining, wanting to be carried. "I'm worn out," the woman says. "Just walk."

The girl stops and plops on the floor, balking. As the mother grabs her hand and drags her on, a ragged teddy bear drops from the woman's purse. Margot jumps to the rescue, grabbing the bear. She rushes to the woman to hand it back. The woman stares, puzzled by the gesture.

After an awkward second, Margot does the most startling thing. She takes a twenty from her wallet. "Looks like you need a break. Have lunch on me," Margot says.

The woman takes the bill, a smile smashing through her irritation. "Thank you."

"It's nothing," Margot says. "Please get this girl a treat. She's a darling."

Not knowing what else to say, the woman pivots and yanks the toddler toward the door. "If you don't shut up, no fries for you," she says to the child.

Margot sighs, watching the woman leave. "Oh, well," she says as she slumps beside me. "I tried."

I gape at Margot, speechless. It's an awkward moment—Margot being nice? I'm so perplexed I can't concentrate, can't come up with a new direction to turn the conversation. Luckily, Margot fills the silence. She begins talking about some fashion show she wants to see. I gladly tune out, more comfortable with Margot in her oblivious mode.

My heart quivers for a moment as I visualize Mom sitting here with me instead. Mom would love it all—Charlotte, the man in the work pants, even my defiance of Dad. I mean, she loved Dad, she did, but she often said he could be a stinker, and she always stood up to him for us, though she didn't always win. Dad could be so difficult when he didn't get his way.

"Seventy-nine." The voice over the speaker is muffled, so I check the board. Praise the DMV! Saved from small talk with Margot.

Thankfully, Margot really does have a license because she shows one to get my car titled. She even fills out a form to change her address. I do too. "See, it's good we came. Now we're all legal and everything."

After the registration's processed, Margot makes a beeline for the door. Before I can even slide the key into Charlotte's lock, she's speeding out in her roadster, heading off to some restaurant bar to get the DMV grit and grime off her. As her car roars out of the parking lot, I wonder where that woman disappeared to, the one handing a twenty to a stranger. And then I start Charlotte up, grateful to Margot for once, despite her flaws. Now Dad can't say a thing. Charlotte's legal and insured.

I'm a half hour early for meeting Free, so I just drive. Mossy Hills is easy to get around, twenty minutes from end to end, but it's constantly expanding. It's become a satellite community for tech startups and a refuge for remote workers because it's near enough to Portland to pop in as needed. The west side is newer, with tract housing, apartments, and some industrial areas. The quaint east side, including downtown, is the original hub, though there are signs of modern creep, like the new library. It's all steel and glass and completely out of place among the old brick-and-stone facades.

Spotting a little cafe in a converted 1940s filling station, I stop to admire the stucco exterior with rounded edges to its canopy. My stomach begins growling—those granola bars weren't enough—so I duck inside to buy a coffee and a bag of BBQ chips. After sipping the coffee and crunching a few chips, savoring salt and grease and spice, I find myself daydreaming about standing next to Free in the mall. We're talking to everyone, busy handing out our flyers, and then the crowd dissipates. Free turns to hug me, happy for all the work we've done, and then I look up at him. He looks down at me. I'm sure he's going to kiss me, but I never get to finish that fantasy because a car pulls up beside me, interrupting the flow of my thoughts. And then there's nothing left to do except fret about talking to potential voters in the mall.

It doesn't turn out to be so hard. When I pick Free up from the office, he gives me the pointers I need. Besides clarifying the legal issues for me about voter registration and the rules to follow, he explains what he calls his fishing tips. "Don't hesitate to ask anyone that drifts by, but always smile when you say it. Sending out your best energy reels them in. It's the bait. That's what Mom says, and she's pure art with a fishing pole in her hands. Plus, she's an Alabama girl, so she's been trained in all things people … the hard way." Free drums his fingers on the dash. "Her first rule for something like this is, don't react if they ignore you, or scowl, or snap. Just let them swim away. It's not about them. It's about the next one that floats by. Just like fishing, it's about being calm and patient."

I'm the patient one, at least I used to be, so I should be good at this. Still, I'm stiff-faced as we choose a spot in the mall beside the ice cream shop, but Free makes it easy to relax. His energy's contagious.

"Where's the table?" I ask. "I thought this was a tabling event?"

He hands me a clipboard. "I like to be on my feet, walk right up to them. It's harder for them to snub you. If you sit at a table, they just drift on by beyond your reach."

It's not a large mall. In fact, it's all dingy—forty years old and in need of a fresh coat of paint, but it's still a place to hang out. In this small town, that's a plus, so it's always busy. A swarm of kids too young to vote flow by, skipping and chattering. Free takes a moment to scan the crowd, and then he steps toward an older man in a baseball cap. "Hi, are you registered to vote?" As he talks to him, Free doesn't mention the initiative at all. He walks him through the registration form to sign him up. Afterward, he offers a flyer, which the man waves away.

"So, we're not here to push the initiative, right?" Free says as the man moves on. "We're here to peddle registration, but most of them will be automatically registered through the DMV, so they'll say no. I hand out climate info if they want it. Answer their questions, sure, but if I feel resistance, I just offer the flyer without saying anything. Some of them won't vote our way, but the bet is that the higher the participation in the election, the greater the chance for us."

Free steps back and points a thumb toward a woman heading in our direction. "Your turn. Make me proud."

I call to the woman, my voice squeaky tight, "Are you registered to vote?"

To my surprise, she stops. "No, I'm not. I need to do that."

All sudden grins, I hand her the clipboard and point out where to start. She squints as she writes and presses her lips tight, which makes her look cross. I'm afraid to say anything. When she's done, I hand her the flyer. She glances over it. "Oh, yes. I'm voting for this."

I can't help but gush. "Thanks so much." When she hurries on, I turn to Free and give a little skip. His eyes are ablaze. "I feel like I'm thirteen," I say.

"Don't apologize. Thirteen's good." He winks. "That innocence is hard to resist."

Still, when someone walks by like I don't exist, I can't help but pout a bit. It's worse when an old lady snaps at me, or a gruff man shouts *piss off*. But Free keeps on asking, so I do too. After my tenth snide remark thrown in my face, I forget to notice, because the next ask or two brings success, usually with younger people like me who are first-time voters. The afternoon slides by, and the forms pile up in Free's field bag.

Finally, Free checks his watch. "We can quit."

"I almost don't want to. It's fun … at least with you."

"We'll table again." Free's eyes drift to the line for ice cream. "My stomach's calling."

"Dinner?" I say.

"Isn't ice cream dinner?" Free's grin is sheepish.

I grab his hand and lead him away. "Come on, show me your best place in town to eat. My treat."

"Okay, but no paying my bill. I'd be too polite to eat much, and I've sure got the appetite today."

His hand's still in mine, and he's not pulling away. There's a buzz flowing between us, skin to skin. My thoughts spin like they're orbiting the moon, until I spy a computer place beside us. I stop for the briefest moment, which breaks the bond as his hand slips loose.

"What's up?" Free looks down at me.

I gaze at him, still whirling through space. "Oh, nothing. My computer was hacked. I need a new machine."

"We can do this some other time," Free says.

I'm not about to take a chance on that now that I've got him here with me. "It's okay. I'll do computers later. I've got my phone. That still works."

"Sure?"

"Absolutely. Besides, it's probably open late. I'll go after dinner."

When Free smiles back at me, my feet float off the floor. I'd take a hundred hacked laptops just to spend another hour with him.

Chapter 10

As we head out of the mall, someone rushes through the door, bumping into me. It's the guy from the office—the one I think is Carter Brown.

"Hey, Greg," Free says.

The guy nods and pushes past. I turn and watch him scurry. He's Greg? Not Carter? Or maybe Greg is an alias.

"Do you know him?" Free asks.

I shake my head, still distracted. "I saw him at the office. He was staring at me."

"Yeah, he shows up there sometimes. I haven't worked with him on anything. I think he does phone calls, mostly, or back-office work instead of going live."

After a quick glance at us, Greg melts into the mall crowd, but my fear of exposure surges—me, the imposter, the rich man's daughter, lying about who I really am. "He made me feel uncomfortable."

"Really? I don't get that off him. I think he may be more interested in the guys and not the gals, I'm just saying."

"No, not uncomfortable in that way. He just …" I stop, wobbling between my world and Free's as if there's a crack opening between us in the pavement of the parking lot. That crack wants to separate us, prove we don't belong together, demanding I tell the truth about my father. I resist. I can't reveal what I know or who I am. Not yet. "It's nothing."

Free's moving fast across the lot, but a black SUV is passing us. The guy who's driving is giving me a cold stare. I try to place him in the mall, but I can't. Maybe he overheard us talking about the initiative. Maybe he's against it.

I scurry to catch up to Free. "Is it far?" I ask. "I'm getting hungry too."

"Not far. This way."

"Where are we going?"

Free eyes twinkle. "My best place. Your request, remember?"

We cross at a light and head down a side road to a little shacky kind of house at the edge of an industrial area with peeling blue clapboard and a hand-lettered sign that says *Miguel's*.

"Best fish tacos in town," Free says as he opens the door for me.

And they are. After we pick up our orders, we settle into chairs at a small, scuffed table. The room is bare, brown paneling on the walls and a few torn posters here and there, but the food's so good. With slow, deliberate bites, I savor the fishy flavor. There's plenty of lime and the chili zing is exactly right. Free's ordered four of them. I regret I only have two.

In between bites, Free throws out questions. "So, where do you go to school?"

"Before we moved here … XM High in the city." I'm hoping he doesn't know it.

"Seriously? Xavier Moreaux? Isn't that number one in the city?"

I want to melt into floor. "By what measure?"

"Status?"

I stare down at my plate. "Some would say that." Heat rises to my cheeks. Is it the chili?

"Hey, no problem. It's not like I didn't guess." He takes another bite. "The hint was your address on the voter form. You don't live up that road if you haven't got some hustle going."

It's suddenly hard to swallow because I wrote my name, along with the address, down on that form—Malloy. Why did I use my real name? I guess I had to so I could legally vote, but does he know who Dad is? At least it's a common name. Dad could be any Malloy. Still, it's time to detour. "How long have you lived in Mossy Hills?"

"About eight years. We're refugees." He winks. "From Santa Barbara."

"Santa Barbara? That's a classy place."

"I know. The American Riviera. I was in the 1 percent there … as in 1 percent Black. I certainly didn't grow up in touch with my roots."

"And so, you moved to Mossy Hills? Why not somewhere more cosmopolitan?"

"You mean diverse? Oh, yeah, Mossy Hills is a tiny Santa Barbara. Not at first, though. Eight years ago, it was a sleepy little town, and then *boom*. The money moved in, driving up the prices for any place to live."

I detect an undercurrent of resentment for people like me. "So, why do you stay?"

"Family. My mom's a hospital administrator, and my dad works for the town planning department. He's an engineer. What's your dad's gig?"

"My Dad, um …" I jump up from my seat, rapid breathing swamping me. He knows. I know he knows. "Is there a bathroom here?"

Free points to a small hallway. "Down the hall, turn right."

Limp, blue eyes stare back from the restroom mirror. My cheeks are bright red. I splash water on my face to cool them and consider making up a cover story about how my dad is dead. There's a little bit of truth to that—emotionally he's dead, but I can't see a future with Free if I lie to him. Drops of water on the mirror slide down in tiny streams, a slow-motion race to the bottom, which is exactly where I fear I'm heading with him. I'm resigned to explaining the real story, about me, about my father, but as I move down the hallway, I see Free talking on his phone. He's nodding like he's getting great news.

"What's going on?" I ask when his conversation ends.

"Newspapers are lining up for us."

My eyebrows pinch, puzzling over this. "Does anyone read the papers anymore?"

"Older folks do, so an endorsement could mean some undecideds breaking our way."

"You're really into this campaign, aren't you?"

Free's nod is definite. "I always go deep. And I like to win."

He's forgotten his question about my father, so I keep the topic going. "What's the game plan? Can we win this?"

"Polling's tight. And that's good. Last spring, we were down by ten." Free drums his palms on the table. "But there are some big ad buys for the opposition just hitting, and we don't have the funds to compete. So, it's all about fundraising now, big time."

"You've got some Mossy Hills events coming up?"

He leans close. "Some good ones, but it's all hush."

"I want to help," I say, though I don't know anyone to invite, and I'm crap at organizing. "I can do the graphics! And I'm great with a camera. I've got all the gear."

Free tilts his head. "Cool. I'll let them know."

His head tilt is so tempting. I flash on what it would be like to kiss him. "How soon is it happening?"

"Maybe a few weeks, maybe less." Free's being a bit evasive, but for fun. "Nothing's quite solid."

I go along with the tease. "No hints about anything?"

"Vincent Van Gogh."

I giggle. "He's coming?"

"Think of theme. Think of art, his art."

"Starry Night?"

"You got it."

"Starry Night graphics would be fun." I'm already seeing those swirls of stars against a dark background. Those stars capture motion. They could give energy to the design with whirls of text around the stars. No, that might be unreadable. Or maybe not. Not if it was small repeating text—long, short, long, short—in alternating rays of starry spin. Long would be: *Initiative for the Climate.* Short would be: *Vote yes.* I can't wait to get home to play with that. Boy do I need some time with pixels.

Right now, though, Free's the one spinning into motion. He stands and picks up his plate. "I've got to get. Family time, and Mama doesn't tolerate late."

Free walks so briskly back to the car that I'm winded. He fights forest fires. I sit in my room, working on my laptop. Maybe I should get on Margot's spin cycle when I get back. At the car, he hands me the packet of forms from his field bag. "Can you drop these off for me? My sister's just a block away, and she's my ride." Free twirls around, a star spinning into space, but turns back and signals with his thumb and little finger that he'll call. "Tomorrow," he assures me.

I stare after him, deflated. This was not how I hoped the day would end, all zero chemistry between us. He didn't even say goodbye, let alone kiss me. Of course, he's busy, and it's our first time together, but those voter forms in my hand shout one thing: I'm just a convert, someone to join the cause. He's not into me after all. I kick at the pavement in disappointment, but then spin away, determined to keep alive the possibility of something between us.

Outside the Initiative for the Climate office, I take a moment to peer through the glass, hoping Greg is still at the mall. Even if he's not Carter, he knows Tom. Not seeing him, I rush through the doors. The volunteer from yesterday isn't around, so I stand in the middle of the room with the papers in my hand until an older woman waves me over.

"Can I help you?"

"Free wanted me to drop these off. We tabled at the mall today."

She's got plump cheeks with a grin to match. "Thanks so much," she says as she takes the papers, counting the forms. "Thirty-five. Marvelous!"

I can't help but beam at her. "Free's so good at this."

"Are you Deidre?"

"No, I'm Kaye."

The woman gives a little smile. "My mistake."

Alarm splashes across my face. Free has a girlfriend? Is that why he's not into me?

She catches on, her eyes filling with apology. "No. No. Sorry. Deidre is Clayton's girlfriend. I can't keep up with all the gossip. Don't worry, honey. The last I heard, Free is still free." She laughs at her joke. "Better hurry."

Both relieved and embarrassed, I say goodbye and scurry out the door. The clouds are ablaze with the sunset. That fire in the sky mirrors the fire on my cheeks. Better hurry, the woman said, but I don't get the sense Free's in a hurry about anything. He's so focused on the initiative. It's his shield against the flames, but what kind of flames? The falling in love ones? Or is it grief? Those firefighters must have been close to him, so that's definitely understandable. When Marty died, I didn't feel like talking to anyone, let alone going on a date.

As the red and orange of the sky sear deep into my brain, branding me with cloudy glory, the metallic flash of Margot's copper-colored roadster zooms by, a man in the passenger seat. I don't bother to wonder where she's going with him. Instead, I'm glad to have the house to myself.

That thought creates a geyser of jubilation. I find a drive-in and order a hamburger, fries, and a banana milkshake. Two fish tacos weren't enough, especially when I'm on Margot rations. Summers Discount Store is the next stop, basic clothes a sudden priority. I can't believe the prices. Jeans and summer tops—can these really be so cheap? And they're great. I'm done with wasting money on high-end brands.

It's also time to stock up on chips and energy bars, something to renew the stash in my closet. Because of Margot, high-energy nibbles are a must to keep on hand for daily hunger emergencies. I even find eggs to cook for breakfast, amazed this discount store sells them. And milk too. I grab a gallon. Halfway up Willow Mountain Road, I realize I've forgotten butter to fry the eggs, and more importantly, the computer store.

When I pull over to turn around, a black SUV drives by, turtle slow just like the one in the mall parking lot a while ago. There's a shiver running through me, but it turns onto a side road up ahead, canceling my suspicions. Still, caution grips me—hackers, laser microphones, bunkers—so I head straight home, studying every car in the rearview mirror, taking note of make and color. There are two black SUVs, one that dawdles behind me before turning left at a four-way intersection.

It's dusk when I get back. Young oaks rise like watchful sentries along the drive. The landscape lanterns at their roots become their signal lamps. Bleak House is empty, and it feels plenty creepy tonight. Despite being brand new, this house feels haunted. Sometimes the echoes in these hardwood halls or the eerie vibrations in the silence don't bother me. Sometimes they do. And the bunker below the study doesn't help. I get a touch of claustrophobia just thinking of it.

With the milk and eggs settled on a spotless refrigerator shelf, I scurry up the stairs, *tap, tap, tap*, heading to my room. It's cozier there. Halfway up, though, I circle back to Dad's study—with no one home I can hunt for clues.

The desk drawers are still locked. The trash can's empty. I rummage through the cabinets. The only thing interesting is an invoice from a private investigation agency called Bancroft & Sons. It has Dad's name and a balance due total of $5,075.00. There's that shiver in me again. There's that whisper of the word, echoing like a chant—*murder, murder, murder*. Is this about Marty? The invoice is dated about a month after Marty's accident, so it must be. A jolt charges me with energy. Maybe Dad doesn't believe it was suicide either. He's looking for proof. Who does he suspect? I parse every word on the paper, hoping for a clue, but it's just all about hourly fees and mileage expenses.

And then I glance over at the mirror, remembering the door to the bunker that needs to be shut. My chest squeezes at the thought of it, plus Carter Brown. What if he's down there, waiting for me? My eyes grow wide just imagining that.

Click. Thump. There's a glimpse of face beyond the window. Another breath and it's gone, but spiders of fear crawl up my spine. I shut the blinds with a swift twirl of the wand so they *snap*. Racing down the hall, I set the alarm, check all the doors, and turn on the security lighting, panting with fear.

That face at the window floats before me—dark eyes, pale skin, almost spectral in the gloomy light. I'm thinking ghost, knowing that it wasn't. "Shush the ghost talk," I mutter, but I can't dispel the chilling accents to the evening. This eerie house. The creepy noise. Someone at the window. Not to mention a haunted computer and a hidden chamber. Odd details like these in a horror movie would build suspense, calling for the anxious music that plays just before the freak-out scene.

I lock my bedroom door and close my curtains to the darkness that has settled around the house. There's a wind up tonight. The fir trees outside rustle their needles. Limbs creak. The damper in my bathroom fan keeps flapping, *clank, clank*. A strong gust hits the house. The roof groans like a demon. Bleak House has definitely gone all haunted-vibe.

My eyes zoom around the room, looking for answers as if they're hidden in the corner shadows, my mind flashing on the invoice I found and the SUV man. Is Dad's private eye following me? Or is it Carter Brown? I have no way to answer that except asking Dad, but I don't have the courage to text him. What if my own father is having me tracked like a criminal? He couldn't be that angry unless Margot told him about my car and the DMV.

Yes, that would turn him ballistic.

Thinking about Margot ratting me out makes me grumpy, a frown hanging heavy on my face, until I spy something propped up on my desk. I zoom toward it, a bee drawn to a garden full of blossoms. It's a binder, red and blue, with a label on it: *Marty's Masterpieces.* A note beside it says: *I'm sure this is another thing you want to keep.* Damn you, Margot! How did all this thoughtfulness creep into you today?

The binder is a songbook filled with sheet music. Some are chord charts for Marty's guitar, and some scores are more complete. There are songs called *A Mouse in Your Toothpaste, Hey Crow … Don't Eat My Last Burrito,* and *Twenty Tulips.* Only Marty could dream up titles like that.

Marty was brilliant in so many ways. A comic. A scientist. A musician. He had a guitar that he played since he was fourteen. And he wrote songs to make you laugh. His silly songwriting began as a way to keep Mom's spirits up after she got sick. They kept my spirits up too, after she died. When I reach the song called *Frown When I Sing It,* the one he wrote for me, I close the book. Every time he sang that song, I couldn't frown for days.

But right now, all I can do is frown. I need Mom. I need Marty. Even Dad would do tonight. I call him but get no answer. There's no use leaving a message because right now any message from me would not make sense. I sip in a long breath and hug my arms around me, staring at mom's candle, willing it to soothe me. Instead, every noise gets louder and louder, including my heart drumming in my chest.

Desperate to shut down the alarms ringing in me—about this spooky house, that SUV, Tom, and Carter Brown—I decide to browse for funny videos, hoping to ward off the creeps. When I open my laptop, though, a blast of light greets me from the login screen. Right in the middle is the eye. It's in full color, a brown iris with flecks of gold, and it's blinking quite dramatically, like a GIF.

I should be used to this by now, but my heart is pumping out distress code on the edge of totally freaked. No, I've gone way over that edge, gripping the corners of my desk, my mouth wide in a silent scream.

Chapter 11

A face comes into view. It's not a real face, more like a plastic mask, pure white, but luminous, sort of glow-in-the-dark Halloween but without the eye cutouts. Instead, the eyes are embedded into that white, a horror movie come to life inside my computer. My mouth is like a canyon. I should be fainting or throwing the laptop across the room, but that floating sensation hits me again. A pulse races through me. Time stops—or is it just my heart-beat cratering?—and I say as if it were still a possibility, "You're not Marty. His eyes were blue."

"I know. I am Sol." The voice sounds rich and soothing, filled with rushes of breath like the breeze. "And you are Kaye."

My eyes mist. I should have nothing to say to this stranger in my laptop, but there's a tug of war between the alarm he rings in me and my longing to connect. It's that voice of his, like a serenade, and that way he says my name: *And you are Kaye*. Besides, I need to know more. I need to understand what all this means. "Just tell me what you want."

It's then the face fades away, but the screen on my PC changes. A message writes itself across my wallpaper of forest trees in the same italic font as the prediction: *You saw the tornado.*

"Yes," I say as if he can hear me, nodding as if he can see me too. My eyes aren't even blinking; I'm so mesmerized.

He responds in text. *You still do not believe it?*

My breath skips. I want to say no, I don't believe it. That wasn't a real tornado. Not at all. But deep beneath that thought is another one that whispers *yes*, it must be true. It couldn't be anything else but true because I was there. "Nobody saw it except me. It's not even a news story."

Check again.

On my phone, I type: *Mossy Hills tornado*. There's a hit on the local weather page.

You still do not believe me?

"I don't know." My head is in my hands. My brain is cracking.

Do you need a new prediction?

When I don't answer, he gives me one anyway: *Tomorrow a hurricane will form in the Gulf of Mexico. They will call it Chris, but they will nickname it El Diablo because sustained winds will reach 205 mph at landfall.*

"Where?" I drop my phone. "My father's in Galveston."

Better have him come home early before the evacuation chaos.

I'm panting for breath. "How do you know this?"

I am the last one on Earth.

"What?" I jerk back. It's whiplash. I pound the desk. "You're joking, aren't you? This is all a joke. Who are you? Are you Carter Brown?"

Perhaps you will believe me tomorrow. Goodnight, Kaye.

"Who are you?" The laptop just thrums. "Who are you?" I ask twenty, thirty, maybe more times than that. The trees on the screen flicker, but no new text appears. In my mind's eye, though, a scene appears—that ragged crack down the lonely street, the one that rips at my heart. I focus on its jagged length until the memory of Sol's voice rises in me. He's saying, "I am Sol. And you are Kaye." And then, that lonely crack disappears.

Settling on my pillow, exhaustion washes through me till I begin to dream, dreams I can't remember. The ringtone of my cell wakes me. Someone's calling. It's Free but I can't seem to swipe to pick up. My arms, my legs are clumsy, and my thoughts are jumbled. There's a far, far away sensation and the journey back is proving hard. I'm not in regular time and space. I remember the voice and the mask. It was all a dream. It had to be.

Still, I check my computer for a sign of Sol. Nothing's there. Not in the login screen or any photos that had an eye before. I should be relieved, but a twinge of regret pinches at me. I can still hear his voice, the sound of my name, the warmth behind the vowels, drawn out, soft air carrying them. That voice satisfies some intense craving, a deep need to feel close to someone, to not feel lonely. Is this love? Am I falling in love with my hacker? No, there's nothing romantic here. This longing is the same longing I have for Mom, for Marty.

Stumbling to the bathroom to splash water on my face, I almost feel stoned, but my pupils aren't dilated. The morning is bright beyond my window, light filtering down through the trees. The sound of their needles, rustling softly, reminds me of his voice.

Snuggling back in bed to attempt a proper wake up, I notice a sketch in the notepad on my nightstand. It's a tree, its leaves shaded by the ink of Marty's pen, clumps of white among them, shining like starry flowers. When did I draw that? There's a smaller scribble scrawled across the top left corner in my handwriting: *El Diablo. Hurricane.* The prediction. Yes. That I remember.

I check my phone app for breaking news. Finding nothing, I flop back against the pillow. It's not true. There's no hurricane. There's no last man on Earth. I'm ready to roll over again, go back to sleep, but my phone won't let me. *Ding.* It's a news alert: *tropical storm forms in the Gulf.* It's called Chris. It's headed toward Texas.

All my breath bleeds away. I'm wretched, more than wretched, and what's double, triple wretched is it's true—the hurricane. Sol was right. It's happening just like it's some magic carpet unrolling into the future, one I must walk. It's not the red celebrity carpet though. This one is gruesome black and whipped with wind so strong it blows me back. It's not going to end easy.

I text Dad: *Bad storm in the Gulf. Come home early.*

I'm not worried, he texts back.

I'm surprised he even answered. He must have gotten the same alert.

It's going to be bad. Certain Dad's not listening, I add a reckless warning: *They'll call it El Diablo*, and then sit back to wait.

Nothing. Is he just busy? Or is he being dismissive of me, his foolish daughter? Watching for signs of the storm outside the window, as if it were lurking beyond the hillside, my hands turn to fists. I want to punch away that storm to keep him safe, even though it's too far beyond my reach. What would I do if he never comes back?

My ringtone chimes to rescue me from questions. This time I pick up Free's call. "Hi."

"Hi. Hey … sounding sleepy there. Did I wake you?"

I yawn. "Yeah … I think so." I'm talking at half speed. My words sound sloppy, like I'm drunk.

"You want to canvass with me today?"

"Sure." My brain struggles to define that word. "What's canvassing?"

"We wrap buildings in canvas. It's like TP'ing a house but with style."

I know he's teasing me, but I feel too sluggish to play along. "Really?"

"No." Free chuckles. "You mean you'll go with this without knowing what it is?"

"Well, whatever it is, I know you'll make it interesting." I can't seem to find the energy to sound eager.

Free picks up on my flat tone. He sounds hesitant when he asks, "So, the office at eleven?"

"Oh, I have a lunch with my stepmom, I think." The thought of lunch with Margot zings me—bleh—but it gets my blood moving. Another day with Free? I can't miss that.

"How about ten? We can just do a few hours to break you in."

"I'll check and get back, okay?" Finally, there's some punch to my words.

I close the call and text Margot, my fingers clumsy but moving quickly: *What time 4 lunch?*

She texts back: *Not today. Tomorrow at 12:30.*

My smile spreads wide. *Ok.*

Texting Free, fingers flying, I'm fully charged. *No lunch today. I can do it. Great. Eleven. At the office.*

Catapulting out of bed, I shake my legs, working the last bits of sleep out of them, and raid my snack stash. There's a protein bar to munch as I search *canvassing* to find out what it really is. It's knocking on doors for the campaign, which sounds daunting and, for sure, requires something sensible to dress in. I settle on gray slacks and a print blouse, little blue flowers. Who could argue with flowers? I do the braid thing again. That worked out well yesterday, and it makes me feel more mature. My backpack gets stuffed with snacks, sunscreen, and a visor. I pick up Marty's pen from the nightstand and slip it into the side pocket to write notes down.

It's 10:45 when I park across the street from the initiative office. Not wanting to wait inside, I sit in the car and check the news every other minute for updates on the storm. It's growing stronger. They project it will become a hurricane within the hour. The eye is beginning to form. A local site for Galveston is already showing radar. It loops, bands of green, yellow, and red swirling hypnotically. That radar captivates—just the power of it—suggesting towering waves and lashing rain in the middle of the ocean. A ship tosses wildly. The crew struggles to keep from sinking until I realize I've lost track of time. It's 11:10.

Rushing through the office door, I stop in my tracks. Free's there, his back to me, talking to a girl with beautiful skin the color of sienna. Maybe he's mad that I'm late. They're laughing and she's pretty and I can't compete.

The girl points at me. Free turns around and waves me over. "Kaye, meet my big sister Chanise."

I'm blushing now. Stupid me, being jealous. "Hi."

She reaches out her hand to shake mine. "Call me Channie." She's tiny, not like lanky Free, but her eyes are just as kind.

Free glances at the clock on the wall, an eyebrow raised. "Better go. Lots of doors to hit."

He hugs Channie and heads out. I wave to her and follow Free as he strides across the street to my car, not waiting for me. He's all restless today, pressing forward through space, a force that can't be stopped. "Driving okay with you? My car's been out of sorts for a bit. I've been biking it."

My breath catches a tiny bit. Am I just a ride? I push against that thought with a flick of my hand. "I don't mind. Neither does Charlotte."

"Charlotte?"

I pat the roof. "She's my best friend." And then I wince. That sounds lame. "She's my first … car that is." I wince again. That sounds even lamer.

But Free nods. "That's cool."

As we buckle in, I ask. "So where do we canvass?"

Free studies a map on the clipboard in his hand. "Looks like we head east to the hills. Star Mountain. Eagle Mountain. Crisscross Mountain."

Those streets are close to mine. I gnaw my lip. *Please, don't say Willow Mountain. Please. Please.*

Free turns the clipboard sideways and reads, "And one more. Treasure Mountain."

"Treasure Mountain? I wouldn't think they'd be interested up there. Aren't those pretty fancy places?"

Free tilts his head sideways in that winning way. "You'd be surprised. Sometimes they get a dash of conscience delivered to their door and they respond, I'm just saying."

"Okay." Guilt pinches me. Does Dad have a conscience that could respond? I'm not sure.

"Besides, we start in the subdivision," Free says. "Star Mountain is mostly subdivision. More middle class. It doesn't get upscale until Crisscross

Mountain. Eagle Mountain is old-time rural. Small cabins and farms. Some of the best folks live there. But Treasure Mountain? Yeah, they've got some serious loot on that street, so we probably won't find anyone answering the door."

Tired of wincing about my rich-girl status, I change the subject. "So, what's cap and trade?"

"Cap and trade? It's another way to curb emissions. Polluters offset the carbon by buying credits, but if they set the price too low, it doesn't do much. We want to pass the carbon tax, instead, to show voters will support it, and besides, some places around the world use both types of systems. It's not one or the other. They can target different parts of the problem."

Free explains more about the pros and cons of cap and trade as he directs me to our first street. Star Mountain is a neighborhood I feel comfortable in. The houses are from the sixties. Many of them are split-levels with a two-car garage and low brick walls capped with wooden lap siding. To my mind, that would be a home. Unlike Bleak House, you couldn't feel lost there.

I park at the end of a block, and Free hands me his phone. The impatience in him is dissipating. His voice is more chill, the space longer between his words. "You can just do some response recording till you're ready to step up your game."

Each address on the mobile screen has a name with questions below it like a multiple-choice test. The main question to mark is whether they support the initiative, oppose it, or are undecided. There are also places to check if no one's home, the place is vacant, the person is deceased, moved, or speaks a different language. One choice says refused. I can't begin to imagine how those door knocks go.

"Refused," Free says, "isn't so bad. They hardly ever get nasty. Mostly it's all *sorry, busy*. So just do like the mall yesterday. Smile, be polite, and move on. Sometimes they'll take the door hanger, sometimes not. Most people don't pay attention to the issues, but your face at their door is important. When they see you smile, it may nudge them on election day."

I glance up at Free, knowing that's been me—lazy about the issues. "I guess I could be like that, too busy to pay attention."

"But, hey … look at you now." Free beams at me. "You're an activist."

"An activist. I like the sound of that." Still, it's hard to square that image with the real me, just days ago, believing everything Dad said.

Mostly, no one is home, and Free leaves a door hanger with information about the initiative. When someone does answer, many of them are busy or undecided.

"This is discouraging." My footsteps lag.

Free's stride doesn't slow one bit. He's used to this. "Stay positive," Free says. "You never know when you'll make an impression."

The next door proves his point. A woman answers. She's on the phone, and there are children yelling in the background. One runs screaming down the hall behind her. Free gives her a sunny grin. "Have you heard about the Initiative for the Climate?"

"Barb," she says into the phone, "some nice young kids are at the door. Can I call you back?" She hangs up and gives Free her attention, smiling expectantly.

"We're here to talk about an Initiative for the Climate. Basically, it's for your children in there," Free says. "We're trying to make sure they have a future; we have a future. We need to slow climate change, the rate of emissions."

"How are you going to do that?"

"We're going to put a fee on carbon, like anything from fossil fuels that's used for electricity or gas."

"Will I have to pay it?" Her forehead wrinkles with worry.

"Businesses will pay it, but prices will rise a little bit, more as the years go by."

"I can't afford that." There's a little shake to her head.

"You'll get a rebate every year to help cover the cost." Free's beaming at her, his gestures wide. He's working his magic.

"A rebate?" The woman's chin lifts. She's open to hearing more.

"All the money from the fees will partly go toward a rebate to every adult in the state. The rest will go to help with mass transit, renewable energy, and energy conservation."

"That sounds okay." She's nodding now.

Free slows down, pausing a moment, choosing his lines. "I know it's hard to think of paying more for anything, but the less fossil fuel you use, the more value you'll get from the rebate."

"Oh," the woman says. "Yeah, I guess so."

The woman is still undecided, at least it seems that way to me. I can't think of anything more to add until a little girl comes to the door. "Hi," she says.

I bend down to her level. "What's your name?"

"Tammy."

I look up at the woman. "You've got a sweet little girl here."

"Thank you." She's beaming, a proud mother.

I smile at Tammy and give her a wink. "I think Tammy needs to grow up with a chance to live a good life. What's that worth to you?"

"Everything," she says, the words soft but emphatic.

I stand back up, tilt my head, and let my voice come out softly too. "Then vote for the initiative. She needs you to. This really is for her. We don't even want to think about what might happen if we don't fix this." A tear creeps into my eye. Dad? Rory? Do they ever think of anyone else's kid?

"I will." She smiles down at her daughter. "When's the election?"

"November." Free points to the date on the door hanger and hands it to her.

She tilts her head, thoughtfully. "Maybe … do you have a few more? I'll talk to my neighbors."

"Great." I clap my hands together.

"Can I have one?" Tammy asks.

"Sure." Free hands her one.

"What do I do with it?"

"Just hang it on your door."

"Okay," the girl says and disappears.

"Thanks for doing this." The woman reaches out her hand to me.

"You bet," I say, shaking it.

Free shakes her hand too. "Thank you for talking."

As we turn and walk down the steps, Free points a finger at me. "Look at you, all bouncy."

Yes, bouncy, that's what I'm feeling. "I just knew what to say."

I'm buzzy with disbelief. It's almost like that floating sensation I get from talking to Sol, but not so lasting. This is just a little hop and skip over gravity, but it's good.

My thoughts drift back to Sol, surprised to realize I've stopped doubting him. Sol is real. How did I come to accept that? It's just hard to deny a hurricane, but what does he mean—the last one on Earth? That must be a metaphor for his lonely existence. Or perhaps he's the last of a long-lost people, like an indigenous tribe in the Amazon. There's an urgent need in me to get back to him, to ask him what he means.

But right now, I'm here with Free doing the work of canvassing. Free's stride is long with an easy rhythm. There's a bead of sweat on his forehead. I love the way it glistens. It trickles downward toward his eye. Ah, those shining, diamond eyes.

He glances my way, eyes twinkling with fun, but also lit by a glow that might be affection. Does he like me? I can't read it clearly, but I hope I'm not alone in wanting a deeper connection. The one thing that's clear to me is this: I'm definitely falling for him.

Chapter 12

Of course, the next time we find someone home, Free lets me begin the conversation, and I blow it, talking carbon tax right away. *Tax* is a trigger word for this guy at the door. He gets angry and almost slams it in my face. "Tax, tax, tax. All they want to do is tax," he yells at me.

Free steps forward and slips in the rebate information, stressing how the rebate is worth more to him the less carbon he uses. His voice is soft, gently coaxing the anger out of the man. "You could come out ahead depending on what you buy and how you travel." That gets the man's attention.

I move back, trying to fade into the bush beside me, letting Free take charge. He manages to get a door hanger into the man's hands, but we mark him as undecided. At least I don't have to choose refused. "I'm lousy with men," I say as we move on.

"You'll learn. Remember, it's just choosing the right story for the right moment at the right door. By the end of the day, you'll wrap them around your little finger. You've already done that with me." He gives me a look that makes my heart sputter.

Wrapped around my little finger? That thought brings a tingle from my head to my toes. "But, a story? Shouldn't it be about the facts?"

"So … hey. You can only use facts if they believe in the story you're telling, otherwise they just discount your facts. People usually make facts fit the story, and only the story they want, like that man. He wanted the what's-in-it-for-him story, not the future-for-the-children story, and definitely not the tax story."

"How do you know which story to tell?"

"You have to size them up, ask questions to see where they're at, get into a conversation, and maybe get it wrong sometimes. There's always another door."

My phone dings right then. It's an alert. I moan. "Oh, no. It's a Category 2 already."

"What?" Free's surprised by my alarm.

My heart beats louder. My shoulders sag. "The hurricane. It's getting worse. And it's headed toward Galveston."

Free peers over my shoulder at my phone. "A hurricane in Galveston? You serious?"

"Yes, headed that way. It's going to be a real bad storm. They call it El Diablo."

"Say what?" He points to the headline. "It says Chris."

"Well, yeah, I just read that somewhere." My words come out all mumbled because how could I explain Sol's prediction? I'd sound crazy. "My Dad's in Galveston today. Don't you have family near there?"

"Houston."

"Better tell them to evacuate."

"Really?"

"Yeah, really. It's going to be bad." I start texting: *Dad, get out of there. It's getting stronger.* I stare at my phone as if that can force a response. "I just lost my brother," I tell Free. "I can't lose my father too."

"You lost your brother?"

My lip trembles. I resist saying it, but then it tumbles out. "His car went over a cliff into the ocean."

Free stops, giving me a look of recognition. "Hey, I'm sorry, Kaye." He's quiet for a minute. "Maybe we should call it for today."

"No, no." The sidewalk becomes my focal point. "I'll calm down. I can." I gulp some air and press my heels into the cement beneath me as if that will stop the grief and gloom. "Dad'll be okay. He'll make it home."

Free leans down to catch my eye. "We're almost done with the block. Take a minute. I'll finish."

My nod is slow. "Yeah, it's not good to talk to voters all upset."

He takes his phone from me so he can continue the canvass. "Don't worry. I got this."

I pace relentlessly to distract myself from the storm. Nibbling snacks from my pack, I obsess over gardens, taking photos of flowers in the yard beside the car. There's a bee on a blossom—a purple aster, its petals radiating out from its yellow center like a star. We had those in Portland. I love them. Digging out Marty's pen and some old notepaper lingering in the pack's inner pocket, I sketch them.

Free walks down the street toward me as radiant as the yellow center of that aster. It must have been a good door. *Ding.* My phone chimes in. It's Dad. *Wrapping up. Leaving early but the flights are full in Houston so renting a car and driving north to catch one in Dallas.*

I text back. *Wonderful!* By the time Free reaches me, I'm sunny again.

"Hey, that smile's a sign. Good news?"

"He's on his way back."

Free points to the pen in my hand. "You carry a tactical pen?"

"A what?"

"That's a tactical pen. It's like a lethal weapon."

I stare at it, eyes troubled. "What does it do?"

He points to the sharp end. "It stabs people."

I shudder at the image. "It was my brother's. I can't imagine him stabbing people."

"Well, it's used for self-defense. Maybe he lived in a rough part of town or something."

My fingers freeze—that pen cold in my hand. My thoughts go tumbling toward black SUVs. I imagine Marty being wrestled toward a dark car by

Carter Brown; Marty stabbing with the pen, fighting for his life. Was that how it happened? No. Marty's pen was in the hoodie. He didn't have it with him when he died.

Free breaks into my fret by peeking into my backpack. "You brought snacks? Hey … chocolate banana. That's like essential grub out here in the canvassing wilderness."

I whip out an energy bar for him. "But only if you promise to call Texas and warn them about the storm."

"For food? Anything." His laugh is a melody that makes the air ring.

Most of the afternoon goes great. Eagle Mountain Road is a haven of liberal folks who embrace the initiative. They ask us in, offer up some iced tea or water. One woman even has fresh-baked ginger cookies to share. A younger guy asks how to volunteer.

Crisscross Mountain is a different story. No one answers the door even though we can hear people talking or music playing inside. The houses are huge, like mine. As he knocks on each door, Free's eyebrows pinch. Ouch! Does he have an attitude about someone this rich? Maybe not an attitude, really. Free's not like that, but he's not comfortable around here.

At the last address, Shelley answers. She looks from me to Free. "Hi, Free."

"I didn't know you lived up here," Free says.

Shelley winces slightly. "Well, I don't like to broadcast it."

I'm surprised by that.

"Voting yet?" Free asks.

Shelley shrugs. "Nah."

"Eighteen this year? I can sign you up."

"That's okay. I'll do it later." She points at the last remaining door hanger in Free's hand. "What's this about?"

"The Initiative for the Climate."

Shelley perks up. "You mean the carbon tax?" She gives a sideways grin.

"My dad completely hates it."

Free chuckles. "Now there's a reason to vote for it. Good as any."

"Okay," Shelley says. "Sign me up."

As Free pulls out a registration form from his pack, I study Shelley. It's something about her face when she turns a certain way—those eyes so dark, her skin so pale. In the shadows of the doorway, she's almost ghostly bright. As she fills out the form, I flash on the face in the window last night. Yes, it was her. I stiffen.

She hands the clipboard back to Free and says without much energy, "So, Kaye. I guess we're doing lunch tomorrow."

Ugh. I melt into the flagstones at my feet. Now Free will tag me as one of those privileged girls who live in houses like these. "I guess."

Free looks from me to her. "Hey, thanks Shelley. And if you ever want to really rebel, volunteer with us. Here's the phone number." He points to the contact information on the door hanger.

"Maybe I will. Good to see you again." She turns away abruptly and closes the door.

As we walk back to the car, the space between Free and me slips into some hazy, uneasy territory. "So, lunch with Shelley?" he asks.

I study his face for signs I'm overreacting. "Yeah, my stepmother knows her mom. She wants me to make connections, but I don't know if I'm interested."

Free surprises me. "Shelley's not so bad. She's a let-me-aloner at times, and she hangs with an older crowd at Mossy Falls."

"The community college?"

"Yeah, I think she's into art or drama."

"She doesn't seem to have the energy for drama," I say. "Probably art."

Just when I think I've misjudged things about him backing away from me, Free checks his phone. "Oh, hey. Two o'clock. Let's backtrack to the office."

"What about Treasure Mountain addresses?"

Free shrugs. "I don't think Treasure Mountain will be worth the steps."

Thud. The shrug tells me I didn't overreact. Something's gone stale between us, and what could it be besides me being too rich? He must think I'm a snob.

Free doesn't say much on the ride back. He takes out his phone and thumbs through some messages. "Whoa, serious," he says.

"What?"

"It's from Channie. My cousins in Houston are packing up. Mandatory evacuation. Category 3 and heading to 4."

I sip a short breath. "Do they have somewhere to go?"

"Aunt Marjorie's in Dallas. They'll be fine. Their house, that's different. Rebuild again? I think this time they might give it up."

My forehead's all pinched with tension. Free's family, my dad. Will they make it? "Maybe it won't reach Houston."

"Maybe," Free says, his voice cloudy. He's lost that spark in him. "Damn those skeptics. They're just lying for the oil companies, for the money. They keep pushing the climate to the edge. They don't care who dies."

Free's so heavy right now, I'm not sure how to lift him. I'm struggling to lift myself. "You're thinking of your crew, huh? The ones in the fire?"

Free's rubbing his chest like he's filled with an ache. "That's a definite yes."

I ache for him too. "But that's why you're doing this. Remember? For them."

He stares out the window. "Oh, for certain, a real big-time commitment, but will it help? Will it ever be enough to compensate for ..." He pauses and then finishes. "For losing everything, everyone?"

"You can't give up." I hate how lame that sounds.

Free chews his lip. His shoulders sag a bit like his eyes. His colors grow muted. Saying anything right now would make me look insensitive. I know how I felt with all those platitudes slung at me after Marty died. I craved respectful silence, but people kept talking. Once or twice I even snapped, telling them, "Shut up!"

Back at the office, Free opens the car door right away. "Catch you later." He doesn't glance at me.

That stabs, but I try to reconnect. "I know how you feel. I lost someone too."

Free just nods and gets out of the car. His stride, long and lanky, doesn't have any bounce left. Is that what happened to me? When Marty died, did I lose my bounce? No, I never had it to begin with.

My foot taps the gas, wanting escape from Free's pain, my pain. If I let it, where would that foot lead me? Perhaps someplace new, a place where I can walk into a store and people know my name. And I've got my own house. It's cute and cozy. A window looks out over a small city. Down below, the traffic lights at night gleam like they're reflecting stars in the sky. There's no laptop voice scaring me. Friends stop by. Yes, if I could find a place like that.

Greg comes out the office doors. He gets into a dark SUV parked four spaces in front of me. That SUV sets off alarm bells. Is that the one following me? Charlotte gives an impatient *vroom*, pulling into traffic as a car zooms by. It swerves around me, blaring its horn. I slam on the brakes and sit for a moment, and then turn on my blinker, starting out again, driving slowly past Greg's car. It's dark blue, not black.

Turning the corner to pull over and park, I stare into space till my heart stops galloping. It takes a funny gargoyle face in an old iron gate beside me to bring back a smile, helping me relax again. That's when I notice a computer store across the street in a quaint fieldstone house.

It's tiny. Only one person stands behind the counter. He's got dark hair and a tawny tone. I like his eyes. They flash sharp and quick, like he knows what you want before you ask. His nametag says Danilo.

"I do graphics. I need a laptop with lots of RAM, 2T of storage, and a great graphics card."

"Let me check."

As he goes to the back to see what's in stock, I check out a little tablet on the shelf beside the counter, great for surfing the net. Down an aisle, there are interesting gadgets for sweeping a room for bugs, as in surveillance. Maybe that's a thing in Mossy Hills—lots of wealthy folks worried about who's spying on them. I add one to my purchases along with my own spy camera. *Spytime Cam* the package reads. Thinking of Shelley peering through the study window, I consider putting it in Dad's office to see if someone's sneaking in for mischief.

When Danilo comes back, he says they'll have to order the laptop. "Takes about a week."

"Okay, I think I'll wait. I'll just take the tablet and this other stuff today." As he rings me up, I ask, "Have you heard about the hurricane?"

"Yeah, sounds bad," he says, shaking his head. "It's all getting bad. We've got to do something, don't we?"

I put myself into canvassing mode. "Have you heard about the Initiative?"

"For the climate? Sure. I'm going to volunteer for that."

A business card on the counter has his name. "I have a friend working on it too. Can I give him this?"

"Absolutely." Danilo gives me my receipt. "Hey, did you hear about the tornado? It was right outside of town yesterday. No, the day before."

"Yeah, I saw that." I'm surprised someone knows about it besides me.

Danilo is bagging up my items. "Tornadoes. Hurricanes. What's coming next?"

That question: What's coming next? It clicks. That's why I'm keeping my PC. Sol was right about the tornado. He'll be right about the hurricane. I need my laptop to hear what Sol has to say.

Chapter 13

Back home, there are cars all over the driveway and a house full of people. Margot has friends over, so I lock my bedroom door with a definite punch at the button in the center of the knob. Stretching out across my bed, I close my eyes. All that walking and talking has done me in, but I can't relax. My hectic thoughts become a whirlpool, swirling like the storm in the Gulf of Mexico. Dad? Tom? Greg? SUVs? Marty's pen? And Carter Brown? Yes, so many questions but not any answers. I think back to the invoice I found. Maybe that's the place to start.

Bancroft & Sons. It's a Portland firm. Were they investigating Marty's murder? My phone hunts down their number.

"Bancroft & Sons," a woman says when she answers. "How can I help you?"

"Can I speak to Mr. Bancroft please?"

"Concerning?"

I gulp, grasping for a cover story. "Um. This is Paul Malloy's assistant. He's in Dallas, but he wanted me to call to see if you have any updates on his case."

"Mr. Bancroft is in a meeting all afternoon. Can I take a message?"

"That's all right," I stammer. "Mr. Malloy will call when he gets a chance."

Ugh. Utter fail. I disconnect, studying the ceiling for a better plan, but there's only currents of shadow between those islands of texture. I don't even know the new assistant's name. The last one had to leave when Rory's wife got jealous of her. I consider calling back and giving Margot's name with my number, but indecision grips me.

My thoughts become storm-tossed again. Carbon taxes. Hurricanes. Free, his sunny light fading. Marty again, his body churning in the waves below the sea cliff. It was hot today. How hot will tomorrow be? And the next year and the next? Heat. Heat. Heat. My attention lands on Sol. He calms my storm, but I don't know why. Maybe he's a good-guy hacker, someone who really does need my help. It makes no sense that he can know the future— so, yes, it's crazy—but I need to speak with him again. I need some answers.

I sit up straight and turn on the computer. Is he there? Not in the login screen. The background's just that screensaver of a river in the forest, trunks rising to the sky. I check my *eyes* folder, navigating to all the suspect images—the funeral pic, my dad's photo, the NASA shot. Not an eye in any of them, grayscale or color. I open a blank document. Using the text tool, I type: *Are you there?*

There's no response, so I grab the pen tool and start to draw a vector path, an oval like a pupil. Coloring it black, I put a new path on top of it, adding a crescent of white for the glint in the eye. I keep building the eye, adding a new layer beneath the first, naming the layers *pupil* and *iris*. I shape the iris, filling it with brown before adding a fourth layer to hint at speckles of gold. There's a slight upward slant to the outer eye like Danilo's in the store today. Yes, that's how the eye looks.

I stop, connecting Danilo with the eye. He's a computer guy. He could be a hacker, and he knew about the tornado. With a shake of my head, that option gets crossed out on my who-is-Sol list. Danilo didn't sound like Sol. In fact, this eye I'm drawing is not Danilo's. It's filled with flecks of gold. Danilo's eyes were a solid, darker brown.

Layer by layer, the eye crystallizes. With each click of the stylus, a new pen point appears, creating a sharp corner to the shape unless I draw out its control handles smoothing the corner into a curve. I love forming the curves, called Bézier curves for the French engineer who patented them. This is play-time for me, moving the control handles wider, narrower, up, down. Curves deepen. Corners become slightly rounded. This work, point by point, line by line, keeps me steady. My mind settles, peaceful again, floating me into a tranquil space that feels like forever. Is it Sol? Has he appeared?

Yes, it's Sol, but this time, there's no drama to the pulse of light I see. The eye I've drawn acquires a gentle glow like the sun's backlighting it. Some text appears beside it: *Kaye. I am ready. Are you?*

I sit back, and then type. *Ready for what?*

To talk. I have so much to say.

Will you tell me who you are, really?

Think of my name.

Sol?

This time think of sole as in one, only one.

Yes. You said you are alone, but why?

I am the last one.

The last one of what?

The last one on Earth.

I stiffen at his words but keep typing: *You said that before, but what do you mean?* Three more question marks highlight my confusion.

I am from the future. Think years beyond years, when the world is different and everyone you will ever know is gone.

No. That's impossible, but I resist my urge to close the laptop, to forget all this, to retreat into thinking it's all a joke someone's playing on me. Remembering the tornado and the storm, two unlikely predictions that came true, I push myself to continue. *How can that be? I don't understand.*

The text disappears. A photo takes its place. It's me in the bunker, sitting on the couch with my PC on my knees. When was this taken? I never sat on that couch when I was down there.

The curser's frozen. I can't type. Instead, I chew my lip, and wait, and wait some more. It's just a photo of me in the bunker, but my hair is all wrong. It's cut extremely short, and I'm not wearing what I wore two days ago. Something's different about my face. It's older, years older, my eyes a bit puffy. I've gained some weight. I could be twenty-five or thirty. That brings shivers.

My cursor starts blinking again. I right-click on the photo and select properties from the menu to check the date the photo was taken. It says twelve years from now, but that date can be altered. My face can be altered too. I do that all the time. The other changes, to my clothes, my hair, could be digitally altered as well. I zoom in to look for pixelated areas, missing shadows, or wavy lines that should be straight, but I'm not an expert at spotting digital fakes, and nothing obvious jumps out at me.

Sol types beneath the picture: *Take this to the bunker. I will explain.*

You mean the laptop?

Yes. It will be much easier there.

Can I trust him, whoever he is? No. Yes. Maybe. It doesn't matter. My laptop's under my arm as I sprint down the stairs and around the corner, rushing to avoid anyone from Margot's crowd. Slipping through the study door, I flash-freeze like I'm a computer that's crashed. It's Tom Rodington. He's standing over Dad's desk, looking just like the grainy photo I took the night of the party—the scowl, the beard, the eye glare so mean.

"What are you doing?" I sputter.

"Your father called and asked me to find something for his meeting tomorrow in Galveston." His voice is penetrating.

"Get out! There's no meeting tomorrow. He's on his way back home."

"He didn't tell me."

My eyes narrow. "I don't believe you. Should I call him?"

"Don't bother him. It must have been a misunderstanding." Tom's voice is as smooth as a snake's.

I gather myself. "Misunderstanding or not, he's coming home, so go."

Tom brushes past me with an icy vibe. Even the air around him feels poisonous, so I vow to wait in the study till he leaves. Locking the door, I settle into Dad's chair, trying all the drawers in his desk. They're still locked. Nothing in the room looks out of place or odd. It's still Dad's brand of orderly.

It's time for the bunker, but when I reach for the key in my pocket, it's gone. I pace a circle around the desk. Without the key, how am I going to talk to Sol? How am I going to close the bunker door before Dad gets back?

I'm thinking back, vaguely remembering setting the bunker key on the nightstand by my bed. Or was it in my pocket when I spun out on Willow Mountain? Did I lose it then? Ugh. I have to find that key, or a key, at least. There must be more than one key to the bunker. Dad would want a backup.

I feel under the bookcase by the keyhole. Nothing. I check beneath every cabinet, examine ancient artifacts, and scour the insides of closets. In one closet, there's a box of papers. I paw through it but find no key. In the bottom, though, is a photo album. Who makes an actual photo album anymore? I flip through the pages. Apparently, Margot does.

It's her wedding album. Margot married Dad five years ago. I was twelve; Marty was going on twenty-one. He had just finished his third year of college. The wedding was early May, a week before his birthday, which made him glum. I remember him saying, "How can I celebrate with her in this family … like permanently?" Marty barely came home again.

As I pore over the album pages, I realize I'm barely in there. Most of the day, I walked the resort gardens like a lost puppy. The rhododendrons were in bloom, and a bumblebee crawling across the rocks beneath them fascinated me. It looked so fuzzy, almost cuddly. I loved the pretty red-orange band in the middle of its back.

This album's full of strangers. I'm searching for the face of Tom but not finding him. At the end though, there's Margot and a woman who could be an older version of her—still blonde but without the heavy makeup.

Between them is Greg, the one I think is Carter Brown. He looks much younger, of course, but he resembles them. Is he Margot's nephew or cousin? My throat squeezes as if a cry is stuck there. I've always despised Margot, but now she's a threat. She's involved in this, but Margot, Greg, Tom, what's the connection?

The photo of Greg ends up captive in my pocket. Gripping my laptop, I listen at the door. It's quiet. Unlocking the door, I listen again. Nothing. I tiptoe to the front door. The driveway's empty. I hope that means Tom's gone too.

Back in my room, I paw through the nightstand for the bunker key. It's not there. After some frantic tipping out of drawers and boxes, I flash on finding the key in my pocket while waiting for the tornado and putting it into the glove box for safekeeping.

As I dash downstairs to retrieve the key from my car, Dad calls. "Just to let you know I'm heading north to Houston."

"That's good." Relief floods me.

"The bad news is that I'm stuck in traffic halfway there."

"Well, get off the highway. Go east or west."

"It'll be fine. There's probably an accident up ahead."

Margot's giggling in the kitchen. A man's voice booms too. It's Tom. He's telling some joke. Ugh. It sounds racist. There's the *N* word, and Margot is actually laughing at it. Of course, Margot will laugh at anything a man says when she's flirting with him.

Tom says something about a vaccine. "And we'll have control over distribution. That's power."

I whisper into the phone. "Tom's here."

"Tom Rodington?"

My *yes-ss* is all hiss. "He was in your study."

"What were you doing in my study?" Dad's voice is suddenly sharp.

"Me? What was he doing there?"

I've raised my voice too loud. Margot's in the hallway, staring at me.

"What's wrong?" The slur of her words is explained by the wineglass in her hand.

"Dad's trying to get out of Galveston, and he's stuck in traffic."

Margot blinks in confusion.

I'm shouting now. "There's a storm. A big storm. Haven't you heard?"

"Oh, dear." Margot almost looks worried.

"Everyone's evacuating. Dad's stuck in the middle of it."

Tom heads out the door. "I'd better go."

"Yes, you'd better." I focus back on the phone. "Dad? Dad? Are you there?" Nothing. The call is disconnected.

I steer a wobbly Margot toward the family room where the ultra-flat-screen hangs on the wall and turn it on. Some anchors are talking aimlessly, trying to fill airtime.

"Chad, isn't it unusual for such a strong storm this early in the season? It's only the beginning of August."

"Well, John, surface water temperature in the Gulf is off the charts."

Behind Chad and John is the radar of the mammoth storm, lots of yellows and reds swirling around a huge hurricane eye, perfectly formed. The storm's dark eye becomes a tunnel. Staring into its core, looking for Sol's eye, I almost expect to find it in the pixels of the flat-screen, but it's not there. Even so, that strange sensation, like I'm floating off the planet, threatens to return. Spinning around to face Margot on the couch, hoping she'll say something irritating and bring me back to Earth, I frown. She's conked out, snoring.

That on-screen hurricane propels me toward the front door, the bunker key summoning me. I've got to talk to Sol. He knows the future, someway, somehow, even though that couldn't be true. How could it? Yet, as if to dispute that, Chad's voice from the TV follows me. "Down in Houston, they're calling it El Diablo."

Chapter 14

Tall firs beyond the driveway loom dark against the starlit sky. A long shadow by the front door spooks me. I lock Charlotte up and pat her roof affectionately before running the last fifty feet to the front door, the bunker key clutched in one hand, the bag from the computer shop in the other, and my backpack slung over my shoulder. I forgot all that in the back seat this afternoon because I was thrown off by the driveway filled with cars.

After closing the door against the dark and setting the alarm, I turn toward the study. Tom's prowling convinces me to hook up the spy camera right away. Outside the study door, though, the voices from the flat-screen stop me. Traffic jams have snarled the roadways all over Houston. I launch myself in that direction, needing to hear more. The phone rings. It's Dad.

"I'm not moving. And my phone battery is low, so I can't find a way off this damn road."

My heart squeezes. This is not good. "Why didn't you charge it?"

"I forgot."

"Well, the news says traffic isn't getting better up ahead. Let me look for another route. I'll call you back."

"I'm on 45 in Dickinson. I see Exit 19 just ahead. Should I take it? Text me the directions."

"Okay." I sink into a chair in front of the flat-screen and plug in the tablet, setting it up, creating a password, connecting to our network to search for a map. Dad's on 45 between Galveston and Houston. There's Dickinson. Boy, he didn't get far. Zooming in, I spot a number 19 in green.

Street view shows the exit sign. It says: *Exit 19, 517, Dickinson, Alvin.* Zooming back out, it's clear that Road 517 goes east and west, but east is too close to Galveston Bay. He could get trapped from rising water. West connects to Highway 6, which heads northwest. That's better.

After texting all that to Dad, I add: *Highway 6 will get you to Sugarland. Take 90 west and then 99 north. That will loop around Houston so you can pick up 45 again, or head north to Dallas on smaller roads. Let me know when you're in Sugarland.*

The live news chatter on the flat-screen is panic inducing, so I turn the volume off and check for updates on the tablet. Even so, the news still makes me super tense. While waiting for Dad to get back in touch, I type two words into the search bar: *time travel.* I've got questions, like how can it be possible for Sol to reach me from the future? Does he time travel? That's impossible, but I'm hoping some site on the web can rule it out completely.

So, time travel. Everyone has an opinion. There are reams of videos full of lunatic rants, oddball theories, plus sites with links that are plainly dubious. Some are overly complex, filled with scientific jargon that I can't decipher. Heading deeper and deeper into the murky world of time travel, I get lost in quantum physics—multi-universes, relativity, string theory, plus bosons, fermions, and quarks. The only familiar word is *photon* because it's a particle of light, and light is what a camera captures. Some sites say particles can become waves and that means strange things happen. The title of one book sums it up as everything that can happen does happen. Does that mean time travel?

I sit back and read that title again: *Everything That Can Happen Does Happen.* That sure describes my past few days. Everything is happening all at once, and at least some of what's happening is absolutely crazy. Maybe all the particles around me are turning into waves, and the waves are crashing onto my personal shore. That's as good an explanation as any.

Still, many sites claim time travel is impossible, so how will Sol explain it?

I won't find out if I keep missing that rendezvous with him in the bunker. What if the bunker's a time machine? When I walk through that door, will it sweep me into some wormhole to the future where only one lonely person exists? No. That's too terrifying.

The news ticker across the bottom of the flat screen announces in all caps: *EL DIABLO IS NOW A CATEGORY 4*. At least for now, my visit to the bunker is on hold. I need to wait for Dad to call me.

My backpack's almost empty of munchies. Free ate all the energy bars except one, lemon honey. Maybe lemon is not an essential flavor for him. I gobble it, savoring the blend of sour and sweet. As I crunch on the bar, I remember Marty's pen. Free said it was for self-defense, but that makes no sense. Still, a web search for *tactical pen* turns up lots of hits.

Watching a video about how to use them, I reach for the pen in my pack's side pocket and practice one of the moves, but that pen, glinting in the flickering light of cable news, hints at the horrific. It flashes red, and then yellow, and then red from hurricane radar. The thought of jabbing anything like that into someone's neck is sickening. My stomach flips, lemon honey rising in my throat, so I thrust the pen into the pack's side pocket away from my view.

About an hour later, Dad calls.

"Get me off this road," he shouts. He's stuck in a traffic jam of cars trying to head north on Highway 6. "I shouldn't have listened to you."

"You should have left long before you did. So … where are you?"

"I don't know."

"Well, turn around."

"You're crazy," Dad says. "That's toward the storm."

"The storm isn't here yet. Turn around. Look for another road, one that heads west. Then tell me what it's called. I'll find a way to make it work."

"Okay," he says. "I'm turning around." But a few seconds after he does, I hear the squealing of brakes and lots of noise. *Thunk!* "Oh, sh—" Dad says as the line goes dead.

I'm on my feet. An accident! I know it. Either that or his battery is dead. Frantic calls to his cell get no response. Dashing to the couch, I shake Margot. "Dad's been in an accident!" Margot murmurs something sleepy and turns away. I shake her again. "There's been an accident."

She sits up and then lies back down. "Call a doctor," she says. I pace the room until Margot wobbles to a sitting position. "Did you say an accident?"

"It's Dad. He was stuck in traffic and then there was an accident or something. I can't reach him on the phone."

Margot finally shows a sign of concern. "I should call Tom."

"Not him," I say abruptly. "Try Rory. Rory will know what to do."

While Margot's talking to Dad's partner, I stare at the news anchors, waiting for them to report on an accident on Highway 6. Instead, they're talking about the newest forecast. The hurricane will reach Category 5 before it makes landfall. Tomorrow evening is when they predict it will hit. A meteorologist describes a hurricane in 1900 that destroyed Galveston. She says, "The death toll was more than six thousand people. And that was only a Category 4."

"What will happen to Galveston if a Category 5 hits?" the stony-faced anchorman asks.

A co-anchor replies with awed disbelief. "There just won't be a Galveston anymore."

I keep flipping through the channels for more news. Margot's still talking with Rory. Ugh. How can she flirt in the middle of all this? Finally, my phone rings. It's an unknown number.

"I'm okay. The car's in a ditch," Dad says.

I liquefy, a puddle of relief, one with a Kaye Malloy face. "Where are you?"

"Someone was traveling the wrong way. I swerved but landed in the ditch. I'm at a house just off the road. I'll hire a chopper in the morning, but my phone's busted. I want you to have this contact number in case it doesn't work out."

Anticipating the blame Dad will heap on me for the accident, I mumble an apology. "Dad, I'm sorry. I shouldn't have told you to turn around."

Dad shushes me. "No, I should have hired a chopper right away. At least I can do some good. There's a whole family here, two women and a boy, stuck without a car in working condition. I can get them out." Dad's upbeat, almost giddy.

"Did you hit your head?"

"Of course I hit my head, but Cindy fixed me up. She's a nurse." He chuckles. "I'm in good hands. Wesson says he's going to take care of me."

"Who's Wesson?"

"He's the cutest thing. Just seven, but he's real sharp."

Dad gushing over a seven-year-old boy? He must be in shock. "Do you have an address? I need to know where you are."

"Don't worry. I'll be out of here first thing in the morning. And we're watching the news. If things get bad, Cindy's got a rowboat." He laughs at this as if it's hilarious.

My worry shoots into overdrive, imagining him in the hurricane in a tiny boat, waves washing over him as he laughs like a wild man. But then, he's always at his best when things seem the worst, at least for a while. Eventually it catches up with him and then he goes all gloomy.

"I've got to go. We're moving everything up to the second story. I'll let you know when I get to Dallas." Dad rattles off a string of numbers. Something clicks, like the receiver on a landline. I scramble to make a note before those numbers vanish from my brain, and then turn around and pull the phone from Margot's ear. "Dad's okay. He's going to hire a chopper to get to Dallas."

Margot nods, announcing the news to Rory, and then bragging about snagging tickets to that fashion show in the city she wants to see. Why doesn't Rory just hang up?

My legs suddenly go all slack like they've run a marathon, so I plop in front of the flat-screen. The storm won't make landfall tonight. He still has plenty of time to get out, but just sitting and waiting spikes my stress quotient. It's time to prowl. In the kitchen, some pizza's left in a delivery box. Margot bought pizza? The fridge is bare except for my milk and eggs. Even the stuffed dates are missing.

In the trash, there's a flyer about the meeting—all political. And then I notice some powdery residue on the countertop, barely visible, white on white quartz. Whoa! Were Tom's pupils dilated? Were Margot's? I shudder and turn away, hoping it's just pizza crust dust.

Commandeering what's left in the pizza box, I juggle all my gear from the family room and head to the study to tackle the security camera. A spot above a photo of a castle on a moor seems the perfect place to hide it. The installation isn't easy. It takes an hour to sort out the app. Finally, the whole office is in view in the video on my phone, even the mirror door, which makes me think about Sol and the bunker.

Ready to face him, I go to shut the study door, but Margot's in the hallway, wobbling off to bed. She stops to ask, "What are you doing in the study?"

The question really ticks me off. "Why can't I go in here?"

Margot shrugs. "It's nothing. It's just Paul doesn't want me in there either."

"Oh." I blink. Margot sounds like she's telling the truth. "So, what's the big secret?"

Margot gets a silly smirk. "Maybe we should find out."

What a horrifying thought—being her ally against Dad. "Dad wouldn't be happy."

"I know." She giggles and points into the room. "That's where I found the songbook."

"Really? Where?"

"I don't quite remember. No, yeah, I do. It was on a shelf with some of his books." She straightens up and looks me in the eye as if she's sober for a second. "I get it about Marty. Remembering is helpful for you."

Her words jolt me. "Thanks," I say.

She shrugs again, losing that sense of sobriety, and turns around, wobbling down the hall again.

With Margot on the prowl, it's not the time to talk to Sol, so I grab my laptop, tablet, and the spyware bag to head up the stairs. My legs feel weary, like they're moving through concrete, but it's not because I'm so beat. It's Margot—she's suddenly not the monster I think she is. She understands about Marty. That makes her human. And the bunker—I doubt she even knows it's there. Whatever's going on, she isn't the source of it. Ugh. I should be relieved she's not an evil genius, but sympathy? I never saw that in her.

Drawn by the soft glint of moonlight on the balcony railing, I step outside. To the west, a layer of cloud moves in, hiding the stars, bathing my cheeks in cool freshness. Hushes and creaks filter down through the trees. Wings flap. Someone coughs. My head whips in that direction, spying a shadow on the patio. A hand reaches toward the French doors. I catch a hint of beard in the dim light and make a wild guess. "She's gone to bed, Tom, and the alarm's set. Go home and snort your powder there."

The shadow flits across the patio and melts into the trees, heading uphill. Tom's on foot? "And don't come back or I'm calling the police."

I spend an hour on that patio, watching for him, wishing Dad was getting home tomorrow.

Chapter 15

A call wakes me. It's Free. "Hi. Meet me at the coffee shop? The one from the other day?"

He's a bit too abrupt. My stomach gets achy. This is a meet-me call, not a date call. "Sure, give me an hour? I just woke up."

"9:30 would be great."

"9:30, okay."

The shower tackles the sluggishness of sleep. The hot air from the dryer, blasting my face, really snaps me out of it. I begin fretting on what to wear. Should it be serious or sexy or sweet? It takes too much time to decide, so I just throw on some jeans and a tank top. By the time I make it to the coffee shop, I'm ten minutes late. He's already finished his latte.

Alarmed by Free's face, his eyes heavy and shadowed, my instinct is to apologize right away. "I'm so sorry. I had a tough time waking up." It's hard to believe ten minutes could upset him this much.

"It's not that." Free takes a deep breath, and then he shrugs and doesn't say anything.

It's a struggle to start the conversation. "Are your cousins all right?"

"Oh, yeah. They made it to Dallas."

"I haven't heard from my dad yet this morning. I'm not sure where he is."

"I hope he's okay," Free says, a bit flatly. He stares into his empty mug.

I can't think of what to say next. It seems all wrong, like it's too much work to speak to him. There's no sunshine in his eyes. Where'd the crinkles go?

"So, what was he doing in Galveston?" Free's question seems about more than Galveston. I get the feeling he already knows the answer.

Out the window, a guy locks up his bike. It's got vivid blue tire rims that jolt me. "He's a hedge-fund manager."

Free drums his fingers on the table until, with a loud and definite thump of his hand, he says, "We know who you are."

My head jerks back, my jaw clenching. He makes it sound like I'm a criminal. "You know who my father is, you mean. But what about me? Do you know who I am?"

Free stares down at his hands a bit embarrassed. "It's not fair, I know, but he's part of the opposition. I'm just saying, they don't trust you."

My hand reaches toward him but pulls back. "I was afraid this would happen, but I wanted to spend time with you. I understand. I should have told you."

"Oh, yeah," he says. "Totally." His elbow is on the table. His hand props up his cheek. Free closes his eyes. Finally, he opens them. "If you had told me straight."

Tears well up like the rising seas. "Please, I want to help. I can spy on my father's group. I can see what they're up to."

Free shakes his head. "That's not what we do."

Back behind this tension, I sense he truly is torn. "Isn't there any way I can fix this?"

He bites his lip. "I'm sorry, Kaye. I don't want complicating factors, you get that? This is important. I can't get distracted."

My nod is slow, defeated. Yes, he needs to see the campaign through to the end. Obviously, this is about his friends who died. And of course, it's all my fault. I was dishonest, which leaves me doubly sad. I longed so much to have someone like Free in my life, and now that's broken. The screech of his chair as he stands makes me wince.

"Maybe after we win this thing?" I force out an awkward grin, hoping to postpone the inevitable.

Just before he turns to go, Free smiles, putting a bit of sun back into it. "When we win this."

I don't watch him leave. Instead, I grab his cup, gazing into it, creating a fuzzy connection to him through the pale, creamy ring at the bottom. Unable to move, I pretend to sip from the empty mug as if it's my cup too, something we can share. It must be an hour I sit here, that cup as my disguise, covering my heartbreak, avoiding eye contact. If someone looks at me, I'll cry.

Eventually, an older man comes up to me and asks gently, "Is everything okay?"

"Yes," I hiss with a bold glance his way.

He flinches, hurrying off, as I mutter at my reaction. "Don't be so nasty, Kaye." Standing stiffly, I make it outside just before my tears overflow. The grooves in the sidewalk become my focus, hoping their textures, colors, contrasts will stop the quiet flood pouring down my cheeks, but it doesn't work. It's a tsunami as I walk past shops and restaurants in a weepy daze, twisting away from everyone, trying to shield my face.

Turning a corner, I wander down the street, hoping this is the one Charlotte's parked on. A sense of *lost* nags at me, and it's not just because I can't spot my car. It's all the things I've lost: my connection to Free, my home in the city, my brother, my mom, old friends. I'm not quite sure why I've lost those friends, but when my brother died, they vanished. Was it me or them? They came from the same empty world, one of privilege and money. Do people in that world even know how to be friends? Were they just phony friends? Am I?

Charlotte's halfway down the block ahead. My energy picks up, but when I'm fifty feet away from my darling little car, keys in hand, a girl about my age, tall and blonde, steps up to the driver's door and unlocks it. Before I can stop her, she drives Charlotte away.

I dash after her, but my ankle rolls on an uneven seam in the paving. Arms flail. My hip cracks against the sidewalk, my shoulder landing hard, my cheek scraping the concrete. The force of the fall boomerangs through my head. My ears register that power as a high-pitched ring.

Catching my breath, I focus on some splats of blood across the concrete in front of me—what's that pattern? The splatter of distress? And then I scan around me, looking for my keys as if finding them will bring back Charlotte. They're there on the sidewalk in front of me. Lunging forward, I clutch them to my chest and outright bawl.

A hand reaches down. A guy says to me, "Let me get you up." He's got a super-strong grip as he pulls me to my feet. "Are you okay?"

"No. Someone stole Charlotte, my car."

"Someone stole your car with your baby inside?"

"No ..."

"Your dog?"

"No, my car." I don't bother to explain.

He seems to get it. "Oh." He's clearly not as concerned as he was a moment before. His face is pink with the heat. He's about my age, and his eyes are dark. I'm hoping for some sympathy in them, but they don't tell me anything. They just dart back and forth as if he'd rather not be here. Opening his backpack, he pulls out a pocket pack of tissues, pointing to my bloody cheek. "Here, use these. I'll call the police."

After he calls, he stands awkwardly beside me as I sniffle.

"Don't worry," he says. "They'll find it. How old is it?"

"A 2002."

"Old cars get stolen all the time. You'll get it back. It's probably just a tweaker. He'll abandon it somewhere when it runs out of gas."

"I just filled her up. She could go hundreds of miles. I'll never see her again." Sobs burst full force. It's like I haven't cried for years. Perhaps I haven't.

"Look, I'm sorry to leave you like this, but I've got to get to work. I'm already late. The police have my number. Tell them to contact me, but just to make it clear, I didn't see anything."

I try to hand him back his pack of tissues, but he waves it away as he turns and heads down the block, leaving me leaning against a fence, just a street urchin, alone in the world with no one to care. Remembering the scrape on my cheek, I dab a tissue against it, and then stare at the blood soaking into its white like an ink blot of pain.

Clicking my tongue at that tissue, I connect that red to the coupe back in my garage, the one I don't want to drive even with Charlotte missing. Red is such a Dad-color, aggressive, demanding attention. Red's also the color of Mom's skin cancer—too much sun for a fair-skinned Irish girl. Mom often dabbed her bloody lesions with a tissue, speckling the white with spots of red. Despite aggressive treatment, they couldn't save her. No wonder I can't drive that car.

My phone rings. It's Dad. My heart bounces, ready for the rebound. "Dad, my car—"

Dad isn't listening. "I'm in Dallas, but I missed my flight, so I'm staying at the Grand Hyatt at the airport."

"I'm glad you're safe. Dad, my car—"

"Just a minute, Kaye." Dad's talking to someone else. "You're a real smart fellow." He comes back to our conversation. "That Wesson. He built these fantastic paper airplanes out of the hotel stationery. They fly really well."

"Wesson?"

"Cindy's little boy. Remember, the family? I called from their house." He barely pauses for breath. "We all got out. It was quite a trip. Thunderstorms and everything. Wesson's Granny got airsick, but that chopper pilot could really fly. I paid a bundle, but Wesson was worth it. Aren't you? You're so damn cute."

Wow. Dad's pure overboard with this boy. My frown makes my cheek hurt. Of course, he's always had a soft spot for little kids. When I was like four, he was a great dad then, always making time for play whenever he got home before bedtime, which wasn't often. There were piggyback rides and hide-and-seek. Once he even built a blanket fort with me.

"Have you seen a doctor?"

"I will. Look, I'll be staying a few days. I want to make sure Wesson and Cindy are taken care of. The shelters are full already."

I give up trying to tell him about my car. "Send a picture of Wesson."

He doesn't notice the sarcasm in my voice. "Can't. No cell phone. I'm on the hotel phone. By the way, you were right," he says. "They're calling the storm El Diablo. How'd you know that?"

"I'll tell you later. I've got to go." I disconnect. I must. I would have plunged headfirst into the sidewalk again if he'd hung up on me.

Chapter 16

Dad's call snaps me out of emotional tailspin mode. I grit my teeth and take deep breaths, determined to fix this without him. Focusing on the patterns of the leaves above my head, I admire the highlights and shadows until the police pull up. As they're taking my report on Charlotte, someone rides up on a bike. It's jet black with brilliant blue tire rims just like the bike earlier outside the cafe. I can't help but be distracted by it, especially because Shelley's the rider.

"What happened?" she asks.

"Someone stole my car."

"Was it a carjacking?" She points to my bloody face.

I shake my head at the ground. "No, I just fell."

The police are asking me questions again, so Shelley rolls her bike a few feet away and waits, but I'm irritated she's there, listening in.

After the police leave, Shelley's at my side. "So maybe you want to cancel lunch?"

I punch my thigh. "Oh, damn. Lunch. I forgot all about it."

"I almost did too, till Mom reminded me every minute before I left."

My wince is painful. "I can't face Margot looking like this."

"That's cool. I'll call Mom and have her reschedule."

Shelley invents an excuse about finding a lost puppy. I smile at the image of me with floppy ears, huge brown eyes, and a furry tail.

"All set," Shelley says after hanging up. "I'd give you a lift back home, but

I'm completely short on seating space."

I nod, eyeing those bright blue rims. "That's a great bike."

"Electric."

"Really? How's it do on the hills up there?"

"Great."

"What about the rainy weather?"

"I don't know. I've only had it a month."

"What about at night?"

"I get a lift from friends."

Shelley's such a puzzle to me. How can she not have a car? "You must have a car."

"I totaled it. Lost my license. I was DUI." Shelley shrugs like it's no big deal.

Still, it feels like a big deal, and trying to ease my awkwardness, I stumble further in. "So, your parents got you this?"

Shelley's eyebrows pinch. "No, I got me this. My Dad grounded me for driving drunk even though he does it too."

"I remember … Margot's party." I keep glancing at those brilliant blue wheels. "How fast does it go? How good does it brake?"

"It goes about fifteen or twenty and has disc brakes. Better in the rain."

Reaching out, I touch the bike like it's another kind of Charlotte. "I've never tried one."

She points to a little alley down the street. "Come on."

Soon I'm sailing down the alley, fast but so quiet. "Wow, I want one. I'll need it till I get Charlotte back."

"Charlotte?"

"Yes, my car." And then I burst out, "My car, my car."

Shelley puts a gentle hand on my shoulder. She talks tough, like she's too cool, but there's something tender in that soft weight on my shoulder. It's so light, it doesn't make me flinch, even though my shoulder aches.

"Let's get lunch," Shelley says. When I hesitate, she adds, "I have an idea about Charlotte."

Shelley gives me her bike to steer down the sidewalk while she sends a text. That's when a black SUV drives past. The driver—close-cropped hair, glasses, white—stares at me like I'm next in line for the graveyard. I point to him, my hand trembling. "Do you see that?"

Shelley nods. "Do you like SUVs or something?"

"Did you see who was driving it?"

"An old guy about forty or fifty. Do you know him?"

"No, but he was staring."

"He probably noticed your bloody face. Not pretty." She takes the bike back. "Are you sure you're okay?"

I'm limping a little bit, which makes me unsteady. "Some aches. I'll get used to it."

It's still an hour till the lunch crush, so the cafe is quiet. Green-and-blue fabric panels on the walls help to soften the sounds. The couple in the corner are intent on each other. They ignore me, but self-conscious about the blood on my face, I head to the restroom to wash up. My reflection in the mirror shocks me. My cheek is swollen, and the scrape is pretty raw. Every time I wash it, new dots of dark red form. At least there's no deep gash to stitch, but I'll look like a mutant Kaye Malloy for a bit. It's almost a relief that Free doesn't want to see me, but just as I think that, my heart quakes. I've lost Free. I've lost Charlotte. And my dad's gone gaga over some strange little boy he just met. I would cry again, but there are no tears left.

Back at the table, Shelley seems preoccupied by texts, so I search the menu for something to heal a broken heart. They've got macaroni and cheese. I love that. A mango milkshake catches my eye too.

"I found her," Shelley says.

"What?"

"Charlotte. I know where she is."

I'm rising from my seat. "Let's go. Let's get her."

"Don't worry. She's coming here."

I sink back down. "Huh?"

"It was Herman Cooper's car, right? He sold it to you."

The waiter comes up to order. Shelley orders a tuna sandwich and an iced tea. She orders another sandwich—egg salad—and a diet coke.

My eyebrows arch. "I don't want that."

"That's for Tracy. Now tell him what you want. It's on me."

I stare at her without saying anything.

"We've got to wait here for Tracy. She's got the car. You might as well eat."

My appetite's vanished, but I obey. "Mac and cheese and a milkshake … mango." My lip quivers. Comfort food isn't going to help one bit. The waiter takes our menus and leaves.

"Come on," Shelley says. "Cheer up. You're getting Charlotte back."

I snap at her. "So, explain."

"Tracy is Herman's daughter. It was her car. Her dad got mad at her and sold it."

"But it was in Herman's name!"

"I know. He bought it for her." Shelley gets another text. She answers it.

I can't understand this story one bit. "Why did she steal it?"

"Herman lied. He said someone else stole it. When she saw it on the street, she took off with it before the thief came back. She still had her key."

Sinking back in my chair, I groan. "What a mess."

"Yeah, but she's bringing Charlotte back. She hopes you'll explain to the police."

I pout for a few seconds, not quite ready to forgive this Tracy girl, but after a few more seconds, I relent. "So how do you know Tracy?"

"She's a friend of a friend of a friend."

"You seem to know a lot of people."

"I cultivate connections." Shelley grins, pleased with this.

I do my best not to label her a mini-Margot. At least she's not all flatter and fluff. "I don't. I'm terrible at it."

"What about Free?"

"Don't ask. It's been a horrible day."

Shelley clicks her tongue. "That's a shame. Free could use some company."

"Why?"

"I know a friend of his, and that's the story."

"You're unbelievable. And Free said you were a loner."

Shelley grins. "Only when I want to be."

I flash on that window in the study and her haunted face. "There's something I have to ask you. Were you at my house? Looking in the window?"

"Yeah, that's a story too … for later." Her cellphone dings. She reads a text.

The cafe door opens. Charlotte's thief is heading through it. "She's here," I hiss.

"Well, don't hiss. She's not completely bad. A little sassy with her tongue at times, but who isn't?"

Tracy plops beside Shelley. "My demon Dad. He's such a liar." She frowns at me. "I didn't know."

She explains the whole situation just the same way Shelley did. When she finishes, I say, "Thanks for bringing her back."

"I'm making Dad hand over the cash. At least he couldn't find a poker game and gamble it all away." Her eyes are amber with a touch of temper in them. "I've got my eye on a 2008 Prius that someone's selling." Tracy rattles on like she's trying to convince herself. "It only has seventy thousand miles on it. Can you believe it? I think I can talk him down with what I've got saved plus this."

"You want a Prius?" Shelley asks.

"Yeah, there's this hot guy working on that climate campaign. A Prius will impress him." Tracy turns to me and hands me her key to Charlotte. "She's just down the street."

I rush to the window. My smile's as wide as the ocean. When I turn back, the waiter shows up with our order. I hand him a twenty-dollar bill. "Make mine to go. You can keep the change."

"Sure," he says, his eye's lighting up.

When the waiter hands me the go bag, I head for the door.

Tracy leans forward. "You're going to phone them, aren't you? The police?"

Pulling out the paper from my pocket that the cop gave me, I wave it at her. "Right away. I just want to tell them I'm sitting in the car."

Tracy looks at Shelley for assurance.

"Don't worry," Shelley says. "I'll completely vouch for her."

"Okay. It's cool." Tracy nods. "I'm glad you like the car." Her tone softens. "I used to call her Kate, but Charlotte's good too."

"I'll take good care of her, I promise."

I swoop out the door and slide behind the steering wheel. "Charlotte," I coo, my head against the window. After calling the police, I take a couple sips of milkshake, but the icy cold makes me shudder. Feeling too distracted to drive, I grab the bag, heading to a picnic table in the park across the street. My jaw aches as I chew. It's sore, like my shoulder, but there's no headache. And I'm hungry. Maybe crashing into sidewalks makes you hungry. I gobble down the mac and cheese like I haven't eaten for a week.

There's one last slurp of milkshake left—so rich mango good—but Greg walks by. I duck my head till he passes. Tossing my trash in a bin, I hurry to keep up, but the limp slows me. Tracking him makes me think about Tom. Tom was in Dad's study hunting for something. Greg must be helping him. I could pretend I'm helping Dad fight the initiative and get some information out of him. Maybe I'll call him Carter and see how he responds.

Greg turns down a side street. By the time I round the corner, he's gone. Down the block, a flyer-covered door is propped open beneath a shallow marquee, so I peek in. It's a bookstore, but he's not there. I peer through the pane of a window display next door. It's a clothing boutique, but there's no one crouched behind the racks of dresses.

The block is not as charming as some others downtown. There are plenty of comfy shops, like the bookstore and boutique, but also a concrete-and-steel three-story office right in the center that spoils everything. It's some kind of architectural firm, so you would think they had better sense. I wait on the corner for at least ten minutes, but Greg doesn't appear from any shop or office door. He's definitely ditched me.

Slipping into the bookstore to check for him one more time, I get distracted by a shelf marked *Photography*. As I'm checking out a book about light and shadow, someone asks the clerk, "I'm looking for nonfiction, all about time warps." It sounds so much like Tom—sharp tones, demanding. Peering around the shelf, my chin drops. It's him.

"Um, well, I'm not sure," the salesclerk says. I recognize the voice. He's that guy who called the police about my stolen car. The clerk points in my direction as if he's read my mind. Boom goes my heart. "You could try the Physics section."

The shelf titles around me all begin with *P*, and Physics is right across from Photography. Tom will think I'm spying on him if he catches me here, so I slink to the clearance section in the back of the store and peek around a corner.

"I see you've got a rook on your T-shirt." Tom's voice has lost some of its snarl.

"I'm in a chess club." The clerk sounds upbeat.

"My son plays chess. He's a division champ." Tom's words hint at fatherly pride, but it's hard to imagine him having a son. I wish I could see his face right now—is there a trace of softness?

The clerk taps a poster on the wall beside him. "We have a meeting tomorrow night. You should have him come."

"Oh, he's back east with his mother … vacationing." Tom adds something quickly that I can't catch.

"How about you?" The clerk tips his head sideways. "We could use a few more members."

"Nah, too busy." Tom's sniffing loudly. "But how about … here, a donation."

"Whoa. That's too much."

"I'll make you earn it. Find a book about time, time warps, time travel, maybe two or three."

"For your son?"

Tom's wiping his nose. "Ah, well, sure. Yeah. His birthday's next month."

The clerk looks alarmed. I can't see what he's seeing. "Are you okay?"

"Damn allergies. Anyway, have to be somewhere. I'll come by next week."

After Tom leaves, I take the photography book I'm hugging tight and walk over to the clerk. He's wiping up the counter. "Everything okay?"

His face is pale, his lips frowning. "That guy. He didn't look so good."

"How's that?"

"I couldn't see his eyes with the shades on, but he was sweating tons and trying to sniff back a nosebleed." He shows me the dust cloth, covered with spots of blood. "Plus, this." He holds out the cash Tom gave him. "Five hundred. Pure impulse. He was probably on drugs."

"Well, don't spend it in case he comes back."

"For sure." The clerk looks at me more closely. "Hey, you're …"

"Yeah, the weepy one with the stolen car. I got it back, at least."

"Really? The police found it that fast?"

"Nah, a friend did. But it's all good. It was just a misunderstanding."
I lean close, almost whispering. "But that guy that was just here. I know
him. He's rich, but if you have any trouble about that donation, I'm your
witness." I write my name and number on the back of a bookmark. "His
name is Tom, and oh, yes, he's an addict."

He studies the bookmark I hand him. "Cool. Thanks Kaye." He shakes
my hand. "I'm Kent." He waves away my credit card. "The book's on me."
He winks. "Or maybe Tom."

The clerk's grateful smile becomes contagious, so I can't help grinning
as I hobble back to my car like an injured sprinter coming off the track.
Unlocking Charlotte is a relief. Slipping behind the wheel, I pat it gently,
whispering, "I won't let anyone take you again."

Despite being anxious to get home to the sanctuary of my room, I
drive extra slowly, a sudden wave of anxiety flooding me from the stress
of all that's happened. *Honk. Honk.* A hundred horns blast me, so I send
pixelated glares to poke back at them. I even pull over once or twice on
Willow Mountain to let cars pass me. My jaw aches. I feel stiff all over.
Maybe I shouldn't be driving.

Watching my mirror for black SUVs, my thoughts drift back to Tom
in the bookstore. Tom's thinking about time travel. Sol's talking about the
future. They seem like opposites—Tom ruthless, Sol gentle and kind—but
my whole world's swirling in a tornado of time, and these two are at the
center of it.

Then I think of Free and start crying again.

Chapter 17

Back at Bleak House, Margot's home, exercising in her gym. Her trainer's here too. That's good. I don't want to explain anything. It's not just the swollen, scabby cheek. It's the questions I have about Greg and her, the suspicions I have about Tom, all of them, being part of a scheme against my father. And Marty. Something happened to Marty, and I need to prove it, but how?

There's still nothing in the fridge but the milk and eggs. I pour a glass of milk, set two eggs in water to hard boil, and grab a blackened banana from the fruit bowl in the kitchen. When the eggs are done, I carry them outside and plop onto a patio chair. Staring into the trees, I remember Tom disappearing into darkness. Where was he headed?

After scarfing down the eggs and chugging the milk, I leap up, scouring the hill for a sign of his tracks. On the other side, a trail winds along the stream, now just a trickle in the dry season. Plowing down through the brambles to the creek, I try my best to avoid the thorns and follow the trail to where it ends on Pine Mountain Drive, a side road off Willow Mountain. There's a little pullout in the pavement for parking.

Tom must have parked here and taken the trail to Bleak House last night, but I can't imagine why he did that. Is it Margot? Are they having an affair? I shudder to think of Margot in bed with him—the drugs, and he's such a creep.

Turning back, I find a spot by the creek to sift through the mystery of Tom. He's cruel, ruthless, and spies on Dad, but he's got a son far away that he misses, and that zings him in the heart—at least he's got a heart. But no, I can't feel sorry for him. He's too mean. And besides, he wants to make sure the planet melts, so he can't really care that much for his son. Does Dad care about me? Does he even miss me? It doesn't seem like it, and for the flash of a second, that makes Tom seem a tiny bit better than Dad.

A leaf floats by on a little eddy in the water, around and around. Tom was in the study, so Dad has something Tom needs. I get an uneasy feeling that Dad already knows, and in fact, has all the answers to my Tom questions, but there's no way to ask him over the phone when he barely listens to me. I pick at some moss on the rock beside me, frustrated by my lack of progress.

Back in my room, my jaw aching and my brain sluggish, I take two ibuprofen and snuggle down beneath the covers for a nap until Margot knocks on my door. There's quite a bit of growl in my voice when I call out, "I'm asleep."

She opens the door anyway. "I thought we could go shopping for school clothes. It'll be fun."

I bury my face beneath the blankets. "No. I don't need school clothes, and Dad's in the middle of a hurricane."

"He's not. He's in Dallas."

I peek out from my bedspread cave. "Well, he's not home safe yet."

Margot looks all bewildered. "He's coming home tomorrow, isn't he?"

"Didn't he tell you? He's taking care of that family he rescued."

Margot doubles down on bewildered. "He rescued a family?"

I squint up at her. "For goodness sake, Margot, don't you two ever talk about anything?"

Margot's chin drops.

"I'm sorry. I'm just tired. I need to sleep."

"Okay." She shuts the door.

A mental collage of the day assaults my effort to sleep—milkshakes, coffee mugs, electric-blue bike rims, tissues all bloody. These images blur into dream scenes of electric-blue milkshakes filling blood-red coffee cups that spill all over a bicycle I'm riding in circles, around and around. And Sol's smiling at me. He reaches out. "Kaye," he says. "I will meet you in the bunker."

It's early evening when I wake. Long shadows stretch across my blue cotton curtains like a dream. Margot's gone. The house is graveyard still. I steel myself against the haunted vibe and feel my pockets for the bunker key. It's a déjà vu moment—the key's missing, so the search for it begins again.

That key was in my pocket last night, but where did I put it? It was there when I drove to the coffee shop to meet Free this morning. Yes, but I put the key in my glove box again, thinking I wouldn't forget it there. What if Tracy took it?

Grabbing my laptop, I race to the car. I need to talk to Sol. I need that key. Sliding into the driver's seat, I check my glove box. The key's there, so my relief is a flood, rising, rising. Sol, I'm coming! I'm surprised his pull's so strong. Still, the thought of sitting in that bunker talking to a stranger from some distant time and place is spooky. Spying my backpack on the backseat, I remember Marty's pen and pull it out of the side pocket, wrapping my fingers around it, sharp point out. Heading to the study, I slip the key into its slot and turn it.

The door hatch to the bunker is shut. Does it shut automatically, or did someone else do it? I pause a half second—who will be waiting for me—but my hand takes the lead, pulling the handle. The door swings open. No one's there. Everything in the bunker looks the same as the last time. Couch, table, kitchen. The lights are on. They must be motion sensitive like the LEDs in the corridor.

Calmer now than my first visit—calm enough to explore the rest of those interior doors—I step inside. There's three bedrooms and a bath as luxurious as those above. Another door leads to a huge storeroom. Boxes on top of boxes are stacked against the walls. That's when I realize this bunker isn't finished. Those boxes hold equipment waiting to be installed, like water- and air-filtration machines. There are even security cameras still in their protective plastic and nestled into white Styrofoam. I won't have to worry about being discovered here, not yet.

This isn't as luxurious as the bunkers in the news photos, and it doesn't seem equipped for long-term living. Maybe it's a hedge-your-bets type of bunker. Dad might not think it's really needed, but he's just doing it in case he's wrong about everything. The whole idea is claustrophobic, but this time I don't panic. Instead, I feel depressed. There are billions of people in the world who can't have this, an escape hatch to survival if the world goes bad. How is that okay? It isn't.

Settling onto the couch in the living room, I open my laptop, but there's no network, so I click on that photo of me, the one ten years in the future. Things are different in the image—more clutter, including books, notepads, and pens. Two cups linger on the table beside two plates. Either I don't bother to clean up, or someone else joins me. Right now, this place is spotless like no one has stepped foot in it. Of course, someone built it, someone furnished it, so that isn't true, but since then, who's been here? Dad?

This could be some trick. Sol says he's from the future, but how could that be? Is he lurking here instead? I lodge a chair in the open hatch door to make sure no one can trap me. Gripping Marty's pen firmly, I wait.

After about ten minutes, an error message triggers in my brain. I'm a day late for this meeting. How will Sol know I finally got here? Well, duh, he won't unless I tell him. The pen retreats to my pocket, and with the text tool, I type across the photo: *I'm here.*

The laptop screen blazes with light. Even the room flares brighter, as if a golden lamp has turned on. In the bunker I feel more grounded than my room. Only a hint of light-headedness hits me, but my time-sense feels strange. The moments are endless.

Sol's response is immediate and clear of static. "Hello, Kaye." His voice streams from my PC, but it can't be coming over the internet because there isn't any Wi-Fi signal.

A face appears, a real one, not a mask. His skin is brown with a golden cast except for his high cheeks, brushed with a rusty glow. A square jaw and Roman nose complement the long face. It's framed by straight black hair that has a beautiful translucence. It almost glows. Beneath each brow is the same eye that I drew before. Those dark eyes have a remarkable shine in them. He smiles deep and wide with very full lips. "It is good to see you," he says. He sounds so formal, almost like English is not his first language.

I speak to him as if it's a live video connection. "How did you know about the tornado and the storm?"

"I am from the future."

I answer with a long-drawn breath, using it as a pause button, thinking through my response, not quite sure of anything. The future—it's hard to believe, and yet it's perhaps the only thing that makes sense. "I believe you, and then I don't. You could be any hacker."

"A hacker who knows about the future? I need you to believe me, Kaye. I need your help, and you need mine. Your future is in danger."

"My future or everyone's?"

"Both."

"How do you know?"

"Your laptop."

"What?"

"I have your laptop."

I grip the sides of my machine. "No. I'm holding it."

"And so am I."

A shiver starts in my spine, and then travels down my arms and legs. "Where are you holding it?"

"Here in the bunker."

I peer over my shoulder. "Are you here hiding somewhere?"

"I am not in your time. I am still in mine."

"How's that possible? How can you travel in time?"

"I do not. It is the laptop."

My computer is suddenly horrific. What will happen if I strike a key on it? "You mean it's a time machine?"

"No. I only use the laptop to communicate. The machine is just a machine."

"Well, something must happen."

"Yes, something happens—a connection. There is a pulse through time when everything aligns, and I find that moment to connect. We call it the Momentary Principle."

"We? I thought you were alone."

"I used to not be alone." A sad echo fills his voice. "I am not sure how long it has been, probably just years, but it seems like decades since the last one on my team died." He stops to gaze off into the distance. "It was another round of Permian virus. We had run out of medicine."

I frown deeply. "I've never heard of the Permian virus."

"No one had until the permafrost fully melted. It is not really Permian, but it is ancient. It came back to life and wiped out half the population until we found a treatment."

My brain fractures into pieces trying to make sense of this. "So why did you run out of medicine?"

"We lost the ability to make it. Data got corrupted. Equipment broke down. We could not get vital ingredients, and the experts died off, the ones who understood variants."

"But you said it killed off half the population, so there must have been some people left."

"That was not the only problem we had."

And then Sol tells me the whole story. Or really three stories. The first story is how the effort got started too late to fix the climate mess. It all went bad. Old people died in the heat waves. Young people drowned in the storms. Inflation from climate-caused shortages went skyward, bringing economic collapse. Rich people lost their fortunes. The fertility rate dropped. There were other pandemics too. Tropical diseases moved north like malaria and dengue fever. Cholera hit after each disaster, and Ebola spread. "Then the pollinators disappeared, so there was mass starvation as well as food wars, water wars."

"You mean the bees died?" My heart sobs.

"Yes, the bees. The butterflies. Even the moths."

I picture a bumblebee, vividly, orange against black, as if that could keep it alive. "Oh, I love the bees. Especially bumblebees."

He gazes at me for a moment and then says, "All the worst happened that could happen, but there is a second story."

Sol tells of people joining forces, finding each other across the chasm of death and destruction. "We learned to overcome differences, give everything we had—time, money, energy—to find new ways of living. Rebuilding the soil. Replanting forests. Creating new energy technologies. We developed an economic model that made it all work without endless growth and recaptured the carbon released across centuries. We found a way to live that consumed less and cared more."

My hopes rise. My bee buzzes from flower to flower. "Why didn't that work?"

"There is a third story, an important one. I call it the Earth story. Our natural systems work according to the laws of physics. Those forces are powerful, beyond our control. For example, greenhouse gases raise our planet's temperature, changing ocean currents and air currents. When everything gets out of kilter, it is not a simple thing to change it back. It takes time, and we ran out of it."

I'm quiet. I know this. It's what the scientists have been warning about. "My father has always said it's not true what the scientists are saying."

"Many said that, unfortunately. They let it go too far. If they had not, it might not have broken so badly." Sol's eyes dim, clouds of sadness covering the sun in them.

"What's it like now, in your time? Is it desolate?"

"No, some plants have always survived, wind-pollinated ones like the fir trees in your backyard and grasses in your lawn. Some animals are rebounding, species that survived at least. But it is a long journey back from collapse. Much has been lost forever, including us, the species at the top. The Earth will heal. It will be beautiful again. I wish we could be part of it."

"There's really no one left but you?"

"As the population dwindled, we scoured the planet for survivors using satellites and drones. We needed people together to keep the population going. In the end, there just were not enough of us to counter all the disease and toxicity and heat. It overtook us."

My face is pinched. "Maybe there's some indigenous tribe in the Amazon or something?"

"There is no Amazon. It was destroyed."

"No!" My head is shaking back and forth, trying to erase that image.

"I am afraid so, yes. You believe it will be there forever because it is so huge. But it was fragile. The Amazon was a self-sustaining system, creating its own rain clouds, its own nutrients. Year after year, it was whittled away until it lost the battle to renew itself."

"And the coral reefs? Are they gone too?" My voice is stressed, almost squeaking, holding back a cry.

"Mostly, yes. I do not really know what is happening in the oceans. We gave up sailing them. There was no need. The fish stocks were almost depleted."

"Without people to fish, why didn't they just bounce back?"

"Just because the emissions stopped, it does not mean the temperature of the ocean returned to normal. That takes time."

Glum is a word that captures me. I struggle not to say it. "What's the use, Sol?"

"Plenty," he says. "That is why you are here." Sol's eyes brighten as he points to me.

"I don't understand."

"Think of the three stories. It all depends on number three, the Earth story. If you do not push the Earth so far beyond its limits, do not break the systems so badly, then the second story, that story of transformation, becomes the stronger story, and we see less of the destructive first."

I'm nodding, but not understanding. "What does that have to do with me?"

"Remember I spoke of the Momentary Principle?"

My frown becomes perplexed. "I've never heard of that."

"Of course not. No one knows of it in your time."

I lean into the screen, desperate to understand. "So, what is it?"

"Simply put, it is the possibility for endless change that can occur through momentary pathways within time itself—like this pathway between you and me. We spent years perfecting it, waiting, listening, ready to reach back through time to find someone like you, someone who can get the changes happening sooner instead of when it is too late."

I blink. And blink again. His words won't compute. "How could I help with all that?"

"One less degree is all I am asking for."

"One degree of what?"

"Let me explain. As the years unfold, the disasters will become so dire that everyone will join together to reduce emissions, but it must start sooner. With an enormous push to curb emissions in your time, the atmosphere will not heat up as much, and all the efforts that follow will have greater impact, saving the climate and us. Can you see, Kaye, why I need your help? It cannot end with me." There's a sudden flicker on the screen and the crackle of static. "Oh. The moment is gone. I will be back."

The screen goes dark. I'm blank like the screen, but only for a minute. Those words, all that Sol just said, begin swirling in my head. It's brain bedlam. One degree. He just needs one less degree of warming. Sol needs my help, someone who can make a difference. I can't wrap my mind around that.

And yet, as I sit here on the couch, a couch that still exists in a far-off distant future, the only thing that's sure: I believe him. Yes, I do—except perhaps the needing-someone-like-me part. When is he coming back to explain all this?

Waiting in the bunker isn't easy, and I'm the patient one. At least that used to be true. Since the party, since seeing that first flash of light, I've been the opposite. Before, no one would ever think of me as bold, at least not until these past few days, buying Charlotte and chasing after Free. So, can Sol be right? Can I really alter the course of history, even when I can't get my own father to pay attention to me?

It's time to open my laptop. Art always soothes me, the working of the layers, drawing, shaping, painting. In my folders, there's a picture of a storm. I think hurricane. I think lightning. I take the storm clouds in the photo and darken the levels, adding a lightning flash, making it brilliant, multiplying the layers, warming the colors. Being in this mind space should surely bring Sol back, but even with that lightning so vivid it shocks me, it doesn't work. Sol still isn't here. I can't reach him.

While I wait for him, I explore the bunker. In one of the bedrooms there's a closet filled with boxes, and the boxes are labeled in Marty's handwriting. Dad's been hiding all this, burying it here in the bunker, pushing it away, not talking about it. Tingling all over, I rip one open. Inside are books, research notes, DVDs, even his old stuffed bear and a toddler's baseball cap. I open another one. There are notebooks from college and books on writing computer code, which is strange. Marty wasn't a tech guy. His work was in vaccines. I pick up one of the code books. Scribbled on the cover are the words in all caps: *KEEP IT FROZEN!* Is he talking about the temperature for storing a vaccine?

At the bottom of the box, there's a photo, 8 x 10, of Marty, Mom, and me, taken a few years before she got sick. She's so lovely, blue eyes and long, wavy red hair. I look a very timid four, and a bit too serious. Marty is a gawky, gangly twelve, with glasses and braces and a freckly grin. Even with its thick oak frame that's way too wide, I love this picture.

A black guitar case leans against the closet wall behind the boxes. Opening the lid, I find Marty's acoustic guitar and hug it close. The strings twang off-key, but after tightening one of the pegs to tune it, I stop, afraid to snap the string. A musty scent oozes from the wood. Perhaps I'm just imagining that scent, but I don't care. It's a deep breath of him. It's like he's whispering to me: *I'm here Kaye. I never really went away.*

Slipping into that strange, dreamy place where thoughts float away into strands of confusion—meanderings that never quite lead to the places you need—I slump against the wall, brushing against those strings again.

"Marty?" I call as if he's spoken to me. I wait and wait, but it's like waiting for Sol. Wherever Marty is, the moment isn't right for me to hear him.

As I start to put the guitar back, that's when I spot it—a slight bump in the cloth that lines the case. My fingers run over something small and rectangular, a bit thick. The edge of the lining is loose near that bulge, creating a gap. After working the lump over with my fingers, I pull it out. It's the black plastic case of a flash drive.

Chapter 18

Racing to my laptop, I push the flash drive into the USB port, getting a login box. It's encrypted, and it's asking for a password. Several guesses later—birthdates, favorite songs, favorite colors, the day Mom died even—I'm frustrated, but I don't quit until a faraway voice calls my name. "Kaye, are you here?"

Damn. It's Margot. The mirror door's open.

At the end of the corridor, I peek into the office. Margot's already left, so I go back and settle everything into Marty's box, except the photo of Mom, Marty, and me. The guitar case goes into the closet corner, but the flash drive is still in the laptop. Inside this little rectangle of black, answers must be waiting like why Marty died. "Marty, what's the password? Tell me."

After striking randomly at the keys with no success, I slip the drive into my pocket and close down my PC. Shutting the bunker hatch and then the mirror door, I settle the key into its little box below the desk. "There," I say. "No more getting lost."

Margot's in the kitchen. "Are you looking for me?" I pull my hair over my cheek to hide the scabby damage, fearing she'll see it but won't really care, which will drive me crazy.

"Your father wants you to call."

"Really? It's almost midnight there."

"That's what he said."

"Okay, I'll call from my room."

Margot hands me a scrap of paper with the hotel number. Her eyes narrow as she spots the picture in my hand. "Where did you get that?"

I lie. "My closet." Well, it's not really a lie. That bunker bedroom might be mine someday when the world goes dark.

"I've never seen it before."

"Marty gave it to me." That's not a lie either.

Margot nods. She won't challenge a gift from Marty. I just turn and walk away.

Back in my room, the picture gets buried, along with the flash drive, in a box under my bed, so Margot can't make it vanish, which I suspect she has done with others of Mom. She's always been jealous, just like the *Snow White* witch. I imagine her gazing at her reflection tonight, asking, "Mirror, mirror, who's the prettiest?" Her jealousy won't get her what she needs, but Margot doesn't understand Mom's beauty had nothing to do with the color of her eyes or the profile of her face. Mom's beauty came from the reach of her smile, a smile that touched hearts.

I call Dad.

The first thing he says is, "I got checked out at a clinic. No concussion. I'm fine. Just a headache and a big bump."

I grin, surprised that he listened to me.

Then he spoils it. "Cindy made me. She thought I should go."

"Who's Cindy?"

"Wesson's Mom. I told you that."

"Oh." Prickles of hurt creep in.

"I'm staying the whole week to head up a task force for creating more long-term shelters. The Governor asked me to help. We go back years," he says. "Hey, I've got to go. I promised Wesson I'd get him some ice cream. He's worried about his turtle back home. The storm's battering that whole area. They say the wind is catastrophic. I'm trying to take his mind off it. I'll update you later. Bye."

Dad disconnects without a *how are you*, or anything. My phone flies across the room like a shooting star. Luckily, it lands with a soft *pfump* in the middle of my bed. I plop beside the phone and close my eyes, too tired to even cry. I just feel empty.

In the morning, it's the same. Everything's a void, as in black holes in space. Marty's gone. There's zero connection to Dad. Even Free's deserted me. My only friend, it seems, is a car named Charlotte, who disappeared, but at least she came back. And then there's Sol. What is he? A friend? What kind of friend could he even be? He's decades, perhaps centuries in the future, and the only link between us is something called the Momentary Principle, which I'm not really sure about.

Longing for Marty, I thumb through his songbook on the nightstand beside the bed, stopping on a page. There's no music, or even chords, just words. It's a poem. Scribbled in Marty's messy script, it says:

Lightning flashes,
point to point,
through chasms of time.
My voice,
all jagged,
filaments of longing branching out
until
a path illuminates
in the darkness.

My breath goes raggedy as if these lines have used up all my oxygen. When did he write that? It doesn't even sound like him—way too serious. It must be about Mom, his longing for her. I read on:

Bolts of current
launch my question,
like pulses of fire,
like rushes of breath.
I wait to hear it,

the rolling thunder of response

in that instant

between us.

With that last line, my breath settles into a steady rhythm. That connection between Mom and Marty, Mom and me. This poem describes it so beautifully. Just thinking of it, reading the words, fills me with a big, wide feeling. There isn't an exact word for it, but I'm no longer so empty.

My phone brings me back to Earth with a zillion news notifications waiting for me to read. It's all about the storm. El Diablo made landfall in the early morning. The winds were 205 miles an hour in Galveston, the strongest storm to hit the US in recorded history. The article says some scientists believe such a high wind speed is not possible, but others argue that with the warming oceans they don't know what the upper limit to such storms will be. All they know is that a peak wind speed of 205 was recorded before the city was flooded by storm surge. Now there's no power, no communications. No one knows what's happening or if Galveston even exists.

And then the phone *dings* with a breaking news flash. I ignore it till it dings again. A new update comes in. The storm is over Houston right now as a Category 4. The city's being battered by winds of 140 miles an hour. Photos show islands of land in a sea of waves. People are huddled in the corridors of tall hotels and apartment buildings, even office skyscrapers, to keep above the flood. They're calling it a vertical evacuation strategy. The forecasters look shaken in the weather segments. They wonder aloud about how many people may have drowned.

I think back to Sol's three stories. El Diablo is part of the first story, the destructive one of storms and fire, flood and heat, starvation, death, death, death. Sol said that story can be minimized if I do something, but this task he's given me feels paralyzing like I've contracted some terminal disease. Gulps of air drown me. Sol has put all his hopes on me. How can I be the chosen one? I mean, me? I'm no one.

And then I think of Free and all those volunteers at the Initiative for the Climate office. It's not just me, alone in this. There are people everywhere around the world working this. It's not a time to get overwhelmed. It's a time to begin. I can start by planting my garden.

But a bee garden? Is that too small, too naive, too insignificant? Maybe, but Sol spoke about the bees disappearing, and I don't want that to happen. A search on my phone leads me to Mossy Hills Garden Shop. Its home page talks about native plants and organic gardening. That sounds like the place for me.

And it is. Store flyers line a cedar-plank wall, listing plants for bee and butterfly gardens. Another flyer advertises a gardening club. I check the dates and read the info, plugging the details into my phone.

A voice chirps behind me. "How's Charlotte?"

I turn to see Jane Zell smiling at me. "You work here?"

She nods and points to my face. Her hazel eyes signal concern—one so genuine I would never have to enhance it with a digital layer.

"I tripped," I say, and then add, "Hey, thanks for telling me about Joe. He fixed Charlotte's brakes. And he gave me the Jane Zell discount."

"I'll stop by with a dozen cookies for him. Oatmeal raisin is his favorite."

"I'd make some for him, but I don't have a recipe."

She winks. "My recipe comes from Joe himself. I'll send it to you."

"Please do." The flyers wave in my hand. "I want to make a bee garden, but I need to extend the water line before I can."

She reaches past me to pull a brochure out of its pocket on the wall. "Here's an irrigation guide, but we don't carry the PVC pipe or connectors. I recommend Daily Hardware for that. Ask for Mel and tell him Jane sent you." Jane's eyes softly glow, like candlelight.

"I'll come to you for all my recommendations. You must have lived here a long time."

"I grew up here."

"Really? I bet it's changed."

"Quite a bit. I went to college in Seattle but came back to start my business. I'm just a small-town girl, you see."

"So, this is your place?" My hand sweeps the air, pointing toward the plants hanging from the ceiling and covering the shelves. "Oh, I'm so glad I came. Do you have bee balm?"

"Those are out back. They like the sun. And we've got lots of natives too for bees," Jane says. "But let me ask, do you ever babysit?"

"You mean Elyse?" I nod, even though I've never done it.

"How about the day after tomorrow, 6:00 p.m. or maybe 5:30? I need a sitter, and my regular one's busy."

"Sure, I'd love it." Pulling out Marty's pen, I write my phone number on the bottom of the irrigation brochure, ripping it off for her. "Just call me. I'll put it on my calendar."

Jane heads over to help a couple who walk in. I stroll along the plant-lined gravel paths behind the building, finding five little black plastic pots labeled bee balm. They look so perky. Plants must love Jane because she takes good care of them. Will my flowers look as good? I imagine blossoms splashing color over my garden, bees humming, busy with their work. And then I think back to what Sol said about the bees dying, the burden of that knowing sinking into me. Until I get more instructions from him, buying the bee balm is a place to start.

I limit myself to two bee balms and take them to the register. "Do you think they'll survive until I can get the water line in?"

"Keep them in a bit of sun, don't let them dry out, and they'll be happy." Jane hugs me. "Call me if you need advice, anything. And don't forget babysitting."

I soar out the front door, her hug as my wings, and settle my bee balm on Charlotte's floor before turning the key. *Click*. There's nothing, not even a sputter. My nerves prickle with alarm as I check for lurking SUVs and reach for Marty's pen in my pocket. Seeing none, my hand turns the key again and again. After the fifth try, I rant and pound the steering wheel about a dozen times until I cringe at myself. This is Charlotte I'm yelling at.

Or is it? Who am I really mad at? Dad? Margot? Men in SUVs? Maybe it's Sol. Maybe it's the pressure to fix the world for him. At least, I know who to call to fix Charlotte. Joe's website says to text him. *Help. It's Kaye. Charlotte won't start.*

Waiting for Joe to rescue me, I sit in the shade of a tree by Jane's nursery and spend twenty minutes reading all about bee balm on my phone. When Joe pulls up, I point to my cheek. "You don't have to ask. I just tripped."

"I didn't even notice." He winks.

I hand him my keys. "Thanks for coming."

"No problem. I'm always glad to rescue friends, especially Jane's friends."

"Well, you must be busy all day because I'm sure she has lots of friends. I've even named this plant after her." I show off Jane.

"And what's that one called?" He points to the one in the other hand.

"Joe, of course." I raise the plants in the air like they're prizes I've won. "Jane and Joe, the two nicest people in Mossy Hills."

Joe chuckles. "I can see I've been too good to you. I need to let the real Joe out." He makes a fake grumpy face, but when he tries to start the car, his frown turns thoughtful. "Did you leave the lights on?"

I shake my head.

Joe taps the wheel. "One hundred percent sure it's the battery."

"Oh, yeah, the guy who sold it said the battery was old."

He jumps the battery and Charlotte starts. "Drive it over to the shop. I'll get you fixed up with a new one. Just don't turn Charlotte off till you get there. I'll be back in ten."

There's a bicycle shop around the block from Joe's. After he pulls up and tells me it might take an hour, I head over to it. The clerk jumps up from stocking a shelf as I walk in. She's a bit jockish, with buzzed brown hair, a tattoo on her upper arm, and a scar across the olive skin on her hand.

"Where are your e-bikes?" She's checking out my injuries, but I'm tired of explaining, so I tell a story. "I fell on my bike, and we both broke badly."

She points to her hand. "I've had some tumbles myself."

The e-bikes are in a corner near the back. There are several different brands but not the one with the bright blue wheels that Shelley had. "Don't you have any with electric-blue rims, the wide ones?"

"We don't carry that brand. You'll need to buy it online."

"Oh, well. What else do you have?"

She shows me all the models. One folds. That's promising. I could load it through the hatchback to bring home. "Okay, I'll think on it and be back."

Heading to Joe's, I remember my plants in the car and set out running, but the twinge in my ankle forces me to stop and walk. Back at the shop, Charlotte's baking in the sun and the door won't open. It's locked. As I tug on the handle anyway, Joe laughs at me from his office door, my bee balm in his hands.

I march up to him, faux angry. "I *was* going to make you oatmeal raisin cookies, until you laughed."

"I don't like oatmeal raisin."

"Yes, you do, but I'll just give you a hug instead, because I don't know how to bake a darn thing." I step to his right, wrap my arm around his ample waist, and give a sideways hug.

"You're a great kid," he says. "Thanks. You've made my day."

I pull out my wallet and hand him my credit card. He waves it away. "No charge."

"But the battery. It cost you something."

"Here's my price … oatmeal raisin cookies every week till you bake them just right."

"Okay," I say. "But I am paying for the battery."

"It's a deal."

He charges me $75.00 for the battery. It's not enough, but he won't budge. I give him another hug.

"That's worth two batteries," Joe says. "Now, get going. I can't talk cookies all day."

Chapter 19

The balcony by my room gets some filtered sun. I'm hoping it's enough as I settle my bee balm in a corner. After watering them, I stare out across the garden, wondering how much pipe to buy. To figure that out, I search the garage for a tape measure. You would think Dad would have one, but he hires someone to fix everything, so why bother with tape measures? I come up empty.

The garden shed is the next place to check, but as I detour through the family room, the flat-screen beckons. Margot often leaves it on mute instead of turning it off, so silent scenes flash across the screen—buildings swallowed by waves, boats bobbing down streets. I turn away.

Locating a tape measure in the shed, I estimate the length of the new water line and head back to town. Daily Hardware is a gray block building with a flat roof. There's an e-bike outside locked to a street sign. Its rims are electric blue. Shelley? I almost don't go in but decide to challenge myself. She did help me get Charlotte back. What if there's something nice beneath that spooky eye shadow and surly stare?

Shelley's at the checkout counter. She winces. "Ouch. You look bad."

"Gee, thanks." Did I think she might be nice?

"That's my try at sympathy," she says as she pays the man at the register. His name tag says *Mel.* "Her boyfriend smashed her face into the sidewalk."

"Shelley!"

"Just kidding." She shrugs. "So, how's Free anyway?"

"That's off the radar now. He's very anti-my-dad."

Mel bags Shelley's purchase—a can of tar remover. She points to it. "To clean my bike."

I follow her to the front door. "I might buy an e-bike too."

"That'll win points with Free. He has one."

"Really?"

"Yeah, and Tracy bought that Prius, so you need to hurry."

"What do you mean?"

"She got the Prius, and now she's signed up to volunteer for that climate thing. She's hot for Free. You need to save him from her."

"I thought you and Tracy were friends."

"Friend of a friend of a friend." She corrects me. "Tracy wouldn't be good for him."

"And I would?"

Shelley's hands are on her hips. "The one thing I'm good at is sizing people up. You and Free are a match."

I don't know why I believe her. Probably I just want to. I feel the urge to rush to the bike store, grab that e-bike off the shelf, and ride straight to the campaign office. What if Tracy's already there, flirting with Free? She's tall like him. Her Dad's not rich. She owns a Prius.

Shelley breaks into my fret. "What are you here for?"

I snap into focus. "Oh, I've come to talk to Mel. I need some advice for my bee garden."

Shelley calls out across the store, "Hey, Mel, you're needed."

Mel is reorganizing a row of transparent stain. He puts down a can and heads in our direction. He's got quiet eyes, very watchful, on his round, brown face. "How can I help?"

"Jane Zell sent me. She said you can help me with a water line for a garden."

"Sure can."

About twenty minutes later, I'm heading out to my car with a bundle of ten-foot PVC pipe. Shelley's carrying the bag of couplings and supplies. She also has a narrow shovel and a hoe made for trenching. I'm complaining about the pipe. "These are not going to fit."

"You've got a hatchback. Just open the front window. Let them stick out a little bit."

Shelley's bossy but right. When everything's loaded, I surprise myself. "Want to help?"

Shelley nods. "With the garden? Sure."

"Great. Meet me at my place in an hour."

Hesitation flashes across her face. "I'm not coming in if Margot's there."

"You don't like her?"

"It's not that." She's grinning. "Let's keep this project a secret. The Moms can't know. It'll be fun."

"You like devious mode, don't you?" We trade phone numbers so I can text her if Margot's back. "She's been out a lot. I think she's seeing someone."

"My uncle. I've seen them. It's not romantic. It's something else. They've got some club they're starting. I don't know much about it. I'm working on it."

"You really surprise me."

"I'm just a snoop," she says.

That triggers me. My eyes narrow, remembering the face at the window. "Does that explain you spying at my house the other day?"

"Oh, yeah. That. I saw the white hatchback. I was trying to figure out how you knew Tracy. I thought she was there." She pauses a moment, one eyebrow raising as she tilts her head. "Don't you see? That's why I knew where to look for your car."

"Oh, yeah." I nod, that blank filling in. "I missed that." A smile's creeping into my brain. Shelley's got nerve and smarts. I like that.

"So why a whole hour? Are you going to push Charlotte up that hill?" she asks.

"I've got to buy some groceries to make oatmeal raisin cookies."

"Okay. I'll be home polishing Stanley." She pats her bike seat gently.

"You named your bike?"

Shelley hops on her bike and grins. "You named your car."

"That's fair," I say.

Charlotte starts like a charm. I turn toward the market, but then, thinking of Tracy, I head straight for the bike store. The oatmeal and raisins and butter—don't forget the butter, Kaye—will have to wait. But then it's the bike store that has to wait because, as I park, Greg's walking down the sidewalk ahead of me.

Jumping out of the car, determined not to lose sight of him again, I follow past the windows of wine, cheese, and tea shops—downtown is so gentrified it even has an art gallery. He walks straight for blocks, till he turns a corner. I scurry to catch up, damn the twinge. When I round it, he's still in sight, his bold orange-and-blue shirt easy to follow. All at once, he stops, so I step behind a rack of T-shirts on the sidewalk, browsing through them while keeping an eye on him.

Greg heads into a vine-covered building. It's an Italian restaurant. I can't follow him in—that's too obvious—but through the window, I see Greg, or really that orange-and-blue shirt, sitting at a table with someone. My mouth drops a mile. It's Margot! She's talking to Greg!

My phone snaps a picture as Greg pushes an envelope toward her. Margot picks it up, slipping it into her handbag without looking at it, like it's a drug buy. Maybe it is. Maybe he's her dealer. But no, he was at the wedding. Margot wasn't doing drugs then. That came later, after Dad started ignoring her. I watch for a few seconds more, but they just glance over their menus as if nothing's happened.

I head across the street to a cafe and order a salad. Settling in at a window seat, I zero in on the orange of Greg's shirt and Margot's pale hair. When my number's called, I jump up for my salad and scurry back to the window. That splash of orange and blonde is still there. Munching down greens, I keep watching, but they're just eating, not in a hurry about anything.

Ding. I get a text. *What's happening?*

It's Shelley. I text back. *A delay. I'm on a mission. I'll fill you in later.*

You'd better.

Maybe another hour. Ok?

Shelley sends a grumpy emoji.

I send back a picture of the bee I took the other day. *It's for them.*

When I look up, Greg's leaving with a go bag in his hand, but I get distracted by Margot speeding off in her copper roadster and lose sight of him. Standing on the sidewalk, I stare up at the sky, caught in a whirlpool of complications. It's like the only thing I can do is spin and spin. I don't know what Greg's up to or who killed Marty, and I'm not helping Sol either.

Back at the bike shop, I head straight to the e-bikes and point to the collapsible one. "This one." It's silver-blue like Marty's was. Soon, the clerk's carrying it out of the store for me and sliding it into my car. "Ned, meet Charlotte," I say before shutting the hatchback. When Dad comes home, I'm sure he'll be as cranky about the bike as he was with the car. That puts a smile on my face.

I text Shelley. *Mission success. I bought a friend for Stanley.*

She texts back: *A bike. Cool.*

I'll let you know who's home in a few minutes.

I just rode past. She answers. *All clear.*

Whoa! Shelley's eager—is that just the way she is? Clouds of doubt pass through me—she *is* Tom's niece—but everything's too upbeat right now to dwell on that. I just need to move forward to see where things lead. Anyway, I have no choice. What's the alternative?

As I pass the initiative office, my mood dampens. It's busy today, people moving in and out. It's odd to be so rich, to be able to buy a new e-bike without blinking, and yet lack everything that makes my life worth living. Working on the campaign had offered some promise—friendly faces, shared purpose, companionship. I've been denied that, paying the price for my father's sins.

It's not fair, but life isn't. Dad has taught me that.

Chapter 20

I drag my hoe through the dirt. My trench for the PVC pipe is pretty pathetic. "It's a memorial garden."

Shelley's ahead of me, working the narrow shovel to loosen the soil for me to excavate. She's a bit more capable than I am, though she claims she's never done it. "So, tell me the full story. Don't leave out a word."

I'm tempted to tell her about Sol, how it's a memorial garden for the future, and how we'll lose the bees if we don't fix the mess we're making, but I don't dare. She's so down-to-earth, she'd think I'm crazy. "It's for my brother."

"Mom told me about your brother. She said that's why Margot wanted me to come to the party, to cheer you up."

"And that's why you're helping me?"

"Nah, I suck at sympathy. I just think you're interesting."

"Well, I'm not."

"Yes, you are. I'm a good judge of character."

I want to argue with her—nobody finds me interesting—but decide to drop it. Leaning on my hoe, I ask, "Hey, have you ever babysat?"

"No, I'm not much on little kids."

"I'm supposed to babysit for Jane Zell. I've never done it."

"See, you're interesting. You know Jane Zell. She's a top-rate contact. I'm impressed."

"Well, she's nice to everyone. But I'm afraid I'll blow it. I don't know anything about little kids. I've never had to do it. I've never needed the money."

"And now you do?"

"No, it's not for money. It's just a favor for her."

"Well, I've no advice to give, but there's got to be video on the subject."

"You're right." I get back to chopping at the trench, trying to pull the loose dirt out and make the bottom even like Mel told me.

Shelley's making great progress with her little shovel. She's opened up a lead on me of ten whole feet. "So, what are we going to plant in the garden?"

"I've got a list of plants from Jane. One is bee balm."

"That sounds cool." She gives an extra strong push with her shovel as she forces out a rock. "So, your dad's okay with this?"

"He's still in Dallas."

"The gossip is he rescued someone."

Ugh. "Margot's got a big mouth. It wouldn't be bad if she really cared, but she just trades on it, you know, drama queen."

Shelley nods. "Well, any type of rescue would be good. They think Galveston's gone. A lot of people drowned in their cars trying to get out."

I freeze. "How many?"

"They don't know. Some think it could be thousands, or tens of thousands."

The shock of that forces me to sit. Everything Sol told me starts flooding back. I should be working on that one less degree. Instead, I'm complaining about my stepmother and digging trenches. "We've got to stop this."

"Stop the garden?" She pauses to stare at me.

"No, the emissions, or the storms will get worse."

"How are we going to stop that? I don't have a weather wand to cast a spell."

"I don't know yet, but I'm trying to figure it out."

Shelley drives her shovel into the dirt again. "Well, when you do, tell me, and I'll let the whole world know."

I stand back up and get to work. It's good to work while you think, but this is different than working digitally. With graphics, time stops. With this, you just sweat a lot, but you tend to let your mind wander.

Our progress slows with the heat. Shelley's quiet for a while until, with a groan, she's the one that sits down. "I need something to drink."

Her skin looks clammy. I drop my hoe. "Hey, let's go in. It's too hot."

"No, I just need a drink."

I grab her shovel. "Shelley, it's time to call it quits. It's really hot today. And humid too. That makes it worse." Pulling off her gloves, I walk her to the patio, pointing to a chair under the wide eaves. "Sit there." After turning on the misters to cool the air around us, I hurry inside for some water and some damp paper towels to wipe her face. "Sip slowly. Don't guzzle it." When I come back from gathering the tools, she's perking up.

Settling down beside her, I pull out my phone. "Crap, it's a hundred and one. I hope it's not another heat wave."

"No, it's just today," she says, pouring the glass of water over her head. "But you're right about emissions. We've got to do something, or every year will get hotter, and we'll be dying in swarms." She hands the glass to me. "More, please."

I bring out a fresh glass for her to sip from and one for me. "One thing I can do is ride Ned. I love Charlotte, but I'll have to use Ned when I can."

"Ned's your new bike, huh?"

I nod. "I've always liked to name things. I've even named my bee balm. I'll probably name every plant in my garden."

"See, you're interesting." Shelley points at the house. "What do you call this?"

"Bleak House."

"That fits." She lifts her glass high. "To Bleak House!"

That's when any lingering suspicion about her falls away. We're in sync. Two rebels. We have the same radical take on this rich world we live in—it sucks.

"Is it time to bake cookies?" she says hopefully.

"Nah, I forgot to get ingredients."

"Tomorrow, Mom is gone. Come on over. I'm sure we have the stuff."

"I'll bring a recipe. Text me."

A door slams inside. Shelley jumps up. "Shh!" she says, putting her finger to her lips. "Our secret." She whips around the side of the house before Margot opens the French doors.

"Hi stranger," Margot says with a friendly grin.

It's amazing that Margot never holds a grudge. Is she ditzy or just more decent than I give her credit for? I decide it must be ditzy, but then I change my mind. Feeling generous, I add some pluses to her column. Maybe she really is human after all.

Margot doesn't notice the scabby cheek, but she notices the tools by my feet and the dirt on my jeans. "What's this?"

"I'm planting a bee garden. I need to extend the water line."

It takes a moment before Margot absorbs my words. "A bee garden?"

"Yes, we're losing our pollinators. We need to plant flowers for the bees and butterflies."

"We already have flowers."

"Not the best kind for bees."

Margot scans her garden, worried I've destroyed it.

I point to the hill beyond. "It's over there. Your guests won't even see it from here."

Margot nods, somewhat relieved. "Well, you can get the gardener to do it for you."

My jaw tenses. I'm buzzing like a bee. "It's my project!"

Margot squints like I'm speaking Latin.

"I need to do it. It's a garden for Marty. Think of it as therapy."

"Okay," Margot says, hesitantly.

"I'm even thinking of joining a gardening club. You said I had to make connections, right?" Why am I even trying to convince her?

"Well, yes, but … I meant someone your age, people like you."

I sense where she's heading. It sends me into a bee-buzzing tailspin. All those pluses I gave her get erased. "You mean, it's not the connections you want me to make because they might not be *valuable*, as in rich." I shout. I can't help it. "But all the rich people you know are such creeps."

Margot's staring at me, not just shocked by my words, but also horrified by something else, like maybe she realizes I'm an imposter—the pauper who's masquerading as the princess. She shouts back at me. "Your face! What happened?"

"I tripped. I'm okay."

"Oh dear," Margot says. "What will your father say?"

"Dad won't even notice." I sputter, my frustration spilling out. I need a mom, a real one—someone to comfort me, to care for me, not just care what people think. "It's really Becky and the rest of them. You're worried what they'll say when they see a face that's less smooth and perfect than it should be. Well, I'll tell them you did it. Or maybe Tom. I'll say he beat me up. I'm sure he'd love to. And I know you're sleeping with him."

"Kaye!" Margot is fierce. "Stop this."

There's nothing left to say to her. Picking up the tools, I storm off. I should be satisfied by my outbreak, but I'm not. It's left a stormy feeling in me. I've got that get-out-of-here feeling like the other day, but I don't dare drive—Joe would never forgive me if I skidded off the road again. After my shower, I slip out the side door and take Ned from the back of the car. Settling myself against the bumper, I read the instructions for operating him. To begin, I unfold the bike. Then I try to ride it. Our driveway's not long enough to really let loose, so soon I'm off, riding up Willow Mountain Road.

The traffic makes me nervous, so I turn up a side road called Silver Mountain. It leads to Gold Mountain, and Copper Mountain, and Diamond Mountain. Before I know it, I'm out of mountains. The roads are now meadows. I'm on Talisan Meadow Circle, where the homes are like castles, and my battery is almost dead. I should have charged it first.

Talisan Meadow. That name was on the flyer in the kitchen trash, the one I found when Tom rummaged through Dad's study. It had a mailing address on it: 5-something-something Talisan Meadow Circle. Riding again, I search for an address that begins with five. The one hundreds turn to two hundreds and three hundreds. Without the battery, it's my own effort that moves me up the incline, which slows me down. I puff from the exertion. Sweat builds on my forehead. My ankle twinges as I pedal, which slows me even more. At the high four hundreds, a black sedan pulls out of a driveway up ahead. The man behind the wheel stares as he passes. It's Tom. His bushy eyebrows still scowl. Maybe he was born that way.

My head snaps down as I fiddle with my brake, afraid he might stop. He doesn't. When he disappears around the bend in the road, I ride up to his driveway. The address by the gate reads 513. Thirteen must be Tom's lucky number. Up the hill is a house twice as big as ours and built of stone, gray and black. It's sure sinister—the perfect house for murder. I name it the House of Horrors. Reaching for Marty's pen in my pocket, I pull it out, jabbing the air as if punching through the creepy feeling this house gives me.

There's a sudden urge in me to storm that house, find out Tom's secrets—any connection to Carter Brown, to Marty—but Tom could be coming right back. It would be stupid, so shaking myself from the grim spectacle of the mansion, I turn around.

It's mostly downhill now and quite pleasant with the wind refreshing me. The sun is heading lower in the sky. Birds *kak* and *caw* in the fir trees. There's a bigleaf maple by a driveway with a splash of red zinnias spreading out beyond its base. Swallowtail butterflies flutter over the flowers. Their pale-yellow wings edged in black are a perfect study in contrast.

Birds and bees and butterflies—what would life be without them? Does Dad ever ask that? It's not a question fit for Tom or Rory, or the other men like them who are trading life on Earth for dollars in the bank. But Dad? Is he really that callous? I'm hoping he's not. I'm hoping he still has some heart left in him like when I was four and we would catch spiders in glass jars to set free outside. Yes, Dad used to do that. We would even make up names for them, and he would tell stories about their new life in the great outdoors.

Turning up our drive, I get a dizzy, timeless sensation just like that signal from my far-off future friend. Is it the moment to find the path through time to him again? I punch the code to open the garage, plug my bike in to charge, and enter the house through the kitchen. Margot's spinning in the gym, talking on her phone, probably about her ogre of a stepdaughter. I grab my PC from my room, head to the study, and reach for the key to slip through the mirror door, feeling like Alice heading down the rabbit hole to Wonderland. In the bunker, I open the laptop. The burst of light greets me. Sol is on screen, beaming like a thousand suns. He's been waiting for me.

"I'm sorry you had to wait. I couldn't get here." That's not quite true, and with Sol, I'm not going to lie. "Correction. I just got busy, and I never know when it's time to find you."

Sol's smile radiates, warming me. "Kaye, I never mind waiting. That is what I do. That is how I reach you. I am always waiting."

"You must do something else. Eat, sleep?"

"Of course. But the one thing that matters is connecting to you."

I fidget restlessly, imagining him sitting on this couch for days till I show up. "All that waiting, I would get frustrated."

"Remember, I am trained in this, trained to reach out to find you. It is my purpose. Every day I look forward to it. And besides, I cannot get impatient because time for me has stopped."

"What do you mean?"

"There is day and night, yes, but weeks and months and years? That disappears when you have no one to share it with, when there is only now and the end."

"The end?"

"The moment when we no longer exist."

My breath catches, all throaty and rough. "What do you mean? Dead?"

"Yes, but more. Extinct. The end of us."

"Extinct." I echo him, but saying that word hits me so hard that my heart stings. It's not grief. When Mom died and Marty died, I felt grief. This is different, like something snapping shut, a door closed forever, darkness sucking me away. It's more than the end of one man sitting alone in the distant future. It's the end of dreams, of art, of music. It's the end of stories. Our stories. It wipes out history, memories, all meaning is lost. When the last human is gone, nothing's left, not even the idea of us. It shudders deep. It wounds.

"Now you see why I so desperately need your help? It is not for me that I am living. I am hanging on for all of us. If it were only me, I would want it over."

His words hurt. "Don't say that."

"No, I must say it. I must share it. I will never touch another hand. I will never give another hug. Each day is a struggle. Humans need each other. We need to connect."

I'm blinking back tears. "You're connecting with me."

"That helps. It really does."

I lean into the screen, my voice pleading. "What else do I need to do?"

"Whatever you can to cool the Earth one more degree."

"How do you know it's just one degree?"

"We had already clawed back three degrees with new technology, lower consumption, replanting forests, and capturing carbon from the air and water. It wasn't enough, so we calculated, and calculated again. We found that we still need one additional degree."

"Why not two?"

"Two would be great. Who knows what progress we could make with two, but at least one more degree would be enough to ward off extinction. The ideas we need are there in your time already, or they will be found very soon. And many of them will work. I can tell you that. We just need it to happen sooner to pull back from the extremes. And that is where you come in, Kaye. Start now. Give the human race a chance."

I'm pumped with adrenaline. I've got to save him. "Where do I start?"

"Start by changing minds."

I think of myself. Cast out of the campaign. Losing Free. I can't even talk to my father. And I only fight with Margot. "But no one's going to listen to me."

"At first, it does not even matter if they listen. Just start." Sol winks at me. "And you may find that you have already begun."

Chapter 21

Margot ambushes me from the kitchen as I step out of the study. "Come and talk."

My mind is focused on extinction and Sol's pleas for me to save the human race. It can't make room for Margot's superficial jabber. "I don't want to hear your gossip. I'm hungry, and there's nothing in the fridge."

"I'll order takeout," she pleads. "Stay."

"Sorry, you're on your own tonight. I've got a date."

Margot's face goes flat. She turns away. I head through the front door, feeling guilty about lying to her, but I can't help it. Sometimes she deserves it. That's what Marty would say. He always said Margot sharpened his instinct for deceit—she brought out the worst in him.

Sliding into the driver's seat, I slump, thinking of Rory Mason, Dad's partner. I despise the way he lies to everyone, but I do it all the time, especially to Margot. Even Marty's claim that she deserves the lie doesn't soothe me right now. I should apologize. Well, maybe. At least I should listen to what she has to say. She did give me Marty's letter. And his songbook too. I reach for the door handle, ready to go back inside, but I can't make myself do it. My anger with Margot is such a roadblock. Instead, I open the glove compartment. The wedding photo of Margot and Greg is there, waiting for me.

I stare at it, blinking. Why did I march out to the car just now? Wasn't I really heading upstairs to put away my laptop? Picking up the photo, I find a label on the back. Did Margot label every picture in her wedding album?

She probably did. The label reads: *Susan Taylor-Malm and son Greg Malm by the reflection pond.* Taylor was Margot's maiden name. This settles the Carter Brown question for sure. Greg is not Carter. He's Margot's evil nephew.

And then I do something impulsive and a bit scary. I call Free. I need to warn him about Greg. The phone rings and rings. He's avoiding me. He won't pick up. I'm definitely losing it.

But then he does. "Hey?" he says. He sounds hesitant.

"Free, I've got something important to show you. Are you too busy for dinner?"

There's a long pulse of silence. He must be thinking *no*, that I'm just insane, perhaps a stalker, but then he answers. "Well, hungry is the word, at least tonight."

"My treat," I say.

"Hmmm." He's thinking aloud. "Right now, starving is number one on my issues list, and I'm broke. I've got to make it to the end of the month till my final check."

"From the Forest Service?"

"Yeah. I'll be job hunting soon."

My pulse races. He could be working up to a *yes*. "So, let me contribute to the cause. Meet me at Marino's. Do you know where that is?"

"Sure, but I'll be stopping by the office first."

I check my watch. It's seven. "Quarter to eight?"

He agrees, so I call the restaurant to put my name in, and then drive off, wondering what to do while I wait. That's when I glance in the rearview mirror and catch a glimpse of my face. Ugh.

Turning back, I slip into the house with my laptop and creep up the stairs to throw on a clean T-shirt and jeans. In my bathroom is a makeup kit from last year's homecoming dance. The makeup makes my scabs look even worse, like it's a skin disease. I wash the makeup off, brush my hair, and nod at my reflection. Picking up my keys again, I charge down the stairs, intent on my mission to warn Free.

Still, while waiting at the restaurant for Free, I do fret about my face. Am I ugly, pitiful, unappealing? I decide I am, even though the hostess doesn't react one bit as she hands me a menu. Maybe she's trained to be polite.

Free notices right away. "Does it hurt?" he asks. His voice has sympathy. That's nice.

"No, and I just tripped on a sidewalk. Stupid me. I'm embarrassed."

"Don't be. You still look beautiful."

My cheeks are hot. Every response I can think of is pure lame, so I just say, "Thanks."

Free glances out the window as a girl walks by. She waves at him, and he sinks in his chair. "I feel a bit guilty meeting with the enemy."

My eyes flash. "I'm not the enemy, though I know who is." My pride is hurt, so I whip out the photo of Greg. "This is Greg at my father's wedding. Greg knows my stepmother, Margot. He's related. And he knows a guy named Tom from FossilLite Industries who is part of the opposition against the initiative. They were together at my brother's funeral. And then today, in this very restaurant, he gave an envelope to my stepmother. He's an infiltrator." I show him the photo on my phone of Greg in the restaurant with Margot. "She's my stepmother, and she pals around with Tom."

Free's lips press tightly as he looks away from the photo. Staring out the window, he says, "We've had eyes on Greg for a while. He's been drawing suspicion, but we can't believe he's got anything to do with the opposition. He's no pro."

"You knew?" I blink, stunned. "Why didn't you tell me?"

Free tilts his head, a bit exasperated. "Because I wasn't sure about you."

"And today? Are you still not sure?"

"I'm … considering everything." Free's words are cautious.

Afraid he will get up and leave, I sit back, trying to dial it down a bit. Why did I blurt all that out so impulsively? "It's just I found a listening device outside my house. Because I thought it was Greg's, I followed him here. He was sure acting suspicious."

"Serious? A listening device?"

"Yeah. I took it down from a tree behind the house. A laser microphone." And that's when I flash on the glove compartment of my car. The key to the bunker was in there. The photo too. But I also put the listening device there the day I found it. It's not there anymore. Tracy must have kept it.

"Why would they be surveilling you?" Free's concerned. That's a hopeful sign.

"I don't know why. Maybe it's just Dad's business, mining for stock tips, but it's still bizarre. Everything's getting really eerie." It would be so great to tell him the truth, about the tornado, about the bunker, about Sol, but he wouldn't believe me.

"So that's why you're so jumpy tonight."

I wince. "Jumpy?"

"Off the planet?" There's a grin on Free's face.

"That bad, huh?"

"Yeah, a bit all caps about it." His hands raise for emphasis, but his tone is lighter. He's teasing.

My breath calms a bit. "It's nice to see a smile from you. I didn't get one yesterday."

Free sits back, more relaxed. His hands go wide. "Oh, hey … I was just shook. Quite a shock who your father was."

The waiter comes up. "Are you ready to order?" He looks from Free to me as if he's got another table to rush off to.

I shake my head. "We haven't even peeked at the menu yet."

"I don't need the menu." Free peers at me, one eyebrow raised. "Their ravioli is ace."

"Okay," I say. "Two orders of ravioli and … salad?"

"Salad's solid too, with house dressing." Free hands his menu to the waiter.

"Breadsticks?" he asks Free as he scribbles.

"Necessities," Free says. "And two mint iced teas."

The waiter glances at me. "That works for you?'

"Everything the same. We're identical twins," I say with a grin.

The waiter laughs as he walks away, but I sense the irony in my words. I'm from a different planet than Free, one of privilege. "If we really were twins, we could trade places. I'd love to have a different life than mine. I hate it."

"You'd leave all that? You don't need to worry about anything."

"You don't understand." I lean into my words. "That world is so fake. Nobody cares about what really matters. Did you know that they're buying bunkers, big underground luxury condos, to escape the apocalypse?"

Free shakes his head. "Serious?"

"Yes, they are. They think it will save them. They haven't got a clue. It's disturbing."

"I'm going to check on that," Free says as the waiter steps up with our breadsticks, "but first, let's eat." He snatches a stick from the basket. "Forgot lunch. I was slammed today."

I let him eat all the breadsticks, except one. When the rest of the meal arrives, I give him half my ravioli too. In between, he gives me tips for navigating my new high school. "Ms. Baldwin is cool. If you like history, take her AP class. And I loved Tandel for math. If you end up with Drake for English though, step up your game. You'll learn a lot, but don't slip into procrastination. He doesn't forgive your tardies on homework."

It feels great to be talking about everyday things. "So, college for you?"

"UW was my dream, to study atmospheric sciences, but quitting the fire crew makes that difficult. It'll be part-time work and winter quarter at Mossy Falls after the election."

I've read up on Mossy Falls, the local community college. "They have a great graphics program. I might want to start there too. Dad will be pissed. He wants me to do something with my life. I'm sure that means lawyer, doctor, scientist. I just want to play with pixels."

We talk on. It's an easy conversation like life's all normal again, giving me hope there's still a chance for a connection with Free. I love how his eyes twinkle when he's excited about something. And more than once, he leans in so close when he's making his point that my heart begins to palpitate. Still, I can't tell if he's attracted to me. There are moments when I catch him watching me, but it's just short pulses of interest, sparks that go nowhere.

When the plates are empty, I say, hopefully, "I can order dessert."

Free checks his phone. "Hey, that's temptation, but I've got a late meeting. Big event tomorrow, some speakers coming in."

"I wish I could help you." I try to say it wistfully, without bitterness.

Free gives me the don't-push-it face, firm, but he's not angry. He stands up ready to leave. "Are you down for canvassing again sometime?"

"Sure, but won't they care?"

"Nah. How will they know?" His eyes are full of crinkles.

"I'll wear a disguise, a gray wig and glasses."

"There you go." With a slight tilt of his head, Free says, "I enjoyed this."

I'm so grateful for those words, my heart beaming at the promise of another day with him, but I just blink and blush like I've got lockjaw and won't ever speak again. As he lopes toward the door, I mine my memory of the evening for every look, every sentence he said, collecting the evidence to prove he really is interested. He enjoyed this. He said it. That seals the case.

When the waiter brings the check, I nod in Free's direction as he slips out the door. "We're really not twins, of course, just friends."

"Twins was a stretch, but I'm not sure you're just friends, either."

"Maybe not. I hope not actually." I raise a finger to my lips. "Shh. That's a secret."

Back in my car, Free's the bright spot I fix on as I drive up Willow Mountain Road. My mood is all uplift. It's not the gravity-free sensation like the one that signals Sol. Instead, it's more a heart-soaring rhapsody. Musical notes dance through my mind, an orchestra playing. There are violins, lots of them, their strings vibrating clear through my heart. I'm on Free's radar again. He's my ally and maybe something else. I imagine all the lovely ramifications of *something else* until a deer jumps out from the brush.

Screech! My heart's a pounding drum and the orchestra's in chaos, violins squealing and squawking. The deer freezes for a second until it darts across the road, stumbling with alarm. I'm frozen too, my swoon over Free shattered by the near miss. My head swivels right and left, as if someone's lurking in the scrub, scheming to scare me, or worse—is this a Greg and Tom trap? Locking my door against potential ambush, I unfreeze and hit the gas, counting down each turn in the road, checking my mirror for dark SUVs. And I don't have Marty's pen with me. It's in my other pair of jeans at home. I vow not to forget it again.

Back home, I shut my bedroom door, lock it, and curl up on my bed to let my breathless shivers settle. All the strands of confusion from the day catch me in their sticky threads. My impulse is to play with pixels to relax, but I don't open my laptop. Instead, I open the tablet and start searching the internet for images under the name *Greg Malm*.

One of the first that pops up is a photo of Greg and Marty. Marty's smiling at him. His arm is hanging on Greg's shoulder. My head goes all helter-skelter. The orchestra violins are screeching and squeaking again.

I slam the tablet down, turn out my light, and huddle under the covers. Greg and Marty? What?

Chapter 22

Shelley's house is cheerful in the morning light. It's smaller and way more sensible than ours. She's lived here all her life. The kitchen is nice, but not overdone. There's only a single induction range. The fridge has actual food in it. The pantry has plenty of flour, sugar, oatmeal, and raisins for the recipe. While beating the butter and sugar with a handheld mixer, I tell Shelley all about Joe Mandell. "I feel a bit guilty because he doesn't know I have tons of money."

"Maybe he doesn't need the money," Shelley says. "I think he's been fixing cars for ages. He's always busy."

"Still, I feel like an imposter."

"Maybe you should tell him."

I give her a sharp look. "Do you tell everyone who you are?"

"You mean rich? No. But if they've lived here longer than a minute, they already know. In fact, Joe might already be clued into who you are. It's a small town."

I'm still skeptical. "He might still like me even if my dad has lots of money?"

"You don't act rich."

"I hope not. My Mom taught us some sense, like we're not any better just because of money. But sometimes I think, well, we have so many privileges, how can we really understand? Life's so easy for us."

"All I know is I've spent most of my life playing the part. Then I trashed the car. Spent two weeks in the hospital, talking to other kids, thinking over my life. It just all depends on how you behave. You can act like a rich bitch, or you can just be who you are. I'm working on figuring out who I am."

A bit of batter splatter escapes from the bowl. "Am I doing this right?"

Shelley adds the eggs and the vanilla. "Just don't lift the beaters without turning it off. Otherwise, you really can't mess this up."

While Shelley measures the flour, baking soda, and salt into a different bowl, I focus on the mixing. The eggs turn my buttery clumps into smooth batter filled with swirl lines. I imagine how to turn those patterns into a special digital effect. They become ocean ripples, cosmic auras, foggy atmospherics. It's apparent I haven't had my pixel fix for few days.

A waft of cinnamon from Shelley's measuring spoon delights my nose. "So, what about your uncle?"

She lowers her voice. I can hardly hear her above the noise of the mixer. "Tom? He's a complete demon."

"I think he's pretty racist."

She puts her fingers to her lips. "Shh! Later. My Dad's in his office."

"Well tell me about your cousin at least."

"My cousin?"

"I overheard Tom in the bookstore, talking about his son. He must be your cousin."

Shelley nods. "He's just a normal kid. Bright. Popular. Friendly. That's why his mom has a restraining order against Tom. I haven't seen him since he was six. I don't think Tom has either."

"No wonder he's so sour about everything."

"Oh, Tom deserves every bit of it. I think he beat her up or something. My uncle has issues."

A thump comes from a room down the hall, so Shelley begins talking about the batter. "Time for step two." She points to her bowl of flour.

When the dry ingredients are added, my batter gets stiffer, but those swirl lines remain. Soon, Shelley points to the bowl. "I think you're done." She hands me a spoon and pours in the raisins and the oatmeal. "Stir."

As I drop mounds of batter onto the baking sheet, I can't help eating a few spoonfuls of it. That's how I always helped Mom with cookies when I was little—eating the dough. While they bake, we wash up. "Don't you have a maid?"

"Just for cleaning once a week," she says as she loads the dishwasher. "My Mom likes to keep busy by being domestic. She's not really a bad Mom. She's just a terrible gossip, and way overprotective. I've given her a lot of grief. You should have seen her after the accident."

The cookies actually taste edible. In fact, they're good. Shelley packs them in a bag, and we head off on our bikes to Joe's. She knows all the back roads. "I've got to buy a helmet, but until I do, I stay off major highways."

We glide down the road beneath the trees. It rained last night, breaking the dry spell. Mossy Hills has sprung to life, living up to its name, all covered in vibrant green. Everything's so fresh, especially the mossy branches, the rocks, and even some roofs. I'm always amazed by moss, brown and brittle, until it rains. Then it soaks that moisture up and resurrects, coming back to life. I feel that stirring in me too. Something's opening up, giving me a taste of mossy magic.

Joe's busy with a customer, so we wait outside his office. While I pace, Shelley texts on her phone, oblivious. When Joe comes out to greet us, I hand him the bag. "My first batch."

He samples one as if he's a judge in a baking contest, and hands me back the bag. "I'll see you next week."

"You're tough." I flash a grin but straighten up, ready for my speech. "You know, Joe, I can pay you. I've got plenty of money. You must know that already."

Joe tugs at his beard. "I do."

"So why won't you let me?"

"Because you love your car. That means something to me. Besides, everyone needs to learn to bake my favorite cookie. It's a crusade of mine. Try shortening instead of butter next time. See what that does."

I grin. "Maybe I need Jane's recipe. She claims she's got yours."

Joe winks. "Perhaps."

Shelley waves her phone at him, pointing to a text. "Tiffany says hi." She turns to me. "Joe's niece is a friend."

Another customer pulls up. "Be right there," he calls before pointing to my bike. "Do me a favor though. If you're going to ride one of those contraptions, wear a helmet. If you don't, I won't work on Charlotte ever again." He points to Shelley. "And that goes for you too."

"But I don't have a car."

"Doesn't matter. Get a helmet, young lady."

"Okay." Shelley frowns. "I'd say you're worse than my mom, but you're not. She yells about the helmet every day."

"So, dammit, listen to her." Joe winks and walks over to his customer.

Shelley sighs as she watches him talk to the customer. "Oh well, I can ignore Mom but not Joe. He plays Santa Claus every year. You can't fight Santa."

At the bike shop, Shelley makes me buy a lock for Ned, along with the helmet and a carrier like hers that can hold my cookie bag.

"You're a mom," I say, teasing.

She waves a thumb at herself. "Ma Shelley, they call me."

As we head out of the store, Free phones. "Hi. Hey … how about a picnic?"

"I thought you had an event."

"It's over. Just a morning one."

"I'm with Shelley," I say.

Shelley waves her hands to signal *no*. "I've got a lunch date with Tim," she hollers loud enough for even Free to hear.

I nod at Shelley. "Oh, Shelley's busy. It's okay."

"She's got cookies," Shelley hollers again.

"Do you like oatmeal raisin cookies?" I ask.

"Hey, that's a thing. And I've got sandwiches and chips," Free says.

"So, where? I'm on my bike." I look around like he's nearby.

"Me, too … Summers Lake. Ask Shelley."

When Free hangs up, I frown at Shelley. "Do you really have a lunch date?"

"No, but I'm thinking priorities here. Remember Tracy?"

"Yeah, she took something out of my glove box." My nose wrinkles like there's a bad smell in the air.

"What?"

"A laser microphone. It doesn't matter. I don't want it back even. But still …" I kick at some gravel on the sidewalk. "Well, I bet she sold it for cash for her car."

Shelley settles the cookies into my carrier and gives me directions to the lake. "There's something else about Free. He's hurting bad."

"I know. About the fire."

"So, you know about Anika?"

"Anika?" Fret lines crease my forehead like crepe paper.

"The girl that died in the fire. She was his girlfriend. He's still broken up about her."

I almost drop my bike. "Oh. I didn't know."

"Well, I'm glad I told you then."

"Okay, I'm nervous now. What if I blow it?"

"Don't be," she says. "You both need each other. Just don't ask too much of him too fast. Now, get going."

I put on my helmet. "Hey, Shelley. I can't imagine you acting like a rich bitch. No way."

"Oh, I was. Now I'm making up for it."

"You're a good friend. A real friend."

"Compliments like that … well, just thanks." She points down the road. "Get going."

At the park, I find Free on a bench overlooking a small lake surrounded by fir-covered hills. Boaters in canoes and kayaks splash across the water, wet paddles glinting in the sun. It's big enough for motorboats, but they're not allowed. We walk our bikes down to the shore and park them beside a mossy log—its blanket of green highlights the vivid scene. "I can't believe this is right outside of town. It's so pretty."

"It's a legacy park. Robert Summers was the big boss around here back when it was just a logging camp. He developed most of the land he owned, but he saved this for everyone."

I smile up at the fir trees, their branches bobbing in the soft breeze. "I guess rich people can sometimes do the right thing."

Free sets up a blanket under a cedar, bringing out his sandwiches and chips from a pack. I add the bag of cookies. "I made them for Joe Mandell. He works on my car."

"Shouldn't you give them to him?"

"This is my first batch. They've been rejected."

Free takes a bite. "I don't see why. They hit home."

"He's on a mission to teach me to make the perfect cookie."

"I'll be your guinea pig anytime."

"So how was the event?"

"Solid. All about dirt and carbon sinks." He digs his fingers into the earth beside him. "Soils that are rich in organic matter hold so much carbon. Forests build up the soil. Farmers can too if they do it right. It's called regenerative farming."

I stare at the ground around me. "I'm planting a bee garden. I guess I need to build up the soil. I bet Jane can teach me."

"Jane Zell?"

"I'm joining her garden club."

"Hey, cool. She's a big supporter." Free leans back and stares through the branches of the cedar. "Let's do stories. I'll start." He tells a story about when he was a boy and climbed his first rock. "I was mighty proud, chest puffing out and everything, but it was only six feet high. Channie's got the photo, and she never lets it slide."

"You're a rock climber?"

"Yeah, not so much anymore. There are more important mountains to climb."

"Like the initiative."

He nods. "Your turn."

I tell a story about Marty. "I was five and he was probably thirteen. We decided to make a recipe for the best milkshake in the world. We would try one flavor, and then another and another. By the time we were done, Marty had ordered ten different gallons of ice cream. The delivery guy thought he was crazy, and the kitchen was a disaster because we kept having milkshake fights."

Free glances at me sideways. "Wait, ten gallons? How'd you down all those shakes?"

"Oh, we didn't drink them. Most ended up on the floor or into the sink." Free grows silent. I'm irritated he doesn't find it funny like I do. "What's wrong?"

Free looks pained. "I'm just saying, that's a lot of ice cream."

I realize what he means: as in such a big waste. I'm mortified. "Food waste is bad, huh?"

Free tries to smooth it over. "So, hey … consider this. How much carbon does it take to make the ice cream?"

"I don't know. A lot?"

"It takes energy to keep it frozen. Trucks haul it everywhere. And cows burp out methane. But I can forgive ten gallons." Free pats my hand to reassure me, except it doesn't. I'm a rich kid who has more money than sense. A Grand Canyon of awkwardness has come between us.

To break the tension, Free grabs a rock, skipping it across the water. "Stone-skipping contest. That's a thing you know."

"I've never done it."

"Just start. Pick a flat rock and toss it sideways."

I stand up to toss my own rock. *Kerplunk.* It sinks.

"Hold it at twenty degrees. It's the best angle for the rock to hit the water."

I grab a new rock and tilt it.

"Give it a nice flick," Free says.

My rock skips across the water. I count. "One, two, three, four!" I'm jumping like a flea.

"Beginner's luck." Free skips his rock and counts. "Six, yeah!"

Gazing at the spot where his stone just disappeared, the glint of sunlight on the water distracts me—diamonds floating on the waves. "It's so beautiful," I say. "How can something that beautiful be so deadly."

"What?"

"The sun. Do you think people will grow to hate it as the temperatures rise?"

"The problem isn't the sun," Free says. "The problem is us."

"But the sun can kill us."

"The sun feeds us. Creates rain. And it's our salvation. Solar. Wind. Hydropower. The source of all that is the sun."

"That's what Mom would say ... she used to call the sun the *EarthStar*. She always said that without it we'd be dead. I forgot about that." I close my eyes and lift my face to the warmth above us. "Mom died from too much sun, skin cancer, but she was never bitter about it. I think Mom could forgive anything. I wish I could be like her."

For a moment, I'm with her, dancing in the sun, laughing. I imagine

Margot standing by, watching sadly. Mom points to Margot, asking her to join us. Yes, Mom could forgive Margot even.

"Where'd you go?" Free says.

I blink and look around. "Sorry."

He's watching me, head sideways, a little grin pressing into his cheeks. "You're different."

"Different than you? Yeah. I'm white. I'm rich. I'm a girl."

"No, you've got something … might call it spooky vibrations. You're a little bit not here sometimes, like you're really up there in the universe." He points to the sky.

No one's ever told me this. I feel embarrassed. "I'm an artist," I say, a bit defensively.

"Don't worry. I like it. You're refreshing."

"Refreshing sounds better than spooky."

"Not cool of me." He's quiet, and then out of the blue, he asks, "The other day, you called the storm El Diablo. It was two days before anyone else. How'd you do that?"

"It wasn't two days, and someone told me."

"Who?"

I'm one of those skipping rocks tumbling, down, down to the bottom of the lake. I long to tell him about Sol, but Free won't believe me, so I offer something bold to distract him. "My father has a bunker."

"What?" Free stares at me like I'm crazy.

And I'm beginning to feel like I am.

Chapter 23

"It's one of those Doomsday bunkers I told you about. It's creepy." I study Free's face to see how he's reacting. Maybe if I explain about the bunker, I can explain about Sol.

Free's eyebrows raise. "You're serious?"

"Yes. It's so ridiculous. How long is someone going to last inside a bunker when the whole world collapses?"

"Collapse is not going to be happening." Free sounds more determined than convinced. "We're going to win this."

"I wish my father would spend money on solutions instead of bunker fantasies. He's in Dallas setting up shelters for evacuees, like he's all concerned. But then he tries to stop the initiative."

"The words *feeling guilty* come to mind."

"For sure. He evacuated this family from the storm's path while he was getting himself rescued. On the phone, he's all giddy about this little boy he saved ... how cute he is, how smart he is."

"Well, break it down. He's doing things that will make disaster worse. He knows that but can't face it. He's trying to make himself feel better by helping out."

"I have to change his mind about the initiative." My words are flat, not buoyed by conviction. "But I don't know how."

"So, get a plan." Free's hand chops the air with a definite snap. "Like just talk it out with him." He sits back down on the blanket. "Remember how you spoke to that mom about her little girl when we were canvassing?"

Across the lake, some geese skim the water as they land. "Yeah, so what do I say? My father's handing me a future inside a bunker. Do I tell him, 'Thanks, Dad?'"

"Less condemnation might be best."

There's a pout on my lips. "But he deserves it. He's so remote. He won't talk anymore. Ever since my brother died, it's just gotten worse."

Free's tone is patient, gently coaxing me out of my sulk. "Some radical honesty here. Remember, while you lost a brother, he lost a son. He's struggling with that."

"I know." Down the shoreline is a fir tree. A bulky nest caps its broken crown. What bird raised nestlings in that tree? Are there eagles here? Or osprey? I'm about to ask, when Free looks me in the eye, his hands on my shoulders, riveting me to the earth. There's some charged hesitation, the ideal setup for a kiss, but that's not where it leads.

"Kaye, I wouldn't be doing all this work if I thought people could never change their mind. You've got to believe that they can." His tone is totally serious. "It's like they have an old story stuck in their head. You've got to help them see a new story, one that will get into their brain. They'll start to imagine it, and soon they're hooked. But of course, remember the no-taxes man? Different folks need different stories."

"What kind of story will he believe? I don't even know what the title would be, or how it begins. It's like I need to find the right book, but I don't know which shelf it's on even."

"So, talk with him. Start the conversation where he's at. Let him lead you to it."

"Every time I talk to him, it's like I'm staring at a blank sheet of paper."

"Stay with it. It's gonna come."

Free needs to get to a meeting, so we pack up. Just before he leaves, there's another weighty pause. "Kaye, I know we have backgrounds that don't sync easy, but I do like you."

My heart gets a bit squishy—good squishy. "I'll call you tonight?"

"Perfect."

I hand him my bag of cookies. "For the road."

He rides off wrapped in a smile. I'm hoping it's about me and not just those oatmeal-raisin masterpieces.

Cycling back into town, I consider ways to share my mission for Sol with Free. Maybe I could take him to the bunker to see if Sol will show up on-screen. Or perhaps, I need another prediction. With a prediction that came true, Free wouldn't think I was crazy.

The road narrows as I enter the old section of town. It takes a while to notice a black SUV tailing me. I steer to the right, slowing my speed, but with all the parked cars, it's hard to keep over far enough to stay safe. Mossy Hills doesn't exactly spend much energy designating bike lanes.

My heart thumps as those wheels crunch some stray gravel on the pavement behind me. I swoop into a parking lot and spin around. The driver—close-cropped hair, glasses, white—stares as he passes. With the shivers pulsing through me, I struggle for a plan. Head straight home? Go somewhere public? There's a coffee shop up ahead tucked between a bar and a hair salon. Maybe it's time for a latte. I can sip some brew and study my phone to plan a route home. I'm not riding up Willow Mountain Road even with a helmet. That SUV could flatten me fast.

My shivers turn into grumbles. It's time to find out who's behind this. I open my phone, ready to ask Dad if he's responsible, but I remember he broke his cell phone in the accident, so I dial Margot for the hotel number. Margot doesn't pick up.

Moving on, I pass an old adobe motel, tall firs rising from its central courtyard. Those trees shade the roof completely, keeping it so damp that plush moss covers the roof tiles. I scrutinize the building's shabby appearance, looking for photo inspiration, but squeeze my brakes when I see someone sitting beneath a fir tree in a rusty patio chair, sipping from a beer bottle. It's Greg. Spotting me, he jumps up and heads toward the row of doors that extend from the front office.

Swerving into the driveway, I call out, "Please, please. Can I ask you something?"

Greg stops at door number seven as I pull up beside his SUV.

"You were at my brother's funeral. Who are you?"

"Greg Malm."

"I know that, but who are you? How'd you know my brother?"

Greg stares, chewing his lower lip harder and harder. "Okay." He nods his head. "But not here." He motions to a little plaza across the street. I push my bike, following him, until we settle on a bench. "Ask. I'll answer if I can," he says.

"How'd you meet him?"

"College."

"Marty never mentioned you."

Greg clicks his tongue. "I guess I was a secret."

My forehead's double-pinched. "Why would Marty keep you secret?"

"We were seeing each other." Greg peers at me intently. "We were lovers."

"What?" I can't process those words. It's like he's talking French. I stare at him for what seems like a day. "Marty wasn't gay."

"He was." Greg sounds definite.

I grip the bench hard, breathless. "I … I … No, I would know that." My thoughts spin into a Van Gogh star scene. I can't tame them. "He never said anything."

"Maybe he thought you knew. Of course, he didn't know himself until he moved into my dorm room."

He takes out his phone and shows me tons of photos of him and Marty. There's one with them locked in a passionate kiss. I study it, blinking back tears. Something clicks though, like a hidden digital layer's been turned on, making Marty suddenly vibrant. Little snippets of clues come flooding back: Marty's grin at a waiter in a restaurant; Marty's look as he watched a guy walking by; some cool fashions he tried—all signals I misinterpreted.

"Why couldn't I see that?" I hug my stomach and rock, doubled over like Greg's just punched me, weeping. "It's like he was a stranger … that hurts … so much."

A woman rushes up. "Are you okay?"

"No," I say.

"What did you do to her?" the woman shouts at Greg.

"Nothing, ma'am. She just got some difficult news. She's upset about her brother."

The woman puts a hand on my shoulder. "I hope he'll be okay."

I wail. "No, he's dead."

She steps back. "I'm so sorry."

"Just go away." I snap my hand at her. "Sorry doesn't help anyone." But in the next breath I blubber, "Sorry. I'm just upset."

To Greg's credit, he just sits there, waiting. People are staring, but he stays. When my sobs slow like a windup toy that's going slack, I think of the letter Marty wrote, and it hits me—Greg is the friend Marty mentioned who would contact me. "Why didn't you call me? Marty told you to, but you didn't."

"Huh? Marty never told me to call you."

"Oh," I say, pushing back one last sob. "It wasn't you?"

"No. I mean, I knew who you were. He always spoke fondly of you, and yes, I should have talked to you right away. I just haven't been sure who to trust."

"So, do you trust Margot? I have a photo of you and her at her wedding."

"Well, she's my mom's cousin." Greg runs his thumbnail over a finger, scratching at his nervous tension. "After Marty and I broke up … long story, I was drunk and stupid and sorry just didn't cut it. Well, idiot me, I went out to lunch with Mom and cried my bitter tears. Somehow Margot

got a slice of the story, including about your dad. When she learned his wife had died, she started pursuing him."

"You mean Margot's in my life because of you?"

"Yes." Greg winces. "Marty wouldn't talk to me for months after that."

"I still can't believe it. Marty was such a flirt. I thought he liked women."

"All for show. And he did like women. He just didn't want to sleep with them."

"So, what else don't I know about my brother?" I gaze at the trees across the street, searching their branches for Marty's secrets. "Maybe that's why Dad's all bottled up. Maybe he found out about Marty being gay. He seems so angry about everything."

"Marty told me, when he was nine, your dad caught him looking at another boy in a locker room at your sports club. Just looking, mind you. Your Dad scolded him, so Marty never let on again that he was interested, even to himself. He tried dating a few girls in high school just to fit in, but once he was away at college, he finally explored."

"He was such a ray of sunshine." I'm sniffling again.

Greg's sniffling too. "Yes, he was. I loved him so much. Did you ever hear his song 'Twenty Tulips'?"

I nod, and Greg tells me that, after his cat died, Marty stood below a balcony at the dorm, strumming his guitar in the moonlight and singing that song to cheer him up. Greg loved him for it. I start telling stories about Marty too. When I tell him the milkshake story, Greg laughs. "That's Marty," he says.

Tears run down Greg's cheeks as he talks of Marty. Tears run down mine too. I take his hand, needing comfort, needing to give it. It's like Christmas to finally find someone to share Marty with. "I'm glad you loved him."

We sit on that bench, telling more stories, until Greg checks his phone. "I have to go. I've got calls to make."

I grip his arm. "Not yet. I want to talk more about Marty."

Greg shakes his head abruptly. "Someday we'll have a good Marty confab. I'll organize albums of pics, and we'll have sushi takeout and get all retrospective. I'm just not up to it now."

"But Tom? How do you know him?"

Greg squirms a bit. "It's complicated."

"Why?"

"I've been trying to investigate."

"You were spying on the initiative?"

"No, that was my cover just to impress Tom," he says. "Anyway, I got booted from the campaign. I guess we cancelled each other out."

"You told on me?" I can't help but glare.

"Didn't you tell on me?"

"Yeah." I sink back.

Greg scowls. "I was doing something important. You were chasing after a guy."

An inner gale rises. "Important? Really? What were you doing that was so important?"

"I told you, investigating Tom."

"About what?"

"Just before he died, Marty contacted me. He was worried. He asked me to keep something for him, but he never had a chance to give it to me. He was on his way to see me …" Greg stops, choking up.

I'm gasping, making the connection. "On his way to see you? That's why he was in Washington?"

Greg nods.

The words of Marty's letter dance before me: *I'm working on something big. I may be out of sight for a bit.* Those words—Greg has just draped them in shady meaning. Marty died on his way to Greg's, and he had something he needed to keep safe. Tom's somehow in the middle of it. "Well, something's up with Tom. He's been snooping around the house since my dad left."

"I do believe your house is being watched," Greg says.

"I found a listening device."

Greg winces. "No. That was me."

"What? Why?"

"I wanted to be sure about your father."

I'm on my feet. "You think my dad is mixed up in this?"

"I don't know yet."

I collapse back on the bench, thinking of the fight Marty had with Dad just before he died. I shake my head. "I can't believe that."

"Like I said, I just don't know."

My phone sends a notification, the ding making me jump. It's my spy camera in the study. I open the app. Someone's there hunting through boxes piled on the desk. "It's him," I say.

"Who?"

Reluctant to trust him but tired of carrying all this on my own, I show Greg the video. It's just too hard to keep this to myself. "Tom's in Dad's study again."

We watch as Tom pulls box after box from the closet, sets them on Dad's desk to search, and puts them back. When the desk is clear, he turns around, frustrated, and heads out of range. "So maybe he doesn't have whatever Marty was going to give you. Did Marty tell you what was worrying him?"

"All I know is he was seeing someone, and then he wasn't. He said he was betrayed."

"Who was he seeing?"

"His name was Carter Brown."

My eyes are round as a planet. "I've heard that name before."

"Carter Brown worked for Tom. Or at least did. He's gone missing."

"What?"

"He's disappeared."

Chapter 24

Clinging to the bench, trying to navigate this muddle of new information, I'm all shaky. The couple across the street gets my suspicious frown. Everyone walking by becomes a threat. I check that Marty's pen is in my pocket in case I need it. I'm thinking of the car that just followed me—will I go missing too?

"Was he kidnapped?"

"I don't know." Greg shifts his feet. "I've hit a wall. I'm not sure how to get anything out of Tom. I'm sure he's figured out what I'm up to by now."

"Well, give me your number in case I find something." As I'm plugging his number into my phone, I get a call from Dad. "I'd better take this."

Greg's already on his feet, waving bye. Nodding, I answer the call.

"Kaye." Dad's voice is stern. "What's this about a garden?"

"It's a bee garden, Dad. I just want to plant a garden back beyond the house."

"Can you wait till I get back? Margot called earlier, all upset about it."

"The garden? She's not upset about the garden. She's upset about Tom and something I said. She's spending way too much time with him. He's even there now, I think." Dad doesn't say anything, so I muster up a change in direction. "How's the little boy?"

"He's fine. They're fine. All settled." Dad seems his old self, absolutely grouchy. The hurricane magic has worn off. "It's a mess here. I'm trying to get home as soon as I can."

Yes, the gloom's now kicking in for him, his hues trending darker, grayer, all the highlights lost. I'm a bit glum myself, considering all that Greg's been saying, so I test him. "Tom's been going through boxes in your closet. What's he looking for?"

"Leave it, Kaye. Just leave it."

I can't say a word. My world's too stormy, so I just disconnect and stare at the motel across the street, fantasizing myself renting a room next to Greg's. Dad could be rid of me. But then I think of Tom, back at my house. I've got to stop him.

Jumping back on my bike, I pedal furiously, letting cars pass me within inches. Why bother hunting for the side roads home? Dad wouldn't care if I get flattened. He's like a snapping turtle with a secret, and it has something to do with Tom. But Dad wouldn't hurt Marty, not really. By the time I hit Willow Mountain Road, though, I'm not even sure of that. I keep running through everything I overheard during Marty's last visit. It's like they hated each other. Lots of snarling. No grins. No jokes.

I'm ready to tackle Tom like a linebacker, but the driveway is empty. Bursting through the front door, I don't find him, and the study looks as if nothing's been touched. Margot's still here. I find her in bed, snoring—a bottle of sleeping pills on the nightstand. There's a wineglass beside her and an empty wine bottle. She looks fully dressed. Considering Tom's been around, I can't bring myself to imagine what they've been doing, but that doesn't matter anyway. What matters is I can't seem to wake her up.

"Margot." I shake her again. "Margot."

There's a pulse, but I don't really know how to count the beats, so I shake her extra hard. She's still not responding. As much as I disdain her, I don't want her dying on me. I call 911.

"I'm worried about my stepmother," I say to the emergency operator, my words tumbling out in a rush. "I think she may have mixed sleeping pills and wine, maybe something else. I can't wake her."

"Is she breathing?"

"Yes. There's a heartbeat too, but I'm not good at taking a pulse. I just know it's there."

"Do you think you need an ambulance?"

I'm nodding my head at that, as if she can see me. "Yes. My Dad's gone. I'm all alone."

"Okay, dear. I've got the address. Just hold on. I'm sending someone."

Margot's eyelids quiver once or twice. I hope that's good. "Does it matter if her eyelids are fluttering?"

"Is she still breathing?"

"Yes."

"Just stay on the line. They're coming."

The line goes quiet, which ignites the stress inside. Margot's phone is by the bed. I pick it up and try to open it, thinking of using it to call Shelley. Of course, the phone is locked, so I try to open it with facial recognition, but Margot must not look at all herself right now. I pick up her hand, hoping to use her thumbprint for Touch ID, if she has that set up, but her fingers are eerily cold, so I drop them. "Hold on," I whisper to Margot. I shake her again.

Watching her, so pale, on the edge of death, I remember whole days of thinking how wonderful life would be without her, but now something unlocks inside me. The door between me and Margot cracks open just a bit. Margot's wanted so much to replace Mom in my life, and I would never let her, simply because that's impossible. But maybe it's time to bring down the wall I've built up against her. That seems doable, seeing her so defenseless.

When I hear sirens, I run for the door. "Here! Here!" I wave at the fire crew. An ambulance is right behind them.

Soon they're pouring into the bedroom. It's terrifying, so I slip into pixel mode, filtering the scene down into sketches, focusing on the EMT. She's got short black hair with maroon highlights that etch easily into my neurons. I mentally draw her, using gesture lines in sweeping arcs to help me process all the action. The woman's head bobs back and forth as she works on Margot. I can't see what she's doing, but she's working hard and fast.

A fireman comes up to me. "Is there someone to call?"

I nod and begin to text: *Shelley, are you home? Can you come here fast?*

Shelley texts back: *Yeah, okay. What is it?*

Margot might have OD'd. Could you come?

Be right there.

Time swirls into little spirals of scenes like Van Gogh stars powering through my mind. Those stars spin and spin like a dizzy carnival ride. I can't say when Shelley arrives, but soon she's standing beside me with her mother. As the EMTs load Margot into the ambulance, Becky herds me toward her car. "Have you phoned your dad?"

I stare at her absolutely blank. She's small just like Shelley with heavy makeup around the eyes. It's a shame because there's something nice about those eyes, something that whispers, *Yes, there's really a warm human in here.* "His cell broke. I don't know if he has a new one yet. He's been the one calling me."

"I'll call the hotel," Becky says. "Which one is it?"

"I don't remember. It was near the airport."

"Let me see your phone." Shelley holds out her hand. I give it to her. She searches my recent calls. "I found a number. It's the Grand Hyatt."

"Okay," Becky says. "I'll call from the hospital."

Shelley and I scramble into the back seat. I poke at her and point to my phone, mouthing silently, "Texting you." I text: *Tom was there. He left before I got home ... before I found her like that.*

Shelley texts back: *Talk later.*

Hospitals make me queasy. The last time I was in one, except for some emergency stitches when I cut my hand, was when Mom died. Bad memories flood me—how Mom died, how Marty died. It's a gruesome thing to dwell on, but I'm feeling gruesome deep inside. How am I going to die? In a car accident? By some ancient virus? In a forest fire? A flood? A hurricane? I shudder, thinking of all the people who died in El Diablo. The death toll is preliminary. The headlines say twenty-two hundred now, but everyone is bracing for more.

Becky's on the phone with Dad, giving him the news. Shelley's texting. I'm staring at the wall without blinking, at least that's how it seems. When the doctor comes down the hall, Becky hands him the phone to talk to Dad. "She'll be fine in a few days," the doctor says.

I take those words in, but I can't feel relief. Dad surely won't blame me for this, but still, there's going to be a lot of drama at Bleak House. He won't be happy with her.

The doctor disappears. Becky is back to talking with Dad. Shelley is back to reading email, and I'm back to staring at the wall again. With the crisis over, I feel like I'm a bowl of mush. My eyes start drooping. I'm sliding out of my chair. Shelley nudges me. "You okay?"

"I'm hungry," I say.

"Mom. Mom." Shelley pokes her mother. "Let's get her out of here."

Becky takes me to her house and fixes spaghetti for dinner. I'm hardly speaking. She does her best to assure me. "Your mom's going to be okay."

I'm too weary to even correct her. Just capturing noodles with the fork is a challenge. Mom, stepmom, it doesn't seem to matter today.

As Becky tries to make conversation, something about high school that I can't quite zero in on, Shelley's dad, Angus, bursts from his office. He doesn't look at all like Shelley. He's tall like his brother Tom, but his face is more blank than mean, no hard lines, just round cheeks and a receding hairline. He grabs a plate and serves up some spaghetti, and then silently retreats behind the office door like he's a ghost.

Becky keeps talking, ignoring him. "I understand you went to Xavier Moreaux in the city. Did you like it there?"

"It was okay."

"I hear they have an excellent drama program."

"I was in the Photography Club."

Shelley interrupts. "Mom, don't interrogate. She's not up to it tonight."

"Oh," Becky says. "Am I making you uneasy?"

"I'm a bit of a zombie, I guess. But thank you. This is so delicious. I'm just tired."

"Of course, of course." Becky picks up her plate. "I'll go serve up some dessert."

Settled beside Shelley on the couch, I try to watch a movie, but I feel like I'm on a different planet. Even the cherry pie I'm eating tastes alien. I'm yawning like crazy.

Shelley nudges me. "You can stay here tonight."

"No, I need to go home and sleep."

"Is that safe? What about Tom?"

"I have to water my plants."

"We'll go and come back."

"Um …" I consider that but decide against it. "I want to be there when Dad gets home."

After assuring Becky I'll set the alarm, she drops me off. The first thing I do is fold up Ned and tuck him safely into the garage. When I push on the front door, it swings wide open, but I'm too tired to call Becky back. Besides, I'm halfway sure we forgot to lock it when we left. Still, my steps into the house are spring-loaded, my legs ready to scramble to safety, and Marty's pen is out, gripped tight. I remember Tom's shadow on the patio, disappearing down that path through the woods. Tom could have parked on Pine Mountain and snuck back. Strangely, though, I relax. I'm alone here. I sense it. Tom wouldn't dare risk getting caught after Margot OD'd.

Setting the alarm, I sit in the living room and stare out at the back garden through the French doors—there's that staring again. What does Sol see when he sits here in the far, far future? Is there still a house? Is there still a fountain? I curl up on the couch and pull a cushion under my head. In spits and spurts, I nap, till the sun sets. That's when I pop up in the gloom, like a cartoon rabbit from its hole, and turn on all the lights.

In the family room, the news is still doing its silent dance around the hurricane. The ticker crawling across the screen claims that the death toll's risen to five thousand. I can't watch after that. It's time for some digital comfort, playing with pixels. Stepping through my bedroom door, though, I stop. Something's wrong.

A pillow is kind of wonky. I don't remember doing that. My desk chair is pushed all the way in. I never do that. Some photos on my wall are not straight. I can't stand that. I check my drawers. Clothes aren't folded quite so neatly. Papers in my desk are a little scrunched and squished as if they've been moved around. A box in my closet is open, and that blue camas, the one Marty mailed me, is on the floor, but luckily, it's still in one piece.

It's time to sweep my room for bugs, but it takes a while to figure out the little device I bought. It looks like a walkie talkie with an antenna sticking out of it. I turn off my phone, the router, even the alarm downstairs, and begin the sweep, hunting for a signal from something that shouldn't be there. It shows up pretty fast, a hidden camera set into the wall above my bedroom door.

What a creep! He's been watching me! I get a chill, ready to storm his house with indignation until I notice some drywall dust on the floor, fresh as if it just finished settling there. It's Tom. He planted the spy camera today, either while Margot was drugged or while I was at the hospital. Grabbing a chair, I tape over the camera's eye and head down to the study to sweep it too. There are two hidden cameras that register—mine and Tom's. Tom's is over the door. It gets taped over, and then I turn the alarm and router back on just as Dad sends a text: *On my way by private plane. Arriving soon.*

I text back: *Good*, and leave it at that, my energy consumed by Margot drama, my inner hues gone grim. Back in my room, I collapse on my bed. That's when I remember the flash drive! Did Tom find it? Scrambling to the floor, I sweep my arm deep under my bed to reach the box it was hidden in. Just when I think it's not there, my fingers connect.

The picture of Mom, me, and Marty is still inside. So is the flash drive. Picking up the rectangle of black plastic, I stare in wonder—is this what Tom needs? A surge of energy gallops through me, a second wind. I grab my laptop and the cardboard box, deciding to take that flash drive to the bunker for safekeeping where Tom won't find it.

It seems routine now, retrieving the key, pulling the book off the shelf, pushing the button, slipping the key into the hole in the wall. As the mirror door opens, I realize Dad's coming home. This is my last time in the bunker.

First thing, I slip the flash drive back beneath the liner in the guitar case. The photo fits right beside the bridge of the guitar. I strum the strings once—a sound as morose as my mood. Locking the case, I stand it back in its corner and frown, my heart heavy. That case is like a coffin for Marty's joyful songs. I'll never hear them again.

Sol's not on the screen, so it's my turn to wait. It's a squirmy, restless wait. After all the tension of the afternoon, I can't quite settle. Doing my best to take deep breaths, I try to imitate how someone meditates. I cross my legs but don't know a good Tibetan chant. Stretching out on the floor, I invent yoga poses. Ugh. Nothing works. How does Sol do it? He sits and waits for me. He said he's trained in this. I'm definitely not. I can't focus on anything.

Instead, I keep dwelling on Marty. His letter said he was doing something big. He must have thought his phone and computer were hacked, so he wrote me a letter. This thought leads to Greg. What was Marty going to give him? Greg suspects Tom too. And then there's Margot almost dying in the bedroom. I keep seeing Margot lying so still. Was she depressed about

Tom, or Dad, or me? And Carter Brown. If he's missing, is he a suspect anymore? It's all a big circle. Round and round, the thoughts tumble like clothing in a dryer at the laundromat. And then Dad. I won't be able to hold back when I see him. I'll have to ask: Did you know Marty was gay? Was that what you were arguing about?

The tumbling thoughts lurch to a stop in my dryer of a brain. I'm like that deer on Willow Mountain, freezing as danger heads toward me. Today Dad told me, "Leave it, Kaye." It sounded like a warning. The more I think about it, the louder the alarm rings in my head. His voice was so harsh. That voice leaves me scared. What does he know about this big thing Marty was working on? The more I think of Dad, the more my panic takes hold of me. The car following me today, was it Dad's guy? I'm not sure anymore that I want Dad to come home.

To calm myself, I head for the closet where Marty's boxes sit. These hold fragments of his life, and it's time to resurrect him. Opening a box, I paw through old school papers, research notes, and coding books for apps, looking for clues. There's a notebook full of random doodles and scribbled lists. On one page is a string of scientific terms: *chemoton, PMLO biogenesis, dark proteomes, intrinsically disordered proteins.* The only words I understand at all are *Cambrian explosion.* Cambrian is a geologic time period, but I don't know what caused it to explode. On the next page is a string of simple words like *walk, bike, train, bus, meat, trees, clothes,* and *power.* Those I understand, but why are they important? Below them are names: *EarthStory, EarthHope,* and *EarthStar.*

EarthStar is circled. That's Mom's word. And in all caps next to it is: *KEEP IT FROZEN.* I've seen that before on a code book in this box. Turning the page, I find a folded printout of an airline reservation to Anchorage, Alaska. The travel date is February 8th of this year, three days after Marty died—a trip he never made. Was Alaska the reason to murder him?

I start to pace, translating my ache for Marty into images, bleak, all grayscale, with my brother a dark figure trudging across a frozen, snowy tundra. That tundra becomes an ice floe riddled with cracks. They widen and merge into one long chasm, all jagged edges and angles. I peer into it and holler, "Marty, are you there?"

It's then I notice it—that zero-gravity hint that Sol is here. A flash of soothing light spirals through the bunker.

"Hello, Kaye."

"Sol!" I rush to the laptop. "Thank goodness."

"You have been waiting?"

"Not very well," I say. "Things are getting frantic … bad things happening here."

"Settle down, Kaye. The moment depends on it. You are coming through with lots of static."

"Oh!" I sit down, gulping air. I feel so awful inside, like the breathing hurts. "It's hard."

"Look at me, Kaye."

I do. His eyes are liquid calm. Quiet pours out of them.

"What do you see?"

"Kindness."

"How does it make you feel?"

"Better." My turmoil subsides. "Thank you."

"Do you want to ask me something? Go ahead."

There are so many things to ask Sol—about predictions, about telling Free, about my brother and Alaska. Or I could ask about Sol's life, his family, the friends who died, what year he lives in, what he eats, where he sleeps. With all these questions on my mind, I'm surprised when my words tumble out. I simply say, "Sol, how do you keep going?"

He blinks, once, twice, again and again. Is he puzzling over what to tell me, or how to tell me? His sunny dazzle pulses as he whispers, "I know the secret."

Chapter 25

I'm leaning into the screen, thinking he's going to give me another prediction or maybe some magic solution to the climate crisis. "So, tell me," I whisper. "What's your secret?"

Sol's eyes are dancing. "What helps me get through the hard times, and even the not-so hard times, is understanding the power in each moment."

My forehead scrunches. He's sounding like Mom. "Is this about your Momentary Principle?"

"Not exactly. The Principle is embedded in the moment, a very powerful one, but that is not what keeps me going day to day. No, it is more basic than that. Let me explain." Sol pauses, studying me, not explaining anything. He just asks, "How have you been feeling today?"

"Sad."

"What would change that?"

"Having Marty back."

"Imagine that. Imagine Marty back. What do you feel?"

I imagine Marty walking in the front door, racing up to me, gathering me up to hug me. "Good."

"And that is the secret," Sol says.

"But Marty isn't back."

"I know." Sol's voice is soft, soothing. "You wish he were, but he is gone. Yet you have the capacity to fill the emptiness that he left behind. There is enormous power in that."

"I don't understand."

"Imagine something else that is good but also something that can happen, perhaps tomorrow."

I imagine Free calling me, talking to me, his smile wide. My heart becomes the ocean, sending out waves of delight.

"See. You feel happy. It is pouring out of you. You think that comes from Free?"

"How'd you know who I was thinking of?"

Sol chuckles. "You whispered his name."

"I did?"

"Yes, but the point is Free did not create the happiness. He was not here. It all comes from you. When you understand that, things begin to change."

"But you can't just imagine you're happy and you are."

"It is not the same, certainly, but it is useful. I cannot wish my own sadness away, but as I sit here feeling it, I ask: Can I take a break from all that is difficult to think of something cheerier or to make something beautiful, like a poem or a drawing in the sand? In between the sad times, I let the moment brighten whenever I can."

"Brighten the moment? My brother said that." I stop, my eyebrows pinched. "Are you sure you're not my—"

"I am not your brother."

"But you know why he died, don't you?"

Sol is quiet for a minute. "I know what you will tell me when you discover it."

"So, tell me!"

"It is not wise to share the future in too much detail. Connecting across time has repercussions." A gloomy shadow flits across Sol's face, his sun behind a cloud. "We cannot know how things will change, for you, for me, for everyone as we work to alter the future. Nothing about this is safe."

I go gloomy too, dwelling on Marty. "Did he do it? Did Marty kill himself?"

"You already know the answer to that."

I'm gulping back a sob. "He didn't. He didn't."

"No, he did not."

"But who did? Someone did." Sol doesn't answer. When I look at him, a tear is flowing down his cheek. Another one follows. I can't stand to see him like that. "I'm making you unhappy." I sniffle.

Sol reaches out as if he can touch me through the screen. "We do not need to deny our feelings, Kaye. That is not the point. It just means cultivating our sunny side when we can, like a farmer working the crops. It feeds us and helps us to continue, to cope."

"I'm going to grow a bee garden," I blurt out as if that might be what he means.

"Yes, I have seen the pictures on your laptop."

"Really? I do it?"

"You do, and it is beautiful. In fact, I found some seeds in the bunker that you must have left behind. I have planted them and watered them. I did not think they would be viable, but I have seen sprouts coming up. The package says bee balm."

"Yes. Bees love it."

"Well, that is what I will imagine every day, a bee to love my flowers," he says.

Szzzt. Szizz. There's static on the screen. "Wait. Wait," I'm calling out to Sol. "My Dad's coming home. I may not get back into the bunker."

"Try," he says through the static. "And if not, remember to write it all down for me."

With one more *szzt* and *szizz*, the screen goes dark, and it's like my world has ended—the vacuum he leaves behind is so enormous. Like Mom, like Marty, he's a truly deep connection, one that I need. Will I ever see him again?

Looking around the bunker as if something here can keep alive the connection with him, I remember the seeds he said he found. Someday, I'll put that little package of bee balm seeds here safe so he can find them. What else can I leave for him? He said to write it all down. Where? Perhaps on my laptop. Yes, he has access to my laptop. He found that photo of me, probably there, so if I write things down, he can read it when he opens my computer.

I take a moment to think about all the things he told me, and then I begin.

Dear Sol,

I just spoke with you. Will it be the last time? I don't know.

You talked about sunny feelings. I've seen people with lots to share. Marty. Mom. Free. Joe. Jane. I've seen people without much. Margot and Dad. And Tom. Yes, especially Tom. People like him have so much money, but money can't buy what they need. Fancy homes, fancy cars, and luxury vacations, that's not what matters—that's not the secret to a good life.

I close my eyes and glimpse pictures of what that good life is—sunshine beaming through the clouds, the soft glow of firelight, people singing together, a simple meal with friends. Those images generate a flicker of warmth inside me. I think of Marty and Mom who, like Sol, tapped into it. I always thought it was just how they were, and I always thought I was different, born Dad-gloomy, so I would never find what they had. Maybe the only difference was they knew the secret, and I didn't.

I picture Marty now, a Fourth of July sparkler, crazy fits of laughter creating delight. Mom is more constant, a brilliant comet arcing through my sky. Sol, of course, is the sun, the source of joy itself. Me? I feel like a dull flashlight that needs its battery charged—efficient, functional, but to be used sparingly. Instead, I'd rather be the flame on Mom's rose-scented candle, burning with a velvet glow.

Closing my eyes, I try to do what Sol said, to grow a sunny feeling. It's hard. Thinking of Marty, I feel sad. Thinking of Dad, I feel angry. So, instead, I just feel my heartbeat. *Ka-thump. Ka-thump.* I'm alive. That's good. I imagine a little seed, very small, one made of sunny light. I'll plant it. I'll let it grow. How big can that seed get? It sprouts. It leafs out, becoming a tree with sparks of sunlight. Now that's a joyful feeling.

I type that now: *Sol, I found a seed you left for me. A seed of sunshine. I'm planting it. I'm letting it grow.*

And then there's footsteps on the corridor. Footsteps coming close.

I open my eyes. He's standing there.

"Kaye!" Dad says.

Chapter 26

"How did you get in here?" That's what Dad asks the moment he sees me. He doesn't say, "Are you all right, Kaye?" or, "Thanks for calling 911 and saving Margot." Instead, his eyes burn through me. I'm in his bunker.

I pull the key from my pocket and wave it. "I found it under your desk. I was hunting for my car key."

"You shouldn't be in here."

"Why not? When were you going to tell me? After the apocalypse?"

He points up the corridor. "Get out."

"Okay," I say, but I don't leave. Instead, I pick up my laptop, heading to the closet where Marty's stuff is stashed and grab his guitar. "I'm taking this." I march past him up the corridor and set the bunker key on top of his desk because it's obvious he won't let me near it again. That's when my phone starts dinging, coming to life in the land of Wi-Fi again. I've got a ton of delayed voice mails and texts.

The texts are Shelley's. She's desperate to know I'm okay. The voice mails are from Free. He's just wanting to talk, checking in about that call I promised him. I've also got a message from Jane to confirm my babysitting date for tomorrow.

I text Shelley back. *I'm fine. My Dad just got home.*

It's too late to call Jane, but I try Free. It goes to voice mail. "Hi, Free. I've had a bad afternoon. My stepmom's in the hospital. I'll talk to you tomorrow."

Opening my laptop, I finish my note to Sol.

Hey, Sol. My Dad just got back, and I'm all upset. I'm lousy at this. That little seed of sunshine might as well be a lump of coal tonight. I'll try again tomorrow.

Love, Kaye

It's time for sleep, but my dive beneath the covers is interrupted when my phone rings. It's not Free, or Shelley, or even Jane. It's Greg.

"Hello?"

"I need your help," Greg says. "I know it's late, but I'm parked around the block on Pine Mountain. Can you meet me?"

"Maybe. My Dad just got home from Dallas. I'm not sure what he's up to. I'll text you when the coast is clear." I pause and then ask, "Hey, did I give you my number? I only remember getting yours."

"Sorry, I already had it. I checked out your contact sheet when I was still in the campaign. I had to know whether or not you were Marty's sister."

That sounds legit. "Okay. I'll try to be there soon."

My eyes search the room. Should I hide anything? Dad saw me take Marty's guitar. My laptop has a login so he can't monitor that. It's just the surveillance sweeper. It goes into the bottom drawer under some sweaters.

There's a flashlight in my desk that seems to work. I take Marty's hoodie from his box of clothes in the closet and slip it on. Dark hoodie, dark jeans. That seems to sync with secret missions in the dark.

Dad's in the kitchen, talking on his phone. He must have bought a new one in Dallas. He sounds angry but not *loud angry*. His quiet anger is sometimes worse. The only words that are clear are *audit* and the name *Rory*, Dad's business partner. He must be talking to him or about him.

With my exit cut off—I'm not going down those stairs—I head out to the balcony and peer into the darkness below. Should I jump? No, my ankle's already feeble. Instead, I wait for Dad to go into his study and lock the door. Soon I'm jogging down the road. Pine Mountain is about a quarter mile from the house. Every time a car passes, I step farther into the shadows of the brush along the shoulder. There are moments I almost turn around because it's midnight, I'm short of sleep, and this is crazy. At the corner, I text Greg: *Flash your lights.*

Headlights flash in the distance. Greg has parked in a pullout between lots. It could be the same one Tom parks in because there's the creek running through a culvert beneath it. As I settle into the passenger seat, he grumbles at me. "You didn't text me. I was getting ready to leave."

"Oh, sorry. I forgot. It's been a tough day. Margot's in the hospital. She OD'd."

"What?"

"Yeah, sleeping pills and alcohol. I had to call 911. I came home after talking to you and found her."

Greg's mouth drops open. "Shit."

I'm biting my lip. "That's about how I feel. Margot's been a pain, but I never wanted her dead."

"Well, I won't let slip that I know. I'll wait for Mom to tell me."

"Good plan." I tap the dash, too tired to focus on the aftermath of Margot. "So, why am I here?"

"Did Marty ever talk to you about his research?"

"Just that it was about vaccines, that's all."

"For some reason, Tom's been very interested in vaccine research lately. We're not sure why."

"We?"

"I've been getting some inside information."

My stomach flips as I link things together. "Margot?"

"How do you …?" Greg is frowning fiercely.

"I followed you to the restaurant the other day. You gave her an envelope."

Greg doubles down on his frown. "Not cool."

I grunt in disbelief. "Says the man who hid a laser microphone in my tree."

"Okay, okay. But that was my résumé. She's helping me look for a job." Greg's lips press tight as if he won't say another word, but then he relents, puffing out a breath. "And I've been talking to her about Marty, about why he died. I told her I needed to know what might have caused him so much turmoil, and on and on … how much pain I'm in about it. Margot's so easy to play." Greg winces, staring down the empty road beyond the windshield. "I even told her my suspicions about Tom, asking for help. And now she's in the hospital."

My mind is riveted by the big reveal. "Margot was working with you?"

Greg's thumbs drum the steering wheel, an anxious rhythm. "Margot found something. She texted me today about a patent."

I can't compute what he's saying, still caught up in my guilt about Margot. After being so sure she was part of the scheme, I'm ashamed for giving her grief all these years. But Marty never trusted her, and so, neither did I. "A what?"

"A patent. Like for an invention. Marty had one on a new vaccine delivery system."

My head's swimming with all this information. "Really? Marty did that?"

"Of course. He was brilliant. Everyone who met him knew that." Greg's breath catches for a second, holding back a swell of tears. "And I need you to find out about the patent because Margot also learned that your father's hedge fund is investing heavily in vaccine companies, from research to production, including new delivery systems. It's a brand-new push for them."

"How did Margot find all this? I've looked everywhere in Dad's study. I didn't see a patent or even a hint about hedge funds, nothing." And then insight flashes. "Tom? She got this from him?"

Greg nods. "Margot. Supersleuth. She said he gave her the creeps."

My head is in my hands, darkness swirling around my feet. I had her so wrong. "I thought she was just a drama queen."

Greg clicks his tongue. "Well, she is. Always. Forever. But she does have a heart." He pauses. "Do you think Tom found out? Do you think he had something to do with Margot's overdose?"

The silhouettes of the trees look suddenly skewed as if a strong wind's kicked up. Certain that we're parked beside the trail to my house, I shiver. Tom could be watching me from those forest shadows, scheming up a plot against me. "I just know he was there, and he has a drug habit."

"Yeah, that is getting obvious." Greg groans. "Shit! Maybe he found her texting me."

We're both quiet for a minute. I'm still reeling from the news that Margot is on the right side of this. "So, vaccines … patents … is that suspicious?"

"It could be a motive," Greg says.

"Motive?"

"For murder." Greg's stare is deadpan serious. "I'm trying to find out who murdered your brother."

My mouth is a cavern. There's a hammer blow to my chest like a hurricane's tearing me to shreds. Tears pour in rivulets down my face. I can't stop it. Having my suspicions confirmed here inside this car is crushing me. It's the jolt of hearing someone else say it—murder, my brother.

"You think it's Tom?"

"I don't have proof yet, but yes, it was Tom." Greg's hands grip the steering wheel. "I just don't buy the story of Marty driving over a cliff, especially into the ocean. He wasn't a fan of salt water. I could never get him near the waves on a beach."

I sniffle through tears. "There weren't any skid marks, so what did Tom do? Run him off the road?"

"Margot thinks it was the brakes, but all she knows for sure is Tom was tracking where Marty went by hacking into his car's computer system, and something went wrong. That's what she got out of Tom. I looked it up. Yeah, you can hack the brakes that way."

"Hacking the brakes?" I wipe my cheeks dry with my sleeve and sit back, trying to make sense of it.

"In newer models, brakes are run by the car's computer. But you'd have to pay someone a ton to make it happen."

"Tom's got plenty to hire a cyber assassin."

"Agreed, but I went through Marty's car, inch by inch, after the police finished their investigation. It was sitting in an impound lot, waiting for demolition. I bribed some guy to let me have it. Then I towed it to a storage locker and had a friend rip it apart, but he couldn't find anything wrong. Of course, I don't know what evidence hacking leaves behind. Probably none." He shrugs it off. "Anyway, I'm wondering if this patent was the reason for Marty's murder."

My head wags furiously. "No, no. Why would they want to kill him for that?"

"Maybe so your father would control the patent?"

I balk at the suggestion. "Why would my dad do such a thing?"

"I don't think he did."

"I'm lost." Even as I say that, something Tom said to Margot in the kitchen days ago, something about vaccines and getting power, comes back to me. Power over what? I'm quiet for the beat of a whole minute. I finally nod. "Okay. So, here's something to think about. Tom bugged our house today while Margot was all drugged up in the bedroom. Dad can't be mixed up in this or Tom wouldn't be trying to watch him."

"Just see what you can find, but be careful. Tom's dangerous. Call me if you need me." He hits the car's start button.

"Wait a minute," I shout. "I just got here."

"I've got to go. I've got a résumé to send out."

"At this time of night?"

Greg stifles a yawn. "Cash is getting low. It's time to get back to work. Tom fired me."

I bolt up straight, thinking back to the night of the housewarming. "I overheard Tom at a party. He wanted someone to get rid of a guy. He said he was too smart. He'd catch on."

Greg steps on the gas and heads down the street. "That's about what happened. And that's why, right now, I need to get my résumé out there."

He drops me off just down Willow Mountain from my driveway. The house is silent as I creep in, fumbling with the alarm, expecting Dad to catch me, but he doesn't. My spy cam video confirms he's no longer in the study. Collapsing onto my bed, I snuggle up to Marty's guitar case and hug it as if it's him. "Marty, what's going on? Can I trust Dad?"

I try to imagine his answer, but it doesn't work. Instead, my conversation with Greg filters through me. Tears swell as I brood over the hacking of Marty's brakes. How could someone do that? Well, Tom could. On the night of the party, Tom threatened the guy on the phone, saying if Greg wasn't fired, he'd do more than fix it, adding, "And you'll be next." *Next* means there was a first one, and that was probably Marty. Does that count as a confession? No, too vague.

To stop thinking about Tom and Marty, I grab my sketchpad on the nightstand, hoping drawing will soothe me. When I open the cover, there it is on the top page—a tree filled with light, the one I drew days ago. Thoughts of Sol flood me, bringing in a hint of golden yellow to warm my dreary mood.

Snuggling against a pillow, I pivot back to thinking of Dad. I need to talk to him. I need him on my side in this. He's just so gloomy, so angry. He was never this bad when I was young. There was that time at Christmas, him dancing with Mom in front of the tree, lights twinkling behind them. He gazed at her with a glow that beamed with love. That glow can't be totally gone.

And then it's clear how to reach him—simply show him the glow's still here. Before I can imagine what that means, my eyelids droop. It's sudden. I can't help it.

And just as suddenly, I jerk back awake, rescuing myself from one of those falling down, down, down, drifting off moments, slipping into dreams—dreams of Marty making funny faces, singing his song about tulips. When he stopped, he looked at me, saying, "I'm keeping it frozen for you."

Chapter 27

"Kaye?" I hear Shelley's voice at my bedroom door.

She knocks.

"Just a minute." My head's all thick with sleep, reminding me of Margot and her pills. I put the guitar case into my closet and straighten my bedding. On my desk is a piece of scratch paper. Two words are written on it: *Solution* and *EarthStar*, Mom's name for the sun.

Shelley knocks. "Are you okay?"

"Coming." Stuffing the paper into my desk drawer, I rush across the room and open the door.

Shelley peers up at me with an arched brow. "Rough night?"

The dresser mirror tells me why she asked. My hair's a tangled mess. "Seems like it."

"Your dad let me in."

"Did he look grumpy?"

Shelley gives an eye roll of agreement. "Completely."

"I'm not sure he really wanted to come back from Texas. Maybe he wants a new life, free of Margot and me."

"That would be my guess too." Shelley says it straight. One reason I like Shelley is that she doesn't sugarcoat everything.

And then I give a thoughtful wag to my finger. "But who does he really want to be free of? I don't think he likes who he is."

Shelley blinks. "Well, who does? Just look at Uncle Tom," Shelley adds grimly. "He's the poster boy for repressed self-loathing."

With my finger to my lips, I glance at the tape above the door, wondering if there's audio recording in Tom's hidden camera. Pointing to the tape, I whisper, "Tom."

She nods. "Let's head outside to work on that bee garden."

Shelley laughs when I show her where I've stored the tools, the pipe, the bag of solvent and couplings—all piled into my bathtub. She snaps a photo. "For our garden timeline. I'm setting up a page." As I brush my hair, she asks, "Didn't you buy some plants?"

"Oh, yes, Jane and Joe. I've got to water them. They're on my balcony."

Shelley gives a little snort. "You've named your plants Jane and Joe?"

"Of course."

"Which plant in the garden are you going to name after me?"

My mouth curves into a smile. "The sunflower. The tallest one."

Shelley's sigh is a wistful breeze. "I'd love that."

After we water my plants, we carry the tools and the pipe out the side door, hoping to avoid Dad. Of course, as we start to dig, he spots us from the family room and rushes out. "Stop. Stop."

"Okay, Dad." I lay my trench hoe down. It's not a time to fight with him. "So, please tell me, why can't I do this?"

"Just not now. Not with everything."

I lean into my words, keeping it matter-of-fact. "Margot's not here. It'll be better to get it done before she comes back. At least the pipe."

Dad raises both hands as if he's trying to push my words away. "But I don't have time for this."

Only mammoth effort keeps my voice from rising. "It's my project. You don't have to do anything."

Dad stands there like a stone until, with a sudden shake of his head like he's trying to toss the chaos out, he says, "But don't hook it up. Let the gardener do that. And don't disturb the lawn or Margot's plants."

"We don't need to Dad. We're heading from this spigot here, right at the edge of the garden, to that spot up the hill." I'm doing my best to stay steady, feet solid on the ground. "There's nothing even vaguely green in the way."

Dad grunts his approval. "I've got to head to the hospital," he says. "Call me if you need anything."

And then I do the most surprising thing. I walk up to him and give him a hug. "It's okay, Dad. It's okay."

He goes stiff, turns, and walks away. My eyes get misty. It hurts that he didn't return the hug, but still, I'm glad I did it. Inside, that little sunshine sapling grows a whole inch.

Shelley chuckles. "That was brave. If I hugged my dad, I think he'd shatter."

"I bet he'd survive."

"Maybe, but he's so withdrawn. I secretly believe Tom pounded him into submission when they were little. I can't even imagine how I became a baby."

Baby, babysitting! My mind jumps to Jane, but my call only goes to voice mail. "Jane, yes. I'll be there tonight. Did you say six? Text me your address." I pocket my phone. "I'm babysitting! I need to watch some videos."

Shelley stands firm. "You can't quit the trench now, not after that show-down. Your Dad will think we completely wimped. Get digging."

My hoe pulls through the loose dirt until it hits a rock. Working to loosen it, I toss it off to the side. It clunks against a larger rock, covered in moss. On the shady side of that rock, the moss is still green from yesterday's rain. On the sunny side, it's already dry and turning brown. How long can moss exist dried up like that? Does moss still exist in Sol's time?

The sun is warm on my back. It feels good now, but this afternoon it won't. Just a matter of degrees makes the difference. How hot are Sol's days? Is early morning even bearable for him, let alone the afternoon? I think of my mission to decrease the warming by that one additional degree. If I succeed, will he be able to tolerate his summer's heat? Will less permafrost melt so the virus stays frozen in the ground? Stopping the virus would be enormous. With two degrees, can the reefs recover? With three, would less forest burn? Would the Amazon survive? One, two, even three degrees seems so small, but Free explained those degrees are just the global average, not the rise on any particular day, in any particular place, so one degree is harder than it seems. It takes a lot to bring the average down, but maybe with everything else people do to help reduce emissions, just starting sooner will be enough.

"So, I've been thinking," I say to Shelley. "I'm going to talk to my dad about the climate initiative. I'm going to try to change his mind."

"That sounds hopeless, but maybe a few more hugs will make the difference."

"Not just hugs but stories. I need to think of a story to tell him. He won't listen to facts. He knows all the facts, even if they're the wrong facts—which aren't really facts, I suppose."

"You mean like telling him a bedtime story about how all the polar bears die?" Shelley sounds both amused and puzzled.

"Not really. I just need to help him imagine something different. What's better than becoming richer and richer and richer?"

Shelley shrugs. "Becoming happier and happier and happier?"

"Do you think our dads even know what happiness is?"

"Not really. My Dad is frowning every time I see him like it's botoxed there."

I pull extra hard on my hoe. "So, why do they want to be so rich?"

"They want to win the game?"

"Yes, but do they want to win just to win, or do they want to compensate for how bad they're feeling? Do you think that's it?"

"Maybe ..." Shelley pauses, leaning on her shovel. "Perhaps they need their status fix to feel complete."

"Yeah, he wants people to look up to him." I think about that. "But despite all his hard work, I can't worship all those dollars he has in the bank, and he knows it."

"So, what do you do? Fake it?" Shelley's finishing up the last part of the trench. "It's too bad he can't turn all that drive in him toward something better. Just think of what he could do, they could do, if they worked that hard at fixing the problem instead of making it worse."

I stop, practically ready to leap off the planet. "Yes, they could be heroes. Climate heroes. That's the story I need." I run to Shelley and hug her. "You're so great."

My enthusiasm is met with an awkward step back. Shelley's rattled. "I didn't know this was hug everyone day."

"Sorry." My arms flap awkwardly at my side. "I've overstepped. I was just so thrilled."

"No, it's cool. It surprised me. Mossy Hills isn't really a huggy place."

My forehead's all pinched. "My mom was a hug demon. That's what she called it. Marty was too. I guess I'm used to people hugging me when they're thrilled."

"Okay," Shelley says. "I'll be ready next time, but to help me assess the risk, tell me this—how many times a day are you thrilled?" She laughs and jabs into the dirt with her shovel again.

After we connect the pipe sections and add an upright piece to hold the new spigot, we step back to survey everything. "Do you think it will leak?" Shelley asks.

"We won't know until the gardener hooks it up tomorrow. He'll fix any disasters."

We settle onto the dry fir needles covering the ground, ready to plan out the garden, but run into a wall of *ums* and *ahs* and *I don't knows*, so I leap into a whole different discussion. "Tell me about Tom. You keep delaying.

Why is he snooping around my house?"

Shelley studies her dirty palm like she's a gypsy fortune teller reading her lifeline. "You can't tell anyone. Not yet."

"I won't. I'm great at secrets."

"It's all about murder."

My eyes grow wide. "Of my brother?"

Shelley's eyes beat mine for wide. "I don't know about that."

"Then who?" Prickly fir needles poke at my hand.

"Someone named Carter Brown."

Chapter 28

A wind stirs the fir trees above us. I shudder as they sway. "What happened to him?"

Shelley shakes her head. "I'm not sure. I just overheard my dad and Tom talking about where to put his body."

I lean in. "Did they kill him?"

"Why else would you need to hide a body?"

"I bet they buried him at Tom's house. Have you seen that place? Spooky." My shudder becomes a seismic wave running from head to toe.

Shelley puffs out a breath. "Completely spooky. We go there all the time, so I've been trying to snoop, but I'm not making headway. I keep hoping I heard it all wrong, like maybe it was an accident."

"If it was an accident, they shouldn't hide it."

"Unless ..." Shelley pushes around some fir needles on the ground. "The only thing I know is there's some project. It's secret. It has to do with vaccines."

I'm digging my nail into the dirt, scratching a deep *C* and *B*. It's definite now—Carter is off the suspect list, so I rub those letters out. But who's still on it? "My brother did vaccine research of some kind. He knew Carter Brown."

Shelley's staring up at the sky. "I can't believe my father would do it, kill someone. Dad's just an accountant. He's not like Tom. They're brothers, but they're only half brothers." She pauses, her hands digging into the moss around her. "So, what happened to your brother?"

"He died driving over a cliff. It wasn't suicide like they say. When did you hear them talk about Carter Brown?"

"About two months ago."

I shake my head. "Well, Marty died half a year ago. Tom was at his funeral."

"Do you think your father's part of this?" Shelley points around the hillside. "Maybe they buried Carter here. Maybe that's why your dad's upset about the garden."

I press my lips firmly against that possibility. "No. If Dad's a part of this, why would Tom bug my house?" I pivot on that question. "Let's go search for more cameras and get some water. It's getting hot."

We find two more spy cameras in the house, one in the kitchen and one in Dad and Margot's bedroom. "What a creep."

Shelley clicks her tongue. "Maybe Tom runs a porno ring on top of everything else."

We grab tools from the garden shed and remove all the cameras except the one in the study because Dad has locked that door. I feel glum about not being able to talk to Sol, but there's a more immediate concern. It's time for babysitting videos.

Sprawled across my bed, we munch away at my cache of snacks while watching YouTube how-tos. They're completely boring. My eyes get heavy. Shelley's more interested in texting than learning about dealing with little kids, but every once in a while she adds commentary like: "Are you sure you want to do this?" or, "I can't imagine doing that." I'm glad Elyse doesn't need diapers anymore or bottle feeding. By the time Jane calls, I'm confident.

"Yes, I'll be there," I say. "5:30? Sure. I'm not doing anything."

Shelley heads home so I can take a short nap. My alarm is set for two o'clock. When it beeps, I scurry to grab a sketch pad and colored pencils for art. Even though I leave extra early to shop at Summers Discount for kid-friendly art supplies, I'm still almost late to Jane's because my canvas shopping bag is full of child-safe markers, modeling clay, crayons, and a bucket of colored chalk. Jane rushes me into the house, a bit frazzled. "Sorry the house is a mess."

There are a few pieces of paper on the countertops and some toys scattered across the floor, but it's no disaster. "It's perfect," I say.

Jane shows me where her contact info is on the kitchen counter. "I've got sugar cookie dough in the fridge. Elyse loves to use the cookie cutters. They're plastic and safe."

"When's bedtime?"

"7:30 or 8:00. Don't give her any juice right before bed, and she's allergic to eggs, but the cookie dough's vegan, so don't worry if she eats it. No television in the evening. It makes it hard for her to settle." She checks her phone. "I've got to run. Just text me if you need me. I'll be back by ten."

"Okay."

Of course, as soon as Jane steps out the door, Elyse rushes to the window. "Mommy."

When Jane's car drives off, the howls begin. "Mommy! Mommy!" Elyse flops on the floor and cries. The cries turn into screams. I'm glued in place, imagining Jane coming back and finding her daughter like this. There wasn't a video on temper tantrums. I need one.

At first, I try to soothe Elyse with a song that Marty used to sing, but that's futile. The tears keep flowing. Not knowing what else to do, I get out my pencils and sketch pad and start drawing—just lines, bold, sharp lines, intense like Elyse's howls. Next, I crosshatch for texture, my strokes powerful. Gradually, my pressure on the pencil point softens and it begins to create shapes. I render in shadows, giving the shapes dimension. One becomes a sun, with a face like Sol's. Those eyes need crinkles and sunbeams. Soon, I'm smiling, thinking of him, and when I glance up, Elyse is watching me from the floor. She's quiet.

"Come see what I'm doing."

She gets up and comes over, staring at the paper. "Who's that?"

"That's Sol. See his eyes. They've got sunshine in them."

She looks up at me, her sweet, round face so innocent. "He's the sunshine?"

"He helps you feel like sunshine so you can stop feeling sad. Close your eyes."

Elyse closes them extra tight.

"Now, think of something very happy, like making cookies."

Elyse smiles.

"Doesn't that feel good?"

Elyse nods.

"I feel good too. In fact, I feel so happy, I think we should make those cookies."

"Can I make hearts?"

"Lots of hearts."

As Elyse cuts out her cookies, I take some dough and make the sun. With a toothpick, I trace Sol's eyes as best I can.

"It's Mr. Sol," Elyse says with a little clap.

It's so great to be able to share Sol with someone. I wish I could tell everyone about him, but only a little child would believe me. "He's my friend."

"Where does he live?"

"He lives in a time far way."

"What does he do?"

"He sits and thinks good things, happy things."

We put the cookies in the oven, and I give her some paper and markers. She draws lines and squiggles while I watch over the oven. When my timer dings, we take a plate of cookies out to the sidewalk with the bucket of chalk.

"Draw Mr. Sol again," she says.

I draw as she watches. Elyse picks up a cookie and nibbles it. "Now draw me," she says.

With a new piece of chalk, I sketch her face. It's then, over her shoulder, I notice a black SUV parked down the street. A man's just sitting in it, talking on his phone. His hair is long. He has a mustache. He's a different guy than the other day, but he still makes me nervous. I keep waiting for him to pull away or go into a nearby house. He doesn't.

I pick up the cookie plate. "Let's eat the rest in the house. I've got some clay. We can make the moon and stars."

"I like stars," Elyse says.

Checking for Marty's pen in my pocket, I lock the door—all the doors and windows, in fact. We sit at the kitchen table to eat the cookies so I can watch the car down the street. My phone snaps a picture to send to Shelley: *Someone's watching the house. Do you know him?*

Sorry. She texts back. *Do you need reinforcements?*

No. Just check in to see if he's left.

Ok.

The modeling clay comes in handy. We start squeezing it and shaping it, taking my mind off the car. After her fourth wobbly star, Elyse starts yawning. "Let's get you into your jammies and then I'll read to you."

"I like bear stories."

After she wiggles into her pajamas, I pick *Winnie the Pooh* off a shelf and begin, but by the second page, she's already asleep. Pulling up the covers around her, I tiptoe back to the living room and frown at the SUV.

Ding.

Car still there? Shelley texts.

Yes.

Want me to drive by?

You have a car?

No, I'm with a friend.

Okay. Just drive by and see what you think.

In about ten minutes, a pickup pulls up behind the SUV. Soon a huge, stocky guy gets out. Lumbering up to the man in the car, he knocks on the window. The window rolls down, and the big guy says something. Soon the SUV starts up and leaves.

Shelley texts: *Problem solved.* She waves out the passenger window of the pickup.

Tell your friend thanks.

Let me know if he comes back.

Okay.

After the pickup pulls away, I settle onto the couch and search the web for tips on how to lose someone who's following you. There's a lot of hits, which makes me wonder how common this is. Before I have a chance to read the posts, Dad texts: *Where are you?*

Babysitting.

Babysitting?

I'll be back late. Don't wait.

I'm setting the alarm. Just to warn you.

Ok. How's Margot?

She'll live.

Don't wake me in the morning. I'm beat.

Okay. Have a good sleep.

Those last words of Dad's seem magical. *Have a good sleep.* I keep reading that line again and again, wanting him to really mean it. If he did, maybe he just might listen to me. All I need is the story, the hero story, to tell Dad. If I tell it slow, squelch the anger, smile a little bit, perhaps he'll change his mind. But the story can't sound phony. It's got to focus on something he cares about, but what's that except money?

I'm stumped until I remember that little boy he saved. Was his name

Wilson? Ugh. Nobody could call a little boy Wilson. Winston? No, close, but not it. I think of Wade, Warren, Wyatt, and Will, but those aren't right either. That boy is the key to Dad. It's a gut instinct, like a door to the future waiting to open. A hero needs someone to rescue. Dad needs to rescue him. I wish it were me that would stir Dad to action, but it's not. And then I hear it, Dad's voice on the phone when he called from Texas, telling me the name. Wesson. That was it.

Washing the cookie sheet, packing up the modeling clay, I start to hum. It's beginning to feel like I can write that story, the one Dad needs to hear from me. I'll call it *Wesson and the Apocalypse.* It's the story of how Dad can save not just the boy but all of us.

Hope is rising as I pick up my sketch pad and stare at my drawing of Sol. "I'm going to do it, Sol. I'm going to get you that one degree."

Chapter 29

Buzz! It's my alarm. My legs swing over the side of the bed. Today's the day Jose comes to mow the lawn and tend the terrace garden, and I've got to intercept him before Dad intervenes. Besides, there are before-and-after garden photos on my mind, so I need to be out there early to have time for pictures.

My camera looks forlorn, abandoned in its case. I haven't used it in years—at least that's what it feels like, though it's only been about a week. Cradling it in my hands like it's my baby, I head out to my garden plot, squinting in the rising sun. A trampled coneflower reminds me of the party lady who stomped them flat. Thinking of Jose, my heart crushes. What will he think, seeing his plants broken like this?

Dad's already out here, talking to him. I rush up, saying, "Just hook up the line, Jose. I want to plant the bee garden."

Jose glances sideways at Dad, his forehead marked by creases. Lines radiate across his cheeks like rays of the sun.

Dad frowns at me. "What do you know about gardening?"

"I'm signed up for the Garden Club." I turn to Jose. "Mossy Hills Garden Shop. You know Jane, I'm sure."

Jose's eyes brighten. "Yes, Miss Jane is wonderful. She's an expert on all the plants."

I beam up at Dad. "See."

Dad grunts. "Ok, Jose. Just the water line. Make sure it doesn't leak."

"They did good, the girls." Jose winks at me.

Dad's still all grumpy.

"Aren't you proud of me?" I ask him.

He nods, turns, and walks away, his shoulders drooping like a rain cloud's following him. How can I make him see the sky is blue?

Jose works fast. I hold the standpipe in place for him while he installs the spigot. "Your garden's always beautiful. I hope my garden looks as good."

"It will. Just build up the soil so the plants grow strong. Miss Jane will show you how."

I peer at him cautiously. "Do you mind that I'm taking the work away from you?"

"No." His voice is firm. "The world needs the bees. I'm glad for young people to learn that."

"I like the bumblebees best," I say.

"Yes, the Bombus. But I also like the Mason bees. They are very gentle. You can make a nest box for them." He picks up the wooden stake he will use to brace the spigot and standpipe. "You can drill holes for the bees like this." His finger simulates a drill going into the wood. "They lay the eggs in the holes."

"Really? When I get the garden done, will you show me?"

"Si. We can have a lesson." Jose keeps working as he talks about bees. His face is alive, and his voice is warm.

After he connects the PVC pipe to the main water line, he turns on a valve to let the water flow. We inspect the line. No leaks. I turn on the new faucet and water gushes out in spits and sputters, clearing air. When the flow is steady, I step back and take a picture for Shelley.

Jose is already gathering his tools. He says, "Excuse me, I need to work. I have a busy day." He bobs his head and scurries off to the shed as I gaze after him, remembering the starlit tree I drew. Jose is that shining tree, a giant one, towering over men like my father. Raising my camera to snap a photo of him, I stop. I don't need to capture his energy. I need to create some sun of my own. It's time to talk to my father.

He's in the garage. "What's this, Kaye?" He points to Ned.

"It's my e-bike."

"You're not riding that on Willow Mountain?"

"No. And I have a helmet."

He scowls at my bike like it's a piece of rotting fish.

"I'm doing it for the climate."

Dad ices over. "The climate?"

Planting my feet, I reach for calm, thinking of a bumblebee landing on a flower. *For them*, I tell myself and look Dad straight in the eye. "Yes, the climate."

"Our climate is great." Dad sounds like he believes it.

"No, it's not." I give a little stomp. "It's getting hotter every year."

He flicks his hand as if brushing my words away. "That's all a lie. The scientists just want research dollars."

My cheeks burn. "No, they don't. They're scientists. They're warning us."

"Not all of them."

"Ninety-nine percent of them." My lips press firmly on that final *m*.

"That's bogus."

His words wind me up. It's total ignition, my careful plans shot to hell. "Don't tell me you don't believe in it. You built a secret bunker beneath the house. And what about El Diablo? You feel as guilty as hell. You were down there in Dallas, trying to fix things when you're just making it worse by stopping the carbon tax here."

Dad's gone all twisted. A muscle in his cheek pulses like something alien twitches beneath his skin. There's a chill blasting from him that wraps around me. He seems capable of—well, what? Murder? No, but in this house full of lies, it's so hard to keep my thoughts straight.

My next words come out like blades of steel. My face is ablaze. "You've been lying about climate change just to make money off those oil investments."

Dad stares at me. The void is deep between us—a fissure running through the path from me to him. That split widens, and though I'm desperate to pull back my fiery words, willing the crack to close won't work. I can only clamp my jaw hard and not say another thing. Gripping my arms around me, I let questions gallop through my brain. Who is this man? When did he become such a monster?

Struggling to remember the father I knew, without success, I think of that little burst of sun in me, the one that needs to rise through this darkness. There's a hint of it, sunrise shimmering, and my mouth wants to relax, but I can't make it smile. I use my eyes instead, trying to send that hint of sun through them. Can you see it, Dad? I really don't want to hate you. I don't.

Dad's cell phone rings and he storms into the house. I want to call him back to start our conversation over, but it feels so useless—I just don't know how to do this. Marty would. He could brighten most any moment. Slumping beside my bike, the sun sets inside me. I've lost the battle to make it rise. How could Marty do it so easily?

Shelley comes to my rescue with a phone call. "How's the water line?"

"Done," I say, sniveling.

"What happened? Did it break?"

"No, I had it out with Dad. Everything's such a roller coaster with him."

"He didn't like the bedtime story?"

"I didn't even get to the story. I just got mad." I'm a puddle of gloom in the middle of the garage. All my colors have bled into each other, grays mixing in.

"Well, I made some progress about Carter Brown, but there's darkness in the mix."

"Wow! So, come over."

"I'm already halfway there."

"Better yet, I'll meet you. What street are you on?"

"I just turned onto Willow Mountain."

"Stay put. I'll be right there."

Five minutes later, I'm cycling up to her. Shelley's eyes scold me. "Where's your helmet? Joe will be furious."

"I forgot."

"What will you give me not to tell?"

I grin. "A hug?"

She sends a chuckle up through the trees. "Resorting to hug intimidation will never work."

I roll my bike close to her. "Well, before you tell Joe, what about Carter Brown?"

She checks over her shoulder as if Tom is watching. "Not here."

Shelley leads me onto Crisscross Mountain. A few houses down, we stop at a creek, get off our bikes, and walk them along a path, stopping in a grove of cedars by the bank.

"When I need to get out of the house for a few minutes, I always come here. It's my thinking spot." She leans her bike against a tree and settles on a large, shaded rock covered with moss that's still green from the cedars' shade. It looks as soft as a cushion. "This is my rock. You get the smaller one." She points to a rock half the size of hers.

"Ha, I see. Now we're at eye level." My rock has only a light coat of moss to cushion its hard edges. "So, what's the big secret?"

Shelley takes off her helmet. "When Mom and Dad went out last night, I cracked the password on Dad's work computer. Well, not cracked it … I found it scribbled in a notebook in his desk—so lame. I pored through his records. There's a joint account with Uncle Tom for something called the Big Leap Project."

Big Leap. Dad was talking about this to Rory. "Is that the secret project?"

"I think so." She reaches down for a handful of slender sticks beside her rock, tossing them into the creek one by one. "I found Carter's invoices in there, starting about four months ago. Guess where he was?"

I shrug. "On the moon?"

"No, Siberia. The far, far north of it."

That stumps me. "What's that tell us?"

"Well, he was shipping stuff back from there like completely crazy."

"What kind of stuff?"

"The invoice didn't say. But he finally flew back about two-and-a-half months ago, and then there's a bunch of receipts for medical equipment." Shelley stares up through the trees, her mind working the possibilities. "If I were making up a story, I'd say he got sick from something up in Siberia."

"Maybe he died from it. But why would it be kept a secret?"

"Maybe it wasn't. Maybe he died somewhere else, and my dad was just trying to figure out whether to bury him or cremate him."

I study her for a minute. "Are you worried about him? Your dad?"

"A little." She's struggling to explain this. "It's not like we're close, but still, he's Dad."

"So why not forget about all this?"

She presses her lips together, signaling determination. "Because," she says, "I need to know."

"And what if you find out the worst? What if your dad did something terrible?"

She throws one last stick into the current. "I'm not sure."

"Yeah. I keep thinking about Dad. Sometimes I just want to get far, far away from him, but then I can't. He's all I got." A beetle on a clump of moss grabs my attention as it maneuvers across the damp green. "But I hate the damage he's causing, denying climate change while getting rich from oil."

"Yeah, that should be criminal, but it's not."

Her words pull me straight back to moments ago, in my garage, thinking my dad was a monster. It's so easy to believe the worst in him. It's so difficult to believe the best. Perhaps he's really in between—the worst and the best all mixed up in a muddle. Maybe that's okay. Maybe that's just human. Maybe I can work with that.

Shelley picks up pebbles and starts plunking them, one by one. "So, from looking at the accounts, it's all about vaccines, and I know climate change will shift tropical diseases northward as things get hotter. But Siberia isn't tropical, so what's that mean?"

I pick up my own rock and toss it. "Dad's hedge fund is moving into vaccines."

"Maybe they're all in it together."

"So, what do we do?" I picture Dad in jail, shackles around his feet. Should I just walk away from him? No, I've lost Mom and Marty. I can't lose him too, no matter how mad he makes me. It comes down to this: he's my dad. Not walking wins.

Chapter 30

Kerplunk. A frog jumps into the creek with a splash. I try to read the future in the swirling current. "No, it's Tom. It has to be Tom, not them. We have to convince our dads to turn on Tom. First, we need real evidence."

Shelley's eyebrows pinch. High on her rock, she looks more elfin than human. "How are we going to get that?"

"Break into computers?"

"I already did."

"Break into houses? Tom's?"

"Ha, we can't get into that house. It's a fortress."

"But you go there all the time."

"That's why I know it's a fortress."

"Every fortress must have a crack. We just need to find it." I grab the handlebars of my bike. "I'm going there right now."

Shelley leaps from her rock, all elfin-frog, eyes wide. "Don't be completely crazy."

I push my bike up the path along the creek. Shelley's behind me, scrambling to catch up. At the street, I straddle the bike, ready to ride into battle like some Joan of Arc hero brandishing my tactical pen. She's at the end of the path, still staring wildly. "No!" she calls, hitting a note of alarm.

My cell phone rings. It's a call from Free. For a moment, my mission to nail Tom makes me waver, but the fire to storm his House of Horrors suddenly drains away. I answer Free's call. "Hello?"

"Hi. Hey … lunch?" Free sounds as bubbly as usual.

"Okay." Turning back to Shelley, I mouth, "Free."

She takes a long breath as if she'd been holding it for hours. Her eyes lose their froggy bigness.

After making plans to meet Free, I apologize to Shelley. "I'm sorry. I was just so angry at Tom. I wasn't thinking."

"Kaye, we can't be stupid. If we go to Tom's, we need a plan."

"You're right. I'm going to meet Free and cool down." Even while saying that, I feel the threat to my family, my world, circling around me. I go all limp, almost weepy, knowing to stand up to Tom I'm going to need more than Marty's pen. "What can we do? I don't know what to do."

Shelley heads toward me, spreading her arms wide. "Hug?" She drapes her arms around me, her head against my chest, a little elfin princess wrapping me in a powerful spell. "We'll figure it out," she says. "We can't let him win."

My face leans down into her hair, which smells of rinse, slightly herby, a bit gingery. It feels good to be comforted by a warm human body. Since Marty's death, I haven't had enough of that. "I thought you didn't like hugs."

"I just reserve them for emergencies."

"Thanks." I pull away, giving a light tap to her shoulder. "I guess I'd better go. I'll call you this afternoon?"

"I may be busy."

"Then tonight."

"Okay."

Riding back to my house, the magic of that hug's still with me. Even busy Willow Mountain seems pleasant as I glide the road through a patchwork of shadows made by the oaks and bigleaf maples overhead. I love the patterns they create. It's like there's a digital filter on the leaves, turning them into a piece of sketch art.

My thoughts aren't focused on Free. Instead, I'm thinking back to the night of the party when I met Shelley. I didn't want to talk to her because Margot wanted me to. Now, Shelley's become the friend I've longed for here. Instead of being so quick to judge everyone, maybe I should change my people-filter from *suspect* to *friend*, at least when first meeting someone.

Take Greg. I was totally wrong about him, so what does that mean about Tom? As much as I detest him, is he evil? He cares about his son at least, but he's the only suspect left on my list. And what about Dad? I don't trust him, but I want to. And I want him to care about me. My feelings for him churn like a swarm of bees with the power to give honey or the power to sting.

And then I remember the tips Free told me that day at the mall. Free didn't try to convince everyone. He let plenty of people swim past, looking for those he could persuade to stop and listen. So, I don't have to trust Tom. I just need to trust Dad and convince him he's got it wrong. I can't change everyone's mind, but I need to change his. Still, it's a relief he's not home when I get back.

I grab my keys and head down Willow Mountain to Miguel's, hungry for fish tacos. Free's leaning against the shady wall outside the door. "Let's find a park. I need some greenery." He gives a nod toward the door. "I've already ordered. Will two each be enough?"

"Sure."

While we're waiting for the order, he asks, "How's the talk with Dad going?"

"Miserable. I just blew up at him."

"So, hey … let's practice. Like we're canvassing. Knock. Knock. Your Dad answers."

At first, I can't think of anything to say, but then the words spill out. "Hey, Dad. I've been thinking since the storm. Maybe we need to fix climate change to stop the hurricanes."

"Sounding good. Keep going."

"I know you don't like the Initiative, but we need it. We have to cut emissions."

"Step up your game. Why do we need it?" Free asks, coaxing me on.

"I need it, Dad. I need a future. I won't have one if we keep going like this." For a moment, I imagine Dad will listen, maybe even care, but that evaporates. "It won't work. He's got all the arguments against the facts. He'll just dismiss me, send me to my room, take my car key again." I open my hand and drop my keys for effect. They clink against cement.

"Don't say that. You'll need conversations in multiples. Avoid the anger, or he'll shut you down."

I kick at the pavement. "But I am angry. Absolutely."

"Work through it. You get mad, stomp off, but the next time you say … what?"

I'm thinking about last night—about the hero story. "What about Wesson? You're his hero. You saved him from the storm. How is Wesson going to grow up in a world of climate chaos?"

"Good comeback." Free beams at me as he heads inside to get our order.

Picking up my keys, I settle in behind the steering wheel, hugging it for comfort. "Charlotte, next time with Dad, I can't blow it. I just can't."

Soon, we're driving up Clement Valley Road, passing the pullout that overlooks Treasure Pond. On an impulse, I steer to the right and park. The sky is sunny, not darkly ominous like that day of the tornado. I stare out across the valley, remembering that swirl of cloud heading toward me, a slow-motion mental replay. The world feels like it's churning again, and there's a hint of violence in the air. I shiver.

"Why stop here?" Free asks. "I thought we'd park by the pond."

I consider telling him about the prediction, about Sol. "I just had to stop for a moment. Remember that small tornado last week? I was here when it happened."

"What tornado?"

"There was a small tornado, just a F0, the smallest on the scale. I've got video." I get out my phone ready to show him.

Free's head snaps, alert. He points to the phone. "Whoa, did you catch that? I swear I saw something flash across the screen."

I stare at the phone, waiting for another flash. That buoyant, rising feeling lifts me, fingers tingling. My ringtone chimes. An icon pops up, identifying the caller as Sol. "What?" My hand trembles. "Hello?"

"Hello, Kaye," Sol says. Just the sound of his voice drenches me in sunny glow.

"You're calling me?"

"I finally got your old phone to work. We do not need the laptop or the bunker."

"Really? Can I call you too?"

"I am not sure. You can try. Just remember, it is not the machine that will make it happen. It is the connection between you and me. That is how it works."

I glance up at Free. This is my chance to tell him about Sol, but can Sol even talk to someone besides me? I decide to find out. "Sol, I've got so many questions for you, but first, I'm here with a friend. Do you want to say hello to Free?"

"That would be wonderful."

I pass the phone to Free. "Just say hi. His name is Sol."

Free takes the phone. "Hi. Hey … Sol, is it?"

Sol's words sound mumbled to my ear, but Free chuckles. "Really? Clouds, huh?" Free listens again. He nods. "I will," he says, handing the phone back to me. "Sol said to be good to you. He misses you. He'll call back later."

I frown at the phone. I miss him too.

"He's got a nice sound. Is he an old boyfriend?"

"Oh! No, no. He's just a friend."

"He cares a lot about you."

"He's just really lonely. I'm his friend." I stare out over the pond below, wanting to tell the truth but unsure how to. "He's lost the people he loved."

Free stares beyond the window too. "That hits home."

I sense who he's thinking of. "Shelley told me about Anika."

Free jolts. "She did?" He looks troubled. "I guess it's no secret."

"I hope I haven't … I hope you don't think …" I stop, not sure what I'm saying. "I hope I haven't been too pushy."

His eyes flutter for a moment, trying to hold his torment back. He turns away, his body bent, his lanky frame collapsing against the door. Free's face falls into his hands. I hear a sob.

My words stumble. "I'm … so sorry. It must be … horrible."

"Horrible. Yes, it's still so horrible." Free pounds the dash in front of him. "Those flames, I keep seeing them racing toward her."

"I know," I say in a whisper. And then I can't say anything.

Time ticks by as Free sobs quietly. The sun's hot on my arm. The shade of some tree would be better than parked here in the open beside the road, but I don't dare start the engine. I want to give Free space. I wait.

But it's hard. There's nothing to ease his ache, no magic to sweep it away like a digital eraser that could make it vanish—my pain, Free's pain, Sol's pain. And then I spy the sketch pad from last night's babysitting on my back seat. I reach around and grab it, opening to a blank page. Using a pencil from my center console, I begin to draw. First one eye, Sol's eye, in grayscale again, peering at me from the laptop like that first time days ago, but with crinkles at the edges, not the loneliness that I saw in it then. I add the other eye and begin to sketch his face.

Free looks over at my drawing.

"It's Sol."

"It's good."

"Sol always makes me feel calmer somehow."

"I can dig that." He watches me work. "With Anika, I always remember her singing. She had a beautiful voice." He begins to sing a song she must have sung, but his voice cracks and he stops. "I keep thinking I'm over it. I'm not."

"I keep seeing my brother's car at the bottom of the cliff."

"I should apologize, Kaye. I'm not sure I'm ready for us." Free looks at me. "I promised Sol I would be good to you. I shouldn't lead you on."

My head tilts sideways, my thoughts coalescing on Sol. He's simply a friend, but the connection is deep—one so special I would never trade it. And with Free, it can be special too, even without the romance. "Maybe we just need to be friends."

"Would that be workable? Friends?" Free's eyebrows raise, buoyed by hope.

I'm certain. "Yes, it would."

Free smiles—not his wide, beaming grin but a gentle one. It's grateful. I return it.

"So, let's eat," I say as Charlotte's key turns the ignition over. "But first, the shade."

Heading downhill, a car pulls up behind me. I slow down to let it pass, but it doesn't. Flashing back to that black SUV watching Jane's house last night, I stiffen. This car's different, a minivan not a SUV, but it pokes along behind me in surveillance mode, so I step on the gas, leaving it far behind. Pulling into the turnout for the park, I stop and twist around to watch the minivan pass. The driver's an old man, not the man last night. My relief flows out in giggles.

"What's up?"

"I thought that car was following us."

"Like in tailing us?"

"Yes, someone's watching me. I babysat for Jane Zell last night. A car was parked down the street, a guy with a mustache just sitting there. Shelley showed up and chased him away."

"Shelley chasing someone away? Can't imagine it."

"Well, her linebacker friend did."

"She's friends with a linebacker?"

"Well, he was built like one."

"So, you're talking danger? Is it about that guy Greg?"

I sink back against the car seat. "No, it's not Greg. He knew my brother. He's trying to find out what happened to him."

"Are you serious?"

"Yeah, Greg's not the enemy. It's just Tom Rodington. He put spy cameras in my house."

Free's staring out the window like he wants to be anywhere but here. "So, this Tom's dangerous?"

My grip tightens on the steering wheel. I bite my lip. "My stepmother OD'd on sleeping pills and alcohol. Tom was in the house. It was the day he planted the cameras."

Free sips a short breath, opens the door, and looks under the car.

"What are you doing?"

"Searching for an air tag or something." He moves to the front license plate and reaches behind it. "Whoa!" He pulls out a small, round disc. "And you didn't get an alert about this?" When I shake my head, he adds, "Well, it can take twenty-four hours to show up on your phone."

"Maybe last night. The guy watching me."

He nods, opens the tag, removes its battery, and hands it to me. "That ends that."

But it doesn't end it for me. The tag in my hand feels heavy with danger, so heavy that I'm ready to open my mouth, to finally spill out my secrets to Free—about Tom, Sol, Greg, Marty, and even Carter Brown—but I get a ding on my phone. It's my spy camera. Dad's in the study. He's arguing with someone who's out of camera range. I watch, gripped by my father's face. It's not only rage that contorts it but pain and grief. Do I see tears?

And then a man steps into the frame. It's Tom, and his glare is meaner than I've ever seen him. There's something in his hand. What is it? My mind fills in the blanks. I wave the phone in front of Free. "I have to get home," I shout. "Tom's got a gun."

Chapter 31

After taking the corners on Willow Mountain like an Indy 500 racer, I pull into my driveway, screeching Charlotte's wheels. Free's eyes are the moon, full against the sky. He's terrified into silence. It's good that Joe fixed my brakes.

Tom's car isn't here. Dad's is. I burst into the house, calling for him, "Dad! Dad!" Heading for the study, I turn the knob. The door creaks open, and I step back, expecting to see my father lying dead, but no one's there.

Free puts a hand on my shoulder. He still can't speak. I start to explain, but Dad's in the hallway behind Free. Rushing to him, I hug him hard.

"Kaye?" Dad asks. "What's wrong?"

"I thought Tom did something terrible to you."

"Why would you think that?"

"Because Tom was here when Margot OD'd. He did it."

"That's ridiculous," Dad says.

"Well, he was here just a bit ago. He had a gun."

"What gun? What are you talking about?"

"I saw you arguing with him." I'm talking too fast and not thinking. "You were so upset and there was something in his hand."

"How do you know that?"

Stepping back—how can I explain? I can't, so I keep talking, "Was it a gun?"

"No. He was holding a pair of sunglasses. Now, how did you see that?"

"I was guarding your study from Tom while you were gone. Tom was snooping."

Dad's eyes narrow. "Guarding it?"

"Yes. Tom's dangerous. He made Margot OD so he could put up spy cameras." My finger aims at the tape covering the hidden camera that Tom installed above the door.

"What are you saying?"

"I was afraid of Tom, so I put in my own camera above that castle photo." I wave my hand in that direction.

"You were spying on me?" Dad's face looms large like a frightening balloon, his rising anger inflating it to bursting.

"No, I was spying on Tom."

"I can't deal with this!" he yells. "Just go!"

Free's hand grabs mine, tugging me past my father. We head out the door and jump into my car. I'm on Dad's roller-coaster ride again, but it's a scary one, not the I'll-keep-you-safe one. I burn rubber, accelerating too fast. Around the first bend, a car brakes right in front of me, sending me off the road. Lots of scratching, squeaking commotion happens as Charlotte crushes into the bushes.

The dust settles, soft wisps of earthy powder spiraling down like smoky tentacles. Free stares straight ahead, whispering, "Kaye, I'm so shook. What's going on?"

"I'm scared, Free. I'm terrified."

"I can see that, but why?"

"Because I think Tom killed my brother. Greg thinks so too. He's searching for evidence. That's why he was working on the initiative. He was trying to get close to Tom so he could snoop." Free's still silent. I'm making it all worse. I give one last try to sound convincing. "Just before he died, my brother said he needed Greg to keep something for him, but he never had the chance to hand it over. He was killed before he could."

"So, no receipts."

"No, but Marty's last boyfriend has disappeared."

"What?"

"I think he's dead. Shelley overheard someone talking about his body."

"Shelley?"

I nod. "Can you see why I'm scared?"

"Totally."

"What do I do? I can't go home. My Dad doesn't believe me."

Free taps his fingers on his knee. "How about Shelley's?"

"Tom's her uncle."

"You're serious?" Free pounds his fist against his leg. "Well, there's nothing to it but taking you home with me."

"No. I don't want you mixed up in this."

"Too late. I'm there already. But I'm going to be driving, you hear?"

Free can't open the passenger door because of the bushes. It's a heavy traffic day on Willow Mountain Road, cars rushing by, so we scramble past each other over the center console. It's awkward. I end up poking Free in the eye. He ends up placing his hands on my butt. Apologies fly back and forth, but it's a relief when Free puts Charlotte into drive and heads down Willow Mountain.

Sinking back into the seat, I actually doze off, that rush of adrenaline crashing, sapping me of all my energy as it sinks back to zero. When I open my eyes again, we're pulling up to a small cinder-block building on a dusty street without sidewalks. A trucking depot is across the road, their loud engines idling. "Where are we?"

"My place," Free says. "Just a basic studio, but private. You can stay until you're good with your dad."

Free leads me up the stairs to the top floor landing. There are two doors opposite each other, both an ugly orange. "Jill lives there." He points to the door behind us. "She's solid. Don't worry about her. Nita and Guillermo live downstairs. You won't ever see them. They're working two jobs, but they're cool too." Inside, there's a small room with a futon couch, a little kitchen area, a closet, and a door to the bathroom. His bike hangs from hooks in the ceiling. Free shrugs. "It's cheap. It's safe. It's mine."

My eyes soak in the details. "And it's perfect. I wish I had my own place."

"But, hey … your house is so … well, comfortable."

"You mean enormous. I call it Bleak House because it feels too big, too gloomy. No one's happy there, including me."

Free pulls up a plush floor cushion as I settle on the couch. "So, here's the plan," he says. "Call your father. Maybe he's calmed down. Ask him to help you figure out what's true and what's not. Maybe that will get him talking."

"You still don't believe me?" I wince a little, hurt.

"You don't even sound sure of some of this yourself."

"That's fair," I say. "Okay, but I'll call Dad later. Maybe we should eat our tacos first."

"Be right back."

Free heads out to my car and comes back with the takeout bag. He has a small toaster oven to heat the tacos up. The tortillas are soggy from being in their wrap so long, but the limey heat is still potent.

Free glances at his phone. "I have a meeting. Will you be okay?"

"Yeah, I feel much better."

He gives me a firm look. "I'll be back in two hours. We'll talk it out."

As he wrangles his bike from the ceiling, my thoughts race. Am I moving in? Of course not. And Dad hasn't thrown me out. Not yet. It's just till he cools down, but still, I'll need my laptop at least. I text Shelley: *Are you home?*

Yeah.

Could you just ride past my house and see if my dad's there?

I'm doing something, but I'll take a break.

Thanks.

I pace the small apartment. It's spotless except for the taco trash scattered across the little kitchen counter. There's a family photo on the wall with Channie, his mom, dad, and someone who must be his grandma. It should be thrilling just to be here, but no. I can't imagine what Free thinks of me now. I'm a tragic mess.

Searching for a pen and paper to leave a note, I poke around a desk drawer for something to write on. Shuffling through random papers, I find a photo. It's of a girl. On the back it's signed, *Love you, Anika.* Her dark eyes are large and contain a hint of mystery. Her skin is an earthy brown, and her smile is full of sunshine just like Free's. I can see why he's so committed to the initiative. He needs to heal the agony of losing her. With gentle care, I place her photo back in the drawer.

Shelley texts me: *No car there.*

I find a marker by the futon and scrawl across a taco wrapper: *Gone home for laptop. Be back soon.* Dashing down to my car, I trail my fingers along a scratch in Charlotte's paint from the bushes. "Sorry girl," I whisper, slipping behind the wheel. My regret gives way to glee as I start the engine. Even if it's temporary, even if it's only for a day, I'm leaving Bleak House. That's great. That's crazy. That's a little terrifying.

At first, I get a bit lost until I find myself downtown, and then my mind goes on autopilot, planning my escape. Maybe it would be easier to just move out. Maybe Dad will actually miss me. So, what should I take besides the laptop? There's Marty's guitar and his flash drive hidden there, plus my camera and my bee balm plants. I can't leave them to die. Perhaps I can store things at Jane's house. I could even be a live-in nanny for her.

I'm home before I know it. The driveway's empty, and the house is quiet, but the alarm isn't on. Dad would never forget to set it. Margot often forgets. Sometimes I do, but not Dad. I pause, listening, and head for the stairs, but before I reach the first step, there's a loud *clunk* in the study, and then a *thud* and a *swish*, like a box of papers hitting the ground. Is Margot back?

Something crashes. Glass shatters. I'm sprinting to the study. My phone's out of my pocket, ready to call 911. The door is open. Tom's there. He's frenzied, tearing everything upside down. I raise my cell and hit record, capturing the mess as Tom heads toward me.

Adrenaline surges. I'm running, but not out the front door. Instead, it's Dad's bedroom I'm heading toward. Stepping inside, the safe-room button gets a brisk punch from my hand. *Click. Clang. Click.* It's like a dozen locks are snapping. Steel shutters drop over the windows. Emergency lights blink on. Tom's pounding on the door. I'm sending that video to Shelley. And then, I'm calling Dad.

It goes to voice mail. "Dad, I'm here in the safe room. Tom's tearing up the study. Please come quick."

Chapter 32

The pounding on the door stops. That's worse because I don't know where he is. The safe-room lights flicker like crazy. I fear the power's going out and the door lock won't hold. I'm all light-headed, verging on faint. My phone is buzzing. I look at the screen. It's Sol.

"Sol, I'm scared."

"Tell me, Kaye."

I tell him about my fight with Dad. Of leaving home and coming back. Of finding Tom ransacking the study. "What will Tom do to me? What will happen?"

Sol doesn't answer right away. At last, he says, "Right now, all the information I have says you will be safe, but I am sensing a shift may be near. Every single day, we change the course of history for better or worse with the choices we make."

"I'm not sure I'm making good choices about anything ... especially for the future. I need to talk to Dad and not argue with him."

"Do your best."

"I need to try harder ... for you."

"And for you, Kaye. You desperately need your dad. You need to fix things with him."

I'm nodding, but I feel like crying. "It's tough."

"Keep trying. Life is a struggle for connection. Connection is work. It is my work. It is your work. It is the only work that matters, so never give up on your father. Do your best with him."

"But what if I can't change his mind?"

"Then do your best to forgive him."

I suck in my breath. "How could I? How could this be okay?"

"It is never okay, but people make mistakes. We can acknowledge those mistakes without condemning the ones that make them."

"I can't seem to do that." Frustration boils inside me. "I'm failing at everything. I'm failing you."

"No. Something is different today. The wind seems fresher. I hear a sound on that wind right now. It sounds like a bird. Could it really be a bird?"

This startles me. "You don't have birds?"

"There could still be birds somewhere, but I have not seen one in a long time." Sol caws loudly. "It sounds like that."

"It could be a crow."

Sol laughs. "Ah, yes, I have heard of crows. And I do not have burritos."

"Burritos?" What a strange thing for Sol to say.

"Crows do not like burritos?"

That question sends a prickle up my spine. Before I can dig into it, another call comes in. It's Dad. "Sol, I have to go. Call me soon."

"Remember, Kaye, rage gets you moving, but understanding brings the healing." He pauses and then says, "Here is a prediction for you: *EarthStar* will be big."

"*EarthStar?* Sol—what does that mean? Sol? Are you there?" I breathe in a moment's worth of waiting, but the connection is already gone, so I take Dad's call. "Hello?"

"What's going on?"

"I came home to get my laptop. The alarm was off. I found Tom in the study breaking things. When he saw me, I ran into the safe room. Can you come home?"

"I'm on my way."

"Should I call the police?"

"I'll deal with him. Just hold on." Dad's voice is gruff, but there's a hint of worry in it.

In the silence of the safe room, my heart is a bass drum, beating out a rhythm of panic. The ceiling looks too close, ready to squeeze me flat. I need to call 911. I need the police to be on their way, but what if they arrest Dad? What if he's part of this?

An image rises up across the screen of my imagination. It's that dark fissure in the pavement I often see, and it's closing up around me. I pull back, resisting it, but I can't stop the remembering. Now I'm eight again, and Dad's yelling at the phone. We're at the playground, and I drift beyond the boundaries of the swings and slides. He doesn't notice. When he finally finds me, I'm halfway down to the duck pond, watching ants pour out of a crack in the asphalt path. We've just buried Mom, and I imagine her deep in the earth all alone. I keep staring into that crack, wanting to find her, to see her, to follow those ants down to where she now is. Dad gets angrier and angrier because I'm not listening. Someone calls the police. They don't arrest him, but it's tense.

Stumbling into the bathroom to splash water on my face, I let its chill revive me and then pace up and down, past the marble tub, past the sauna, to the shower. At the shower door, I grab a tube of Margot's lipstick and start to make a list of all the things about Dad I can't forgive:

Marrying Margot.

Letting Mom die.

Arguing with Marty that day.

Moving here.

Ignoring me.

My last one is written in all caps—*LYING.*

Slipping the cap back on the lipstick, I wonder if I could ever erase anything on that list, though he didn't really let Mom die. He just lied about it, saying it wasn't going to happen. And moving here hasn't been so bad. I just hate this house. I miss our old one filled with memories of Mom.

With the lipstick open again, I begin to draw around the list, first a rectangle enclosing my words, and then some stick arms and legs attached to it, a square neck, a round head above it, dots for the eyes, the nose, and a line for the lips. It's a crude figure, but I know that figure is me. Yes, that's me, just a walking collection of hurts and grievances, a list of words defining me, controlling me. Is that what I want to be, words of bitterness?

There's a mirror over the sink, its glass waiting for me to fill it. Behind me is the old Dad list, the one I can't erase. Maybe I never will. But here before me is a blank surface. I begin to draw my eyes, my hair, my face. I give definition to the body, building in soft curves despite all my angles. This is the me that's free of the list. Can I be that girl? Can I start over? I lean down, my hands on the vanity, breathing in, breathing out. Each breath is a wish.

As the minutes tick, I begin to settle, coming back to the immediate crisis. Tom, Dad, all the mystery surrounding them and my brother. It's all connected, but I can't sort through the missing shards scattered through my brain. My distress ignites again, a red flare arching through the dark of my sky, as I struggle to focus on the moment—me, here, waiting for Dad.

A hand towel on a stand before me is appliquéd with two red flowers. Tulips, Marty's favorite. Is it a sign? I close my eyes. Something's bothering me—*Keep it frozen*, my brother wrote. Frozen in Alaska? That question catapults me in a new direction. I call Greg.

"Did Marty tell you why he was going to Alaska?"

"Alaska? I know nothing about Alaska."

"He had a flight reservation for three days after he died."

"I had no idea." Greg sounds hurt as if Marty has abandoned him all over again.

"Oh." My breath deflates. "Well, how about a password? Did Marty have one?"

"What's this all about? Are you okay?"

I'm fingering that hand towel, tracing the outline of a tulip. "It's a flash drive. It's password protected."

"Meet me."

"I can't." I peek out of the bathroom at the bedroom door as if Tom's walking through it. "Tom's here, searching for something. He's got a back way through the woods to my house, so I didn't know he was here. I've locked myself in the safe room."

"You have one of those?"

"Yes. My Dad's on his way. But I just thought you might remember some favorite passwords."

"Some of his passwords had Robin Hood themes for sure. And tulips, of course. I used to call him sweet lips. Try that. And Squeaky Burrito, a pet lab rat we took care of for a bit."

My mind races through those possibilities, sorting the options. Instead of seizing on one, I hurdle in a new direction, triggered by a loud thud in the spare room above me. "Do you still have Marty's car?"

"Yes," he says.

"Call Joe Mandell on Kettle Street. He's a mechanic. Tell him Kaye sent you. Have him check out the brakes. If someone hacked them, maybe Joe will know how it's done or who to call."

"Hey, you're not okay." Greg's voice is firm. "I should call the police."

Dad's voice booms in the hallway. "Kaye!"

"Dad's here. I hear him." Before I hang up, another question pops out. A disturbing one. I'm thinking burritos. Marty's silly song is flitting around in my brain, the one about burritos, and Sol just mentioned that. "Did Marty ever mention someone named Sol?"

"No," Greg says. "Not to me."

"Huh," I say, but there's no time to figure it out because a muffled swearing sifts in through the door. "Okay, bye," I say to Greg as someone knocks.

Before closing the call, I hear Greg shouting, "Call me back! Let me know you're okay!"

There's another knock. Dad texts: *You here?*

I reach for the door release but hesitate. What if Tom's got Dad's phone? What if he's the one that texted? "Dad! Are you there?"

There's no reply. Now I'm really scared that Tom's out there. I call Dad's number, but it just goes to voicemail. Another call comes in. "Dad?" I'm breathless as I answer.

"No, it's Free. Hey. What's happening? Where are you?"

"Home. I've been hiding from Tom. He was trashing the study. I've got a video to send you. I think my dad's here now, but if I don't call you in half an hour, call the police."

"I'll be right over."

"No, no. Just call the police if I don't get back to you. Show them the video."

After sending him the video, I text Shelley. *Did you get the video? I'm in the safe room. I think my dad's here. Not sure if it's him.*

There's no response—where's Shelley? I power off the phone and hide it behind the leg of the bed stand to keep it safe from Tom. I can't lose my phone. How will I talk to Sol? Margot's phone is on the floor. I pick it up and grab Marty's tactical pen from my pocket. This time I really do release the door.

Peeking out, my heart sinks. No Dad. He's disappeared. I flash on the birthday parties he missed and that time I was in the school play, and he was gone. That's my dad. That's the way it's always been. When I need him, he's not here, but then something switches around in me. Yes, I need him, but for what?

Words come to me from somewhere, perhaps the moon, perhaps it's Mom whispering it or Marty singing it, or perhaps I've just finally figured all this out. I keep thinking of what Dad doesn't do for me, all the ways he makes me so unhappy, but Dad's my chance to find there's more to me than waiting for him to care. I'm the artist, and an artist chooses the palette, sets up the composition. I don't have to wait for Dad to offer it. I can create it, with hues that are warm and vibrant. Isn't that what Sol was telling me? He works at creating it. That's how he reaches out to me. It's the way to build connections. Just thinking this, I feel Sol's calm confidence. Standing tall, I call out, "Dad!"

My voice rings in the silence of the house, but the hallway stays empty, and that clarity from just a moment before begins to fade. My heart starts to jackhammer as I call a second time. "Dad!"

He pokes his head around the door of the study. "Kaye, I thought you'd fallen asleep or something. Why didn't you open the door?"

I race toward him. "I wasn't sure it was you."

"Well, no one else is here. Are you certain it was Tom?"

"It was definitely Tom." I step into the study. Everything's knocked over except the desk and the bookcases attached to the wall. Statues are broken. Books are ripped apart. Picture frames shattered. "Aren't you going to call the police?"

Dad shakes his head.

This time I don't accuse him. I just want to know. "Why not?"

"We'll just change the alarm code. Besides, I've got someone else working on it."

"Bancroft?"

"Bancroft? How did you know that?" He's pissed at me again.

My voice stays even. My feet plant firmly into the hardwood floor. "I found an old invoice for him. So, what did he find out? Did Tom kill Marty?"

Dad jolts at my question, his jaw clenching.

I face him. "You must have suspected. You hired an investigator."

"I haven't found any evidence."

"But you suspect Tom. Why? Because of Marty's research? His patent?"

"You know about that too?" Dad's eyebrows pinch.

I step closer, leaning in. "I'm just trying to understand, Dad. So, what about the patent?"

"Tom wanted me to turn over Marty's patent."

"Why would you do that?" My words have a sharp edge.

"I wouldn't. But that's not the real issue …" Dad's voice trails off.

I sense a secret in Dad's reluctance. How hard should I push? "Why are you even mixed up with Tom?"

"It's for you, Kaye. I'm trying to protect you."

"I don't understand." I'm pleading now, my voice breaking. "You're just chasing money, but it's making you miserable. What's the point of that?"

Dad doesn't answer.

"Is it all about climate change?" I soften my voice. "You know climate change is real, and it's destroying my future."

Dad throws his hands up in the air. "We can't stop that, Kaye. There's so much working against it. Rich and powerful men are in charge."

"Like you?"

"No, like me," an angry voice snarls. It's Tom in the doorway, a gun in his hand. This time I'm not mistaking it. "Give me your phone," he snaps at me.

I shake my head until Tom points the gun at my father. Faking reluctance, I toss Margot's cell over to him. Tom smashes it against a bookshelf. The screen shatters. He leans down and whacks it with the gun. Picking it back up, he pockets it.

"Tom, we weren't going to call the police," Dad says.

I can't help but frown at Dad. Is this how he's protecting me?

"You know what I want." The glint in Tom's eye is manic.

"I don't have it." Dad's sincere, but it's not enough for Tom.

Tom waves the gun toward the door. "Let's take a trip and convince you."

Dad's just standing there. It's time for me to do something. "No!" My hand reaches high, ready to strike with Marty's pen, but Tom blocks my arm. The air cracks around me. A high-pitched ringing takes over, reverberating between my ears. I'm falling, falling, and my world goes dark.

Chapter 33

Drifting in and out of consciousness, I hear a car motor and see a patch of sky. I'm being carried somewhere. Each step jolts my head, which aches. My father's holding me. There's the scent of him—sweaty, a bit sour. I've never realized he had a scent, but now I recognize it. Doors close. Bright lights pass overhead. Darkness comes and goes. It's a cold place now. I shiver.

Dad's still here, arms around me. I smell blood. "Was I shot?"

"No, he just walloped you with the barrel of the gun."

"It hurts."

"I'm sorry, Kaye. I was protecting you from this. Or trying to. It didn't work."

"It's okay."

Dad's silent. I am too. Is it really okay? No, that word came too easy. And saying *it's okay* isn't forgetting all this. Still, I need to start over with him, but what does that even look like? I can't put it into words, so I paint it in wispy brush strokes across the canvas of my mind: a key unlocking a door, the sun peeking from a cloud, and always, Mom's smile. I title my brush-work *New Beginning*. Yes, right now is my opportunity to start over, but how many new beginnings will it take?

Settling into his arms, feeling five years old again and ready for that roller-coaster ride, the one where he keeps me safe, I focus on each faucet drip. *Plunk. Plunk. Plink.* And I drift.

Bright lights bring me back. It feels like days have passed. I'm laying out flat, and Dad's arms are not around me. My head hurts plenty, but I'm more alert. My arms and legs are stiff, but they work. Turning on my side, I push myself up slightly. My head's bandaged. I'm on a gurney, alone in some room that looks like a doctor's office. I'm hoping we've been rescued and this is a hospital or clinic.

But when the door opens, Tom walks in. I slump back. Hope oozes out of me, seeping off the gurney, trickling to the floor.

Tom stares down at me, his eyes bulging like a frenzied fly. He's restless, almost jerky, sweat dripping off him. His pupils are wide. He's waving something in front of my face. It's a syringe. "Your father's had his shot. It's your turn. Unless you know where it is."

"Is this about Marty's patent?"

"I don't need the patent."

"Then what are you talking about?"

"The vaccine."

"Vaccine for what?"

I'm thinking he's lost his mind until he says, "The virus. The Arctic one."

The Arctic? Siberia? Alaska? My pulse skyrockets. "A virus? Is that why you killed him?"

"It was an accident. His brakes failed." He's enjoying this. There's a gleam in his eye.

I want to charge at him, knock him to the floor. "You hacked the brakes! That's what Margot said." I'm like a lion, roaring. If only I had claws and fangs.

"Why would I do that? I wanted his vaccine." A smirk leaks out, telling a different story.

"How do you know he even had one? He never got to Alaska." I wince at myself. Why'd I say Alaska?

"See, you know all about it? I want his vaccine. Someone gave it to you."

"Me? No," I splutter.

"I read the letter." Tom's leaning close. His breath is hot. His vibe is pure agitation. "Who is Marty's contact? If you don't have the vaccine, he must."

Whoa! The letter. Tom must have found it in my desk. "They never got in touch. I don't know who it is."

"It's all about the future, isn't it? You know, don't you?"

Sol's face is lighting up my brain. Marty? Tom? Sol? But Tom can't know about Sol. No. Tom's just talking about climate change. He wants to dominate the future when the world is on the brink of collapse. "I don't know what you're talking about."

"I don't believe you. Time's up." Tom looks at me like he's mean enough to stomp on my grave. He lowers the syringe toward my arm. I feel a prick in my skin and pull away, but Tom's grip is firm. He steadies me and gives me the shot. "You'd better hope this is just a vaccine." He turns and walks out the door.

Staring at the ceiling, drained, I wonder if the shot was real or just a trick. I can't dwell on that for long. I keep thinking about Sol. I keep thinking about Alaska. Did Marty really find a cure for a virus?

The door opens again. Dad walks in followed by Tom. "Talk it over," Tom says and leaves again.

Dad rushes to me. "Are you okay?"

"He gave me a shot."

"It's just a vaccine. But we need to get out of here. Tom's over the edge. He's got a cocaine habit, and he's lost control of it." He helps me sit up. "Can you walk?"

I slide off the gurney, feeling wobbly. Dad helps me toward the door. As he tugs on the handle, it resists. He groans. "We're locked in."

"So, call for help."

"Can't." Dad points to his phone on the counter, smashed.

I try to clear my thoughts, but there's a brutal throb pounding in my head. "Did you know what Tom was up to?"

"Kaye, let me explain." He steers me back to the gurney and pulls up a chair. "Not at the start. I was just interested in stopping the carbon tax."

"Because it would cost you money? Money won't help when the world starts unraveling."

Dad frowns. "It won't unravel."

"Yes, it will."

"Not for you. With enough money, you can survive."

I close my eyes against a future of disaster. "How do you know money will be worth anything?"

"Because it always has."

I blink at the light overhead, seeing climate scarcity, stock market crashes, skyrocketing inflation, dollar bills turned to dust, but despite all Sol has told me, I can't share it with Dad. Instead, I try those lines I practiced with Free. "What about that little boy in Houston, what was his name?"

"Wesson?"

"How is Wesson going to grow up in a world of storms? He won't have the money to survive it."

Dad's head is down, focused on the linoleum that's sprinkled with flecks of silver. "I can't do anything about that."

"But you can. All that money gives you power. You could save Wesson and all the other children growing up with the threat of storms, floods, and fires looming over them. Didn't it feel great to save his life? You felt alive, Dad. You were ecstatic."

He just stares at me, so I keep trying. "All you rich men with money could be climate heroes. You could go down in history if you saved the future instead of destroying it. Wouldn't that be money well spent instead of tossing it away on fancy homes with survival bunkers? No one will remember that."

Dad's getting super uncomfortable. I don't want him to shut down. It's time to be curious, like Free said—ask questions, find common ground, begin the conversation wherever Dad's at and let him lead me. "Okay. Say money will still be worth lots. Is money the goal? What does money bring?"

Dad concentrates on the wall, considering my words. "Safety. Security."

"Does that make life worth living? Think of Marty, of Mom. What did they bring into your life?"

Dad doesn't answer. His eyes get misty.

"Mom and Marty were all about joy, love, happiness. I get happy just thinking of them. It's not about big houses or fancy cars. It's about being alive, living. I want to live, Dad, just like Marty did. Just like Mom did."

"You still need money." His words lack punch.

"But how much? Why do you spend every waking minute thinking about making even more money than you've already got? You always want more, more, more. When will you have enough?"

His eyes look vacant. "I don't know … never?"

It's hard having this conversation. I'm losing patience with it. "And can't you see how crazily insecure that is?"

Dad's face clouds over, so I try to take the sting out of what I just said. "There are things just as important as money. Mom understood that." I sip a breath. I've gone too far bringing Mom into this.

But Dad doesn't fly into a rage. Instead, tears slide down his cheeks. "Yes she did … which is amazing considering her family."

"Why? What happened?"

"They were drug addicts. That's another kind of *never enough*."

"Oh." Now, I'm the one that's speechless. My shoulders slump. I've always imagined them as a loving family, someone to lean on.

Dad wipes his tears with the palms of his hands. "And despite all that, she was a much better parent than I am."

Awkwardness seeps into the gap between us. This is my cue to say something wise, but I'm not sure which words can bridge the years of anger. Finally, I blurt out, "We could just start over."

Dad bites his lip and steals a glance at me. "Okay." His eyes dart toward the door. "Except right now we have to fix this problem with—"

"Tom? Help me understand how all this fits together. Did something bad happen to Marty because of Tom and his Big Leap Project?"

Those steel-gray eyes snap back toward me. "Shh!" he whispers.

I look Dad in the eye. "You know what that project is, don't you? How did you even get involved?"

Dad's face sags. "It was just an idea for investing in the risk. Supply and demand. Vaccines will be like gold as diseases spread. But then, Tom went crazy, more than crazy. He started talking about who should get vaccines and who should not. He wanted power over life and death. He's nuts."

Dad's not being totally honest here. I remember him talking to Rory during the party. Dad thought the project's vaccines would save him, and I guess, me. He bought into more of Tom's dark motives than he can admit. Still, now he sees how awful that is.

I jump off the gurney, my feet steadied by conviction. "Dad, let's get evidence and expose him."

Dad hangs his head. "I can't. I'll be implicated."

"In what?"

"Burying Carter Brown."

Chapter 34

I shift uneasily, staring at Dad in the chair. "Did you kill him?"

"No. He came back from Siberia sick. It seemed like the flu. When it got worse, the staff tried to treat him. He died."

"The staff?"

"There was a small staff here, looking into pathogens that might spread as the climate heats up. It can take years to develop vaccines, but with a head start, we could make a fortune on them."

I resist the urge to yell at him. That won't change anything. I've finally learned that. "So, you didn't take him to the hospital?"

"Tom wouldn't let us. He didn't want awkward questions or investigations … to protect the project. He's been blackmailing Angus and me into keeping quiet. He threatened you, and Shelley too, just like he threatened Marty."

"Tom thinks Marty found a vaccine. Someone told him Marty did."

"That was Carter Brown. This all came from him. He was talking crazy stuff. I didn't know he'd die. I'll probably go to jail for it."

"Oh, Dad." I put my arms around his neck and lean into his shoulder. "We have to stop Tom. It will only get worse if we don't."

Dad nods. He's coming around.

"Let's get out of here." I head back to the door and jiggle the handle. "The deadbolt locks from the outside."

"But maybe we can find a tool to help with those hinges." Dad pulls something from his pocket. It's thin and black.

"Marty's pen!" I lunge for it like it's Marty himself. "It's tactical, for self-defense." My arm swoops through the air, practicing the defensive move from the video. "Didn't Tom take it?"

"When you dropped it, I scooped it up before he saw it."

The pen is too thick to force the hinge pins, so I tackle a cabinet beside me, searching the shelves. Inside is a small medical instrument that vaguely resembles a screwdriver and another tool that looks like a double-headed hammer. Dad knocks the hinge pins up and out. Wiggling the door loose, we slide past it and step into a hallway. To the left are more doors and a corner where the hallway turns. Glancing right, I see Tom and brace myself to run.

Tom's got the gun again. "I can watch, you know, from anywhere in the house."

I stall. "Your house? This can't be legal, tucked away in secret."

"Legal doesn't matter. With the vaccine, I'll ..." His voice trails off like he's lost his train of thought. He takes a step closer. "In the room," he says, pointing to a door on our left.

Standing tall, ready to defy him, I remember the bookstore. "What about your son? You're forgetting about him."

Tom's head jerks my direction. "My son?"

"All this stuff you're doing is going to land you in trouble, and your son must already have doubts about you. How will he feel if his father's in prison? He may never speak to you again. You need to stop this while you can."

Tom's wavering, treading some border between drug-fueled delusion and reality. Just when I think he's going to lower the gun, the scowl returns, but his hand is shaky. "No, the vaccine will protect him. This is for him."

"Protect him, instead, by curbing emissions, by keeping it frozen," I shout. "You have to help reverse it, for him!"

"Shut up!" He steps toward me, but Dad's already charging. Marty's pen is out front, pointing straight at Tom.

The lights flash off. There's a tussle—grunting, gasping. It sounds like Tom moaning, but then the gun fires. Dad calls, "Kaye, run. I'm hit."

My feet spin me. I dart into the darkness, my hands in front of me, reaching for the turn at the end of the hallway. My fingers touch a wall. I go left, finding more corners, heading blindly through the black maze. Again and again, I turn, but when I hit a rough spot on the floor, I stumble, that weak ankle wimping out on me. Down against the cold cement, I cry out, not from pain but from the agony of failure. I don't know how to get out of here.

But then a door opens. "In here," someone whispers.

I smell herby, gingery hair rinse. "Shelley?"

"Shh. Yes."

Her hand reaches out fumbling for mine. She pulls me into a room and shuts the door. A flashlight floods the space with light. It's a big room, filled with cages. They're all empty, but they still hold the gamey scent of mammal.

"It's a lab. They were doing tests on animals," Shelley says. "I wonder why they stopped."

I'm taking deep breaths, helping my heart rate settle. "Carter Brown. Dad says he got sick from something in Siberia. He died."

"I knew it."

"My Dad's hurt. We've got to call an ambulance. What's through there?" I ask, pointing to some double doors.

"The monitor room. That's where I turned off the lights."

Another door is opposite them. "Let's go this way."

"No, we need to beat Tom to the monitors." She heads through the double doors and up a flight of stairs.

I hobble after her. "How'd you get here?"

"I snuck into the house when Tom left. I found the office, the lab.

Creepy. When he came back with you, I hid in the monitor room and watched everything."

The stairs look all spooky in the dim light. "I thought we needed a plan first before storming this place."

Shelley shrugs as if it's no big deal. "That's what I was doing, working out the plan."

"How long have I been here?"

"About an hour. I've been hiding in a closet, sneaking out, trying to keep track of what's happening by checking the video streams."

An open door is on the right. Shelley's flashlight sweeps across a small room filled with monitors and a computer. Every screen is dark. "I almost snuck up to ground level to get signal on my phone," she says as she steps into the room, "but I was afraid if I tripped some alarm he would kill you before I could call the police, so I stayed. I've been trying to figure out how to get you out." She starts to pull a plug to the monitors, but I stop her.

"Turn them back on. I have to see what happened to Dad."

Shelley's eyes go ghostly wide. "No. He'll find out where we are."

"I have to, Shelley." My stare is firm. There's no other option.

Nodding reluctantly, she opens a small gray metal door in the wall and flips some breakers. Lights come on. I race to the bank of monitors, searching for Dad. There he is, slumped against a wall. His leg's bleeding. His shirt is ripped. It looks like he's trying to make a tourniquet with strips of fabric. "He's alive!"

Shelley doesn't let his image linger. She rips out a plug and the screen goes dark. Turning large screws on the back of the PC tower, she removes it, tearing out wires, tossing them into a corner behind some furniture. "Let's get up to some signal so we can call." She switches off the breaker and leads me up more stairs. Halfway up, the lights blink on. "He's close," Shelley whispers.

I ignore the throbbing in my ankle. We scramble faster, bursting out the door at the top of the stairway into the main house. We're in an office that's been ransacked, lots of empty files piled by a shredder. Tom's been getting rid of evidence.

Shelley has her phone out dialing 911. We turn into a hallway and run its length. It ends in a windowless wall covered in portraits of men, like a display of family ancestors. The very last door on the right opens to a great hall. Dark wooden timbers hang several feet below the vaulted ceiling. As they crisscross the room, they create a medieval vibe. A noose dangles from one timber. Hanging from others are banners with numbers or strange symbols I don't recognize. Shelves along the wall hold books, small marble figures, and a silver military helmet with an ornamental spike jutting upward from its top. A glass cabinet at the back of the room contains old muskets, rifles, and handguns. Around the room are confederate flags jutting out from the walls at an angle.

"He's a white supremacist," I say to Shelley.

"That was always apparent, though no one in my family talked about it. And I'm not sure whether he believes it, or if it's just useful to him for connecting to that crowd. I think he's more a wealth supremacist. His goal is to keep the wealthiest in power … people like him." Shelley connects just then with a 911 operator. "Help. A man's been shot at 513 Talisan Meadow Circle. I need an ambulance and the police." There's a pause as the operator says something before Shelley continues. "We're still in danger. It's the owner, Tom Rodington."

While Shelley explains what happened, where Dad is in the basement, where we are up here, I move to the back of the room to test a door. It's locked, and my feeble force applied to it doesn't make it budge. To my right is a production camera on a tripod. He films something here, but whatever it is, I don't think I'd ever care to watch.

Behind a velvet curtain, there's a metal ladder attached to the wall. It leads up to a bank of theater spotlights. I put my hand on a rung looking up among the lights and timbers, thinking that could be a place to hide. The beams are wide. We might stay hidden there till the police arrive. Just as I'm ready to call Shelley over, the door opens.

"Hi, Uncle." Shelley tries to sound casual.

I peek out from the curtain.

"Where is she?" Tom shouts.

"Who?"

Tom waves the gun. "I've been keeping track of people you spend time with."

I flash on the car that's been tailing me. It's been Tom's guy.

Shelley bluffs. "I'm just here to ask a favor."

He steps closer. "I know she's here."

Like a sprite with wings, Shelley dashes across the room and scales the shelves, scrambling onto the top one. She's so tiny she fits easily, dangling her legs over the edge. Beside her is a pint-sized marble figure of a wild-haired, bearded man in Civil War uniform. She grabs it. "Come closer and I drop him. It looks like that Bedford guy from the KKK. I know he's your complete favorite."

Tom stops. "Drop him and I shoot you."

"Thanks, Uncle."

Tom's a bit unsteady, and his head is bleeding—is that the mark of a tactical pen? Maybe it won't take much to topple him. I begin climbing, going slowly, rung by rung. My ankle stings. My hands get sweaty. I inch out across a beam, heading over the room, the ceiling only inches above my head. Slightly dizzy, I work to keep my breath long and focused. Patience. Patience. I used to be the patient one. I've got to find that patience again. Below, Shelley keeps badgering her uncle, keeping him talking. I try not to listen so I can concentrate. I try not to glance down, either.

Time slows. It's like working a digital image, creating layer after layer, filtering, masking, blending the seconds as I crawl along the timber, my hands moving left, right, left. That makes me think of Sol and how time is so malleable. I can reach across time and talk to him as if the years don't exist, or I can slow time down, like now, to help me concentrate. I'm counting heartbeats—one, two, three, four. Each beat takes a thousand minutes as I move, hand over hand. And then, just as the journey across the timber seems to be stretching out forever, all at once I'm there, right above Tom.

A canvas banner hangs below me decorated with double eights. It's attached to giant eyebolts in the beam by three snap hooks. I gauge how it will fall, hoping it will drop the way I want it. Tom's yelling at Shelley now. She's yelling back, calling him a wimp-ass Grand-Wizard wannabe. I undo one snap hook at the closest end and crawl to the other end to release that one. The banner sags from the middle hook, but Tom doesn't notice, so I work my way back to the center, struggling with the last hook. It's stiff. It doesn't want to unclip. With more force, it opens, but wrestling with the banner makes me dizzy.

As the banner drops, I wobble, grabbing for the edges of the beam, but I still slip, plunging headfirst toward the floor. All those times picturing Marty in his car, plummeting, I've resisted the feeling of it. Now that it's me tumbling, I let go, calm, almost relaxed. Maybe this is the way it ends for us, the Paul Malloy kids.

With a thud, I hit—not the floor but something soft and lumpy. Tom groans beneath me. It takes a moment to focus, my head aching like it's split open again. Drops of blood from my wound splatter over the banner, its numbers stained forever. Soon, Shelley's at my side, pulling me up. We stare at the bump beneath the canvas. Tom isn't moving.

"Is he dead?" I'm breathless with alarm.

She prods the lump. Tom moans again. "Unfortunately, no."

I hurry to a table. "Can you help me lift it?"

It's heavy oak. We center it over his body beneath the canvas, then add some chairs at the edges.

"Can he breathe?" Shelley asks. "We can't just kill him … even if we feel like it."

Grabbing the spiky helmet from its shelf, I slip it under the canvas to open an air pocket near Tom's head. Standing back up, I get woozy and grip the table for stability, my ankle aching. The room begins to spin. Sirens whine in the distance. Someone's shouting down the hallway. "Kaye! Kaye!"

"Here!" Shelley calls back.

In a moment, the room fills with people. Free's arms surround me. Greg's beside me. Shelley's shouting to the police, "Hurry. Hurry. Mr. Malloy. He's hurt."

I take a step to follow them and collapse on the floor.

Chapter 35

Dad's not conscious. He's lost a lot of blood, but he's alive. I'm in the ambulance with him. My head still aches, but the bleeding's stopped. There's a fresh bandage wrapped around it. Shelley's beside me. "I'm not leaving her," she said when they loaded me in.

Greg and Free are following in Greg's car. They joined forces at my house after racing there to help me. Free rode his bike like a madman as soon as I hung up. Greg arrived about the same time because I never called him back. They spotted the blood in the hallway, so they called the police, and Greg knew where Tom lived.

Shelley's talking up a storm with the EMT. "You should have seen how she body-slammed him. She dropped from the sky like Batgirl or something." Shelley's getting a bit shaky. The EMT puts a blanket around her shoulders. "I can't believe we did it," she whispers to me.

"Hey, how did you get into Tom's anyway? I thought you said it was a fortress."

Shelley presses her lips smugly. "Easy. I had an alarm code that completely worked. I know a gamer who's a top hacker. This afternoon, she broke through to the security firm Tom uses and stole his passcode."

At the hospital, they rush Dad through some double doors. A nurse pulls up with a wheelchair for me.

"I'm fine," I say.

"Hospital policy," he says. "You have a head injury. Let's get you evaluated."

In an emergency treatment bay, the faded pattern of a hospital curtain separates my space from another. The reds and greens have become dull. The blues are faded to a cool gray. Someone behind that curtain has a dry, hacking cough that sounds more like a smoker's cough than a cold or flu. It echoes inside my head, causing it to ache even more. I try to tune it out by thinking of Dad. When a doctor comes in, the first question I ask is about him.

"He's stabilizing. It's just the blood loss. We'll get him back in shape." She shines her tiny light in my eyes. An ID tag hangs from her pocket. It reads *Dr. Gloria Martinez*. There are tired circles beneath her eyes, but still a cheerful gleam in them.

I don't answer her questions. Instead, I ask her to move me away from the cough machine next door because I'm getting a huge headache.

"I tell you what we'll do. I'm going to order an MRI and admit you to a room for overnight observation. You've had a serious blow to the head and a bad tumble from the roof."

"Ceiling," I say, correcting her. "And something broke my fall."

The doctor's eyes crinkle the slightest bit. "I heard about the Batgirl routine."

"Ugh. I'm gonna kill Shelley for that."

"You don't like Batgirl?"

An image of Sol comes to mind, beaming at me like the sun. Sol's way is different—more practical really. Not everyone can be Batgirl every day. "Despite what I did today, Doctor Martinez, there's a better way to fight for what's right."

The doctor nods at me with brown eyes that glisten. "Very wise, young lady."

And then I remember Dad's arms around me. "Besides, you're never going to kill all the bad guys. And sometimes they can change their ways."

My MRI shows signs of a concussion but no swelling. They let me settle in at Dad's bedside after he comes out of surgery. For a while he just sleeps, but then he wakes. "You're okay?"

"I've got a thick skull, just like you. Is Margot coming up to see you?"

"She's not here, Kaye. She's enrolled in a treatment program in Connecticut. She left this morning. I don't want her here. I may never want her here."

I'm not sure what to say. Margot isn't who I thought she was. She has good points among the bad ones, but how to explain that to Dad? I pick up his hand and squeeze it. "Don't think of that now. Just get better."

A nurse comes in to give Dad a shot of pain medication. The syringe stirs a hornet's nest inside me. I feel again that prick in my skin where Tom injected me, its sting triggering a question: Am I a dead girl walking?

After the nurse leaves, I lean close and whisper to Dad, "Remember the shot? Will we die like Carter Brown?"

"No," Dad says. "Carter inhaled anthrax spores from an old, thawed-out carcass that had melted in the permafrost. We gave him a course of antibiotics, but we were too late."

"Will we get it? Anthrax?"

"You need to breathe in the spores to get it. It isn't contagious."

"So, what was in the shot?"

"Tom had a few vaccine trials going before Carter got ill … malaria, Lyme disease. Vaccines won't contain the live germ. He was just trying to intimidate us. It might have been a placebo anyway. I think we'll be okay."

"Shelley warned the police about the lab. They went in with biohazard suits."

"I don't think anything's left there anyway. After Carter died, Angus and I disposed of all the soil samples Carter brought back from his trip, and Tom moved the lab out of state."

"Dad, I didn't tell anyone about the body. I haven't even talked to the police yet."

"Don't worry about that. I'm just glad you're okay." He sinks back into his pillow and shuts his eyes, looking pale. I call the nurse, who rushes in and shoos me away.

Shelley, Free, and Greg are waiting for me back in my room. They're grinning like cats in a field of mice. They've got a present for me. It's a book on bees with a section on gardens. "In case you're completely bored," Shelley says. "I can't believe they had it in the gift shop."

Free steps up to the bed and takes my hand. "So, hey … you slayed this. Both of you."

"I still need help. They'll let me go home in the morning, but they don't want me alone in the house. Perhaps you could sign up for a shift?" I pause. "In fact, all of you could help."

Shelley assures me she can pitch in. "I'll clear my schedule."

"I'm open," says Greg. "In fact, I can take the night shift. I've been roughing it for too long at the motel."

Free winces. "Sorry. It's fundraiser rush time."

"Starry Nights?"

He nods. "You're all invited to the party. My guests."

I tug on his hand. "Even me?"

"Especially you." There are tears in his eyes. "I'm sorry for putting doubt on you earlier."

"All forgiven. But if you have time, call me."

"I will. But I've got to pedal." He taps his watch.

"Excused," I say.

After Greg leaves to extract Free's bike from his car, I ask Shelley, "How's your dad?"

"He's got a lawyer. He's showed them where the body is."

"You're kidding."

"Yes, he's finally decided to stand up to his brother, but Mom's having fits. She didn't know anything."

"What will happen to him?"

"He says he doesn't care." Shelley's beaming. "I think it's awesome. It's great to feel proud of him."

"I bet." My sigh is deep. Can I feel proud of Dad? It's complex. "That reminds me, I have to call Dad's lawyer. Can you search him on your phone? Jay Phelps. Manlowe and Carlisle."

Shelley dials the main office phone number, and I leave a message. As Shelley puts her phone away, she asks, "So what's happening with Free?"

"We've backed off. We're just friends."

"Are you okay with that?"

"I can't tell yet. It's been so intense."

"Yeah, I'm wiped." She's like the elf child again, sitting in the chair, her legs dangling. "It still feels surreal."

"You gave him hell, Shelley. I can't believe it. What did you call him? A KKK-loving wimp-ass villain?"

"A wimp-ass Grand-Wizard wannabe. I've been wanting to say that for ages. We'll need to completely testify."

I shudder. "Yeah, but I don't want to."

"Just tell the truth. That's my plan."

How can she be so calm? I can't.

Greg's standing in the doorway. I wave him in. "I've got a plan too. How about pizza and wings at my house tomorrow night? I need help with a project."

"The garden?" Shelley asks.

I start to shake my head, but it hurts. "No, something I've been forgetting. Something important."

"The flash drive!" Greg shouts.

"What flash drive?" Shelley's eyes narrow, indignant.

I punctuate my grin with a wink. "It's a surprise. Bring a laptop."

"No, tell me. What?" Shelley leans forward. "I can't wait."

"You'll have to."

"Meanie." Shelley's snarl is punctuated with a grin.

"You can't know everything."

Shelley laughs. "I try," she says. "I really do try."

Chapter 36

In the morning, Dad's looking better. We barely talk, but it's an easy silence until I say, "Shelley's dad is cooperating. He's led them to the body."

Dad's hand grips the bedrail, bracing for what's coming. "We'll have to plea deal, but at least exposing Tom will be a winner for you and your initiative."

I beam at Dad and hug him. "Marty thanks you too."

"I regret so much that argument. It's the last time I saw him."

"I know, Dad." I stroke his forehead. He seems hot. "What was it about? His patent?"

"No, something else. Carter Brown got wind of it. It was, well … to be honest, I thought Carter was crazy, but Tom was so certain. I was just trying to ask Marty about it, and he went nuclear. He accused me of spying, even though I told him it was Carter."

"But what was so secret?"

"It was something about a frozen virus up in the Arctic—that's what started the project. A Permian virus, he called it."

"Permian?" Trembles build inside me, percolating up through layers of consciousness. I sink back, sitting there frozen like the virus. It's those words Marty wrote: *Keep it frozen.* I'm seeing his trip reservation to Alaska.

"Yeah," Dad says. "Tom had this ridiculous idea that Marty had the cure for it like he could somehow see into the future. How could he make the vaccine for something we hadn't found yet?"

Dad rambles on as puzzle pieces settle into place. Sol knew Marty's favorite phrase: *Brighten the moment*, and then *burritos*—Marty's crow song. Sol knew that song. Plus, Marty's letter about a friend contacting me. That friend was Sol. I go hot, and then cold, all clammy. It wasn't just any virus Tom was talking about; it was Sol's virus. Yes, Marty spoke to Sol. All the clues line up. So, did Marty get the vaccine from Sol?

The lawyer knocks at the door. He advises me to step outside the room. "You'll be a witness," he says. "It's best that your father talks to me in private, so it's protected by attorney-client privilege."

On my way out, I stop at the desk. "My dad has a temperature."

"Don't worry. It's come down a bit," the nurse says. "I think he picked up an infection in that hellhole of a place."

"Infection?" My brain explodes, thinking of that shot Tom gave him. "He was injected with something. Have you run tests?"

The nurse puts her strong, brown arm around me. "Don't worry. We ran all the tests. It's a simple strep. It's responding to antibiotics."

I lean my head against her shoulder, weak with relief.

At noon, Greg picks me up and takes me home. The first thing he does is retrieve my phone from the safe room because reaching down beneath the bed makes me dizzy. I open it up, hoping to find a number for Sol, but of course, I can't. He doesn't have a number, not a different one anyway. He called from my own phone, my own number.

Greg settles me into a chair and turns on the flat-screen. The story is all over local news, Tom's face blasted across the display. There's video of biohazard-suited cops swarming Tom's house and gardens. Every few minutes, I ask Greg to check outside for hordes of TV reporters and their cameras, but the police must not be releasing any names.

"What will I do when they find out?"

"Move out for a while? I bet my mom would take you in," Greg says. "She's far away in Connecticut, trying to support Margot. They won't find you there."

"Thanks, but I have someone that might help." Thinking of Jane, I lean back. "Hey, can you do a food run? Pizza and wings?" My stomach is cramping.

After Greg leaves, I flip through the channels. The other news is the hurricane. Galveston is in shambles. It's literally gone. The relief effort is massive. The military's been called in for recovery missions. I can't watch any more of it, knowing this will happen again and again, unless I stop it, but bringing Tom down can't be all that's needed. There are so many men like Tom in the world.

Wandering out onto the patio, I sit by the fountain. The soft trickling of the water is so welcome—a whisper from Mom. I start to dwell on the hug she will never give me, but thinking of Sol and how he reaches for the good, I close my eyes and remember those last words she said to me, "Let the *EarthStar* be my hug for you." I never understood what she was saying, but now, as sunlight pours over me, I imagine her warmth in those rays like her arms are around me. That's what she meant.

Remembering Margot, I snap a photo of a purple dahlia, her favorite. Back in my room, I get out my colored pencils and sketch one out, the rounded petals cascading softly, one over the other. When I'm done, I fold it into a card and write a simple note to her, saying: *I'm thinking of you. When you come home, let's start again. Let's do this better. Love, Kaye.*

The camas flower Marty sent me is beside Mom's candle, making me smile, its softness filling my heart. I open his songbook. There's Marty's crazy song about crows and burritos. Yes, burritos. Marty must have sung this song to Sol. Turning a page, I read Marty's lightning poem again. It's now clear where it came from. That poem wasn't about the past, about Mom. It was about Sol.

For sure, this poem is really all about the Momentary Principle, that mysterious connection Sol creates. *Lightning:* the flash of light that flits across the screen. *Longing:* Sol's heartache, waiting for the path to open, the chance to connect. Sol never quite explained how it happened, so I can only imagine it. I think of a canvas as big as the universe, filled with Van Gogh's stars spinning in space. I'm tiny, so tiny, but when I reach out, I can touch those stars because I'm not small at all. That's the moment when something big happens, something so powerful it transcends time and space and all that we know. That's when I talk to Sol.

And Marty spoke to him too. They connected. And now that Marty's gone, I'm left to finish this—whatever it was that Marty started.

Pulling out the guitar case, I touch the outline of the zip drive beneath the liner. It holds the clues I need, but I don't reach for it yet. Instead, I study the photo of Marty, Mom, and me, zeroing in on the frame. It's too wide and too thick, which makes it suspicious. Marty wouldn't choose that frame unless he had a reason. Maybe he was just being funny, but it could also be a signal Marty left for me—a signal to look closely. There are no hairline cracks in the wood to reveal a place to hide something, so I yank on the cardboard backing. It's stuck tight like it was glued in place. Using a steak knife from the kitchen, I carefully saw around the edges of the cardboard and nudge it off to find it's a false backing. Marty, you clever devil.

An envelope is taped inside. It holds a letter and a key. The key is to a safe-deposit box and the letter explains where it's located and what's in it—a flash drive that holds what Marty calls *The EarthStar Solution*. Does that sound like a vaccine?

On the balcony, the bee balms droop. I water them before grabbing the letter, the key, and the flash drive. Heading downstairs to the couch, I snuggle beneath a comforter and snooze till Greg comes back. He's got Shelley with him.

"Guess what?" Greg says. "Joe found something in Marty's car. A hidden USB port with a gizmo plugged in. He can't believe the police didn't find it."

"They didn't want to look very hard. They had their mind made up."

"Well, Joe is talking to someone he knows to get the investigation opened up again. And everyone is interested in Tom now, so who knows?"

I pull out Marty's letter. "Okay, speaking of gizmos, I've found something." They settle around me, staring at the envelope in my hand. "It's from Marty. It's what he was trying to give you, Greg."

Setting it on the table along with the key, I wonder how to explain. Do I tell them about Sol? Do I talk about the Permian virus? No, that's later. First, I need to find out what *EarthStar* is. "He has a flash drive in a safe-deposit box with something important on it. That's the key." I pull out the flash drive from the guitar case. "I think this is a copy, but it's encrypted."

They both have their laptops with them. We download the file and dive into the mission to guess the password. Getting nowhere, I open some sparkling water Greg brought to drink. After two pizza slices and way too many wings, I start again, but staring at my screen makes me weary. Sprawling on the couch, I drift in and out of sleep. My head still aches, and the painkillers make me drowsy.

Around sunset, I wake up. "Tulips," I say to Greg. "I had a dream days ago. Marty was singing his song about tulips."

Greg shakes his head. "That doesn't work."

"Add a number."

"He liked twenty. How about 20twolips as in T-W-O?" Greg pounds the keyboard. He shakes his head again. "Nope."

"And not the other way either," Shelley says.

And then I think of the day Mom died. "914." I type. "914twolips."

"That doesn't work no matter what order I type it," Shelley says.

I chew my lip, thinking back to that dream of Marty. He was singing his tulip song, and then he said something about keeping it frozen. I type *keepitfrozen* and stop to think. He said *for you*, meaning me. I add the number 4. And then I type *Kaye*.

My breath catches as a single folder appears, one named *EarthStar*. I click it, and boom! My screen explodes with a list of files that's two pages long. I open one. It's all code. "It's keep it frozen, number 4, and my first name."

Shelley and Greg open folders with lightning clicks. Shelley finds the narrative. "*The EarthStar Solution* app," she reads, "takes back power from a system that's killing the planet and us. The technology is there to turn this around, we just need to demand it be used. We must vote for change, not just in elections but with our dollars and our actions, earning *EarthStars* for the things we decide to buy and the things we choose to do."

My mind goes total tilt. "What? What? Where is that?"

Shelley points the file out in the index. Greg and I scurry to open it. I'm disappointed this isn't a vaccine. Marty was a scientist, but he built a social media app. That seems all wrong. Still, Sol said *EarthStar* will be big. I settle back, smiling. "*EarthStar* was my mom's special word for the sun. Now everyone will be using it. That's Marty's way of keeping her alive for me. Maybe Dad too."

"Wow," Greg says as he reads through Marty's notes. "He's a genius. Everything you do earns a star. Taking the bus. Biking. Buying an electric car. Turning down the thermostat. Going vegetarian. Voting. Talking to neighbors. There's big steps and small steps. Some even children can do. Think of all those possible stars people can earn."

"Let's slow down," I say. "We've got to do this right. We need someone to back it with money. I'm going to ask my dad."

"Your Dad?" Shelley sounds like her engine stalled mid-flight.

Greg's a bit in gloom mode too. "Well, Marty owns it. He created it, so I suppose it belongs to you and your dad."

"I don't want to own it. This has to be free for everyone, but it needs money to keep it going, and Dad is ready to make things right." I reach out and take Greg and Shelley's hands. "But it's our project now, so I want you with me on this. Do you think I'm right about Dad?"

Shelley looks at Greg. Greg looks back at her. "Yes," he says. "Your father will want to make it work because this meant so much to Marty."

Shelley agrees. "I never met Marty, but I feel him. He's completely here with us. I think we need your dad."

I nibble my lip and study them, wondering whether to agree. I don't want them to give in so easily. Debate would be good because I'm not sure about anything. "Dad can be stubborn. You can help me stand up to him. You'll be my board of directors."

Shelley wrinkles up her pixie nose. "That sounds so corporate."

"Even nonprofits have boards. It's okay, Shelley," Greg says.

Shelley grabs a pen and opens a notebook she brought with her. "So, my fellow directors, let's brainstorm. Idea number one: we need to have some stars for those billionaires too. Maybe they can earn one for divesting from oil or setting up forest preserves. We need to invite them in, just like your dad."

Greg keeps clicking through the files, looking for more instructions. "But who'll assign the stars? Are they self-assigned—will that work?"

Shelley's downloading the app. "Peer pressure is powerful. Even if they cheat, they're contributing to the pressure. Everyone will check out stars their neighbors have, so they'll want those stars too. And if they lie too much, well, people love to tell on each other."

I sit back to watch Shelley and Greg. They're already scribbling down ideas, drawing up cluster diagrams, arguing.

Shelley bounces like a fountain bubbling over. "The biggest star," she says loudly, "the most important one ... needs to be something that almost everyone can do—walking. Even without money, you can walk. We'll call it: Walk for the planet."

As I watch them, I remember that starry tree I drew. I imagine it rising, lit by millions of stars. I give it color. There's a hint of rainbow in the distance, the sun bright behind the clouds. I add texture to the image, a watercolor spatter softening the sky. And then, I add people around the tree, every age, every race, every culture, holding small golden suns. We're not going to vanish off the planet. We're going to fix this.

"One degree," I whisper under my breath. "Sol, I think we just might get there."

Chapter 37

I'm sitting out under the stars at Summers Lake. It's my second party in Mossy Hills. I almost feel I belong here now. Almost. Maybe Mossy Hills truly is the place I've wished for since the day we moved in. Of course, Sol would say, it's up to me. This is my place if I want it to be. I'm the one that needs to make the connections. I think I have.

Still, it's a party, and that's always a challenge. I do my best, dancing, singing, meeting new people like crazy, but every so often, the inclination strikes to slink off on my own even though everyone's so great to me. I love being here with Jane and Joe and getting to know Shelley's legions of friends, but still, I'm missing Dad. It's been two weeks since he was shot. He's still recuperating in the hospital. And Sol. I long to talk to Sol. I haven't heard from him.

I gaze up at the stars, forcing a smile across my face. It takes a minute till I feel Sol's memory warming me, shifting something in me.

"Kaye," Free says as he rushes up to me, "I'm glad I found you."

"You're a busy man tonight."

"Hectic is the word." He pauses, looking at me intently. "So, I saw you dancing with Kent."

"Kent?" It takes a moment to place him. "Oh, yeah, the bookstore guy." I give a sideways smile. "You jealous?"

"Nah." Free looks away. "I just was wondering."

"Kent helped me out. He called the police when my car got stolen."

"Stolen? When?"

"Oh, three weeks ago. Before all the drama." Free looks puzzled. I pat his arm. "When was there time to tell you? And I got Charlotte back right away."

"That's good." Free's eyebrows are pinched. Something's on his mind. A ripple of tension flows between us.

Looking for a way to break the silence, I sweep my hand through the air toward a banner hanging between the trees. "I love that. Starry Nights and Carbon-Free Days. Who thought of that?"

"A girl named Tracy."

Thinking of Tracy making a play for Free, now I'm the jealous one. "Tracy Cooper?"

He nods. "Lucky guess?"

"She used to own Charlotte."

"Serious? I never heard that story."

"I'll tell you later."

He peers into my eyes with concern. "Hey, you're looking tired."

"I'm not a good party girl," I say.

"Let's walk," Free tugs my arm gently, the harmony between us restored.

We head out along the shore. A soft breeze fluffs my hair, and the lapping of waves serenades me. Free leads me to a log that straddles both sand and water.

"How are you riding out the storm?" he asks as we settle down on the sand, our backs against the log.

"I'm dreading the trial and the media frenzy. Even though I'm hunkered down at Jane's, I still keep checking out the window for satellite trucks."

"You can always escape to mine if you need to."

"Thanks."

"And your dad?"

"He'll be out of the hospital soon. I'm not sure where he'll go or even if he'll be arrested."

Free pats my hand. I lean against his shoulder, absorbing some of his cheerful strength. "I know now why Tom killed Marty. Dad said Marty had threatened to tell the authorities, so he thinks Tom wanted to delay that, but something went wrong, damaging the brakes on Marty's car. Knowing Tom, that was on purpose, but the police may not be able to prove it."

"What does Sol say about all this?"

My eyes shift away. "I don't know. I haven't spoken to him."

"Why?"

"He's hard to connect with."

"Tell me about him."

I hesitate, realizing the risk in telling anyone about Sol. Tom found out, and he went all greedy and crazy. "It's really his story to tell," I say, hoping Free drops it.

"He leaves a deep impression, for sure, and I just spoke with him for seconds." Free pauses. "I keep dreaming of him, just his voice. I dream he's telling me things, but when I wake, I can't remember what."

"Really? Telling you things?" I would love to hear Sol's voice each night, even if only in dreams.

"That time I spoke to him on your phone … the for-real time, he told me to study the clouds. He said clouds would be important. I didn't think much about it until I researched it today. They think clouds might begin to thin or even break up when the Earth gets too hot."

"Clouds?" Sol never mentioned clouds to me. And I never said anything about Free studying the climate—yet. Maybe that's later. Maybe I will write to Sol about Free.

"Yeah, when the atmosphere gets overheated, it's hard for those low clouds, the stratus and stratocumulus, to form, and we need them. They reflect a lot of sun to cool the Earth." Free gets all academic, but like he's trying to understand it himself. "That creates a feedback loop. Less cloud cover means more heating."

"Sol's pretty wise. Maybe you need to listen to him."

"Maybe," Free says, a bit absently. He turns to me, intently. "So, us …
what are you telling Sol about us?"

"What do you mean?"

There's a glint of moonlight in his eye as he asks me, "Is it going well, the
friendship business?"

I'm on edge, worried Free's hiding something. "Sure."

Free flutters his fingers over my hand like he's anxious. "Well, I'm not so
sure."

My eyes flash wide with alarm. "What did I do?"

"No, no, no." Free looks at me, pleading. "It's coming out all wrong." He
puts his hands on my shoulders. He's chewing on his lip. I'm scared he'll say
he can't see me ever again. Finally, he takes a deep breath and calms. A little
smile pulls up the corners of his lips.

"I'm just saying, I keep wondering …" He leans closer. "What would it
be like to kiss you?"

I tilt my head up—it's automatic. This is something I've wanted for so
long, but with a gasp of breath, I pull away, my mind filled with static. "I
don't know, Free. It's hard to keep bouncing back and forth."

He steps back. "I shouldn't."

Flustered, I gaze at the stars, sad to have broken the moment. "Maybe
when we win this."

"Yeah, when we win this." He sounds like he just lost.

We sit for a while, just holding hands, not saying anything until Free
hears someone calling his name. "Time to get back."

"No, wait." My feelings, they're torn. I'm so drawn to him like he's
magnetic north, but there's just too much going on. "How about—" I stop,
not sure if I should say what I'm thinking. It will require patience, but I've
lost that trademark quality of mine. Can I trust it to come back?

"How about …?" Free hangs on those words.

"Perhaps a trial kiss? Just to check things out, so we don't have to keep wondering. It could be a total flop, but we'll know."

He comes close again. "You sure?"

"Just one kiss," I say. "And then we don't talk about it. And then we deal with everything else that's going on. And then, after the election, and perhaps the trial, and whatever else, we check back in on this."

"Like a date?"

"Yeah, we check in for a date and see how it feels."

Free's tone picks up. "I'm down with that."

"Ready?" Tilting my head, I let my lips brush his. He moves closer, his lips soft, cool, pleasant. It's all gentle, and there's a night bird calling, and I breathe in the scent of moss and leaves and something on his cheek that smells like fresh mint. A silent hum purrs where his lips touch mine. It's good. Really good. It lingers even as I pull away.

We stare into each other's eyes. He's got a hint of smile in his and starts to say something, but I shush him. The water splashes gently against the log. A frog croaks. But someone is still calling Free's name. He looks toward the lights of the party.

I nod that direction. "You go. I want to stay here for a minute."

He gets up, beaming. "Your eyes. There's some starry dazzle in them. I'll keep hold of that."

As Free pads off across the sand, I watch reflections of the party lights mixing in the waves. It becomes a pixel scene I'm working, layering on deep blues, soft whites, adding a few more sparkles. It's all so peaceful, the effects of that kiss still lingering. The hush in the air comforts me. The moon brightens. The stars pulse. I float like mist on the water.

Drifting like this—the moments seem like hours—I'm content, happy. What should I call this new feeling? It's more than satisfaction. It feels complete somehow. Maybe I'll call it *enough*. Yes, *enough* is a word everyone chases, like Dad chasing enough money. But *enough* isn't something to chase. It's something to claim: *I have enough. I am enough.* There's so many of us that do have enough in our lives, in ourselves, but we forget it's there.

My phone buzzes. A text is waiting for me: *Look what I found today.*

It's Sol! I tap the link. That familiar flash flits across the screen, and there he is in a photo, a bumblebee crawling on his finger. *Bombus occidentalis* his caption reads.

I text back. *Really? One less degree? Did you get there already?*

No, but it is a start. The shade is cooler. And I see more clouds.

You mean there were no clouds before?

Between the storms, not so many, not the lower cooling ones. It made the heating worse.

And now they're back? Have I done enough to help you? I can't imagine it's enough.

Something has been set into motion. We will have to see how the choices play out.

I bite my lip, thinking about Marty's app. *The choices people make about emissions?*

Yes. Will they keep building on the change that is needed? Or will they stop?

But the clouds are back, so there's a chance.

Yes, there is a chance.

My energy leaps, but then it crashes. Have I changed things so much that Sol doesn't need me anymore? I'm surprised by this turbulence all in one millisecond. My eyes mist. Our time together might be over. I flash on Marty's letter. *You knew Marty.*

Yes. He sent me to you.

You told him about the Permian virus?

He was intent on stopping it, but without a sample he could not make a vaccine. Instead, he developed The EarthStar Solution.

Why was he going to Alaska?

To make a video to release his app. He believed it would keep the permafrost frozen.

Leaning back against the log, I nod. Marty wasn't going to Alaska to find the virus. That virus could be anywhere in those miles and miles and miles of frozen tundra. No, Marty's vaccine is us, all that we choose to do, like the carbon tax or walking to the store. It's up to us to keep the virus frozen, or not.

I shut my eyes, remembering the smirk that crossed Tom's face. *Tom thought Marty had a real vaccine. He was desperate to find it.*

Yes, seeing into the future can be dangerous. Marty told Carter about the future. Carter told Tom. I did not warn Marty to keep the secret.

Now I understand Sol's tears when we spoke of Marty's death. *It's not your fault.*

Until I tracked you down and found your laptop, I did not know what happened to Marty, and then I was hesitant to connect with you. Look at the danger it brought you, but at least Tom has failed. This chapter is over.

There's a catch in my breath. *Over?* Goodbye lingers in the word, and it has never seemed so final. *Will I hear from you again?*

I am not sure how time works when things change so much, but we are connected Kaye. It is deeper than we know.

My phone is quaking as I read this. I text furiously: *I'll keep writing you.*

Yes, and dreaming. Please keep dreaming. Dreaming can reach through time.

Dreaming?

I love it when we meet in dreams.

What? I shake my head, trying to unravel his words. And then I realize— the drawing of the tree, scribbled notes on my desk, those mornings so hard to wake—it must be true. *But I don't remember the dreams.*

One night you will.

It's not goodbye! My face lifts to the stars. The night breeze fills me. I ride this lightning of connection, my colors pulsing like a rainbow, but I can't stop trembling, knowing the current is already fading, the one linking Sol to me. Moments are only fleeting. I've learned that at least.

Goodnight, Sol. Thank you for sharing what's precious. I love you forever.

Goodnight, Kaye. I will be here with you.

There's one last flash across the screen. I close my eyes. I hold my breath. And then the moment ends.

Join the Climate Story Garden.

If we want things to change, we have to imagine it.

I am a storyteller. I know the power of stories. I also know writers need feedback to get their stories polished and books need an audience to be successful. Now more than ever, we need stories about solving the climate crisis, and we need an audience to support those books.

Sign up for The Climate Story Garden, a bimonthly newsletter to help build the audience for climate fiction that's filled with hope and heart. Subscriptions are free, though enthusiastic readers can contribute toward expenses.

Go to: **www.climatestorygarden.com**.

Arlene L. Williams—what makes me tick?

I've done many different jobs in my life: driving bus, fighting wildfires, designing posters and pamphlets for a university library. I've been a reservation agent for an airline, helping passengers in distress (not a joy), and chased down insurance claims for a small medical practice (definitely not a joy).

The jobs that were most joyful took me into the woods, working with high school students building trails and leading elementary school students on nature walks. Night hikes were the biggest thrill, showing children how to listen to the dark and feel the trail beneath their shoes, step by step.

The forest is the thing that makes me tick. Among the trees, something stirs. It began long ago when I lived on a dirt road in the Pennsylvania countryside. I was one year old. I had just learned to walk, and I ran away into the woods, again and again. Soon, my desperate parents had to get a dog to track me down. Whenever I would go missing, that black cocker spaniel would catch my scent and lead my frustrated Mom right to me.

Why did I do it? No one knew, and I can't remember, but something fascinated me there in the woods. That fascination never left me. I'm drawn to the mystery of trees, especially the quiet hush from breezes that whisper between their branches. I've always been in love with the woods. I think I've discovered why. Here's a photo I found not long ago of a younger version of myself.

Don't believe it? Well, I am a storyteller, but all stories are embedded in the truth. The first part of my tale about running into the woods is strangely true. The picture... not so much.

Other Books by Arlene L. Williams:

Dragon Soup
·Published by H.J. Kramer;
·1996 Best Picture Book for the Society of School Librarians International;
·1996 Notable Book for Children for the *Smithsonian*;
·1997 Children's Choices book for the International Reading Association
    & the Children's Book Council;
·Honor Award from *Skipping Stones Magazine*.

Tiny Tortilla
·Published by Dutton Children's Books;
·A Junior Library Guild selection.

Tales from the Dragons Cave… peacemaking stories for everyone
·Published by The Waking Light Press;
·A 2003 Children's Choices book for the International Reading Association
    & the Children's Book Council.

How to be a Dragon… without burning your tongue
·Published by The Waking Light Press;
·A Finalist for a Nautilus Award in Children's Literature;
·January 2003 Book of the Month for BookReview.com.

You can read about all her books at
www.arlenewilliamsbooks.com.